Just 15
It Could Be Rotterdam!

By Andy Dale

A fictional take on the events of the 1981-82 season and a tribute to
the Aston Villa players and managers of the time

Released 17th September 2024
to celebrate Aston Villa's return to Europe's top tournament

Copyright

Front Cover Design & Illustration

By Gary Dillon – www.dillonart.co.uk

A special mention to three great Aston Villa managers.

Ron Saunders, for taking the club to our first League title
in 71 years and into the European Cup.

Tony Barton, for taking over and completing the
impossible dream.

Unai Emery for making a 57-year-old dream again.

Introduction

Ten months might not seem like a long time but for a teenage boy, it can completely change his world. Key events from July 1981 through to May 1982 have made their mark on history, including the Royal Wedding of Charles and Di, Botham's Ashes, the Falklands conflict and, for Aston Villa fans, a legendary night in Rotterdam. Of course, these milestones are significant, but it's the personal experiences that resonate more deeply.

Witnessing Aston Villa's claim their first league title in 71 years with just 14 players was just the start. Little did I know how much the new season would impact my life and the lives of those around me.

Join me as I recount a teenager's adventures with his first season ticket, romantic endeavours and evolving friendships throughout the memorable 1981/82 season.

Chapter One

July 1981

1:38pm: Morley gets free down the left. There's a good ball in. Oh, it must be…It isn't! Peter, with the goal at his mercy, has struck the centre pole of the climbing-frame. It's bounced halfway down the park. This really isn't our day. How did Peter Aitken miss that one? He was top scorer for the Boys Brigade two years ago.

Morley's playing well, even if he's only up against a freckly 10-year-old in glasses. Morley isn't his real name. I call him that because he moved down from Burnley a year ago. Burnley were the club the Villa signed wing wizard Tony Morley from. His name's really Clive. We don't know his surname. To think I'll be watching Tony Morley playing in the European Cup this season. My Aston Villa could end up playing the Italian champions Juventus, Celtic or even Bayern Munich this season……

Oh dear, that was costly. I was too busy dreaming of Villa's European glory that I let the freckled kid run straight past me. Still think Noddy in goal could have saved the shot. If he hadn't been struck in the face by the ginger boy's flying left shoe. So, 4-4 now in the Castles Park Cup. Really thought we (Harlech Park) could beat Sandringham Park today, especially as most of them are still at Junior School. The Castles Park Cup is played every summer between the boys from each of the parks in the area. Most of the streets around here have names of castles or palaces. Every few streets there is usually a park. So, it's always been known as the

Castles Park Cup. I say "always", but this is in fact the first year we have ever participated.

Last minute now. Mark, my brother, volunteered to be ref. He's had a new digital watch with a stopwatch on since his birthday, which he got along with driving lessons. Looks like the game is heading for a draw. No good to us as we have already been thrashed 11-2 by Buckingham Park. Haystacks scored seven goals in that game pretending to be Cyrille Regis. Haystacks is still furious that Ron Atkinson has deserted the Baggies for Manchester United. He'll be even crosser if Atkinson tries to sign Bryan Robson. Perhaps the Villa should think about signing Bryan Robson. He would be useful cover for Mortimer, Bremner and Cowans.

Come on, Mark, blow up. I want to go and see if England have taken any more wickets at Headingly. I need to clear that. It's dangerous. Damn! It's hit me on the shin. Where's Noddy? No, no, no … The ball has gone between the two piles of jumpers. I've scored for Sandringham Park with my shin! An own goal!

2:54pm: That was incredible. Wish Grandad had been sitting with me to watch that. Mark won't have it, but it's all down to Ian Botham. The best cricketer ever. Well, yes, Bob Willis has just taken 8 for 43, but without Beefy's amazing 149 not out the Aussies wouldn't even have had to bat again. I love cricket, it helps keep me going until the football starts again. Rubbish when it is an odd number year, so not even the World Cup or European Championships to help pass the time. Mind you, World Cup just meant supporting Scotland last time. Next year it'll be different. England glorious in Spain, with Tony Morley putting the cross in for Peter Withe to score to give Ron Greenwood's England the World Cup.

Wish I knew some Australians now to wind up. Take a bow, Ian Terence Botham. Not bad for a Scunthorpe United player.

Grandad used to quiz people, 'Name three England captains who have played for Scunthorpe United?' His answer was: Kevin Keegan, Ray Clemence and cricketer Ian Botham. Still can't believe he's gone. Losing Grandpa in April was so difficult. Didn't expect to lose my other grandfather less than two months later. Don't understand it. His heart was always strong. He used to boast about it. Said he had 'the heart of an ox'. No idea why an ox. One minute he was digging up his spuds, the next we were burying him on top of Nan. Just 14 and already on my last grandparent. Sole survivor Grandma, Dad's mum, was the one I had always worried most about health-wise. Grandad was never ill.

Wednesday 29th July

11:17am: I don't know why Grace and my mum are so impressed with that enormous dress. It must be 20-foot long and looks creased to me. Surely the future Queen of England could get one of the many servants to iron her dress.

Nice of my parents to invite my girlfriend round to watch big-eared Charles marry the far-too-young-for-him Diana. Just wished it didn't mean I had to stay in and watch it too. They haven't even kicked off yet. According to the pullout in the *Daily Express,* the service takes nearly an hour. It's going to be a long day and I'm not even sitting on the sofa with Grace. Worse still, my dad has just given her a cup of tea in my new souvenir Royal Wedding mug, which I was given at school. Was hoping to keep that safe and flog it when I'm 30, along with my commemorative silver coin. Who knows how valuable they'll be. Perhaps I could take it to Arthur Negus on *Antiques Roadshow.* How can Charles be marrying a commoner? She's a Lady and her dad's a flippin' Earl.

At least I get to see Grace's smile. Hope she hasn't got her eyes on one of the other princes. Women seem to swarm over Prince Andrew. I don't trust him, though. At least Edward isn't going to attract any female suitors, perhaps the odd sailor.

Grace Taylor is enjoying this too much. Mum has even opened her birthday box of Dairy Box. I bet there's only a coffee one left by the time it gets to me. Mark's having the caramel one and he's not even been watching the blooming wedding. Grace is probably planning our wedding. She'd better not be getting ideas. I'm not getting married until I'm at least 30 and then it would have to have a Villa theme. I wonder what football team Prince Charles supports. I know he pretends to be into polo, but he must have a favourite football team.

4:30pm: No idea why Grace stormed off. I was only saying that I preferred the wedding dress that Goldie Hawn wore in *Private Benjamin*. Well, that wouldn't have been too big to fit in a carriage. I hope Prince Charles lasts longer on his wedding night than Judy Benjamin's groom did.

Good to see Spud again even if we are the two oldest here. How did Mark manage to dodge this? The street party for the Queen's Silver Jubilee was so much cooler than this one. Food was better. There isn't even any cheese and pineapple on sticks here. And the slow bicycle race was 100 times better than this sack race. We haven't even played kerbie yet. Spud and his family are flying to Spain on holiday at the weekend. Don't know how his dad can afford it. Spud will be getting a tan in Spain and I'll be getting wet in Scotland. Mind you, if I did go somewhere hot, I would just burn and look like a beetroot. Spud reckons he might see some topless women. What do I get to see? Some old ginger bloke in a skirt.

Spud thinks Wolves will be challenging for the top six this season. He's ready to have a bet with me and Hastings again, over which of our teams finishes highest. Surely no contest. Ron

Saunders' Villans will do it again. Although I'm worried that Ipswich might go one better this season. Bobby Robson knows what he's doing. Haystacks is fearing the worst post Ron Atkinson. I still think West Brom will do well. They could have chosen a better manager than Ronnie Allen though.

Can't help thinking Spud is over-celebrating that sack race victory. He was twice the size of anybody else in the race. That was never a fair shoulder charge with that ten-year-old girl either. She blabbing to her dad now. He's giving Spud a nasty look. As Spud is a foot taller than him the father is now walking away.

I wonder if Spud will be the 'cock of our school' again this year. A great ally to have. Although according to Grace – my girlfriend – bully Kenny Bellington is not coming back to school next year. Grace's mum and Bellington's dad have split up. Mainly because Grace's mum caught Kenny Bellington's dad on the back seat of his Austin Maxi with his ex-wife. I hope Charles and Di take their married vows a bit more seriously. Mind you, that didn't have the best of starts, with Diana saying 'Philip Charles' instead of 'Charles Philip' in the vows. Mark said they should have made her marry the Duke of Edinburgh instead. Well, she obviously likes the older man. That would have made the Queen's speech a bit more interesting than usual next Christmas. I wonder if the Villa will be top for Christmas Day. With the opening three games - Notts County (newly promoted), Sunderland (we beat them 4-0 last season) and then Spurs (who we also beat 4-0) - we could be top, when the first league table is in the *Pink*. It will be so odd; we could have nine points. Really not sure how this new points system will work. Why did 'Chinny' Hill have to put his big oar in. Grandad said it would never happen in his lifetime. And sadly, he was right. I miss him so much. Hope you get *Match of the Day* in Heaven. I'm glad it's back on Saturday nights this season.

8:45pm: What's worse, having to sit through three hours of Royal Wedding or the last two hours watching *The Sound of Music*? It's

10

"let's all torture the teenage boys" day. I do like some of the songs in *The Sound of Music* but I'm not letting on to my mum. Dad seems to have fallen asleep. Nice of the Queen to have given him the day off for her eldest son's wedding. Odd having a wedding on a Wednesday, though. I expect the Abbey was cheaper than at a weekend.

Uncle Norman and Auntie Mavis are round from next door. Not really my uncle and auntie, but I've always called them that. They have a big announcement to make. Auntie Mavis can't be pregnant, she's nearly 40! Their daughter Carol is in the year above me and a good laugh. Mum's woken Dad up and sent him off to the kitchen.

Dad returns with a bottle of champagne and what looks like all the posh glasses we own. We're going to toast the happy couple. I think he means Charles and Diana, not the Von Trapps. It seems that my parents have decided this is the point in my life when I should taste my first champagne. Be great if Dad sprayed the champagne around like Nelson Piquet. Or like the Villa fans did at Highbury last May. I was covered in it. Now at just 14 I am going to finally drink this posh drink. Although I've been given the smallest of the glasses and it isn't even full. To the Prince and Princess of Wales, bottoms up!

I'm now adding some orange juice to make the fizz a bit more palatable. I can see now why cup winners are so keen to spray it around. Announcement time and it's a bombshell! Uncle Norman, Auntie Mavis and Carol are putting next door up for sale. The other half of our semi is going to be sold. Life will never be the same again. From the day I was born in this house, the other side of that wall has been this trusted family. Any bangs were from people we knew and loved. Any problems we had, we had a family we could call on. There might be champagne bubbles in glasses and another blooming replay of the Royal Wedding starting on the telly, but this was now a very sad day. We are going to have nobody to look after the rabbit when we go on holiday next year.

Friday 31st July

2:07pm: Spud (Peter Hogan, whose sci-fi mad parents gave him the middle name of Spudnik) is really starting to annoy the couple in front of us. It was my mistake to start booing every time an Ipswich player came on. But now these two mates are shouting 'you're even worse than the Villa' whenever they see John Wark, Russell Osman or Kevin O'Callaghan on the big screen. We're going to end up getting thrown out of the ABC cinema in Wolverhampton again. Thanks to an Albion and a Wolves fan. How did Kevin O'Callaghan get chosen anyway? What about Alan Brazil or Paul Mariner? I bet a few Villa players were asked, but they turned it down because they were too busy celebrating winning the league. Mind you, Ipswich did manage to win that UEFA Cup. A huge cup. Why are all European trophies so massive? Hope Dennis Mortimer is doing some weight training so he'll be able to lift that European Cup in May.

This *Escape to Victory* film is quite good. An action film with football in it but I think Ossie Ardiles should stick to the football. I don't know why Grace didn't want to come with us. I even gave her the choice of this or *Superman II*. I suppose telling her that Spud and Haystacks (Scott Hastings but built like Giant Haystacks) were coming as well didn't help. Grace Taylor struggles to tolerate Spud, but he's my best mate so she'll have to lump it.

I get the feeling we're not going to see the end of this movie, now that Spud has just called the man in front a 'big girl's blouse'. No, I'm right, here comes the scary usherette with the eyes that can see the whole cinema in one glance. She has been known to clobber unruly schoolboys with her torch. Time to make a run for it just as Sylvester Stallone is saving the German penalty. Can't believe that a

12

team with Pele, Bobby Moore and Mike Summerbee in it can't beat this lot. Guess I'll have to wait until Dad can rent it from Blockbusters in 18 months to see who wins.

Chapter Two

August 1981

3:15pm: Can't my parents find a different room to have this argument? Ian Botham's on fire at Edgbaston. He's taken 3 for just 11 runs. Australia are tumbling, 121 for 8. They still need 29 to win or it's 2-1 to us poms. Martin Kent is the only recognised batsman left, but Beefy will get him.

My parents' argument does actually involve me. My dad's fighting on my behalf. My first match as an Aston Villa season ticket holder is still 27 days away. But it's already causing conflict. We're off to freezing Scotland on the 15th of August for two whole weeks. Yes, I miss the chance of going to Wembley to see Villa in the Charity Shield. I've accepted this battle loss. My dad must take those two weeks off from work. But he promised me that we would come back a day earlier on the Friday (28th). So, I would be able to take my wooden seat in the Trinity Road Enclosure on the opening day of the 1981/82 season. Also meaning Mark could go to Molineux to watch his lot get thrashed by European Champions Liverpool. I'm sure this had all been agreed, but Mum is suddenly saying that it's silly to pay for 14 days yet only stay for 13. Well, Mother, it's even sillier to pay for 21 games and only see 20. My season ticket has cost them £40. So, every missed game is a £1.90 waste.

14

What a ball! Ian Botham strikes again. He's bowled Martin Kent. Dad's attention is now fully focused on the telly and the scenes at Edgbaston, much to Mum's annoyance. Peace at last. She has slammed the door and stormed off. Dad considers following her but instead opts for his armchair. One thing I know is that I'll be at Villa Park on Saturday 29th of August at 3pm. Nothing is going to stop that.

It's all over. Ian Botham holds a wicket aloft after bowling Terry Alderman. What a spell, 5 for 11. Loving this Ashes summer, but just can't wait for the football season to start.

Saturday 22nd August

2:28pm: 'Yes Mum! I know it's raining, but this is the only place I can get a decent reception on my lucky radio'. I need to listen to the Villa v Tottenham Hotspur Charity Shield. Even then I still don't know the Villa line-up. Our new signing Andy Blair is on the bench. For some crazy reason, each team is allowed five subs today. Hope this doesn't mean Ron Saunders is taking it any less seriously. We need our first trophy of the season. I suppose at least five on the bench will be good practice for our European campaign. Sounds like Colin Gibson has got the nudge over Gary Williams at left-back. Could be a sign of what Ron is thinking for the new season. Gibbo is more attacking. Gary Shaw is out. Sounds like he's going to miss the start of the season. Chance for David Geddis to shine. Spurs have got both their Argentinian players playing. Ardiles fresh from his poor acting debut and Ricky "I'm named after a great club" Villa. Archibald is playing. So, the two top scorers of last season going head-to-head. Hopefully Peter Withe will outscore him this season. Glad that Garth Crookes isn't playing. He's far too quick.

That sheep is looking at me a little aggressively. Perhaps I'm a bit too near her lambs. I'm getting soaked, but at least I can hear most of the commentary. Sounds like Peter Withe and Graham Roberts are having quite a battle. Sounds totally wrong having Ray Clemence in goal for Tottenham. Clemence has missed it … Goal!! Peter Withe. He's off the mark this season already.

It's no good, I'm getting too wet and it's so cold. Feel sorry for the cute baby lambs. They must be freezing. Radio is all just crackling now anyway.

6:44pm: No, I'm not eating it. I don't care if that's all they've got. I am not eating lamb. Not after seeing those lambs outside this afternoon. I bet we'll find they have mysteriously disappeared in the morning. I wouldn't mind, but why do they have to call it lamb. Bacon and pork are yummy, but they don't call it baby piglet. It's going to take more than covering it in mint sauce to make me eat it now. I'm being accused of making a scene at the dinner table, but perhaps if they'd let me go to Wembley instead today then we wouldn't be having this conversation. I could have been eating a hamburger. You see, they don't call it a baby calf burger. Maybe I'm just cross that we have to share the Charity Shield with Spurs. I don't even know how that works. Who gets it for the first six months? It's not like you can cut it in half. If they aren't going to decide it by penalties, then at least they could make it so it was in two pieces and each team could have a half.

At least Peter Withe managed to make it 2-2 after that Tony Morley cross. Two goals for Mark flippin' Falco and two for our Peter. At least we didn't lose.

There is no way I'm ever eating lamb again. Unless it's a lamb chop in a mixed grill.

Monday 24ᵗʰ August

5:56pm: Why are we sat in the hotel lounge trying to watch a tiny telly which has Scottish news on? It's not even time for *The Krypton Factor* and anyway I'm starving. No choice again with the evening meal. Well, there is a choice of starter: fruit juice or prawn cocktail. Main course is then something called Scotch Pie with mashed potato and gravy. No idea what Scotch Pie is but Mum has promised me there's no lamb in it. She's been acting quite strange this holiday. I know she was sick yesterday morning. She is being very moody. Watching the news going on about Mark Chapman – the bloke who shot John Lennon – being sentenced isn't making her any happier. He's got 20 years. That doesn't sound a lot for shooting a Beatle.

NASA's Voyager 2 has finished taking pictures of Saturn. I wonder what it saw there. Perhaps by the year 2000 we might be able to send people there. We could send our convicts. Like we used to send them to Australia where they'd just become quick bowlers. Banishing Mark Chapman to Saturn would make sense. In the year 2000 I'll be 33. What will the Villa have won by then? Ron Saunders could be guiding us to our 20ᵗʰ consecutive First Division title. Gary Shaw would only just be 39. He could still be scoring goals for the Villa. Mind you I expect my season ticket could be over £100 by then.

Saturday 29th August

7:24am: This is far too early to be up on a Saturday. Even if it is the first day of the season. No *Tiswas* or even *Swap Shop* until September. Still over two hours to *Joe 90*. I've made the decision not to fill in my Roy of the Rovers My Team Performance poster this season. Instead, I'm going to leave last season's completed one up. To mark the magnificent achievement of us winning the league with just 14 players. Anyway, perhaps I'm getting a little too old for football posters. Tucker has a poster up of Cheryl Ladd from *Charlie's Angels* in a Chinese top with the only button being just beneath her breasts. She isn't even wearing a bra. I think it's time I put the First Division teams all in alphabetic order on my new *Shoot!* League Ladder. Or better still, I'll put them in the order that I think they'll finish this season.

Maybe putting the Villa top (again) is a touch optimistic. Liverpool have signed the Brighton defender Mark Lawrenson, so they might regain the title. I mean they are European Champions. So, Liverpool first and Villa second. Arsenal looked good that last game of the season. What a day that was at Highbury. Still can't believe I was there. Okay, Arsenal third and I think Ron Atkinson will do well at Manchester United, so I'll put them fourth. Sorry Hastings, but even with Bryan Robson I can't see the Baggies being as good as last season. I'll put them as seventh. Fifth and sixth I say Spurs and Southampton. Although Brian Clough might get Forest back up there. Mr Walker would be pleased. If Forest are eighth, then Coventry can be ninth. Maybe Leeds tenth. Flipping heck, I've forgotten Ipswich. Perhaps they'll be too tired from last season. Putting them eleventh sounds low but I'm not changing all the other teams now.

Dad comes down to get some water for Mum. Seems she is being sick again. Perhaps it was the long journey back from Scotland yesterday or the delayed effects of that Scotch pie. What is mutton anyway?

Dad is not impressed that I haven't slotted Wolves in yet. So, I tell him they are going to finish thirteenth. He warns me not to show my brother. Above them I'll put Middlesbrough, in support of Bosco Jankovic. After Wolves, Everton and then Manchester City. Dad then pushes in Coventry in the number 16 slot. I think that of the promoted teams West Ham will do best. At least they wear claret and blue. I've always liked Trevor Brooking. Still can't forgive

18

them for cheating us in that 1980 FA Cup quarter-final. Sunderland are in eighteenth place. So, who is staying up? Last four tabs are Notts County, Stoke City, Swansea and the one I refuse to name, Birmingham City. I'm going to save Stoke City. Bottom three are twentieth Swansea, twenty-first Birmingham City and last Notts County – who the Villa play in just over four hours. I'll be there in the Trinity cheering them on. What should I wear?

1:44pm: Maybe my 1975 Villa rosette is not trendy, but I need to show my support for the team. My season ticket seat will be on the front row, so the players will look to me for inspiration. Hopefully, they'll look to Ron Saunders first, though. It's a warm sunny day but Mum insisted I brought my Pac-a-Mac cagoule. Unfortunately, I left it in Dad's Ital. I had hoped it would just be me and Mr Hill in the car travelling to the game, listening to the game previews on the radio and us chatting about football. But no, I'm squashed on the back seat of his Ford Cortina between two quite large elderly ladies. Well, they aren't as old as my grandma. Still probably in their late 50s. Mr Hill, Howard as he insists I call him, is the Senior Steward at our Methodist Church in Bilston. He's had a Villa season ticket for years. I think he saw us win the FA Cup in 1957. I'd always been polite to Mr Hill growing up, but I was still gobsmacked when he told my dad he'd take me to Highbury last May. All the way to London with somebody I hardly knew, but Howard was brilliant. Now he was going to be taking me to all the Villa home games this season.

When Dad dropped me off at Howard's I was unsure what to expect. The house turned out to be bigger than I had anticipated. I was greeted by a very bouncy labrador. The two ladies I was now wedged between are Mrs Hill, who is lovely, and a very chatty Peggy Doubleday. Not sure if she's Mrs or Miss, but she hasn't drawn breath long enough for me to ask yet. It seems we're taking them to the Bull Ring. Which apparently is where all the big shops are in Birmingham. Hence the big shopping baskets they have perched on their laps. I'm a little worried about timing but it seems Howard knows the route well. He notices my worried look and reassures me that we will be parked up before half-past two. In the passenger seat, where I had hoped to be, is the Hills' son. He's quite a bulky chap; I think in his late 20s. He very rarely speaks; I think he goes to a special school even though he's older. Likes to do complicated jigsaws including the ones that have no corners.

I climb into the front after we wave the three shoppers goodbye. Mr Hill turns up Radio 2, apologises for his non-stop talking sister and we are soon chatting about the important things in life, like will Peter Withe get a hat-trick today.

2:31pm: This is it, I'm ready to tear out ticket number one from my new season ticket book. Mr Hill told me I had to do this in full view of the turnstile operators. I wonder if he'll realise this is my first time. I stand and gaze up to the wonderful brick Trinity Road stairs and balcony. Such a beautiful piece of architecture. You can feel the history and tradition. Stepping over a large pile of horse manure, left by a very angry-looking police horse, I join the queue at the turnstile for the Trinity Road Enclosure with the sign over it saying, 'Home Supporters Tickets Only'. Within minutes, I'm through the giant rotating claret gate and entering the holy ground. It's almost as if I have forgotten to breathe as I catch my first glimpse of the Villa Park pitch. As it's the start of the season it is for once in near pristine condition. Looking like a large-scale version of my grandad's perfectly cut back lawn. I think it's the first time I've seen it without the bare and sandy patches that it gets once the season starts. I make my way down the steps, past the rows of wooden seats, right to the very front. Row A seat 108 is a seat that is reserved just for me. My dad has found me an amazing position. Only about ten seats to the right of the Villa dugout. I stand, trying to take in the enormity of the moment. Here was me, just 14, about to play a major role as champions Aston Villa start their defence of our First Division title.

The others on row A give quizzical looks to the newcomer who is joining their ranks. A well-endowed lady, possibly in her late 50s, welcomes me to my seat. She is in A109 and is quickly interrogating me. Asks my name and if I'm on my own. I tell her my name is Jonathan. Did consider giving myself a pseudonym. Maybe Roy Race or JR Stadler. The old lady reminds me of that housewife character that Les Dawson does. She seems friendly enough and soon tells me that old Mr Warrington normally has that seat. Well, it's mine now. Perhaps the excitement of the Villa winning the league was too much for old Mr Warrington. At least I know he didn't die in this seat in the 3-0 win against Middlesbrough. Surely, the well-endowed lady would have said if he had.

Excitedly, I suddenly notice two things. Firstly, an ATV camera down towards the Holte End. So, the game will be on *Star Soccer* tomorrow. This season it's back to being Sunday afternoon because *Match of the Day* is back where it belongs. Second sighting, walking around the pitch towards me, is the programme seller. I need to get his attention. While 35p is a lot, it is my first season ticket game. I'll try and get one every game this season. Then I can save the vouchers on the back in case we get to a cup final.

The programme has a picture of a teenage boy who looks a bit like me on the front with the League Championship trophy. He's wearing the new Villa Le Coq Sportif kit. How lucky is he! Kit looks really smart with the slimming claret sides and the round badge in the middle of the chest.

I lean over the advertising hoarding in front of me to check what the advert is. It's 'DAVENPORTS' and I am exactly behind the O. So, on tomorrow's *Star Soccer* I'll be able to spot myself. I will set the video so I can then pause it when I watch it back and the ball goes near the DAVENPORTS sign. I'll set the speed to SP so I can pause it in colour. Might be jerky but at least I can show it to Mum.

2:53pm: That's the *Theme From an Unmade Silent Movie*. The music Aston Villa come out to. Not sure why they never made it. Here comes Dennis, leading the Villa out. He's holding the League Championship trophy. Everyone is applauding and cheering. This is magic. Best day of my life.

4:47pm: Howard Hill is waiting for me just outside the ground. He shakes his head. How can we possibly have lost 1-0 to Notts County, a team who were in the Second Division last season. I just can't believe it. We didn't play well. Still should have won. Tony Morley hit the crossbar and Peter Withe should have scored. Losing Ken McNaught injured so early didn't help. What a rubbish start to the season. Going to be hell back at school on Tuesday.

Back in the car and Radio 2 Sports Report make the champions Villa's home defeat to newly promoted Notts County the headline news. Followed by news that another promoted team, Swansea, had put five past Leeds. Then the news I feared, Wolves had beaten European Champions Liverpool, 1-0 at home. Terrific, and this season it's crazily three points for a win. We are already three points behind my brother's team. At least the Albion lost at Manchester City. But I think a defeat to Notts County is a lot worse in the bragging rights at school.

Outside the Bull Ring, the three shoppers are ready to jump back in the Ford Cortina. Shopping baskets surprisingly empty as they all climb in. I'm again wedged in between the two ladies in the back. Despite our obviously dejected faces they still ask how we did. Worse still, Peggy Doubleday doesn't believe us when I say we lost. She accuses me of joking. As if I'm ever going to joke about a Villa result. Doesn't she realise how serious this is? My whole school holidays have been ruined by the last 90 minutes. I'd been waiting for months for this game.

Soon we are driving through Handsworth in silence. A site of riots only a few weeks ago. It all looks so bleak, but then everything looks bleak to me now.

5:48pm: Mr Hill drops me off at Grandad's house. I'm determined to keep calling it Grandad's house even though it's nearly four months since he died. My mum has been sorting out the pantry there and starting to empty the kitchen. I miss my Grandad so much. He'd say the right thing now and give me one of his famous cups of tea in my special Jonathan mug.

Grandad's neighbour Randy is waiting excitedly by the front door. He's waving something at me. It's *The Pink*, the *Sporting Star*. He'd gone up especially to Grandad's paper shop to get it. Thinking he had done something wonderful for me. I tried to smile and say thanks but right now the last thing I want to do is read about how the Villa were losing with ten minutes to go. Then look in the Stop Press to see that final 0-1 score. At least Mark wasn't here to gloat.

At that moment my dad and Mark pull up in Dad's car, beaming and celebrating the Wolves' victory. Mark just slapped me on the back and smiled. He didn't need to say a word.

Sunday 30th August

2:33pm: So strange seeing Grandad's house looking so empty. It's stopped smelling of Grandad. Randy and my dad did several trips this morning, in a rickety old van that Dad borrowed from work. I think with Unigate on the side. People probably thought it was an enlarged milk float, or some thought a Humphrey might jump out. Not sure where some of the stuff went but I know my dad isn't going to be able to park his car in our garage for a few weeks. He'll hate that.

We're standing in the front room watching *Star Soccer* on ATV. It was always called the front room even though it's at the back of the house. Mark is really enjoying watching us lose again to Notts County. Even saying what a great player that ape Brian Kilcline is. Jimmy Greaves is talking sense at least, saying that Villa were a bit unlucky. Look at that one-tooth Notts County manager, Jimmy Sirrel. How can he be a First Division manager? He looks like he belongs on *Last of the Summer Wine*. Reminds me of that bloke who's married to Nora Batty and her wrinkled stockings.

Mum said to me and Mark that we could keep five things each of Grandad's. I started with small sentimental things like the plastic deer ornaments from the dining room and the blue formica mug with the name Jonathan on it. But Mark was obviously thinking bigger. He baggsied Grandad's radio tuner, Kodak camera and bedroom table green glassware. So, I decided to up my game and grabbed the teasmade, whistling kettle and the portable colour TV.

Randy and Dad have just filled the Unigate van with the final load. Time to start saying goodbye to my grandad's house. Mark suggests it's time to say goodbye properly. Mum is crying as she sits on the front step. She's been very emotional lately. I guess it's all been quite a lot for her as an only child. An only child in her late 30s who's now an orphan. Mark's idea is a final match on Grandad's top lawn. He's the only person I've ever known with a garden lawn on two different levels. It's certainly not a posh house, but the garden was always his pride and joy. Perfectly flat hedge tops you could probably roll snooker balls across and then bowling green style-lawns that a Wembley groundsman would be proud of.

From Grandad's famous shed Mark gets four garden canes and makes a goal at each end of the top lawn. I find the lightweight yellow ball that we have played with many times. The fifth incarnation of the yellow ball. The earlier four had been burst by Grandad's prized pink roses. It's to be Villa v Wolves. Randy and I

24

representing the team in claret and blue. Mark and our dad would play for Wolves. A winner-takes-all game. The cup final to end all cup finals. Rush-back goalkeepers. I would be Jimmy Rimmer and Mark would be Paul Bradshaw. First to five the winner.

Randy is a lot better than I expected and almost straight from kick-off he has beaten Mark with a headed goal from my long clearance. Mark wasn't happy and without waiting for us to stop celebrating he has blasted the ball between our cane goal posts. Then Dad gets in on the act, bouncing a second Wolves goal in off the apple tree. Surely the apple tree is out of play, but Randy says they can have the goal. It gets worse when I bend down to tie my trainer lace and Mark whacks the ball against my backside. It then loops up and into our goal. Wolves 3, Villa 1. We don't deserve this scoreline. Mum is now oddly sitting at the bottom of the apple tree. So, according to Randy, she's on the pitch. Randy goes on a lazy, Tony Morley-style run and smashes the ball into the cane to the right of the Wolves goal. The cane goes spinning out of the ground. Mark says, 'no goal', but Mum overrules and says Grandad says a goal to the Villa.

Mark completes his hat-trick accompanied with a chorus of 'Oh, Andy, the South Bank sing'. Still seems wrong, Villa legend, Andy Gray playing for Wolves. Randy and I are 4-2 down. Only a miracle will save us now. Just then Mum says, 'It's time we were going'. So, Randy then jumps at the chance to play that traditional rule, "next goal wins". Mark protests, but Dad reluctantly agrees.

Mr Nawaz (Randy) is suddenly one-on-one with Mark. Randy swerves past Mark and sends the ball rolling towards the Wolves goal. Dad dives and somehow palms the ball around the cane. Hold on, Dad isn't Paul Bradshaw. He's not the Wolves rushy goalkeeper. That's not allowed! Penalty to Aston Villa. Chance to win the last ever cup final on Grandad's top lawn. Mark agrees it's a penalty. He tries to argue the law of next goal wins, by saying if we score it's a draw. No way, if we score, we win. Finally, Mark agrees after I beg

Mum to get involved. Deciding in a lightning speed that Clive Thomas would have been proud of, Mum said 'NEXT goal wins'.

Randy hands me the ball. I face up to my nemesis, older brother Mark. I can do this. I'm Sid, Gordon Cowans, taking the all-important penalty kick for Villa. Mark stares me out. I'm not blinking. I know I'm going to place it coolly to my brother's right. It may kiss the garden cane on the way in, but this penalty is going in.

I slip on my run up, blooming cheap C&A trainers. The ball chips up and straight into Mark's arms. Even Randy is laughing as I end up lying on my back on the lawn. The Wolves keeper kicks the ball from his hands the full length of the 20-foot pitch and straight into our goal. Dad, Mark and flaming Wolves have won the cup. I've blown it big time. It isn't Sid's or Villa's fault, it's mine. I'm rubbish. I can never beat my brother. What a horrible way to say goodbye to Grandad's home.

End of August Top of Division One

1.	Swansea City	Pl: 1 Po: 3	+4
2.	Everton	Pl: 1 Po: 3	+2
3.	Tottenham Hotspur	Pl: 1 Po: 3	+2
4.	Coventry City	Pl: 1 Po: 3	+1
18.	**Aston Villa**	**Pl: 1 Po: 0**	**- 1**

Villa August League Result

29th Notts County (a) 0-1 Lost

Villa Charity Sheild Result

22nd Tottenham Hotspur (Wembley) 2-2 Draw (Withe 2)

Chapter Three

September 1981

8:16pm: How did we let them equalise? We should be beating Sunderland. I thought when Terry Donovan gave us the lead that my lucky radio would see us win easily. When the second goal horn went and they said goal at Roker Park, I didn't even take a deep breath. Really thought it was more good news. Ron's going to be giving them hell in the dressing now.

Only one and a half games into the 1981/82 season and we've already used 15 players. One more than we used the whole of last season. Injuries to Ken McNaught and Gary Shaw haven't helped. I guess Ron was right to play Donovan over Geddis.

With Wolves getting battered 4-1 at Southampton last night, with Kevin Keegan scoring, if we can win today, we'll be above them. Even though no league tables will be out. Mike Channon scored two for the Saints. I bet he did his windmill goal celebration.

Just time to drink my cup of tea in my formica Jonathan mug before the second half starts. I bet it seems like a long ten-minute break for the Villa players with Ron Saunders yelling at them.

Goal horn already, it can only be Roker Park or The Hawthorns … Losing, we are losing to Sunderland.

9:41pm: Finding it hard to follow the story on *Shoestring*. Eddie seems to have fallen out with everyone in the newsroom. How did we lose 2-1 to Sunderland? We beat them twice last season. Two games into the new season and two defeats. Could we end up losing every game this season? Could it be the worst ever defence of a league title? At least Albion have also lost two games. If there was a league table, they would be below us. They have a goal difference that's one goal worse. Mind you, Hastings would be first to say they have played Man City and Arsenal, while we have played the great Notts County and Sunderland. I suppose it could be worse. Tucker and Noddy support Walsall in the Third Division and they've lost both their games too.

Friday 4th September

7:51pm: I don't think I've been in Spud's house before. First time I've met his family. His mum seems unexpectedly attractive. An impressive bosom that's difficult not to stare at. Not the type of mother I was expecting. So here we are celebrating my best mate turning 15. He's always been the eldest of the Local Gang (our gang made up of mates who support one of the rival local football teams). The birthday party has a Wolves theme. They even made us all dress up in something orange. They call it old gold, but really it's orange. I'm hot in this orange tank-top and I don't mean hot as in the sexy variety. Spud has dyed his hair jet black and is wearing a bright orange shirt. Only half buttoned up. I can't believe he has got so much chest hair at just 15. At least Grace is here with me. My first proper bona fide girlfriend. She even introduced herself to Mrs Hogan, Spud's mum, as 'I'm Grace Taylor, Jonathan's girlfriend'.

Grace looks extra lovely tonight. She's wearing an orange dress with white spots on. The dress is quite short, and you can see her knees. She's wearing black tights. While I had to shiver in

Scotland, Grace went back to Bournemouth. She's still got quite a tan.

Not surprisingly, Spud has invited the scary Carrie Campton to his party. He's spent the last three years chasing Carrie, when most of us have been running away from her. She's a funny – funny strange – girl. She seems to look like someone in their 30s even though she's only 14. And you'd struggle to find anyone other than Spud who would define Carrie as attractive. She never speaks to Spud and seems to barely acknowledge his existence. Yet, she has accepted an invite to his birthday party. I haven't seen her talking to anyone, although she seems very partial to the cheese and pineapple on sticks.

Tucker (the other Pete in the Local Gang, Peter Jenkins, like the Tucker character in Grange Hill) has performed his normal magic to create the mix tape for the party. He is so ace at stealing songs from the radio and taking out the DJ talking at the end. The current number one *Tainted Love* by the oddly named Soft Cell is currently playing. If I was more confident, I'd ask Grace for a slow dance to it, despite the lack of room in Spud's parents' dining room. I do the next best thing and sit next to Grace and try to sway with her in time to the music. She seems quite happy to do this. Not knowing what to do with my hands I keep my arms folded across my chest. Perhaps not the most relaxed pose. Perhaps Grace will take control, grab my hands and direct them where they should go. She seems more interested in the music. Quickly, the music changes to *Hands up (Give me your heart)*. This song by Ottawan I know has actions and I'm relieved when Grace does grab my hands and starts showing me the action. Admittedly this doesn't involve her putting my hands anywhere near her dress like I would have hoped, but I guess it's a step in the right direction. A good time to try to grab some jelly and ice cream. Tucker is not happy at Spud's impromptu music change. He had Duran Duran's *Girls on Film* up next followed by the appropriate *Happy Birthday* by Stevie Wonder.

Spud seems to be having even less luck with Carrie Campton despite his chest rug being on display. She's not impressed with *Everybody Salsa*. So, Spud puts on his new Gary Numan single *She's Got Claws*. Seems quite right for Carrie Campton, but for the rest of us is a real mood killer.

9:26pm: Grace's dad has just arrived to pick her up. It's home time now for many of us. My dad agreed to pick me up at ten o'clock, still no school tomorrow, and he said it would mean I could help Spud with the tidying up. I say goodbye to Grace and thank her for coming. She gives me a quick peck on the lips and says, 'See you at school a week on Monday'. We've spent quite a long time together tonight. I've really enjoyed it. Good also to spend time with Tucker and Spud. Really hope to see them more outside school this year. Now I know where Spud's house is, it's only a half-hour ride down the canal on my Chopper.

Tucker and I are looking for the birthday boy. We've just realised we haven't given the Wolves fan his birthday bumps. It'll be a challenge for Tucker and me to lift Spud 16 times, but we're willing to give it ago. Not sure if Carrie Campton has gone home yet. Neither of us saw her leave, but we were doing our best to avoid her anyhow.

We finally find Spud and Carrie in Mr Hogan's shed. There is no light on in there, but we can clearly see Pete Hogan's large head. Perhaps stupidly, Tucker and I decided to open the door *Starsky and Hutch*-like and shout, 'Come out with your hands up'.

So, Spud and Carrie Campton both smoke. That was quite a shocker. Spud tried offering both me and Tucker one of his dad's hidden cigarettes but we both declined. I think Spud was relieved as it looked like there were only a few left in the packet. Carrie belittled us and made out she'd been smoking for years. I like her even less than I did when Spud was still 14.

Saturday 5th September

4:27pm: Mum is going on about something happening at a place called Greenham Common. Not a common I've heard about. Certainly less well-known than Wimbledon Common where Great Uncle Bulgaria lives. Woman on the news said a Welsh group, Women for Life on Earth, had arrived at Greenham to protest the decision of the British government to allow cruise missiles to be stored there. Well, I'm sure Margaret Thatcher has her reasons for wanting to store missiles there. There are more important matters now. Can Villa hold out at White Hart Lane? Four goals by Villa. Three scored by Aston Villa players and then Spurs pulled one back through Ricky Villa. Ahead 3-1, but Spurs are fighting back. Terry Donovan scored two. That's three in two games. Apparently both goals were made by Colin Gibson. He's playing as an attacking left-back. The skipper, Dennis Mortimer, got the other goal. The Baggies are winning, though against Swansea, but Wolves are getting hammered by Leeds. The first league table in *The Pink* tonight is going to be interesting. Pity I won't get one.

Sunday 6th September

6:27pm: Sunday People league table shows us 15th. Our first ever three points from a game. I'll start the new school year with my team top of everybody else's team. Hastings' Albion are 16th, only because they've scored one less goal than us. Birthday boy Spud's Wolves are in the relegation zone. Admittedly on the same number of points as Villa and Albion. A team in claret and blue are top. Sadly, West Ham not us. But they are only four points ahead. Still 39 games to play. Over 100 points up for grabs. Amazingly, the three promoted teams are all in the top 6. I think I'll leave my *Shoot!* League Ladder in alphabetical order for another week.

It's odd having the top 40 on a Sunday night. Tony Blackburn is no Gary Davies. *Girls on Film* by Duran Duran is down to 19. Surely Cliff Richard isn't number one. *Wired for Sound* is pants.

UB40's *One in Ten* is playing as I start to contemplate going back to school tomorrow. At least I'm safe in the knowledge that Kenny Bellington won't be there. How could I ever have thought that Grace Taylor would be going out with a headcase bully like Bellington. Her mum must have been bonkers to shack up with Bellington's dad.

Mark barges in unannounced. 'So, you're finally listening to some class and taking an interest in politics', Mark says, plonking himself on my bed. I question what he means about politics. I'm listening to the top 4o. 'You know this song is anti-Tory, don't you? Taking a swipe at flippin' Maggie's "there's no society" speech'. Mark seems surprised at my lack of interest. How many 14-year-olds does he know who are interested in politics? There's a reason why we don't watch Robin Day and his big dickie-bow on *Question Time*. It's not even a particularly catchy song.

'Do you even know why they're called UB40, titch?', Mark continues this uninvited interrogation. I don't really care. I start my O levels tomorrow and still haven't sorted out my pencil case. Trying to show some level of interest, I enquire if it's because one of the band members will soon be 40.

'Pathetic, it's what Margaret Thatcher gives people when she takes their jobs away from them and leaves them on the scrapheap', Mark announces as he pulls my Villa duvet from under me and throws it on the floor.

Monday 7th September

8:57am: It's quite comforting to be back at school with familiar faces. Even Louise Douglas gave me a smile when I walked in. Julie

Duggan wants to talk to me about Aston Villa. Spud and Tucker are in the same class as me this year. All that's missing is Pincher. Still haven't heard from him since he emigrated to Australia. Really must send him a postcard.

Our form this year is 4MC, which sounds cool. Less cool is that our form tutor is Mr McGinn, nicknamed "Jock" because he's from Scotland. He teaches Physics, which is why many of us chose not to do Physics this year. Anyone not standing when Jock enters the room gets punished. Woe betide anyone who sits down before he sits down. He has been known to throw a few dummy sits in, just so he can bawl out the early sitter to show who's in charge. When he bawls somebody out, the nerves on his neck stand out. It always reminds me of Windsor Davies in *It Ain't Half Hot Mum*. Haystacks once tried to appeal to McGinn's better nature and tried to talk football, but it turned out he played rugby for Glasgow Boys and hates football pansies. 'Oh dear, how sad, never mind'.

The bell goes and the door swings open. We all stand up ready for Mr McGinn, but the figure at the door is not the dreaded Scottish Physics teacher. For me, it's much worse. Walking into 4MC is Kenny Bellington. He walks towards me, snarls and then punches me hard, and I mean hard, right between my shoulder blades.

Jock McGinn walks in and is soon grabbing Kenny by the cuff of his blazer. 'I saw that, Bellington, I'll not stand for behaviour like that in my class'. Mr McGinn was fighting my corner.

'Steady on, sir, I'm just giving my old pal Stadler a friendly tap on the back. I haven't seen him since last term. We've missed each other, ain't that right, Jonathan?' Under the influence of Bellington's Vulcan-like stare I crumble and continue the farce that this was just a friendly welcome.

Monday 7th September

12:39pm: Sitting on a wall in the playground catching up with my girlfriend Grace Taylor, I was beginning to regret that Mum had packed me egg rolls in my lunch box. First chance I'd had to talk with Grace since Spud's party. Last time I saw her the Villa still had no points. Grace is in 4WA this year with Noddy and Hastings. She gets to be in Mr Walker's class, the cool Maths teacher who supports Forest. Really hope I get Mr Walker for Maths this year.

Filling in Grace about Kenny Bellington. She accuses me of joking about Kenny being there. Now, there are lots of things I would happily joke about, but Bellington reappearing is not one of them. That wouldn't even be an April Fool's prank I would do. I explain that hopefully it isn't for very long. Kenny is living with his auntie in Mossley while his dad is finding them somewhere to live back in Coventry. The idea of sending Kenny Bellington to Coventry is very appealing. Grace is looking so worried about all this. I take it as my cue to put my arm around her. She seemed comforted by my action, but my miscalculated decision to move my right hand up towards her chest area soon saw me dramatically lose any brownie points I had gained. A stern look from Grace and the slamming shut of her *Dukes of Hazard* lunch box was enough to warn me off.

Saturday 12th September

2:50pm: As I sit watching the big hand on the Witton Lane clock move on to the A of Aston Villa, I feel ready to witness my first Villa home win as a season ticket holder. We can beat Ron Atkinson's Manchester United and start to march up that First Division. There is only one top manager called Ron and he's pictured on the front of today's programme being presented with the huge Manager of the Season cup. You can see our wonderful

Trinity Road Stand behind him. I really feel part of the Trinity now. I was warmly welcomed when I sat down by the old lady and her daughter. We are now even on first-name terms. Doris and Penny. Penny is the daughter, although still probably my mum's age. Seems ages since that first home game. Mind you, this week at school has gone so slowly. I'm sure they added a couple of extra days. We are still without Gary Shaw and Ken McNaught. I like Brendan Ormsby though. I was at Molineux when Brendan Ormsby and 'goody two shoes' John Richards were shown red cards in 1979. Hope Brendan stays on the pitch today. Odd that refs have no yellow or red cards this season. How are we supposed to know if a player gets sent off? Terry Donovan is up front again. He's scored a couple of goals lately. Not sure if he did get two against Spurs though; Brian Moore suggested the second was a Gordon Smith own goal. I never liked Gordon Smith at the Villa. A bit unfair perhaps. Maybe I like him more now he has scored for us.

John Gidman is up against us for Man United. That'll be an interesting battle, Giddy against super Tony Morley. They've got Frank Stapleton and Garry Birtles up front. Mr Walker said that Birtles is due a goal and wouldn't be surprised if he scored a hat-trick against us. I'm glad I got put in the top O level Maths group and have Mr Walker. Quite a midfield for United of Ray Wilkins, Steve Coppell, Lou Macari and Sammy McIlroy. That is like an elite Home Internationals best of midfield.

3:46pm: How are we not winning? Let in a goal again just before half-time. Who was supposed to be marking Frank Stapleton? We were controlling the game after Gordon Cowans scored. This ref is rubbish. Programme says his name is Gwyn Owens, never heard of him. Sounds Welsh, he's probably worried Villa might overtake Swansea.

Wolves v Tottenham will be the score by the letter J on the half-time scoreboard. Looks like still 0-0, same as West Brom at

Forest. Mr Walker was off to that one. Anyone of us in the Local Gang could be top come Monday.

5:06pm: Why aren't they mentioning our blatant penalty on *Sports Report*? Mr Hill was as disgusted as I was with the referee. That was a definite penalty. We deserved to win. At least Spurs beat Wolves so our 1-1 draw is not so bad. Keeps us level with Hasting's Baggies and we've scored more goals. Big talking point seems to be that Man United are bottom. The only team below the Wolves. Man United have only got two points and that's one more point than they deserve. We were robbed.

Driving back through Handsworth it hits me how many shopfronts are boarded up.

Monday 14th September

7:13pm: Can't believe I've four lots of homework tonight. History, Maths, English Language and RE. At least Monday is crap telly night. *Panaroma* or *World in Action* almost makes History homework seem appealing. Do wish I'd written more detail in my homework diary though. I'm sure there was more to it than 'Write about "The Plague"'. Not even sure which of the *Encyclopaedia Britannicas* to look in. Will it be in the one containing words starting with "P" for "Plague" or "G" for "Great Plague"? In less than 48 hours I'll be watching Villa in the European Cup. Playing Valur from Iceland. Perhaps I'll look up Iceland in the encyclopaedias. See if there's anything on Icelandic football.

Mum interrupts my train of thought with an unexpected yell of my name. There are very few permitted reasons for Mum calling me away from my studies. Perhaps Ronald Reagan has declared war on the USSR, or the Beatles have reformed.

The reason for Mum's insistence that Mark and I stop what we are doing and join her in front room is because we have visitors. Mark seems in quite a huff and is firmly gripping his latest copy of *Amateur Photographer*. The visitors are Auntie Mavis, Uncle Norman and a very fit-looking Carol. They have come to say goodbye. Tomorrow they are moving and we are going to have new unknown neighbours. Not sure I was ready for this major change in my life. This trio had always been next door. I know we had nearly three months to get used to the idea, but it still seemed so unreal. They've just always been there. Uncle Norman used to come and watch the cup final with us every May. Auntie Mavis used to bake mince pies with Mum every Christmas. We shared firework displays with each other over the fence. Mark and Carol were sitting close to each other but in silence, almost scared to catch each other's gaze. It's a bit of an awkward feel all round. So, I'm relieved when Dad decides to take the lead. Yes, this moment calls for a speech. Dad clears his throat with a nervous cough.

'What about them suddenly selling petrol in litres not gallons, Norman? It's just to hide the fact they are putting the prices up, I think'. Dad side-steps the speech opportunity, like Tony Morley evading a defender's lunge.

I fear one of my Auntie Mavis's wet kisses as we start our emotional goodbyes. Mark gets a peck on the cheek from Carol. Mark then asks her what the new people will be like.

'Oh, they'll make quite an impression in this street. They'll bring a uniqueness'. Carol delivered the answer to Mark's question with a mischievous smile on her face. What could be so special about our new neighbours?

Wednesday 16th September

7:10pm: It seems odd being back here on the famous Holte End for
Aston Villa's first ever European Cup game. I almost feel disloyal to
my Trinity Enclosure seat. But Dad was happy to come with me
and Noddy had said he's always wanted to see a European game.
Being a Walsall fan, Noddy was never going to get the chance to see
European football at Fellows Park. This is the first time I've been in
the Holte End since the night of the Brendan Batson back-pass. So
much has happened since then: Villa winning the league, losing
Grandad, getting my first girlfriend and the heir to the throne
marrying a commoner.

Noddy seems more excited than me about the start of our
European adventure. He's talked my dad into letting us go right to
the front, against the caging just to the left of the goal. I'm less
excited than nervous. I mean, who knows what level this Icelandic
team are. Is it like Villa playing Walsall or are they more on the level
of Malmo? It was Malmo who shocked everyone by reaching the
final in 1979. It took a Trevor Francis goal to beat them. But we're
from England, and English teams rule Europe. I should be
confident that we'll take a good lead back to Reykjavík. Noddy has
just read where they're from in the Villa News programme. We
wouldn't have known otherwise as both of us have chosen History
over Geography for our O level studies. Perhaps if they had focused
more on which cities European football teams come from instead
of crop rotation in the third year, they wouldn't now be struggling
to fill one Geography O level class. Although History having the
lovely long-legged Mrs Cresswell-Farrington as teacher always
meant Geography was on to a loser in the options. Mrs Cresswell-
Farrington had a look of Sabrina Duncan who was one of the
original *Charlies Angels*.

The first round of the European Cup and I'm surprised that
the ground isn't jam-packed. In fact, we might struggle to get
20,000! Obviously, people have seen that Valur are a team of part-

timers. Dad has pointed out that they include a doctor, a teacher and a radio reporter. It would be like if Tony Butler played up front for the Villa. I feel sick at the thought of what it would be like at school tomorrow if we lose to these part-timers. Surely even without the golden boy Gary Shaw we can score past this lot.

Every single Valur starting players names end with "son". Eleven "sons" in one team. There are another four "sons" on the bench. The only sub whose name doesn't end with "son" is Jon Bergs.

8:50pm: Perhaps we could get double figures. Sixty-nine minutes gone and we are 5-0 up. We all seem to be celebrating less each time we score. It's been plain sailing since Tony Morley scored after just six minutes. Who'll complete their hat-trick first, Peter Withe or Terry Donovan? My money's on Withey but Noddy has bet me 10p it will be Terry Donovan. Imagine if Terry Donovan spent a season in the Icelandic league. He could score 100 goals. I wonder if Ron will make any substitutions.

10:58pm: I guess it was a job well done. Pity we only scored five, but I guess that's enough. We didn't concede any away goals, so they'd need to put six past us in two weeks to knock us out. If they played against us all season, I don't think they would score six. Wish I could sleep. Stayed up for *Sportsnight* and they didn't even show the Villa game. Showing Celtic beating Juventus instead. Be good if Celtic did knock them out. I wouldn't want the Villa to have to face Juventus. Players like Marco Tardelli, Dino Zoff and Liam Brady.

Dreading games tomorrow at school. Bellington says he owes me one and is looking forward to seeing me in the showers. Worried about Grace as well, she seems to be ignoring me. She wasn't anywhere to be seen at lunchtime. I was even planning to share my Trio biscuit with her.

Thursday 17th September

2:45pm: I can't remember last time Spud was off. In fact, I'm pretty sure he has never been. Certainly, last two years he has had a certificate for 100% attendance. He might be a hardcase, but he's also a bit of a swot. He's so determined to make it to be a police sergeant instead of being an ordinary bobby like his brother. Spud thinks that unlike normal police officers, sergeants get to see more of what's happening on the pitch at the games because they are up in the stands. Although the drawback is that you don't get to wrestle with so many lady streakers. So odd today that Spud isn't here. Worst of all, Kenny Bellington is taking great pleasure in the fact that my right-hand man is not here.

Why do they let thugs like Bellington anywhere near a discus? I'm sure he was deliberately aiming his throw at me, even when I was trying the triple jump. If I hadn't tripped over on the frame of the sandpit, Kenny's discus would have struck the back of my head. Mrs Mings just doesn't seem interested in my safety. I guess that's what happens when you let an Art teacher supervise PE. I suppose I'm lucky they don't allow us to use javelins.

This isn't going to end well. Bellington has plonked himself right next to me in the boys' changing room. He pushed poor little Mark Rogers out of the way, just to be next to me. Why couldn't Kenny have left with his dad. I'm not taking my pants off with Kenny Bellington looking. I'll wait for him to go in the showers first.

'Scared of getting your dick out, Stadler? I bet it's as bald as Duncan Goodhew. Probably too small for us to see anyhow'. Kenny Bellington was determined to humiliate me. I wasn't going to be part of his game. I pretend to search in my blue Adidas bag, trying to buy some time. Worse part of this is that blooming Bellington is right! I'm ashamed of the lack of any pubes sprouting and my cock is more like a thumb than a six-inch ruler. I'm what's known as a late developer, but one that is normally very good at hiding it in the communal showers.

Mr Aitken has had enough. He wants us all washed and dressed now. He's got to go to his next lesson. I've managed to escape the shower, but Bellington isn't having it. 'Stadler hasn't had a shower, sir, he stinks. I can smell his pits from here'.

My luck changes as Bellington leaves the changing room while I'm in the showers. Now there is only me and Mark Rogers left. Mark is looking for his lost sock. I help him search for it, with my Villa towel around my waist. I'd wrongly become complacent and let my guard down though. Ron Saunders would have been furious that I'd lost concentration. At that moment, the changing room door is flung open. In marches Kenny Bellington and his sidekick James McMullan. I've left myself wide open. Mark Rogers makes a run for it minus his sock. I haven't got a chance. It's two against one. Like Ford Prefect in *The Hitchhikers Guide to the Galaxy*, I know the importance of my towel. But I soon find myself being dragged out of the boys' changing rooms into the – luckily – deserted corridor. Bellington decides that it's time to separate me from my Villa towel. Bellington and McMullan retreat inside the changing room. Pushing the door closed and blocking it from the inside. I'm left naked in the school corridor just 20 yards away from the Headmistress's office. For once I am quite grateful for my small package, as I can easily hide it with one hand. My attempts to return to the changing rooms are met with laughter from inside. I really have nowhere to go.

What I need now is a friendly face. I need Tucker, Noddy or Haystacks to come to my rescue. Or at the very least Mark Rogers. Then there is a friendly face coming towards me. Well, normally a friendly face and normally a face I'm really pleased to see. It's Grace Taylor, with Louise Douglas, walking towards me. For some reason I do a thumbs up with my free hand towards the girls. Louise gives out a very unladylike snort of a laugh. My girlfriend though has a face like thunder. I've never seen her look so angry. Grace walks straight past me, dragging Louise Douglas with her. Who knows what impression Grace was getting from my predicament. Was she disappointed that her boyfriend's manhood could so easily be hidden by his tightly clenched hand or shocked that her boyfriend was exposing himself in the school corridor?

The next spectators to my unplanned streak were Mr Walker and Miss Tully. Who were engrossed in what seemed like quite a flirtatious conversation until Mr Walker spotted this pale naked schoolboy trying to hide behind a red fire extinguisher. Mr Walker soon whips off his tweed jacket and wraps it around my middle.

Holding back the tears I endeavour to explain to the bemused teachers why I'm naked in the corridor. Making it clear that the evil Kenny Billington was behind this latest humiliation. Mr Walker took control and went to force open the changing room door. Of course, it didn't need any force. Kenny Bellington and James McMullan were nowhere to be seen. The closed door opens easily with Mr Walker nearly ending up on the floor.

Tuesday 22ⁿᵈ September

8:51pm: This new comedy is quite funny. Only the third episode but already I'm starting to like Del Boy, even if he is a bit dodgy. He's the one who was with Ronnie Barker in *Open All Hours*. His younger brother Rodney seems the more honest one. I'm sure he was one of the unemployed brothers in *Butterflies*. Grandad doesn't seem to be in this episode. My dad is really laughing at Del thinking the Hindu God statue is one of India's top wicketkeepers. My grandad would have loved this show. It's his kind of humour.

It's been an uneventful last few days. Even the Villa game at Anfield on Saturday was goalless. I guess not a bad result. Although Spud did remind me that Wolves beat them.

Grace is totally avoiding me following my being naked in the school corridor. Luckily, nobody else knows about it. Well, apart from Louise Douglas, Miss Tully, Mr Walker and of course the two turds who did it. I guess Bellington has got to stay quiet so that there is no proof against him. Don't know if I've been dumped by Grace. I need to find a way to get back on her good side.

The new neighbours are quite interesting. The first Asian family on the street. I wonder if they're finding this curry house episode of *Only Fools and Horses* funny. I'm not sure if I've seen the whole family yet, but certainly two boys and a girl. The one boy is around my age. His name is Asif, well that's what it sounded like when I asked him. He came over to the park and is pretty good at football. He'll be a decent addition to the Harlech Road team. Asif goes to the grammar school, which is an all-boys school. He seemed quite shy when Sheralyn Birch approached him by the climbing frame. Oddly, he doesn't really follow football, but always watched *Superstars* … oh and his dad once met Trevor Brooking. I think I could hook Asif with the Villa. He's like a floating fan. I'm going to let him have a read of some of my programmes. Gently submerge him in all things Aston Villa. I think it's my duty as a Villa season ticket holder to help spread the word. Who knows, Asif might be a way into a whole new continent of Villa fans.

I suppose the highlight of the last few days was when Mark brought his new girlfriend around for Sunday tea. Mum had insisted on meeting Sarah. Mark had resisted for a long time. Even I hadn't met the girl. To be honest I wasn't sure she really existed. Mark met her at art college. So, on Sunday, Mum got her best Eternal Beau crockery out, including for the first time, the cake-stand. We had cucumber sandwiches, which for some reason, Mum cut the crust off. Trying to be posh but it made them almost impossible to eat. We did have crinkled crisps though and chocolate tea cakes. Mum hasn't got an Eternal Beau tea pot, so she put an Eternal Beau tea cosy over Grandad's old blue one. The poshest part though, we had sugar lumps, like they do in hotels. Afternoon tea was planned for half-past four, even though we'd only had our Sunday lunch at one. It was twenty-past six when Sarah finally arrived.

Sarah was not quite what we had expected. As I'd hoped, she was a bit of a punk. Cyan dyed spikey glued hair, quite a few ear-piercings and laddered fishnet tights. But the best bit was that she was probably over 30. She might even be twice Mark's age. The look of horror on my parents' faces was brilliant, but they obviously tried not to show it. Was Mark deliberately trying to shock? Did he find this type of woman attractive? Things just got worse, though, when my mum's offer of a cuppa was met with 'I'd love a Pernod and black' from Sarah. The best Dad could do was a Babycham with a cherry in it. Punk Sarah then broke another house rule by lighting up a cigarette. Not quite sure what type of cigarette it was but Mum's disapproving look meant that it wasn't even seven o'clock when Sarah announced she had to leave. It was all really priceless.

Thursday 24th September

3:56pm: Spud had now been absent from school for six days. Nobody had heard anything from him. I asked Mr McGinn, but he just snorted back, 'How should I know, Stadler, I'm not his keeper'. I get the idea he knew more than he was letting on. So now, Tucker and I are on our Choppers, riding down the cut to Spud's house. After his birthday party I'm pretty sure I know where it is. It can't be more than a couple of miles so I'll be back in time for tea.

Noddy was brave enough to approach Carrie Campton yesterday. He drew the short straw, but she just huffed when Noddy asked if she'd heard anything from Pete.

I remember there was a phonebox on the corner of the road next to Spud's street. Pretty sure it was this one. So, we take the chance to ring our homes to say where we are. I've got ten pence, but Noddy is going to have to reverse the charges.

Looks like I'm on my own. Noddy's mum wanted him home at once because they are going shopping at Asda. I'm suddenly quite nervous. I have no idea what to expect.

I'm sure this is the right house, but no one is answering the novelty doorbell. It seems to be playing *Home on the Range* at a very slow speed. Like a single being played at 33rpm.

The downstairs curtains are closed. It looks like nobody has been home for a while. I can see the Wolves scarf in the small bedroom window above the garage. That must be Spud's room, but it looks empty. I was getting back on my red Chopper when I heard a Gary Numan song being played quite loud. Going through the garden gate I realised that yet again I was going to find Spud in Mr Hogan's shed.

Spud was oddly sat on top of the wheelbarrow that was perched against the inside of the shed. He was smoking, and his black eyeliner had run down his cheeks due to his tears. This wasn't a Spud I had ever seen before. He did manage a smile when he saw me, but there was silence. I certainly didn't know what to say. Eventually Spud broke the silence, 'Couldn't even beat Stoke, hey'.

After I had defended Villa's 2-2 home draw with Stoke last night, we'd talked about *Only Fools and Horses* and the state of Mr Hogan's shed. We finally got to the point. I was fearing Spud was going to reveal he'd got some dangerous contagious disease. But it was his mum, the curvaceous Mrs Hogan. She has cancer and it's quite advanced. I don't know what to say. Should I give him optimism or prepare him for the possible more likely outcome? I want to make a joke to lighten the mood. The kind of thing that Del Boy might say. This is big, though. I can tell that.

'It's in her breast', Spud hits me with more information than I had been anticipating. This was a lot to take in. Suddenly, I need to see Spud's mum's breasts in a different way. Not as something to drool over with teenage fascination, but a functional part of the body that was undergoing unpleasant life-threatening changes.

7:42pm: Mum was being my mum of old. Not the grumpy recent one. I had made the correct executive decision to bring Spud to our house. Quite a squeeze with two on the seat of my Chopper. Spud was very careful not to push his willy against my buttocks. I've seen the size of his private parts and wouldn't want that thing thrusting against the back of my school trousers.

It's the first time Spud's been to my house. My parents have seen him at school events but never really spoken to him. Yet here Mum was comforting Spud. He really opened up to her. Telling Mum, and occasionally Dad, all about his mum's breast cancer. Dad was a little uncomfortable and seemed to take every excuse possible to leave the room.

With his mum in hospital, Spud has really struggled. This is not the super-confident Spud I know. Seems that on three different occasions he has left to come to school, but just couldn't cope. Apparently twice he ended up walking around the Mander Centre in Wolverhampton. I don't think his dad even realised early on that Pete wasn't going to school. Earlier this week he had been approached by a truancy officer in Willenhall. It's always easy to spot those officers. But Spud being tall was able to bluff and tell them he was on a break from his Youth Opportunities Programme job as a brickie. Although I think the weedy little truancy officer didn't fully believe the story, I think he was too chicken to really confront Spud. Probably scared he would nut him.

Spud's promised Mum that he'll go back to school in the morning. Mum has agreed to ring the school and explain the situation.

Friday 25th September

7:40am: We don't normally get a real breakfast in the morning. As Spud's stayed over, we have boiled eggs and soldiers. Not sure what age Mum thinks we are. We even got Frosties as well. Dad took Spud back last night to get his school uniform. Spud did jokingly suggest that he could borrow some of my uniform. I think not. I'm knackered. For some reason, Spud had my bed and I slept in my green sleeping bag on the floor. Well, attempted to sleep. The noises coming from Spud's mouth and bottom made sleeping impossible.

Walking to the bus stop to catch the school bus, I open up to Spud about my woman trouble. Explain how Grace is giving me the cold shoulder. Decided against sharing the detail of Grace seeing me naked in the corridor.

It felt like a "Dear John" letter as I explained my Grace problem to Peter Spud Hogan. He spent time thinking about it as we climbed aboard the 702 school bus. The driver questioning Spud's age and trying to make him pay full fare.

'Dear Hugh' (my nickname in the Local Gang, as sometimes I get called John, so Haystacks linked this to the *Star Soccer* commentator Hugh Johns) '...I think the problem is that there's no romance', Spud starts to answer to my problem. 'A girl needs to be wooed'. Trying to stay serious, I resist the chance to quote Kenneth Williams from *Carry on Matron* when he says, 'you can be as wooed as you like with me'. 'You have been going out with Grace Taylor for four months', the agony uncle continues. True, since Villa won the league.

'Yet, how many dates have you been on? A girl likes to be wined and dined', Spud seemed to be forgetting that Grace and I were only 14 and this was Willenhall. 'Look at Felicity Kendall in *Solo*. She wants more than just the ex coming round for a bit. She wants romance. Comprendo?'

Spud and romance don't really go together but perhaps the old guy has a point. Maybe I do need to do some wooing. Show Grace Taylor that I'm quite a catch. I'm going to do it. I'm going to take Grace on a date. Take her out for a meal. No wine, but I might be able to stretch to a milkshake.

Saturday 26th September

6:58pm: Not totally sure about this new Saturday night programme. It's not quite *Candid Camera*. Some of the pranks they are playing are quite funny. Others a little cringey. I guess some of the people tricked are game for a laugh and others are quite cross about it. I'm reading today's *Roy of the Rovers* comic. Only half watching the telly. Wow, didn't expect a male beauty contest at a nudist colony. On the telly, not in *Roy of the Rovers*. Not exactly the most handsome of men. Be great if Miss World was held in a nudist camp next time. The bearded presenter in the shellsuit is irritating.

Villa just can't score at the moment. We need Gary Shaw back. I was really excited this morning getting ready to go to my first ever Birmingham derby. Really thought we would beat them. Neither team ever looked like scoring. Peter Withe as a lone striker and only Ivor Linton on the bench. That's two 0-0 draws in the last three games. Typical, they bring in three points for a win and we keep drawing. Wolves won against Notts County, so Spud will be rubbing my nose in that one. At least we are still ahead of Wolves on goal difference. Hastings will be hating Albion being in the relegation zone.

11:10am: Get in there! Grace is up for me taking her out for a meal after school on Friday. She even gave me a kiss. Admittedly, only on the cheek but there was some chemistry. Just need to think where to take her now. Noddy suggested the *Berni Inn* in Walsall. But Tucker says he went there for his nan's birthday a month back and his dad had paid over three pounds for a chicken cordon bleu. If we went there, I would have to set the budget at under five pounds each. That's spending all my September pocket money. No, we need to think a little cheaper. Especially as my school bus pass only runs until six pm. I'd ask Dad if he'd pick us up, but Mum was in a foul mood this morning. I think he'll be busy trying to cheer her up. It seemed to relate to her trousers not fitting because she's put on a bit of weight. So where can I take Grace to show her what a great boyfriend I am?

Maths next and the chance to ask Mr Walker what he thinks of Forest's start to the season. They are just three points off top. Just need to check where my scientific Casio Fx-81 calculator is. It should be in my bag. I put it in last night after I finished doing my homework. It's brand new. I'll be in trouble if I've lost that. Not only will I not be able to find the cosine angles of the triangles, but Mum in her current mood will kill me or, worse still, cry.

Bellington is smiling too much. He's not a proper Liverpool fan. If he was, he would be in mourning today because their great former manager Bill Shankley has died. Hastings said he won three First Division titles for Liverpool. He also took them from the Second Division to First Division champions. Like Ron Saunders and Brian Clough have done.

'Lost something, stinky Stadler?', Kenny Bellington whispers.

Rightly or wrongly, I accuse Bellington of taking my Casio Fx-81 calculator.

'Now, I did see a crappy Casio calculator in Mr Harpwell's woodwork class. But that was a smashed up one that looked as if somebody had hit it with a hammer. What happened to that one, Macca?', Kenny Bellington continues to goad me.

The horror unfolded as James McCullan takes out my smashed scientific Casio calculator from his blazer pocket.

8:52pm: The tie was never in doubt after the 5-0 at Villa Park, but good to have my lucky radio working. Commentary is by the Radio Birmingham team, and it's been plain sailing for the Villans. Best of all, 20-year-old Gary Shaw is back. Finally, the Withe-Shaw combo is back in tangent. Still no Ken McNaught, and Andy Blair is in to give Tony Morley a rest. I bet it's cold in Reykjavik. That sounds like a super volley from Gary Shaw to make it 2-0. His second goal. Maybe he'll go one better than Donovan and Withe and be the first Villa player to score a European Cup hat-trick.

Mark's back from his date with the crazy old punk Sarah. He seems quite pleased with himself. He didn't even make a sarcastic comment about the Villa only being two goals up. Seven-nil on aggregate is some start, though. I'm sure that's a love-bite on top of Mark's chest. Struggling to work out how physically glued spiky-haired Sarah would be able to do that, though, without poking him in the eye.

No more Villa goals. Just checking Ceefax for the European scores. Liverpool have gone one better than us. They are through 8-0 on aggregate. Red Star Belgrade did even better, they put eight past Scottish Hibernians today. Glentoran of Ireland, flipping heck, they've won 5-1. Teams to avoid in the draw are Liverpool, obviously, Benfica, Juventus and Bayern Munich. The West German team had got through the first round beating a Swedish team 6-0. Funniest result of the night, though, is Albion being knocked out of UEFA by a team of Grasshoppers. Wait until I see

Haystacks at school in the morning. It wasn't even close, 4-1 on aggregate. Losers!!

What am I going to do about my scientific Casio calculator? I really need one for my Maths lessons. But I can't tell my parents. Mum was crying again tonight when she was talking on the phone to Auntie Mavis. Even though she was in the hall and I was upstairs I could hear her crying. Something isn't right, my dad is walking around on eggshells.

Looking in the massive Argos catalogue Spring/Summer edition, the Fx-81 is £16.99. That's more than the cash I've got in my cashbox and I still must wine and dine Grace on Friday. I've got over £900 in my Staffordshire Building Society account. I'll lose loads of interest if I withdraw any. I got nearly 10% last year. Anyway, I can't get to the Bilston branch before the weekend. It's time to come clean to my brother.

Mark is really understanding about my predicament. Not only is he prepared to help me with the extra money but even offers to go to Walsall Argos tomorrow after his art college class and get me a new one. I'm quite freaked out by his kind gesture and more so when he then gives me three crisp one pound notes to help pay for my meal. It's been a pretty good evening. Think I'll try to set the timer on the VHS video recorder to record *Sportsnight*. They might have the Villa games on. See Gary's goals. 'Gary Shaw, Gary Shaw, Gary Gary Shaw. He gets the ball he's bound to score, Gary Gary Shaw'.

End of September Top of Division One

1. Ipswich	Pl: 7 Po: 17	+ 8
2. West Ham United	Pl: 7 Po: 15	+ 9
3. Swansea City	Pl: 7 Po: 15	+ 5
4. Nottingham Forest	Pl: 7 Po: 14	+ 4
16. Aston Villa	**Pl: 7 Po: 7**	**+ 0**

Villa September League Results

2nd Sunderland (a) 0:1 Lost
5th Tottenham Hotspur (a) 3-1 Won (Donovan (2), Mortimer)
12th Manchester United (h) 1-1 Draw (Cowans)
19th Liverpool (a) 0-0 Draw
23rd Stoke City (h) 2-2 Draw (Withe (2))
26th Birmingham City (h) 0-0 Draw

Villa September European Cup Results

16th Valur (Iceland) (h) 5-0 Won (Donovan (2), Withe (2), Morley)
30th Valur (Iceland) (a) 2-0 Won (Shaw 2)
[Villa win 7-0 on aggregate]

Chapter Four

October 1981

4:55pm: Normally this time on a Friday would be *Crackerjack* time. Today, though, I'm taking my girlfriend out for a slap-up meal. Today is a day to celebrate. The best news ever at school today. Kenny Bellington is finally leaving to go to live with his dad in Coventry. My school tormentor is going to be no more. More great news was that Mrs Cresswell-Farrington has changed her name back to Miss Cresswell, I think she is getting a divorce. But best part of today is being with my woman and buying her a meal.

Great to see the Wimpey in Walsall not too busy. A few too many kids in for my liking but still a reasonable ambience. I give Grace the choice of grill or burger. She selects grill but says I can choose what we have from the grill. It's Friday, so should I go fish? No, I'm going for a Wimpey Grill. Not only a Wimpey Grill but a Wimpey Special Grill. That comes with a fried egg as well as the beefburgers and with a posh star-cut tomato. With a sparkling orange drink that's only just over a pound for both of us. I can then offer her a knickerbocker glory for dessert.

We talk about lots of topics including Spud's mum's breasts, how Grace's mum is coping without Bellington's dad and Villa drawing Dynamo Berlin in the European Cup.

I start to tell Grace about my mum's strange behaviour lately. About her emotional extremes, being regularly sick and her weight gain. I put the weight gain down to eating too many crumpets with jam on.

Shockingly, Grace has another theory for my mother's behaviour. Grace says, 'Have you considered she might be pregnant, Jonathan?'

Is she crazy? My mum is over 40. She'd be a geriatric mother. Surely my parents haven't had sex recently. No, she's way off the mark with this. Anyway, they would have told me and it's only a three-bedroomed house. Well, two and a half really. You can hardly call my box room a bedroom.

6:39pm: It's been an amazing evening. We've got on so well. We've been so close together and just stared into each other's eyes. I really am in love. On the bus on the back row upstairs, we snog quite passionately. My left hand is permitted to penetrate Grace's school blouse. It reminds me of the scene from *On the Buses* when the conductor says to the amorous couple, "You going all the way?". There is nobody within four rows of us. So, my hand can stay inside the blouse and even have a sneaky feel inside Grace's bra. To my joy it touches a very raised nipple. Grace's hands also are starting to roam. Sadly, she's not going to find much down there so I redirect her hand on to my face. We are starting to draw attention, so my hand quickly retreats from Grace's bra and blouse.

Time for Grace's stop and for a final deep kiss.

'See you at school on Monday, Mr Spaceman'. Grace waves me goodbye with a reminder of our first ever date when I took her to see *Gregory's Girl*. The date when we were joined by my grandad. I miss you so much, Grandad.

2:22pm: Nice to have Randy come over for Sunday lunch. He brought not only yesterday's *Pink* but also the *Sunday People*. The paper Grandad used to always bring. Still disappointed that Villa let bottom-of-the-table Leeds equalise yesterday at Elland Road. As I told Randy, I really thought when Gary Shaw gave us the lead so early, we would win. Just our luck that that Leeds bloke Steve Balcombe scored a worldie on his debut. Only one win in our first eight games as champions. Things have got to improve soon. At least good to see we are still above Albion and Wolves. Last-but-bottom Wolves are only a point behind us.

'Are you nervous about Wednesday, Jonathan', Randy asks as he slurps his tea. No idea why Mum insisted on giving him a cup and saucer. He's got a jammy dodger too. I thought we were saving those. I see Mum is having four herself. Maybe she's eating for two.

'We're going to thrash your mob on Wednesday'. Mark towers over me. Speaking for the first time since coming back from seeing his lot lose 5-0 at Old Trafford. At least our game on Wednesday against Wolves is only the first leg. So, if Villa do muck it up it's not all over. Must admit I'm nervous, despite Wolves' enjoyable walloping yesterday. What if Andy Gray does come back to haunt us and I'm forced to watch from my season ticket seat us losing to the Wolves. Dad has paid the money to reserve my seat for the game, but I must show one of the vouchers from the back of my book. If we lose, both home and school life will be hell.

Bryan Robson signed on the pitch for Manchester United before the game yesterday. One and a half million pounds. It even beat the Andy Gray record. What is it with West Midland clubs selling players for record amounts. Poor Haystacks was broken on Friday at school. He couldn't believe that not only had Manchester United stolen the Albion manager but now their best player as well. Haystacks' all-time favourite West Brom player. It's been a pretty rubbish few days for Scott. On Thursday night someone told him that Georgina Ramsey was spotted snogging a sixth-former from King Ed's. And we thought she was too young for Haystacks. He hasn't challenged Georgina over this alleged misdemeanour.

Asif has come round to play Asteroids on my Atari. I said he could in exchange for him helping me with the more complex simultaneous equations in my Maths homework. Randy has to go about three as he needs to be back home in time for *Bonanza*. Randy hasn't long passed his driving test. It took him nine goes. I think they just gave it to him in the end. He is a very careful driver and as yet hasn't been brave enough to take a passenger or even drive with the radio on. When he's driving on a Saturday afternoon, he stops every ten minutes to check the football scores. He doesn't really do right turns. So, Dad is trying to give him instructions about how to get back to Bilston without doing any difficult right turns. It will probably take him twice as long.

Spud has arrived now. Seems he's sick of being in the house on his own while his dad is at the hospital. Even though he's been drinking his dad's homebrew in the shed. It's the first time Asif has met Spud and he's a bit taken aback by the character in front of him. Maybe it's the black eye shadow, massive zits or that he's desperately in need of a shave. Here's me totally hairless in the genitalia department and there is Peter Hogan with more stubble than Worzel Gummidge.

Asif is distracted on the Atari. Very impressive use of a joystick as he is destroying those asteroids. Spud takes me to one side.

'They're going to chop off her tits', Spud just spurts out. I have no idea what to say to this. What is the response when your best mate informs you that his mum has got to lose her breasts to stop the cancer. I'm sure there is a medical term for it, but no idea what. So, I respond in the best way I know and make fun of Wolves letting in five goals to rubbish Man United. Followed by maybe the Villa can put more than five past Paul Bradshaw on Wednesday night.

5:39pm: Teaching Asif the rules of French cricket. Really surprised that a cricket fan is not au fait with how to play French cricket. He's leaving his back legs far too exposed. It needs more of a Chris Tavaré stance than a Mike Gatting one. Spud and Mark are on the same wavelength and quickly the tennis ball is with Spud behind Asif. Spud hurls the ball at Asif's calves with some venom. Grammar schoolboy out without scoring. I'm going to have to go some to save us now.

What a shot! Mark tried to put some underarm spin on his delivery, but without moving my feet I bring my bat forward from the six o'clock position and scoop the ball over the garden fence, into the park and then one bounce against the surprised small girl on the seesaw. Six! What a start to my innings. Spud isn't happy having to go to fetch that one.

What's that chopping noise? No, it can't be. Dad's going to do his nut. Asif's dad is chopping off the branches of our weeping willow tree. The ones hanging over into his garden. That tree has been there all my life. I've stood under there during the rain so many times. My dad loves that tree. Now our new neighbour is cutting big chunks off it.

Wednesday 7th October

7:26pm: We are officially at war with our new neighbours. I'm no longer to let Asif in the house or the garden. Both our fathers are behaving like toddlers and have thrown their toys out of the pram. I think my dad initially overreacted but Asif's dad's response of chopping even more weeping willow branches off really went too far. Mum's being weeping ever since and eating more biscuits.

Time to focus on my own welfare now. Come on, you Villa lads. We must beat Mark's Wolves. I want to go to school tomorrow with my head held high and at home just smile when I see Mark. He's travelled down on the train and is in the away end. I got to come with Mr Hill. The old woman in the seat next door doesn't seem to be getting the magnitude of this game. Why is she giving me some of her granddaughter's birthday cake just as the Villa players are coming out? Glad Ron's recalled Tony Morley. We'll need him tonight.

The boos for Andy Gray are deafening. Even the old lady at my side is laying into Villa's former golden boy. It's the first time he's played at Villa Park since Wolves stole him for £1.4 million in 1979.

8:30pm: Can't believe we let Andy flipping Gray score. He'll probably score again now. One-nil down against this lot. The Wolves fans are making fun of us with their high-pitched Villa! Villa! shouts. I hate football.

That's a bad challenge. Andy Gray on skipper Dennis Mortimer. Right in front of us. Can't believe what the old lady just called Mr Gray. Everyone wants the ref to act … Blimey, I think the referee, Clive White, is sending Andy Gray off. Fantastic, everything is going to be okay. Come on Villa, let's turn this tie around.

They've got ten men. How have we let that old oaf Joe Gallagher score? Two flaming nil. I can just imagine it at school tomorrow. Villa gets stuffed by ten-man Wolves. The team who Man United put five passed on Saturday. What's gone wrong with us? We are Champions of England.

Well done, Dessie Bremner! That gives us hope. Still 20 minutes to go, we can pull this around. Oh, Andy, great goal. Andy Blair makes it 2-2. This is more like it.

10:50pm: That's a front door slamming. Perhaps I should go down and greet Mark. Maybe safer not to. I think that injury-time Tony Morley winner will mean he's not in the best of moods. I'm sure he will argue that Andy Gray shouldn't have been sent off and that that's the only reason we won. The first time I've sat in the Trinity and seen us win. I'm going to enjoy it. Yes, I know it's only the first leg, but a win is a win. Before the second leg at Molineux in two weeks we also must go there in the league. Who knows who'll get the bragging rights then. Tomorrow at school is going to be my day. Thank you, Tony Morley.

Friday 9th October

9:03am: Mr McGinn seems in an even worse mood than normal today. It's zero tolerance for any talking in our form tutor session. Spud has had a shave and seems to be more his normal self, but his mum's surgery is today. Think he's just trying too hard to be normal. Carrie Campton seems to be quite affectionate to him today. I tried to ask him if they were finally going out, but Jock McGinn just threw his whiteboard rubber at me. It hit me smack on the back of my head. It really hurt, but I tried not to show it.

12:43pm: Lunchtime kickabout. Noddy has first pick. Disappointingly he's picked Tucker. I guess these Walsall fans have to stick together. Haystacks then picks Spud. Well, I am bound to get picked before Freddy Gilbert. No, Noddy has picked Freddy. In the end I'm sixth pick. A disgrace, only the two third-years, the Bailey twins are picked after me. Really confusing that the identical twins are on opposing sides. How am I supposed to know if it's Linton or Leroy I'm supposed to pass to. In the end, Leroy agrees to tie his tie around his head.

Spud's gone in goal; that never happens. Haystacks is up front and charging around like a hippopotamus on heat. He's in a foul mood because it's over with Georgina Ramsey. It wasn't the infidelity that finished it, but worse. Georgina has followed Atkinson and Robson and defected to Manchester United. Haystacks spotted that she had a Manchester United, Gary Bailey, poster in her locker. It was like a dagger straight through the heart.

Leroy Bailey is better than I expected. He's scored two decent goals, although I still think one went over the jumper. His identical twin Linton, who's on our side, doesn't possess his brother's footballing prowess. He's just gifted Tucker a goal. Spud seems reluctant to move in goal, so we're just doomed. It hardly seems worth playing. I quickly take the excuse to take a breather when Grace passes by.

'Can we talk please, Jonathan?'. Grace was not exactly flaunting the girlfriend card.

I smiled and went in for a discrete kiss, but the kiss ended up landing more jaw than lips. Something was wrong. This wasn't the passionate encounter of Friday night.

We talked. Well, Grace talked. You didn't need to be a fortune teller to know how this conversation was going to turn out.

Grace had been doing a lot of thinking. She really, really liked me. Time for the but ... Bang! Grace informs me that her O levels must come first. Having a relationship might distract her. She has to focus totally on her studies. She needs good O levels so that she can then get the A levels she needs to go to university. To get a degree to be able to go into Journalism. Wow, she's really got it all planned out. I wonder if she'll end up a sports reporter. Like Peter White in the *Sports Argus*. Problem was that this careers chat was just for the benefit of dumping me. The lad who fondled her nipple less than a week ago. I wasn't ready for this. I'd got plans for other areas of Grace Taylor for my fingers to explore.

How can I play this cool? What is the correct response to a polite dumping on educational grounds? Probably not to have tears in your eyes and just turn around and walk back over to your pals and blast the ball straight past Spud – your own keeper.

It seemed unlikely, but at that moment, there was something more important than my love life. Mr Walker came hurrying out. There was a telephone call for Peter Hogan. His dad was ringing from the hospital.

Saturday 10th October

6:51pm: I'm trying to work out my *Shoot!* League Ladder positions based on the scores from Ceefax. The league table on Ceefax hasn't been updated. Even though the Villa have drawn for the flipping sixth time this season, I'm determined to move the tags around. We always beat Coventry City. But today in that rubbish all-seater stadium. What does Jimmy Hill know? First three points for a win and then a ground with no standing. Both madness. Gary Shaw scored again. That's four goals in four games for him. To think he's only six years older than me. At least we have moved up a place, unlike Wolves. We have gone above Arsenal, crazy. Ipswich are top after beating Wolves, I can't see us catching up the eleven points lead they have over us. Perhaps Bobby Robson deserves the title this year after being so well beaten last year. I saw on *Grandstand* that John Motson was at Portman Road. That means the Wolves game will be on *Match of the Day* tonight. I wonder if Spud will watch it. So glad his mum came through the operation okay. He was going to go and see her this afternoon.

Still don't like Larry Grayson presenting the *Generation Game*. I guess Bruce Forsyth is too old now. *Juliet Bravo* on next for my mum, so I'll do some of my History homework then, before *The Paul Daniels Magic Show.*

Saturday 17th October

11:42am: It's official, Ken's Mobile Trotters basketball club are no more. The committee meeting voted to disband the club. Noddy's dad, Ken, has had to sell his mobile shop. He has joined one of Maggie's unemployed. One of nearly three million now. New Conservative Employment Secretary, Norman Tebbit, told the unemployed 'to get on your bike' this week. Well, it looks like Noddy's dad will have to do just that because he's selling his van. We must walk to the square now if we need a loaf of bread. So, no money to sponsor our team and, to be fair, since Bellington left, we've struggled to put out five players. So, I guess it's twelve games and out for the team. A proud history of nine and a half months. What's the opposite of going unbeaten? We lost every game. Surprised Spud didn't turn up for the meeting. I guess a lot going on with his mum, she's starting chemotherapy this week.

Just leaving the sports hall and bump into Grace. What's she doing at school on a Saturday? The library isn't open and she's not in her uniform. She's looking very hot. A big jacket and a red skirt. Is she wearing shoulder pads? Looks like she belongs on *Dynasty*. I smile but decide not to stop to speak to her.

In the car park waiting for my dad. He's going to drop me off at the Hill's, ready to go to Villa Park. To see the battle of the claret and blues against West Ham. Spud appears from nowhere. He's wearing a white t-shirt and black 501s. Looks like the Fonz from *Happy Days*. What's going on?

'I got the part, Hugh!' Spud shouts excitedly.

So, apparently, the big school production this year is *Grease*. The one that Olvia Newton John starred in. It seems mister big here has landed the role of Kenickie. No idea what he has to sing. Spud tells me the other news. That Sandy is going to be played by Grace Taylor. Brilliant! She dumps me, supposedly to concentrate on her academic pursuits, and then a week later is auditioning for the lead in the school play. Something that will take up considerably more of her precious time than I would.

Girls, who needs them? I'm going to concentrate on supporting the Villa.

1:59pm: Even Howard Hill is slagging off the government today. Norman Tebbit's 'on your bike' comment seems to have really fired people up. I thought it was only Tony Butler who told people 'on yer bike'. Glad we've dropped the shoppers off; we can talk about the important stuff now. How Villa can win their first home league game of the season. West Ham are fourth and their striker, David Cross, is First Division top scorer. Well, joint with Kevin Keegan. Admittedly, Cross did score four against Tottenham. Mr Hill says he's always admired Alan Devonshire. I just hope we don't have to face another Ray Stewart penalty. I'm still furious about that dodgy FA Cup quarter-final penalty season before last.

Howard Hill in his blue diamond Pringle jumper then decides to share his news with me. He's being forced to take early retirement. His engineering firm is cutting 30 jobs. Again, I don't know how to respond. I mean the fact that he won't have to go to work again is surely good. More time to follow the Villa, perhaps go to away European games. Yet, I guess it must be a shock and worry all the jobs that Mrs Hill might get him to do. I also expect that looking after his son isn't cheap. I just nod and say, 'difficult times… what do you think the score will be today?'

3:50pm: Reading my programme feeling quite content. After the nightmare of Trevor Brooking giving the Hammers the lead after two minutes, it's all gone pretty well. Goals by Tony Morley, David Geddis (in for Peter Withe) and the skipper Dennis have put us in control. I can only see more Villa goals in the second half. For the first time ever, I am going to see the Villa win three points. Ron Saunders in his programme notes promised an entertaining game and he's not wrong so far. He says he's confident and of course asks

64

for us and the players to give 110%. Mark always says that this is impossible and only a moron would want more than a 100%. Tickets are available for the Dynamo Berlin second leg. I need to send my dad down to the ticket office next week. He'll need voucher number 32. Good job he works in Perry Barr. It is £3 though. Hopefully he'll forget to ask me for the money.

Old Doris is getting excited and the second half hasn't even started. She's rubbing hard with her two-pence coin on her Aston Villa FC Supa Cash Card. On the 'In The Net' section she's found two goals in her first two balls. That means she'll win a least a pound. Another goal in last two balls would make it a fiver. And if all five are goals that would be an amazing £100. Not surprising that she's starting to sweat. Although, the large coat and cardie she's wearing isn't helping.

Second half is under way and Doris is still revelling in her five-pound win. She's promised Penny a fish supper and a couple of bottles of stout on the way home.

Come on, Villa! We need to get the fourth and put this game to bed. That wasn't in the script. Who was marking David Cross? We've let West Ham back into it. I can see this being another sodding draw. I'm a jinx. My season ticket seat is ruining our season. Maybe I should have stuck to following the Villa at home on my lucky radio. What's going on, Ron? Have you lost your magic?

9:41pm: Decent guests for once on *Parkinson*. Ones I have heard of. Kenneth Williams from the *Carry On* films and *Willow the Wisp*, as well as Windsor Davies from *It Ain't Half Hot Mum*. I've even heard of Vera Lynn, she's a Dame, which I think is a female Sir. Dad said she sang a lot of songs during the war. One about bluebells on a cliff apparently. Mind you, he obviously isn't that impressed as he's gone off for his weekly bath before *Match of the Day*. Pity the Villa game isn't one of the three games on. Would have been good to see if you could see me and Doris during our 3-2 two victory. I was certainly nervous at the end. Didn't think that ref was ever going to blow up. It was nearly quarter to five when he did.

Mark arrives home in a jolly mood. Even though Wolves are in the relegation zone. He's telling Mum all about his wonderful date with Sarah. Think Mum is more interested in Dame Vera Lynn. Probably similar age to Sarah. Wonder who Mum would rather Mark was shagging, Sarah or Vera Lynn? I'm assuming that Mark is having sex. He probably wouldn't tell me if I asked him. Bet he was a late developer too, it's the Stadler curse. I've noticed he shaves every day and even has an extra one before he's going on a date. Although I think he overdoes the Brut. Mark took Sarah to see *Endless Love* starring Brooke Shields tonight. I wonder if she gets her kit off like she did in the *The Blue Lagoon*. It's a 15, so next year I'll be able to go and see films like that. Spud claims that he's rented a few 18 classified films from Blockbusters while his mum has been in hospital. Including *Confessions of a Window Cleaner*. I bet that's an interesting job. Knowing my luck, instead of looking into someone like Barbara Windsor in her bath, it would be Dame Vera, old Doris from football or Howard Hill's sister Peggy.

My thoughts of Babs in a bath are annoyingly shattered by several large bangs. Next door are banging on the wall. Are they in trouble? Dad comes racing down the stairs in his dressing gown. Still fastening it as he storms into the lounge.

'Turn that bloody telly down', comes the shout from next door.

Perhaps Vera Lynn was singing *We'll Meet Again* a touch loud, but no need for rudeness. My dad is furious. Mark is getting hold of the remote control and making it louder. I always forget that this new techie telly can be controlled remotely. At least you can still press buttons on the set when Mum is sitting on the remote. It's now a contest of who can make the most noise. Asif's dad banging or Dame Vera singing. Mark is also singing at the top of his voice as well. Bring back Auntie Mavis and Uncle Norman.

Wednesday 21ˢᵗ October

8:39pm: Seems strange to think of Villa playing behind the Iron Curtain. All I really know about East Germany is the butch women shot-putters. Radio Birmingham commentary isn't too bad. It's only lost it a couple of times. It does seem a long way away, though. Probably the Communist government is putting a delay on the radio waves in case anything they don't agree with is being said. Dynamo Berlin must be decent to have won the East German league. Their manager is called Bogs. We have rejigged in defence. Brendan Ormsby still in for Ken McNaught and now Gary Williams is right-back as Kenny Swain is injured. Ron's playing Colin Gibson at left-back. I think Ron'll be pleased with the draw. Yes, Tony Morley gave us the early lead but it's been all Dynamo Berlin since. No surprise when they equalised. Sure I heard Mark cheer from the bathroom when that goal went in. But 1-1 is better than 0-0. We've got an away goal. We just need to hold out for another 20 minutes. Ooh. Ivor Linton has come on for Gary Williams. Gary must be injured.

In my frustration I kick my lucky radio off the bed. Ivor Linton has been adjudged to have brought down the Berlin player. Penalty to them with only nine minutes left. I guess a 2-1 defeat isn't a bad result. Should be a cracker at Villa Park in a fortnight. Maybe Jimmy will save it. Come on, Jimmy Rimmer, your country needs you.

He's hit the post. Can hardly hear the commentator over the crowd noise. What's happened now? Sounds like an amazing save by Rimmer from the rebound. It's still 1-1, but corner to Berlin. Brilliant Jimmy Rimmer, what a hero. We can still come out of this with a draw.

That's it. Get the ball out of the box. I can't take much more of this pressure. Sounds like Tony Morley has got the chance to get the ball away. Hold on, he's going on a run. What's happening? He's through on goal. Goal!!!!!! A second for super Tony Morley. It sounds like an incredible goal. We're winning. I don't believe it.

9:41pm: I'm nervous watching the game on *Sportsnight*, even though I know we win 2-1. That's an amazing rebound save by Jimmy. How did he get that over the bar? Really like this white away top with the claret shorts. The East German keeper is wearing yellow like an international goalkeeper. How fast is Tony Morley? That's an incredible goal. Probably even better than his Goal of the Season at Everton last year. There was no stopping him. He was faster than Alan Wells. His first goal was pretty special as well. We have one big foot in the quarter-finals of the European Cup.

Liverpool got a decent draw – 2-2 with Dutch side AZ 67 Alkmaar. I was born in the year '67. Apparently, the European Cup Final is being held in Holland this year. The commentator said it will be in Rotterdam and that this is in Holland. I suppose ending in "dam" it would be. The Dutch like their dams. Imagine if Aston Villa reach that final in Rotterdam. Perhaps Mr Hill would take me. The land of cheese, clogs, windmills and ladies of the night.

In the Cup Winners' Cup, Tottenham couldn't even beat Dundalk of Ireland. Be so funny if Dundalk knocked them out.

Friday 23rd October

1:45pm: Sitting on the side of the pool, boring Tucker and Noddy again about Tony Morley's wonder goal, I'm regretting skipping lunch to try to talk to Grace. We did chat a bit, but it was frosty. I said the wrong thing a few times and Grace made it clear that she didn't need all this hassle now. Now my tummy is rumbling and one place you don't want big rumbles is in the school swimming baths.

Can't believe they've made these blue swimming caps compulsory. Mind you, it matches my verruca sock quite well. Pity it isn't a claret one. I'm sure if the club shop started to stock Villa-coloured verruca socks, they would do well. Oddly, from the girls' changing rooms, only Wendy McGregor comes out. Lined up instead on the balcony are ten girls. All apparently unable to swim due to their periods. Obviously, the last Friday in the month is a peak time for periods. Davina Cash must have very heavy periods because it's been over two months since she last swam. Wendy McGregor is getting a lot of attention. I hadn't noticed before what a fab figure she's now got. Very impressive curves. She is really owning that black swimming costume. Pity she's got to put one of these condom hats over her lovely brunette hair. She reminds me of Victoria Principal from *Dallas*. A much younger version, of course. I wonder if she knows I'm now single. Maybe it's time to put myself back out there.

Or perhaps I'm not ready. To my surprise, Wendy McGregor comes and sits right beside me on the edge of the pool. Her lovely long legs dangling into the chlorine-filled water. Flicking her long hair back as she squeezes into her swimming cap. It was like watching the woman in the L'Air du Temps perfume advert.

'I'm safe next to you, aren't I, Stadler?' Wendy McGregor whispered as she patted my slightly chubby bare leg. I just smiled and tried to control my stomach rumblings.

'In pairs please', yells Mr Kellymans as Wendy grabs my arm. 'I want you to practice your breaststroke'.

In our pairs we took turns holding each other's feet as they did the arm actions. I did feel a bit self-conscious when Wendy was gripping onto my verruca sock. Perhaps the more intimate part though was when we had to link hands and both do the breaststroke leg-kicking. This resulted in an unexpected long stare into each other's eyes. Noddy wasn't helping me concentrate as he kept putting his mouth in kissing positions behind me. It obviously wasn't the only me who had noticed Wendy McGregor's closeness to me. I've never really thought of Wendy in that kind of way. Yet here I was fixated with the loveliness of this girl. Her normal overconfidence seems to have melted away.

Saturday 24th October

11:36am: Nervous about this afternoon's latest Stadler family derby. Watching *Swap Shop*. Karen Carpenter from the Carpenters is on it. She looks so skinny. You can almost see her skeleton in her face. So, second of the three Villa-Wolves games in October. Today is the league game at Molineux. I'm feeling quite confident but telling people I think it'll be a draw. We're all going together and I'll be in the North Bank with the Wolves fans. Going to have to stand with Mark, so that'll be interesting. Dad's also invited Spud to come with us. His mum came out of hospital yesterday, but she's sleeping a lot. The first lot of chemo has really knocked her about. We are going to drive to Randy's in Bilston and then go on the 79 bus from there into Wolverhampton. I'm going to have to travel with lots of Wolves fans. No wearing my colours or rosette today. I have got a badge though that's fastened inside my coat pocket. I had it printed on holiday. It says, 'VILLA MAGIC WOLVES TRAGIC'. Mark knows about it and Mum was disgusted when I did it. Randy offered to drive us to the ground, but Dad tactfully got us out of that one. With Randy's driving never reaching 20 miles per hour and his fear of right turns, we wouldn't have got there for kick-off time.

On the 79 bus I'm relieved to see a few with claret and blue scarves on. I listen carefully as one gentleman talks about how great Tony Morley is. Unfortunately, a Wolves fan in a mod coat with a target on the back takes umbrage at someone bigging up Tony Morley. Wolves' fans have not forgiven Morley for the tackle last year that broke Peter Daniel's leg. Out of earshot of Mark and Dad

I'm telling Spud about how attentive Wendy McGregor had been on Friday. How she'd even stopped me after History to check what I thought the homework was.

'Sounds like you're in there, Hugh', came Spud's simple reply. He's still not his normal self. I ask him how it's going with *Grease* and he just shrugged his shoulders and said 'fine'. Changing the subject to the big match and trying to get a prediction from Spud. He's fearing the worst. He predicts a 3-0 win to the Villa. Well, I hope he's right. Spud says that since Emlyn Hughes left, Wolves just haven't been able to defend.

Outside the ground, Dad buys me a programme. On the front is a picture of a boy who looks a bit like me. He's wearing an old gold hat with WOLVES on it.

'Titch, what are you doing on the front? Finally wearing some decent gear as well', Mark sniggers at me.

I get revenge when I point out it says the game is sponsored by Winners Matches. Which is totally inappropriate for the Wolves.

I know I shouldn't, but I do really like the North Bank at Molineux. Maybe because it was the place where I first watched Villa play away from home. Or because Grandad used to stand here when Wolves were a great team. First team to have floodlights and the early pioneers of European football. It's always had a nice family feel to it. Considerably smaller than the more hostile South Bank opposite. Spud is normally in the South Bank, although doesn't get too many games. The new John Ireland Stand is quite impressive. So odd being so far away from the pitch. The plan is to rebuild all the other three sides to join up with it. Rumour, though, that Wolves are skint. Building that stand cost more than they expected; as well as buying Andy Gray. Even if a lot of that money came from selling Steve Daley to Man City. That was a rubbish buy for City. They are about to sell him to a team from America for a fifth of what they paid for him. I guess Villa did the best out of all those deals. At least Andy Gray is suspended today. Not many people here. A few Villa fans, but I expected more. Crowd might only just reach 20,000. Good news, the BBC cameras are here. We are going to be on *Match of the Day*. Don't let me down, Villa.

10:03pm: I'm the only one in the household watching *Match of the Day*. After we thumped Wanderers, seems Mark and Dad have lost interest. Dad is dealing with a bit of a meltdown from Mum. I think it started over him burning her pikelet. It soon escalated. She ended up blaming Dad for the now disfigured weeping willow tree and for Mark ending up with an old obnoxious punk. I'm blaming Mum's hormones and starting to think Grace might be right about my mother having a bun in the oven. Really, I need to approach the subject with my parents. Now, though, it's time to sit back and relive our three-goal thrashing of Wolves under the expert commentary of John Motson. He's already mentioning how the European exploits of Tony Morley will have caught the interest of England manager Ron Greenwood. Morley has played a few times for England B lately. That was harsh comment, Mr Motson, mentioning that in the last three meetings between these teams here there has been three sendings-off and a broken leg.

Sid Cowans played well. Some great tackles. He just flings his legs in. That Joe Gallagher's a dirty player. You can tell he played for the Blues. Great goal by Gary Shaw. Peter Withe backheel into Shaw's path. No wonder Gary applauded Withe's pass. Wolves look so nervous defending. They seemed to do so many backpasses to Bradshaw. Poor Geoff Palmer, he had no option but to score that own goal. Wolves do have a habit of scoring goals for us. Can hear the Villa fans singing 'Jingle bells, oh what fun it is to see the Villa win away'. I was singing with them, to myself, in the North Bank. The 'Going down, going down' chants were a touch mean, though. Perhaps that was a slightly lucky deflection on Gary Shaw's second goal. That's six goals in seven games since he's been back from injury. It's all Villa now. I can't believe we didn't score more. But 3-0 will do.

We are now 13 games unbeaten. Into the top ten and only eight points off the top. Ron Atkinson's Manchester United have gone top but they've played two games more.

Tuesday 27th October

12:49pm: Spud is more himself today. He even grabbed a second-year around the neck for saying how rubbish Wolves are. Tonight is the final part of the Wolves-Villa trilogy. Victorious Villa returning to Molineux just three days after we spanked them. The second leg of the League Cup second round. Andy Gray-less Wolves trailing two goals to three. I guess it's still close. Spud has predicted penalties. He had a dream that Wayne Clarke scored the winning penalty for Wolves. In the dream Spud celebrated with a night of passion with all the Nolan sisters. Font of all knowledge Haystacks then informed us that on the B side of The Nolan Sisters biggest hit *I'm in the Mood for Dancing* was a song called *Let's Make Love*.

Today is Mum's birthday. I think she's 41. That's surely too old to have a baby. In the *Sunday People* they have celebrated geriatric 38-year-old mothers. She seemed pleased with her Eternal Beau teapot. It's a slight second, so was a bit cheaper. She didn't notice though or was too kind to mention it. She was quite taken back that her other son's card was signed, 'love from Mark and Sarah xx'. Seems that instead of going to work today Mum has an appointment at the hospital. I guess if she is pregnant that would make sense. On her birthday she wants Wolves and Villa to draw. Mark and I have agreed not to argue about it. As its Mum's special day, Dad is not going to the game. Luckily, Howard Hill is. Mr Hill is taking me in the Villa part of the South Bank. First time he's stood at a match since Highbury. Mark is going with his mates; he'll be on the other side of the South Bank. But it's not only my mum's birthday today. It's also Gordon Cowans'. Sid is 23 today. He seems to have been playing for the Villa for years. I think Ron Greenwood should be giving Gordon an England cap. He's the best number ten in England. Another number ten, Glenn Hoddle of Tottenham, also shares this birthday.

Grace comes over to us boys and surprisingly gives me a hug. She then wishes me all the best for tonight. The odd behaviour continues when she gives me a card. Well, it feels like a card. It's got 'Mrs Stadler' on the front.

'Have you found out when the happy day is yet, Jonathan?', Grace says smiling and behaving far too much like a girlfriend. I shake my head and Grace Taylor leaves. Even Noddy is taken back by Grace's behaviour.

'Hi Jonny, have you heard the new Queen album? Their greatest hits one. I've got it. Do you fancy coming round to listen to it on Friday night?', Wendy McGregor addresses me in front of the gang.

My response was probably not the most auditable but I'm pretty sure the words 'that would be nice' came out of my mouth. Wendy McGregor laughs and promises to finalise the details tomorrow. The group watch open-mouthed as she walks away.

'Did you see that wiggle of the hips, Hugh? What have you done to all these girls? Is it new aftershave or have you drugged them?' Tucker said, not quite able to take in what he'd just witnessed. I had no idea what was happening, but suddenly I was scared stiff. Perhaps for a late developer like me, "stiff" was not the right term. No, I was petrified. I think I've just agreed to a date with Wendy McGregor.

'I bet it's an amazing album, they've had so many hits', said Haystacks trying to bring me back to ground.

'You can't beat *Fat Bottomed Girls*', interrupted Spud. I wonder if I was the only one in the group then that was now contemplating the size of Carrie Carrington's bottom. It didn't take long for Noddy to take the conversation down a level as he shouted 'Flash' and pretended to expose himself to a passing couple of first-year girls. I was a bit slow. As a Villa fan I should have joined in the Queen songs with a chorus of *We Are the Champions*. I am starting to think that we could be champions again this season.

5:31pm: I have never seen Dad so angry. He's trying to keep his calm for Mum's sake. It being her birthday and the unlikely possibility that she might be pregnant. When I got back from school, I saw that our neighbours had started to build a wall. Well, at least four builders were in their garden laying bricks. It was obvious the intention was to build a wall higher than the current fence that divided our back gardens. A fence that we had played badminton over growing up. A fence that we had lit Catherine wheels on. A fence that was as old as the house and part of our heritage. The building of a wall was a symbol that our two families were now enemies and would never be allies. It was Berlin all over again. Our own Iron Curtain.

We need to get off to Mr Hill's, but I'm waiting for Dad to come back from telling Asif's dad exactly what he thinks of him. Mum has decided she's going to spend the evening knitting. She is no longer in the mood to go out with Dad for a meal at Ye Old Toll House in Willenhall.

Dad finally comes back. Mark has already gone to the game. I'm worried we're going to be late. It's escalated further. Dad has got next door's builders to build a wall in the front of our house now. A small wall to block off the path in front of our houses that joins the two together. None of Asif's family will be allowed to cross the border. This was madness and I wanted no part of it. I need to talk to Asif about this, but first I need to go and support my team. Suddenly I had a very bad feeling about the cup tie. Maybe

Spud's dream will come true. Excluding the part with The Nolan Sisters.

10:30pm: I thought Mum would be pleased that somebody who shares her birthday had done so well tonight. Thanks to two goals from Gordon Cowans, we are through to round three. Admittedly, at 1-1 with two minutes to go, Mr Hill and I were very nervous. Sid never misses a penalty, though. We deserved the 2-1 win.

It seems I'm in Mark's room tonight. My dad really is in the doghouse. He's going to be sleeping in my room. So, I must sleep on the floor of Mark's room. Not allowed to mention the Villa win and must put up with Mark's snoring. There isn't room for anybody else in this house.

Sitting on the sofa packing my school bag I feel a sharp prick in my buttock. I am sitting on my mum's size nine knitting needle. If I needed confirmation of my mother's pregnancy, my left buttock had found it. The knitting was clearly distinguishable as a baby's cardigan. It was yellow, so gender neutral. It could be denied no longer that there was soon going to be two extra tiny feet in our house.

Lying on the floor of Mark's bedroom I'm contemplating so many different topics. The main ones being how I'm going to cope with not being the youngest Stadler child, what the hell I'm going to do in Wendy McGregor's bedroom, and who will we draw in the third round of the League Cup?

If the baby is a girl, guess that's me and Mark back sharing this room. No more Villa pictures up or a place for me to escape. The middle child always gets the short straw. The oldest one gets the benefits of being the first-born, heir to the throne. The youngest one is the baby of the bunch and gets spoiled the most. Then there is the middle child. The one everybody always forgets. Look at The Osmonds. Everybody knows the youngest one, Jimmy. I have no idea who the eldest Osmond is, perhaps that was a bad example.

Which football team would our newest sibling support? Could I cope with another Wolves fan in the family. If it's a girl, will I ever be able to get to the bathroom? Mark already spends enough time in there. Babies cry all the time as well. That'll have next door banging on the walls even more. What about my O levels. Mum, you haven't thought this through. When I need peace and quiet to study, the house will be full of a screaming baby. Hold on, Mum's auntie was a twin. What if it's twins?!

Friday 30th October

4:32pm: Wendy McGregor takes the key from the shoe polish tin hidden under the brick by the backdoor. It seems all our parents hide spare keys in tins. Don't they watch Shaw Taylor on *Police 5*? I had assumed that Mrs McGregor was going to be in when I had accepted Wendy's music recital invitation.

I had tried to get some info on the best way to play my first 'date' with Wendy. The responses had been varied. Hastings had gone for the 'play it cool' approach. Build up to the kiss on the second date. Noddy had been more for heavy petting straight from kick-off. This time, though, I was going to take my big brother's advice. Mark had said let the girl take the lead. Be led by what Wendy McGregor does and look out for any signals she gives off. I'm not sure what kind of signals she might give off. Was I looking for semaphore with flags, smoke signals or will she just blink three times, like Tabitha in *Bewitched*?

Unexpectedly we end up in Wendy's bedroom. I was lured there because she claimed it was where her record player was. Very odd, a record player in a bedroom, not downstairs connected to a tuner and speakers. Was this a signal that I needed to act on? I wasn't ready for heavy petting, so bedroom activity was certainly not on my agenda or within my capabilities.

'Do you want a drink?', Wendy McGregor suddenly stopped going through her box of LPs and asked me. Was she looking to ply me with alcohol? In the hope of taking things to a stage I wasn't ready for? I've only ever had a shandy, port and lemon or that champagne on the Royal Wedding day.

'The Corona pop man came yesterday, so we've got some cherryade. Or there's some flat R Whites lemonade.' Despite being considered tone-deaf, I managed a quick rendition of 'I'm a secret lemonade drinker, R Whites R Whites…..' Had I responded in the right manly way? Maybe I was over analysing all this?

Sitting next to Wendy McGregor on her bed drinking large glasses of pop through bendy straws listening to *Bohemian Rhapsody*. A classic that goes on a bit. I like the song even though it's oddly operatic and really makes no sense at all. I know his mother has just killed a man and now he has a devil for a sideboard. I get distracted about the time someone spits in his eye. Now I'm studying Wendy's bedroom. It's all just too neat and grown up. Where are the posters, the cartoon character duvet, the dolls? It's a little dated. Orange and brown wallpaper just doesn't seem to be very teenage girl. The slightly open wardrobe door reveals clothes that did not resonate with the type of trendy outfits I imagined Wendy wearing.

Wendy insisted on me trying some of her cherryade. I made sure I used my straw and didn't dribble. Perhaps she wanted me to get my lips around her straw. Have my mouth where her mouth had been. These signals should come with a codebook. Sitting on the bed against the wall, our sides were touching. My hip was resting against Wendy McGregor's navy-blue school skirt. A skirt that only last month Wendy had been forced to take the hem down on by our Headmistress, as it was not a respectable length. I do think that Wendy's legs are just growing and the skirt used to be a respectable length. She's wearing tights which look quite thick. I'll have no idea what to do with them. I'm starting to panic. Trying to stay focused on the music and just looking for any major signals. In my head I see the cover of *The Hitchhikers Guide to the Galaxy* with the words 'Don't Panic' on front in large friendly letters. It's brilliant advice and knowing where my towel was now would also be useful as I am starting to sweat. Deep Thought took 7,500,000 years to come up with the answer 42. So, what chance had I got of working out what was going on in Wendy McGregor's head before the evening was out. At least I had the get-out clause of having to be home for half-past seven.

It was during *Another One Bites the Dust* that I had unexpected confirmation that this wasn't Wendy's room. Against my better judgement I'd agreed to Wendy McGregor's suggestion that we lie down on the bed to fully enjoy the immersive stereo experience. The bed wasn't made for two. From the start we were quite pushed together. Our heads were side by side on the pillow. Both looking at the ceiling. Mrs McGregor has missed a cobweb on that coving last time she cleaned. There was something under my neck that was making it quite uncomfortable. An unexpected bulge.

'Sorry! That's my gran's flannelette nightie, Jonathan', Wendy informs me while laughing. 'I'm sure she won't mind if you try it on ... You didn't think this was my room, did you?'

We just had time to play the last track on side two, *We Are the Champions,* where both of us sang the words loudly with our arms in the air. I wish I had my silk Villa scarf with me. Then unexpectedly Wendy was giving me my blazer and school tie. It was only a quarter to six and I was being pushed out of the back door.

'My parents will be home any minute. They'll go crazy if they find I had a boy in the house', Wendy was now being quite assertive. I was left sorting my tie out in her back garden. No goodnight kiss, just a smile and 'I'll see you Monday at school'.

With the lights from Mr McGregor's Ford Escort headlamps heading towards the drive, I decided to climb the McGregor garden fence. No idea why! The sensible option would've been to have waited and then just gone through the gate. But no, despite my lack of gymnastic prowess, I was trying to scale a six-foot-high fence. There was very little to grab hold of. I hadn't calculated the pressure a 12-stone mass would have on a fence with inadequate foundations. With the finesse of an *It's a Knockout!* contestant in a giant wobbly-man suit, I tumbled back into the garden. Whacking my arse against a concrete slab. Good job it's well padded. Luckily, I just missed landing on Wendy McGregor's bad-tempered old tabby cat, Flintstone.

Wendy's parents were now in their porch and Wendy was gesticulating to me through the open bathroom window to get the hell out of their garden. A very different take on the Romeo and Juliet balcony scene.

There's a wall. Why didn't I see that before? Oddly, against the wall is a ladder. Is this left there deliberately for the m   any lads Wendy entertains in her gran's bedroom? Who cares. It's my way out.

Saturday 31ˢᵗ October

5:57pm: Randy slams the door on the rather aggressive 'Penny for the Guy' group. It's still nearly a week 'til Bonfire Night and it wasn't even a proper guy. The bloke had just put his baby brother is a wheelbarrow and told him not to move. I hate Ipswich Town.

Waiting for my dad, I try to defend today's inept home performance to Randy. Beaten 1-0 by Ipswich. Four defeats on the trot against them. What is it that Bobby Robson has got over Ron? Randy's main gripe is that Villa not equalising meant he was one goal too high on his Guess the Goals entry on BBC Radio Birmingham. I really thought we'd win today. I guess that's our defence of the title gone. We are eleven points behind Ipswich now.

We had 82 minutes to equalise Russell Osman's goal. We let somebody from *Escape to Victory* score against us.

Randy is so passionate about the Villa. Even though he's never seen them play live. I really hope one day I can take him to Villa Park. Despite only just passing his driving test he's been working on the motorways for over ten years. He was involved in the construction of Spaghetti Junction on the M6. Where my dad's car crashed last year on the way to the possible title decider. The game when Ipswich also beat us at Villa Park; that was a horrible night. I'm sure Randy's motorway building wasn't to blame for our crash. Randy still hasn't braved driving on the motorway, even though there are no right turns. It was when Randy was building junction 6 that his love affair with Aston Villa began. In the early 70s he would see the AV floodlights of Villa Park lit up at midweek matches. He'd hear the roar of Villa fans and think what a magical place that must be. He talks so passionately about the night that Santos came to Villa Park and even claims that he spoke to Pele. Not sure I believe him, but he cares so much about the Villa and was such a dear friend to my grandad.

1. Manchester United Pl: 14 Po: 26   +10
2. Ipswich Town   Pl: 12 Po: 26   + 9
3. Tottenham Hotspur   Pl: 12 Po: 24   + 7
4. Swansea City   Pl: 12 Po: 23   + 6

13. Aston Villa   Pl: 12 Po: 15   + 3

Villa October League Results

3rd Leeds (a) 1-1 Draw (Shaw)
10th Coventry City (a) 1-1 Draw (Shaw)
17th West Ham United (h) 3-2 Win (Mortimer, Geddis, Morley)
24th Wolverhampton Wanderers (a) 3-0 Win (Shaw (2), own goal)
31st Ipswich Town (h) 0-1 Lost

Villa October European Cup Result

21st Dynamo Berlin (East Germany) (a) 2-1 Won (Morley (2))

Villa October League Cup Results

7th Wolves (h)   3-2 Won (Bremner, Morley, Blair)
27th Wolves (a) 2-1 Won (Cowans (2))

Chapter Five

November 1981

2:19pm: I'll be glad when this French lesson has finished. Glad I'm only doing CSE French. This is so hard. There are only so many places that Pierre can place his blooming bicyclette. Odd that I'm in a room with the linguistic thickies and I can see into the classroom next door where Grace's O level French group is. I can see her with big blue headphones on as she practices her vocab. Very expressive hands. I bet Pierre's probably piloting Concorde in their advanced class. Haystacks has spotted me from the other French class and is now sending me some quite derogatory hand signals. Hand gestures that I think would offend in any language. They get the Lovely Miss Tully teaching them. With that sexy hip-wiggling walk she does. Who do we get? Old cross-eyed Ormondroyd. The only language teacher with a lisp and a lazy eye. He knows nothing about France. Bet he's never even heard of Michel Platini, let alone eaten snails. Isn't it time Pierre moved out of Dieppe? He needs to sell his bicycle and move on with his life.

Grace has looked over at me a few times. She's smiled. Can't believe she's sitting with Wendy McGregor. Perhaps they're sharing notes on how rubbish I am. Wonder if Wendy has told Grace that I'm taking her to the Walsall Arbo Bonfire on Friday night. It's not really a date. Spud's coming too and Wendy's auntie is going to take

83

us. It's odd because Wendy's aunt Linda is only 18. No, idea how that works. She can drive and she's got a car. I know Linda because she was in Mark's class at junior school. Haven't seen her for years.

Would I rather just be going to the Arboretum with Grace? Walking arm in arm as the fireworks light up the romantic sky. I need to focus. My mind is wandering too much now. In only 28 hours, Villa will be looking to finish off Dynamo Berlin.

Wednesday 4th November

7:45pm: This wasn't in the script! The scoreboard to my left displays the shock scoreline Aston Villa 0, Dynamo Berlin 1. Just quarter of an hour gone and our Tony Morley-inspired first-leg advantage has gone. We did the hard work in Berlin. Today should be a formality. We just haven't started. Apart from Gary Williams having to play centre-half we are full strength. This shouldn't be happening. I'm yelling from my front-row seat. Perhaps that verbal assault on Kenny Swain was an overreaction, but he was the nearest one to me. Yes, it was a decent shot but Jimmy went down like me falling off the McGregors' fence.

At least we're starting to attack more. Tony Morley is playing well again. That's now three times that a flaming Berlin bloke has cleared off the line. I'm sure that last one must have gone over the line. Where's a Russian linesman when you need one.

See Steve Austin is at it again. The bloke two rows behind me. He must have a bionic eye. Always shouting for decisions that we can't possibly see from here. He sits next to the man I call Zippy. Call him that because he always seems to have his anorak zip stuck halfway. Not sure where Tim sits. Must be a few rows back. Tim after the Talking Clock. All you ever hear him shout is "Time!

Time!" whenever a Villa player has the ball. I assume he doesn't really want to know the time.

9:07pm: We are hanging on. Doris can hardly look. If the East Germans score, we're out. Come on, Villa! Let's go through on away goals. Wow, great save by Jimmy Rimmer. He's pushed the shot on to the post. Good job we've got Jimmy in goal. He's saved us in both games now. Just five more minutes then surely the ref can confirm Aston Villa's place in the quarter-finals of the European Cup. Just clear it, Allan Evans.

Friday 5th November

6:58pm: Linda McGregor never used to look like this. Wendy's auntie is stunning. She looks like a young Sally James from *Tiswas*. Hope she can't see me staring at her through her driving mirror. She certainly has a firm grip on that gear stick knob. This is a brilliant Mini. Reminds me of the one the mother drives in *Butterflies*, just needs a Union Jack roof. Spud is bumping around a lot in the back with me though. He needs to hold on tighter. Linda is so hot. Perhaps Wendy's not bad but her aunt is in another league. She could be Real Madrid or Bayern Munich. Wendy McGregor is a good UEFA qualifying First Division team. Maybe a Tottenham, certainly better than an Albion. She's being quite assertive tonight. Even pushed me into the back. She's wearing lipstick and smells nice. Spud doesn't smell quite as good. I think he forgot his Right Guard tonight.

He's trying to read his *Express & Star* as Linda manages to hit every bump in the road. It's got the draw for the quarter-finals of the European Cup in it. Liverpool, after Alan Hansen's late winner against AZ Alkmaar, are going to play CSKA Sofia. They certainly like playing teams made up of initials. Our reward is another visit behind the Iron Curtain. Off to Russia this time to play Dynamo

Kiev. I guess we like Dynamos. We are away first but it isn't until March. Ron's team can concentrate on marching back up the league before then and hopefully reaching Wembley in the League Cup final. At least we avoided Bayern Munich and Liverpool. I can't believe Juventus went out to Anderlecht. Spurs have got to play a team of Frankfurters in the Cup Winners' Cup. I think Barcelona will be the favourites in that tournament.

I always like Walsall Arboretum. My favourite is when the Illuminations are on but the bonfire here is always massive. Seems odd a girl who was in the same year as my brother overseeing us. Spud is flirting with Linda. He might have had a chance if he didn't smell so rank. I bet she's got some stud of a boyfriend. She could have her pick of anyone in her sixth form. She goes to the girls high school. I wonder why Wendy didn't go there. I thought she would have passed the 11-plus. She's in the top set for all her subjects.

'Okay, Wend, no telling our mums, but I'll leave you now and pick you up at nine-thirty, right? Behave.' To Spud's horror, Linda announced she was leaving us. She obviously had plans elsewhere. This theory was quickly confirmed when she ran towards a very muscular black guy by the gate to the Arbo. Their passionate embrace reinforced by belief that they had met before.

Sharing a hot dog between three people is not an easy task and I'm sure that the bite Peter Hogan took showed his lack of understanding of fractions. I did manage to find a plastic knife and chop off a generous third for Wendy. Then thinking about Spud's teeth-marks on the end of my remaining bun I kindly gave Miss McGregor my portion as well.

As we got near the bonfire the warmth of the flame hit us. On a chilly night this was very welcome. Spud was kicking an empty Vimto can along the floor. I was attempting to make conversation with Wendy McGregor. Never easy to find things to talk about with girls. I end up asking her if she's seen Kevin Turvey on *Kick Up the*

Eighties. To my delight, she is a fan of this Rik Mayall character. Noddy does a fab impression of Kevin Turvey. We talked about how Kevin Turvey had investigated 'Work' and his joke about Noele Gordon. Well, it ended up not being Noele Gordon, but that still gave me the chance of telling Wendy that Noele Gordon was a Villa fan and sat in the same stand as me. I'm not sure if Wendy was joking when she asked, 'the bloke who presents *Swap Shop*?'

'Grace says you haven't fallen out', Wendy bursts out and stops me in my tracks. Where did that comment come from? What the hell does it mean? I hadn't mentioned Grace Taylor. We were talking about Noele Gordon.

Any chance to discuss the Grace situation in any more detail was interrupted by a Vimto can hurtling towards my head. With cowardliness that would disgust Peter Withe I ducked out of the header. The taunt of 'chicken!' came from Spud. Soon the spectacular firework display was starting. The speakers playing the music from *War of the Worlds*. Sadly, several of the speakers weren't working so the stereo effect was somewhat limited.

The fireworks were impressive. You could see how fast they were being lit. Wendy had managed to snuggle herself in quite close to me. Her arms are wrapped around my waist. Spud gives me a knowing look. I'm distracted by the girl's actions but determined to enjoy the fireworks. My mind was drifting, though, back to last year and watching the fireworks in my garden with my Grandad. So much has changed in the last 12 months. Then we shared fireworks with Uncle Norman, Auntie Mavis and Carol over our trellis fence. Now our friendly neighbours have gone, replaced by an enemy and the fence is now hidden by a high wall.

Applause and cheers follow the dramatic finale of the display, despite the remaining speakers giving out half-way through. Wendy moves away from me.

'So, when are you going to see Grace again, then?', Wendy returns to the previous conversation. What angle was she taking with this? Was it pushing me back to Grace or making sure I'm fully over Grace so I was ready to commit to a new relationship? Before I can respond we realise Spud is missing.

Within seconds, an excited Spud returns. Reason for his excitement, he's bumped into Noddy and Tucker. They're surprised to see me with Wendy McGregor. Tucker whispers, 'I thought it was all finished after she dumped you in the garden'.

It turned out that Tucker and Noddy had crawled under the fence to get in without paying. Hence Tucker's trousers are splattered with mud. Noddy was due to go to his nan's for tea but his nan broke her top set of teeth on a United chocolate bar she'd kept in the fridge. Tucker was grounded for breaking their toilet seat but when Noddy knocked on his door, Tucker's parents said he could go but wouldn't give him any money to spend.

Noddy is hoping Tucker will be allowed to go to Fellows Park tomorrow to see Walsall play Newport County. They've won the last five home games and Noddy really thinks this can be their season. It's weird that Walsall have joint managers, but I suppose Alan Buckley still plays quite a bit, so he needs someone else to manage when he's playing. I doubt Neil Martin is ever brave enough to bring Buckley off. Anyway, I think Alan Buckley is still Walsall's best player.

BANG! A fist hits me smack in the middle of my back. It certainly felt like a fist. In excruciating pain, I fall to the ground. This was an attack.

'I owe you that one, Stadler, you puff', came a familiar voice. I look up, holding my back, to see the ugly face of Kenny Bellington. Before I can say a word or even process what's going on, Spud swings a punch at Bellington. He strikes him right on the jaw. Bellington doesn't go down and instead kicks out at Spud. Within seconds a major scrap had started. Three lads who, I assume, are with Bellington are now joining in. Tucker and Noddy are getting involved. Wendy McGregor strikes Bellington firmly on the head with a toffee apple. No idea where that came from. I am just dazed. Spud has totally lost it. Weeks of pumped-up anger over his mum is now coming out. Within no time the stewards in their hi-vis jackets are jumping on us. Trying to drag Spud off. The on-duty policemen are now joining in to try and break up the fight. Including a very attractive policewoman in her white hat. She looked exactly how you'd hope a policewoman kiss-a-gram would look.

We were dragged out of the Arboretum and into a police van. Sadly, not by the pretty policewoman, instead by two enormous six-foot oafs. I was terrified. I wasn't ready for a police caution. I'm innocent, but I'm not going to let my mate go down for this.

Looking around, I realise there are only six of us antagonists in the police van. A van that contained riot gear and an uneaten kebab. It was much more *The Sweeney* than *Rosie*. I doubt there'll be a fifth series of *Rosie,* there are only so many minor crimes you can have in a small Yorkshire village. Is there really a village called Ravensbay? So, where is Wendy McGregor? How did Tucker escape? And who are these dumb-looking friends of Bellington?

The police officer with a prominent scar across his left cheek was leading the interrogation. In America he would probably have flashed his gun at us, but here his weapon was that he'd be taking us home to face our parents. He wanted names and addresses. Spud was defiant and opted for the made-up name. He took a chance with choosing Brett Sinclair. Has the police officer never seen the episodes of *The Persuaders*? Strangely, Pete gives his real address. Probably just wants a lift home. Noddy is next to be questioned. He gives his real name but conveniently struggles to remember his address. Surprisingly, Kenny Bellington is bricking it. I would have thought he would be used to being in trouble with the law. Is

Kenny actually crying? Looks like he's got quite an egg on his head from where Wendy struck him with the toffee apple.

The police have discovered that Kenny Bellington has come to stay with his Aunt Gabby for the weekend. The two numbskulls with him are his cousins. I do feel that I want some justice here. I was the victim of an unprovoked attack. Probably best just to stay quiet though. Nobody has asked my name yet. If they do, I'll have to tell the truth.

For the third time in a week, I find myself unexpectedly hurtling towards the ground. An emergency radio call meant the police van with riot gear was soon departing. So, six teenage lads were no longer wanted criminals. Bellington and his cousins were quickly off. Although Kenny did turn and give us a double two-fingered salute as he went down the road. Noddy and Wendy McGregor were sitting on the wall opposite ready to greet the returning heroes.

'You owe me a toffee apple, Jonny', Wendy yelled, before rushing over to me and ruffling my hair. Her hand slightly sticky from the toffee apple. 'Quick, we need to leg it or Auntie Linda will go without us'.

My back was still very painful from Bellington's blow. I'm going to have a bruise there, to go with the bruise I already have on my bum from Wendy's garden. Always bruise easy. In the shower next week not only will I be the boy with no pubes but now also two bruises. I'll probably be known as 'Two-Bruises-No-Pubes-Stadler'.

Sitting in the back of Linda McGregor's Mini, I'm feeling sorry for myself. Even though Wendy has climbed in the back with me and has her legs resting on my lap. I am grateful for the fact that still the only police record I have is *Walking on the Moon*.

I am sure that's not the outfit Linda was wearing when she dropped us off. She seems to be wearing a red basque on her top half. It was definitely a polo-neck jumper before. She pops a cassette in and turns the volume up very loud. Spud's eyes light up and he starts to sing. Linda McGregor has only put on Gary Numan's *Cars*. I whisper to Wendy, 'Beam me up, Scotty'.

In my head I was singing Haystacks' version of Spud's favourite song, 'Here in my car, you can take off your bra'. Best to keep this to myself.

Saturday 7th November

2:48pm: It's Villa's turn to have Winners Matches sponsoring their game. Hopefully we'll win against Arsenal. We owe them one for beating us 2-0 at Highbury. Would the title-winning moment have been as good though if we had won that final day? I think the drama in the Ipswich game added to the day. Ivor Linton and Gordon Cowans are on the front of the programme. That Le Coq Sportif blue sweatshirt that Sid is wearing is cool. I wonder if I could get one for Christmas. The voucher on the back is number 10. How can this be our tenth home game already? Our reserves are doing pretty rubbish in the Central League. We even lost to Wolves last week. Would have thought with Geddis and Donovan in attack we'd be doing better. We've used three different goalkeepers in the reserves. Nigel Spink has played most reserve games, but Kevin Poole and Mark Kendall have also played.

Good to see Brian Little still being involved with the club. A new Villa souvenir shop has opened in the Co-op at Tamworth. Brian, Allan Evans and Andy Blair were there at the opening. In the Villa Diary section, it's going on about the wonder goal Tony Morley scored for the England XI at Highbury. He'll get a full call-up soon. Change in the board, Mr Donald Bendall has been appointed Vice-

Chairman. I wonder if that's the Chairman's Ron Bendall's brother or son. Would be lazy of the Bendall parents to call one son Ron and one Don. In the 'THEY PLAYED FOR VILLA' section they are in E to F. All players I've never heard of. One of them is an Alun Evans. Different first name spelling to our current Scotland international. Alun Evans was a forward. Apparently, Wolves once sold him to Liverpool for a record £100,000. He only played 62 games for the Villa. Ended up at Walsall, Noddy and Tucker's lot. Only scored seven goals for them, in the Third Division, so he couldn't have been that good. EWING, Thomas, an outside-left. I guess that's like a left-winger but not sure. My grandad would have known. The only Ewings I know live at Southfork. Kenneth Fencott, another outside-left, was born in Walsall. He was also a wing-half or inside-forward. They're just making up positions now. Whole page on flipping Winners Matches. Who cares that you can get 100 matches for 9p. Spud says it costs 82p for a pack of 20 cigarettes. At least he'll only need 2p worth of matches to light them all.

Arsenal have got nine full internationals. They are still below us in the league though. I think their top five players are Jennings, Sansom, O'Leary, Nicholas and Rix. And they're all playing today. At least Brian McDermott isn't, who scored against us in May. Villa are unchanged from knocking Dynamo Berlin out.

3:39pm: It's déjà vu! Five minutes until half-time and we're losing 2-0 to Arsenal again. We were on top until curly-haired Graham Rix scored in the 26th minute. Then we went to pieces. Letting Brian Talbot score. What's going on, Ron?

Monday 9th November

8:57am: A few more minutes and they'll stop going on about all their teams winning on Saturday and the Villa losing. Wolves beating Coventry at home was bad enough, but Baggies winning at Tottenham? Even Tucker and Noddy can make fun of me because Saddlers beat Newport County 3-1. We're only a point clear of Hastings' Albion now. Blooming Wolves are only one win behind us. At least there are no Bluenoses in the school. Can't believe they have gone above us. Three defeats in a week. Come on Ron Saunders, these players need a rocket up their backsides.

Mr Walker comes in, at least Forest only drew so he can't have to go at me.

'Villa slipping hey, Jonathan. I had them down for a draw against the Gunners on my coupon', Mr Walker says. 'Well, guess I'll just have to keep teaching you lot ... I'm in charge of the lights again for the school Christmas musical. Are you and your mob up for helping again?'

I enjoyed doing the lights for the *Mikado* last year but think I'm bit old for it now. Or was the real reason I wasn't so keen down to the fact that Grace Taylor was playing Sandy in *Grease*? On one hand I would get to see more of Grace, but on the other it might make getting over her even harder. I promised Mr Walker I would ask Haystacks and Co.

12:50pm: It's raining, so Wendy and I are pretending to study in the library. Librarian Miss Carbone frequently tries to 'Sssshhh' pupils, but we all know she has no powers. I'm enjoying hanging out with Wendy. Just hoping this time, I don't end up with a bruise. No idea where this 'relationship' is headed. Can't help thinking that Wendy is just making do until something better comes along. Like Ron Atkinson was doing at Albion until Manchester United showed an interest. Maybe I should make the best of the little time we have together. I invested quite a lot into my relationship with Grace. On the bus with my hand down her blouse I felt I was being rewarded. Then she dumped me. Perhaps you only get a certain amount of time. Maybe I was just too slow, the ref blew the final whistle. So, this time I need to work quicker. Not spend so long on the build-up. Not being too gung-ho though and leaving myself open at the back. I need a plan. I need to know what my end-game is. Admittedly my lack of experience and the fact that vital parts of me need bulking up puts me at a disadvantage. It's important I play to my strengths. My ability to make girls laugh. Show my gentle and sensitive side. Talk about Abba and be up to date with latest Barbie doll accessories.

'Have you heard who's playing Danny in Grease?', Wendy breaks the silence. I guess she means in the school production. Even I know that John Travolta played Danny in the film. I shrug my shoulders. 'Oliver Watkins, from 4PW'.

Wendy means that posh kid who only started in the summer. He's already made quite an impression with the girls. Didn't know he could sing. Spud hasn't mentioned him. I bet Spud is still peeved that he didn't get picked as Danny.

'I guess he'll have to kiss Sandy. I wonder who is playing Sandy'. Wendy is surely teasing me. She knows that Grace is playing goody-two-shoes Sandy. Is she looking for a response from me? I'm not going to rise to the bait.

4:48pm: Sitting on the down-end of the seesaw, in the dark, in Harlech Park, I can see the whole madness of the situation. The park is locked up, so we had to climb over the gates. Here is the only place I can safely meet Asif. At least now he's taken his luminous armbands off, so it doesn't look quite as crazy. The war between our parents is now totally out of control. The poor postman has got involved now. Dad stopped him climbing over the divide in front of our two houses on Monday. Worse still, Mr Mahmood took Mum's Kay's Catalogue hostage. Postman left it in their porch by mistake over a week ago. Asif took it to his grammar school in his satchel today. Just so he could give it me now. I'll blame the Kay's catalogue for the reason of my extra weight on this

94

side of the seesaw. It's too dark even to flick through the pages of the lingerie section. I should have bought my wind-up torch. Or I could just get Asif to pedal frantically on my Chopper so the light stays on. Mind you, that would blow the cover of our secret park meeting. We need a plan to get some kind of truce between our two families. In less than six months we'll have a new member of the Stadler clan. We don't want to bring a baby into a street of feuding neighbours.

Asif hates his all-boys school. He doesn't fit in. They play rugby there and he got crushed in the scrum today. He says nobody ever notices him. He started a chess club, but he's too good at it and beats everyone. So they all left. Strangely, Asif wants to go to my school. I think he'd fit in less there. We haven't even got a Latin teacher.

I am slowly starting to educate Asif in the arts of Aston Villa Football Club. He can now name all the managers since Jimmy Hogan. As well as reciting the names of the 14 legends of last season: Rimmer, Swain, Williams, Gibson, Deacy, Evans, McNaught, Mortimer, Bremner, Shaw, Geddis, Withe, Cowans and Morley. Time now to teach him about the master, who is Ronald Saunders. Villa's greatest ever manager. How he took us from near the bottom of the Second Division to First Division Champions and now European Cup quarter-finalist. Just two rounds from Rotterdam. I take this as a good opportunity to see what a grammar school Geography education is like. I ask Asif what he knows about Rotterdam. It is better than looking it up in one of Dad's prized encyclopaedias.

'It's Europe's largest seaport. The second-largest city in Holland. It lies on the river Rotta. Which in English means "muddy water"', Asif shows a Dutch knowledge that exceeds my expectations. I follow this up by asking what the football ground was like. Disappointingly the grammar school Geography curriculum does not cover sporting arenas.

95

Pretty sure that Asif is the first Hindu boy I've met. He doesn't behave like a Hindu. He swears more than Spud and he eats hamburgers. When I asked if he was circumcised because Noddy said all Hindu boys had to have the end of their knob chopped off, Asif said Hindu's didn't do non-medical circumcision. He said I was thinking of Jews and Muslims. I wonder if Jesus was circumcised. Good job I'm a Christian. I can't afford to lose any of my dick, it's small enough as it is.

Wednesday 11th November

6:41pm: Could this be the day it finally happens? Only a couple of minutes to go and I'm 4-1 up against Mark. My Aston Villa Subbuteo team have been on fire tonight. That last goal from the edge of the shooting area by overlapping full-back Colin Gibson was sublime. Goal of the Month material. Mark does seem to be having trouble concentrating. Mum and Dad are having a very deep conversation in the front room. Probably discussing baby names. If it's a girl I think 'Aston' would be a fab name. I guess if it's a boy I can teach it the art of Subbuteo. Might even let him use my Villa team. Boy or girl, I can see my days of a single-occupancy bedroom ending. Maybe we can afford to move to a bigger house. That would be one way of ending the Stadler-Mahmood feud. How did that go in? Wolves score. In off the bar via Jimmy Rimmer's rod. I need to concentrate. Come on Villa, with 110% effort we can do this.

Mistake by Eamonn Deacy. That pass has left Des Bremner almost snookered on the ball. Need to bend the flick around Kenny Hibbitt. SMASH!! Free kick to the Wolves. It's shootable.

Mark is lying Willie Carr down. Wolves in their all-white away kit have a chance. Mark is going to attempt to chip the wall balancing his player in lying-down position. I would still like to consult with the official Subbuteo governing body to see if this is legal.

Blooming knew it. Four-three now! Jimmy got nowhere near that looping free-kick. He's been fab all season but having a nightmare today. But there goes the kitchen pinger. It's a victory for Aston Villa. Better than that, it's the first time Subbuteo school champion Jonathan Stadler has ever beaten his big brother Mark.

'Second leg then, stinky, back to Molineux', is Mark's response.

Dad comes into the dining room. 'Boys, we need to talk to you. Something serious to say'.

With still over 30 minutes until Villa kick off in the League Cup and with me having no desire to gamble my glory on a second game, I quickly follow Dad into the front room.

8:00pm: Forced to listen to Tony Butler on BRMB. Not sure what's going on with BBC Radio Birmingham. They're just playing the kind of music Asif's dad likes. BRMB is always rubbish reception. I keep losing the signal. Have to keep pointing my lucky radio towards the bathroom. Come on, Villa, our chance to get to fourth round of the League Cup. We still haven't scored at Filbert Street. We must beat Second Division Leicester.

I got things all wrong. Guess I'm baby Stadler forever now. Mum isn't pregnant. I thought she was too old. She's going into hospital in two weeks' time to have a hysterectomy. This is why she's been so crotchety the last few months. I didn't ask for details but I'm pretty sure it means all her womb and womanly bits are removed. Like what the cat had a few years ago. Mum is going to have to take it easy for six weeks. It'll be after Christmas before she can hoover again. We will all have to get involved with the housework. My dad is obviously earning more money than I thought because Mum is going private. Which means she'll get her own room. When we visit her, we'll be able to watch a colour telly. Oddly, I was quite tearful when Mum and Dad told me. Mum thought it was because I was worried about her. Truth is that I'm quite upset that I'm not getting a little brother or sister.

West Brom drew 2-2 at West Ham yesterday, so they'll be in the hat.

Friday 13th November

12:34pm: Noddy has sneaked his dad's Sun newspaper in. So, after quickly ogling over the pert nipples of page three's Sian Adey-Jones, we are studying the League Cup draw. Villa will be away to Fourth Divion Wigan in the fourth round. If we can beat Leicester in the replay. Hastings' Baggies will have to go to Crystal Palace if they get past West Ham. Liverpool will play Arsenal, so one of the big boys is going out. Great chance for us this season.

We are waiting for Mr Walker to tell him we've decided to be the light specialists for the school production of *Grease*. Tucker is on lookout so that he doesn't catch us studying Sian Adey-Jones' assets.

Spud is with us even though he'll be on the stage. He's really down. Mrs Hogan is not doing well on the chemo. Spud says she looks like Kojak and is puking up all over the place. Him and his dad are virtually living at the chippy. He's worried that his mum won't get better.

'What do you think Heaven is like?', Spud randomly asks.

This starts quite a high-level chat about our individual visions of Heaven. I guess, as the only weekly church-goer, I should have the advantage, but I really have no idea. Noddy thought it would be very bright and we'd all wear white shellsuits that never needed washing. Haystacks was worried he'd be bored. He hoped he'd be able to have a nap and didn't have to help with the gardening. Eternity does seem a really long time. I assume you'll be able to get a good view of all the footie games.

Mr Walker leads the way up the familiar ladder to the lighting gantry. Eleven months since we last made this climb. At least Haystacks is a bit slimmer this year. He's climbing quite nimbly. I stop to look at the stage where Grace Taylor is starting to rehearse a song. She's singing *Hopelessly Devoted to You*. How inappropriate. Yes, you are a fool. It was you who "pushed our loved aside". She does look very hot, though. Who is hotter, Grace or Wendy? They're both lovely in their own way. Grace Taylor has the better bosom and Wendy McGregor the better legs. Perhaps the decider is which one has the best bum. I need to study this knockout category in more detail.

Saturday 14th November

5:11pm: What a boring Saturday afternoon with no football. Only the Albion played, but then they haven't got any international players. Not now Bryan Robson has absconded to Man United. With Tony Morley and Peter Withe in the England squad, the Villa game at Swansea was always going to be postponed. Haystacks will not be happy. Albion losing again. Fancy letting Stoke beat you.

Express & Star hasn't got a single mention about the Villa. Back page says that Wolves' Willie Carr might go to Derby. I wouldn't miss him and his dodgy free-kick technique. Geoffrey Boycott scores his 125th career century. He was only playing India's under-22s though. I bet Ian Botham would have scored a triple century against them. Why under-22s? Makes no sense.

Front page is all about another IRA shooting. This time some MP, who's also a Reverend. Surprised he has time for two jobs. Rev Robert Bradford. It's time Maggie sorted this Irish mess out. So many needless lives being wasted. Must be five years since they killed the bloke from Record Breakers.

Just checking what's on TV. I might have time to do my Maths homework. ATV have got *The Pyramid Game* after *Worzel Gummidge. Game for a Laugh* is ten-past six. So, I can do homework after that before Mike Yarwood is on. Says in paper that he's going to do a Romeo and Juliet sketch in the guise of Michael Foot and Margaret Thatcher. I bet it'll be Janet Brown doing the Maggie part. Don't think Mike Yarwood could do that. See tomorrow *Different Strokes* is on the same time as *To the Manor Born*. I can do my Maths homework tomorrow as there's nothing on after those two before *Dallas.* Mum likes *To the Manor Born,* so I'll set that to record while she's at church.

How stubborn is my dad? He's just gone to ring his sister and at the same time Asif's dad has gone to make a phone call. As it's a party line they are both waiting for the other to put the phone down. Neither of them is saying a word. They are both not prepared to put the phone down. A stalemate. Who is going to give in first? Mum is not helping the situation as she's urging Dad not to be a wimp. Dad won't dare put the phone down with Mum hovering over him. Mr Mahmood is now banging on the wall. Mum is now turning up the volume on *Worzel Gummidge.* I have never known Aunt Sally to speak so loudly. Sounds like Mrs Mahmood has now put her industrial sewing machine on. Mark is being ordered to go upstairs and get the hairdryer. I'm not getting involved in this. Oh no, Mr Mahmood is climbing over the front garden wall. He's marching to our door. Thumping on our front door now. Can't he see we have got a chiming doorbell?

'Don't you dare let him in!' Mum yells above the racket.

Dad acts. He's won the battle. Mr Mahmood put the phone down before he charged round. Or somebody else in the Mahmood household did. So, Dad dials my Auntie Deirdre. Mum gives him a kiss and Mark sends a rather unpleasant hand gesture through the window to the retreating Mr Mahmood. With the speed of a Joe Bugner left hook, Mum slaps Mark.

Wednesday 18th November

10:45am: Despite checking for the fifth time, my orange Chemistry exercise book isn't in my locker. I had been up until nearly 11 last night finishing balancing those bloody chemical equations. Must have left it on the dining room table. Wendy McGregor is standing behind me. She's oddly just sprayed some deodorant under her armpit. Not showing much respect for the ozone layer. I only saw her spray one armpit, so it could have been worse for that hole. She's been smiling a lot today.

'Are you going to the School Disco on Friday?' Wendy reminds me that there is a fundraising disco after school on Friday. Not my sort of thing. Don't even know what they are fundraising for. 'It's for *Children in Need*, that thing where they keep interrupting the programmes on BBC1'. Friday telly is rubbish now *It' a Knockout* has finished. Is Wendy asking me to go with her to the disco? 'Am I talking to myself Stadler, are you going to go with me to the disco? Earth calling Jonathan'. I guess no reason to hurry home on Friday and maybe I'll get to dance the *Birdie Song* with Wendy. So, I play it cool and tell her I'll let her know. Maybe I can talk the rest of the gang into coming. Perhaps I can get the DJ to play *Dancing Queen*. An anonymous request is probably best. I'm giving up on that Chemistry book. Just have to face the music.

12:53pm: 'And Keegan scores! A great volley to put England on their way to the 1982 World Cup Finals'. Noddy over celebrates his two-yard tap-in, after Haystacks had been distracted by Miss Tully walking past in a fur coat with a skirt so short you had to look closely to check she was wearing one. And we did. Noddy's celebrations are cut short, as a disgruntled Spud kicks him right up the arse. That must have really hurt. If it had been me or Haystacks our buttocks would still be vibrating now. 'Sod off, Spud. I don't care how ill your bloody mum is. You can't do that. Game over, it's my ball', Noddy picks up his tattered case and walks back towards the Science block. Haystacks and I manage to grab hold of Pete as he tries to chase after Noddy.

It takes a few minutes to calm Spud down. He can't keep behaving like this. He's already had three detentions this term. That's with the teachers being understanding about his mum. He's so angry all the time. Expect having Wolves in the relegation zone isn't helping. Unexpectedly, the passing Grace Taylor stops and puts her arm around my waist. 'Are you going to the *Children in Need* disco?' she asks.

7:39pm: Randy has come round to watch the vital England game with us. It's good to see him and he announces he is dressed in red, white and blue all over. Even his Marks and Spencer Y-fronts. Too much information. I need to lose that image in my head of Randy in just his Union Jack pants. I'm wearing my silk England scarf. I got it at the schoolboys' international at Wembley when I was nine. I'm sure Brendan Ormsby played in that game. I know Wayne Clarke did.

England need at least a draw from this final qualifying game against Hungary. Or we're not going to Spain. Ron Greenwood's fault if we fail for not picking a Villa player in the starting 11. At least Peter Withe and Tony Morley are among the five England subs. Glad Greenwood has chosen Shilton over Clemence tonight. Peter Shilton at least keeps his legs together. Think Terry McDermott is a bit too like Trevor Brooking though. Our full-backs are both nearly pensioners in Phil Neal and Mick Mills. Three Liverpool players, two Ipswich, two Manchester United and even two blooming West Ham players. You can tell Greenwood used to manage West Ham. Don't recognise any of the Hungarian names. But then why would I? One of them has the unfortunate first name of 'Kiss'. I am worried about this disco on Friday now. I seem to have agreed to go with both Grace Taylor and Wendy McGregor. Which one might get a Jonathan Stadler kiss? I must improve my kissing technique. Need to watch more major kissing on telly. The sort you get in a romantic film, not the kind we'll hopefully see these England players doing when they score.

The national anthem is starting. Dad and Randy are both standing to sing it. Mark is refusing to stand but is at least singing most of the words. I do think Randy's salute is going to little far. He only came to England in 1969. He always tells us, 'The year man landed on the moon, Randy landed at Liverpool Docks'.

There are a few perms on display as the teams are being presented to the Duke of Kent. He seems to get tickets for all the best sporting events. I wouldn't mind his job. John Motson says that crowd is restricted to just over 92,000 tonight but record gate receipts for a game in England. Over £650,000. Blimey, you could buy the whole Hungary team for that. It would be great to have a Kevin Keegan perm. I would need to use Mum's heated rollers. I'm feeling quite nervous. So badly want to watch England in a World Cup Finals. Romania failing to beat Switzerland last week means we only need a point. Two points would be even better though. None of Jimmy Hill's crazy three points for a win here.

8:01pm: I've never really liked him, with his girly long hair, but take a bow, Paul Mariner of Ipswich. One-nil to the Engerland. Lucky goal by Mariner. After Trevor Brooking's mishit shot had confused the Hungarians. Surely plain sailing here, all the way to Spain.

'Off to sunny Spain y viva Espana. I'm taking the Costa Brava plane, y viva Espana', Randy unexpectedly starts to sing. Then from his stripey mesh shopping bag he whips out a football rattle. Can't help thinking this celebration is a touch premature.

'Peter Withe would have put it wide from there. You can see why Ron Greenwood picked Mariner', Mark unfairly taunts. I'm not going to rise to the bait. Deciding against asking how many Wolves players were in the squad.

Dad is now encouraging Randy to keep swirling his rattle. Mainly as a response to Mr Mahmood banging on the wall in complaint of the noise.

8:53pm: Hungary aren't even trying to attack. You can tell they have already qualified. Can't believe Mark's gone out to meet crazy Sarah half-way through the second half of a live international football game.

'Our star man is coming on!' Randy is frantically pointing at the telly. He's right. On the touchline, taking his England Admiral tracksuit top off, is Tony Morley. He's going to make his England debut and get a cap. I wonder if they measure the player's head beforehand to get the right size cap. He's going to join the recent list of Brian Little, John Gidman and Peter Withe. Come on, Tony, let's have some Morley magic. Do well here and you can cancel your summer holidays. Steve Coppell is coming off. That means Tony can cause havoc down the left wing. Need Peter Withe on now. To finish off Tony's crosses. Paul Mariner will struggle with that long hair. He won't be able to see when that great mane sweeps over his face.

That deserved a goal. Super shot by Morley. The Hungarian goalkeeper, Meszaros, produced a fine save.

9:27pm: It's all over, England have qualified for the 1982 World Cup. No need for me to support the Tartan Army next summer. England are going to Spain. Tony Morley and Peter Withe must be on the plane and in a recording studio singing our World Cup song. Maybe still time for Gordon Cowans to make a last dash. Or the skipper. He's been close a few times. What about Kenny Swain? I guess Jimmy Rimmer's a bit old now. Hastings said that Rimmer played for England once when he was at Arsenal. But he let two goals in, so they took him off at half-time. I bet they were two unstoppable shots. Maybe it's a little soon for Gary Shaw. I'm sure he'll be a star in the 1986 Finals. Well done, England!

'Me and my rattle are off, before we have to suffer David Steele's Party Political Broadcast. Why do they have to put it on all three stations?' Randy puts his black leather driving gloves on, ready to get Dad to help him reverse his car out. Lots of choke and several failed attempts later, we wave Randy off.

Friday 20th November

4:43pm: This is a rubbish disco. I've paid 50p for this. Don't care if it's going to help give some poor kid a better Christmas. There are nine of us. That includes Haystacks, Noddy, Tucker and me. So much for me having two girls to choose from. Neither Wendy nor Grace have turned up. Grace will probably come after *Grease* rehearsals. Spud is planning to, but he's going to try to get in without paying. Fair enough, as with his mum back in hospital he could count as one of these 'Children in Need', admittedly quite a big child. Only girls here are two second-year girls. Both seem to be trying to pluck up the coverage to ask Noddy for a dance. There isn't even a proper DJ, despite the expensive disco equipment. Miss Tully has just put a tape on of songs she's recorded off the radio. That would be okay if Miss Tully hadn't left before the tape recorder started chewing up the tape. Why didn't whoever organised this fundraiser consider the fact it's November and pitch-black outside. So, we need to have all the lights on.

Haystacks is still struggling to come to terms with his break-up with Georgina Ramsey. It got worse when she confirmed she was now a permanent Manchester United fan. He's been really down. He's back to eating a lot more again. Since school finished, I've seen him eat two Mars bars. Not even the fun-size ones. His belly is outgrowing his school shirt. At the wrong angle you can see his hairy belly button through his gaping shirt. Why has everyone got more body hair than me? You could hide a hedgehog in the bushes under Spud's armpits. Where is Wendy McGregor? This was her blooming idea. Bet she's at home watching *Crackerjack*.

'I've had enough of this crap. Who's up for sharing a bag of chips?', Noddy is first to say what we are all thinking. Haystacks is now frantically searching his blazer and trouser pockets to see if he can afford a bag of chips to himself. We go to leave.

'Sorry I'm late, Jonny. I had to nip home to change first and put some lippy on'. Wow, Wendy looks like a real woman. You could now certainly tell she was Linda McGregor's niece. This was a major effort she'd gone to. Not saying she isn't attractive normally, but this is a whole different level of attractiveness. This is like Felicity Kendal turning into Bo Derek. I guess I could give the disco a bit longer. It is for a good cause after all.

A few more pupils have joined the disco now. Haystacks and Noddy are standing outside the window eating their chips in a suggestive manner. This is made even more off-putting because Hastings has also had a saveloy.

The lot from the *Grease* rehearsals are now starting to drift in. Spud tried to get in without paying but Jock McGinn caught him crawling under the chairs behind the stage curtain. We can now see Spud through the window trying to nab Noddy's remaining chips. Nice just chatting with Wendy. We're sitting on the stage together. Our legs swaying in time to the music. To be honest, I'm just moving my legs when Wendy moves hers. There seems to be a DJ now. Playing actual singles. Can't see who the DJ is, but there's quite a gathering of girls around him.

Einstein A Go-Go is now playing. Spud's type of music. People are finally starting to dance. Not sure I'm ready to dance. No idea how to really bop to this type of techno song. I'm waiting for the *Birdie Song*; I know all the moves to that one. Wendy McGregor seems to be singing all the words to me. She's smiling all the time. I must be doing something right. She must have spent ages putting all those layers of makeup on. She's wearing more than David Bowie wears. I do like her. We get on. She doesn't natter non-stop like some girls. She even understood when I said the answer was 42. We have quite a bit in common. We both list Wellington as our favourite Womble and Wendy also watched Virgina Wade win Wimbledon in 1977 on a black and white TV at school.

Oh no, Wendy McGregor is pulling me towards the dancefloor. *Oops Upside Your Head* by The Gap Band is playing. At least this is one where you get to sit down. Even I can manage that. Pupils are lining up bottoms on the floor with legs and arms out. Seems to be boy/girl/boy/girl positioning. Question is, do I want to have Wendy McGregor between my thighs or be seated in front of her. I'll let Wendy dictate our position. Wendy has decided to straddle me. Well, she has got the longer legs. Also means that I can feel her boobs against my back. Probably should have taken my blazer off. I'm getting a bit hot. I just need to loosen up. Let Wendy move our bodies. All I have to do is concentrate on moving my arms. You have to stretch them out and bash the ground at some point, in time to the music. At least I've got a small second-year girl in front of me to copy. Very rudely she's commenting on how fat my ankles are.

I don't disgrace myself on the dancefloor, but when the next song *Hit Me With Your Rhythm Stick* starts, I make a tactical retreat. To my delight Wendy follows me.

'That was fun! Hope I didn't squeeze you too hard. Why don't we make that our special song?' Wendy says slightly out of breath. Despite the beads of sweat on her forehead her makeup remains immaculate. I nod to acknowledge the odd selection of *Oops Upside Your Head* becoming our song. So, is having a song a form of commitment? Does it indicate that we are quickly approaching the "going out" stage? I decide to test the water. Not with litmus paper from the Chemistry lab but by slowly moving my left hand to link with Wendy's right hand. Wendy does not reject this hand and decides to further enhance the closeness by linking arms. Which did involve loosening hands first before recoupling.

Returning to our place on the edge of the stage. I remove my blazer and my school tie. I'm worried about Spud though. Have I deserted my mates too quickly to spend time with Wendy? Maybe I need to go outside and see what they are up to. I'm generally the sensible one of the gang. I seem doomed to stay at this disco. Grace Taylor has just made an entrance and made a beeline for me. Grace jumps up to the left of me. She seems totally oblivious to the fact that Wendy McGregor is on the other side. Not sure if it's me or Wendy that ended our linkage.

'Sorry I'm late, Jonathan. I had to stay late to work on *You're the One That I Want*. Just couldn't get that "Ooh, ooh, ooh" right.' I just listen as Grace behaves like she never dumped me. 'Isn't the music fab? What an ace DJ Oliver Watkins is'.

So, the DJ that all the girls are swarming around is the infamous Oliver Watkins. The new lad who is playing Danny to Grace Taylor's Sandy. This moment takes another unexpected twist when Wendy suddenly joins in the conversation. She reinforces Grace's assessment of the DJ's record selection expertise. Also, what a stud he is. Have I suddenly turned into the invisible man? That's it, I've had enough. Time I wasn't here and was checking up on my pal. Could murder some chips.

Slick Oliver "pretty-boy" Watkins has read the mood of his fundraising revellers and put on one of the two songs that I know the dance moves to. Wendy and Grace drag me back to the dancefloor just as we hear "It's fun to stay at the YMCA".

I've just done the C in the second chorus when everything goes black. Music stops. My brain takes a moment to process what is going on. It considered the possibility that I've been knocked out by a pupil performing extra vigorous actions to *YMCA*. Before reaching the conclusion, from the many screams, that it's a power cut.

Mr McGinn takes charge of us in the dark. It sounds like Jock McGinn. I have a girl's arm linked to me. Can't be totally sure which young lady it belongs to. McGinn is yelling for us to be silent and directing us towards the fire-door which has an illuminated "Emergency Exit" sign above it.

Outside we can see that the whole school is in darkness. Spud, Noddy and Hastings are loitering a few yards away. Surprisingly, I discover that Grace Taylor is attached to my arm. Wendy McGregor is just behind her. Both are giggling. Probably a cocktail of terror and amusement.

'Wendy, do you want a lift? You live near us', from nowhere Oliver Watkins has appeared and is trying to entice the girl I share a special song with into his mum's car. What is he even doing here? How does he know where Wendy McGregor lives? Surely, she'll say no.

'Oliver, that would be great, thank you. See you, Jonathan, that's an evening we won't forget'. I suppose it saves me having to help her get home. My dad's due in half an hour.

'Is there room for me as well? I can walk from Wendy's'. Grace doesn't want to miss out.

Knight-in-shining-armour Sir Oliver of Watkins comes to the rescue of MY two damsels. You can take a serious dislike to some people.

As I walk towards my fellow Local Gang team members, they ridicule me with very camp actions to YMCA. It was okay, this is where I belong. I'm not yet ready, physically or mentally, for encounters with the fairer sex.

The laughter that greets my recollections of the power cut suggests that my pals know more about this than me. At this point all the lights come back on in the building. The sound of The Village People can again be heard. Moments later a very red-faced Jock McGinn comes running out of the building, shaking his fist in our direction.

'Scarper!!' shouts Haystacks, and we all make a run for it. 'Spud turned off the main tripper switch'.

Saturday 21st November

4:17pm: There goes the goal horn. Please, not a Middlesbrough equaliser. Let it be against Wolves instead. It's Ayresome Park, damn it! Gary Shaw has made it Middlesbrough 1, Aston Villa 3. Surely, three points for the Villa today. Brilliant, made by his partner Peter Withe. I really thought we would struggle today. I need to trust Mr Saunders more. Even after they equalised Peter Withe's goal so early, Villa have bossed it. When I heard that Mark Jones was the sub, I could tell we were lacking players. Having to play four full-backs today because of injuries. Eamonn Deacy is centre-half. Well done, Gary Shaw!

I can relax a bit now and read my *Roy of the Rovers* comic. Somebody is still trying to kill Roy Race.

Another goal horn! Could be number four. Goal at St Andrews. Wolves have scored again. Looks like they are going to beat the Blues. They'll be out the relegation zone. How many flipping goal horns are there going to be? It's the last Saturday ever for Radio Birmingham. From Monday they become Radio WM. It's got a ring to it but hope they don't lose the goal horn. Another goal at Middlesbrough. Come on the Villa. Billy Ashcroft has pulled one back. We are still winning though. Albion are drawing with Liverpool. We must win today.

They'll wear that goal horn out. Let's hope Liverpool have taken the lead. No, Ayresome Park again. I can't breathe. Let it be for Villa.

'Middlesbrough 3, Aston Villa 3, a second goal in five minutes for Billy Ashcroft'. I bury my face in my pillow. Still over ten minutes left, but with the week I'm having I fear things are going to get worse.

6:21pm: Listening to my new Abba album, called *The Visitors,* I'm relieved that we held on for a draw and are still a point ahead of both Albion and Wolves. Mum surprised me with Abba's latest album after tea. Because she is going in hospital, well the posh private one, tomorrow. She bought both Mark and me presents. Very nice but odd. A bit like this Abba album. The tracks I've heard so far are good. Less bouncy than usual. I suppose when you're all divorced it's not surprising. Even the cover is oddly spooky. Could easily be the set of a murder mystery. They are in some kind of mansion. The four are very spread out. There is no warmth. *When All is Said and Done* really sums up the tone of the whole album and probably the band members' broken relationships. Still don't know how anybody could divorce Agnetha. If she's looking for a toyboy, then I'm right here. Hope she likes the smooth chest look.

One of Us is a catchy number, I bet Abba release that as a single. If they do, I'll buy it, but I won't tell anyone at school. They're hardly rock, New Romance or even Adam Ant cool. But like Aston Villa they have got a super symmetrical name. Both start and end with an A.

I can't be bothered to sort the tabs out on my *Shoot!* League Ladder today. My head is still full of thoughts about how both Wendy and Grace ditched me yesterday for that prat Oliver Watkins. Hope he didn't leave them wanting more. How am I supposed to compete with smoothies like flipping Watkins? Bet he never had braces. His belly button fluff probably has strands of pure gold in. I've never heard anyone say which football team Oliver Watkins supports. It won't be a local team. If he even likes football at all. Maybe he's into boys not girls. That would be a bonus. I could ask him who his favourite character from *Are You Bring Served* is. If he says Miss Brahms, I know I'm in trouble, but if Mr Humphries, then "I'm free" to continue my pursuit. But which one am I pursuing? I bet they gave her the name Miss Brahms because the first half of it spells bra. The scene with the inflatable bra, when they pressed the button is one of my favourite ones. I so need to get my hands back inside Grace Taylor's bra. Or a debut inside Wendy McGregor's lingerie. Grace has considerably bigger boobs than Wendy's. Larger cups. We aren't talking European Cup size cups, but a decent League Cup size. Minus the three handles.

I like this song. It would work well for me with my love life. Just checking what it's called. Its title is *Two for the Price of One*. Very catchy, and reading lyrics on the sleeve, Bjorn and Benny had a lot of fun with it, "He had what you might call a trivial occupation. He cleaned the platforms of the local railway station. With no romance in his life. Sometimes he wished he had a wife".

Perhaps I should be more worried about Mum's operation. It's not in Spud's mum's league but they're going to put her to sleep. You hear about people dying on the operating table. Paper's always saying what a mess the National Health Service is in under Thatcher. She's going private. So, I don't think that counts. Hopefully the surgical instruments are more sterile at the Nuffield. The surgeon is unfortunately called Mr Mann. I wonder which one of the *Mr Men* he's like. Hopefully not Mr Tickle. No! I don't want to think of my mother being tickled down there. Not sure which female bits get removed in a hysterectomy. Perhaps I need to find out more. I'll nip down and look in the *Everybody's Family Doctor* book. It's about 30 years old. Some interesting pencil sketches. I'm sure hysterectomy is spelt "hy" but I can just look through all the

H's. There can't be that many medical conditions starting with H. Can only think of whooping cough, hiccups and hamstring injuries.

Not sure what time Mum's going in tomorrow. Hope she cooks the Sunday roast first. It'll take her mind off the operation. Also need to check about Wednesday night. How I'm going to get to Mr Hill's, so I can go the League Cup replay. Surely, we can knock Second Division Leicester out this time.

Wednesday 25th November

5:49pm: So strange listening to BBC Radio WM instead of Radio Birmingham. Mum was cross when our address was changed from Staffordshire to the West Midlands in 1974. I guess the West Midlands is here to stay. Apparently, on Monday, during Mum's operation, there were over 100 tornadoes in Great Britain. It was certainly windy walking home from the bus stop. Sounds like Typhoon Irma, in the Philippines, was even worse. They're talking about over 500 people being killed. John Craven mentioned that yesterday on *Newsround*. Some nurse has also been charged with murdering 12 patients by injecting them with an overdose of some heart medicine. That's in America, though, so think the Nuffield, Tettenhall is safe.

Mum seemed quite with it. In her private room. Surrounded by so many cards, grapes and flowers. Was getting worried that we'd be late leaving for Howard Hill's with Dad having to go in search of an extra vase.

Hope Villa finish off the tie tonight. Baggies must play a third time against West Ham after drawing their replay last night. Be interesting to see which neutral ground they choose. Ipswich went through. Needed extra-time against rubbish Bradford. If we get through tonight, then we should beat Wigan to get into the quarter-finals. Really think we could get to Wembley.

7:20pm: Wish Doris would stop coughing. Don't want her germs passed on to the Villa players. Or me. I can't be taking a cold to my recovering mother. Worse still, I get it, pass it on the Spud and he gives it to his mum who is having chemo. I bet Doris has never missed a game through illness. Old people are built like carthorses and just carry on.

Great picture of the League Cup trophy on the front of the programme. It really is the best-looking cup. To think Villa were the first ever team to win this. Six years before I was born. No other club has won that cup three times. I did think Nottingham Forest would win it for a third time in 1980 until that Andy Gray goal. Manchester City and Spurs have also won it twice.

Looking on the back of the programme I recognise many of the Leicester players. They haven't changed much from the team that went down last season. Mark Wallington with his moustache is still in goal. Not sure I know who Gary Lineker is. He's down as their number nine. Ref is Ken Walmsley from Blackpool. It says he works as a sales manager for a wine and spirit merchant. I wonder what time he had to leave work. The yellow flag linesman is from Kidderminster. Hope he's a Villa fan. Could be Wolves though. Then he'll hate the Villa and give everything Leicester's way.

Nothing beats a game under these famous AV pylon floodlights. No wonder Randy fell in love with the club in the 70s. Pity Mr Hill doesn't come via the M6. I always love seeing the AV floodlights lit up as we come onto the Aston Expressway when Dad brings me. Shame it isn't called the Aston Villa Expressway. In the same way, it's a shame that it isn't Aston Villa University. They'd get a lot more students if they added 'Villa' to their name.

Still no captain Dennis tonight. So Eamonn is again wearing number six. I expect Colin Gibson will play in midfield, with Deacy probably at left-back and Gary Williams playing alongside Allan

Evans. It says in programme that Ken McNaught started his comeback in the reserves last week.

7:58pm: Wow, Eammon Deacy is playing superb. He's in midfield pretending to be Dennis Mortimer. He's running the show. What a start by Villa. Two-up already. Their keeper is making some great saves as well. Loving the way Sid and Gibbo are combining. We could score five or more. Let's save some for Wigan. Just hope Doris lasts the full 90 minutes. She's sneezing now as well as coughing. I hope those dentures are firmly stuck in.

9:40pm: Howard Hill is going to apply for some seats for us at Wigan. There is a very small allocation. You must apply via post to enter a draw. As Mr Hill is now officially retired, he said he could pick me up straight from school and drive to Wigan. If Mum and Dad say it's okay. Be good to see us get through to the last eight and score tons of goals against a Fourth Division side. Thought we would score more than the two tonight, but we were never in any trouble. The wind didn't help us. This really could be our fourth League Cup-winning season. We might be doing pretty rubbish in the league, but a treble this season of League cup, FA Cup and European Cup would be incredible. With Ron in charge, absolutely anything is possible. I don't believe it. Now, Mr Hill is coughing and sneezing.

Friday 27th November

4:12pm: Wendy McGregor was in a good mood today. She helped me with my French homework and even gave me a cake that she'd made in Home Economics. It was a shortcake biscuit with caramel in it. The icing on the top was almost claret and blue. Think she had done it especially for me. Nearly broke a tooth on the very hard biscuit. It tasted pretty good.

'Jonathan, follow your script, blue lights next'. Mr Walker ends my thoughts of Wendy and brings me back to the reality of the rehearsal. Still two weeks to go before the big performance. Good job, as the standard of acting and singing is pretty rubbish. Grace looks fab but is so wooden. She's trying too hard with her singing. Spud, as Kenickie, is having a nightmare. If it was a football match he would have been subbed before half-time. I don't think he's got a single line right. The script says, "A hickey from Kenickie" which Spud turned into 'A thickie from Kentucky'. He should wear glasses but he's too vain. Maybe if Gary Numan wore specs, then Peter Hogan would too. He's trying to read all the lines, including ones that aren't his. There is no way he's going to be ready in two weeks. Mind you, the rest are nearly as bad. All apart from flipping Oliver Watkins. His delivery is annoyingly perfect. He is standing a bit too close to Grace. Hope she kicks him, by mistake, in the dance scene. When I'm in charge of the spotlight on the night, I'll make sure it keeps missing Watkins. I'll have him running around the stage after it.

Perfect Oliver is now singing *Stranded at the Drive-in*. No idea why an American who is old enough to drive a car still goes to school. Perhaps I can blind him by shining the light straight at his eyes. Mr Walker is not impressed with Noddy's Oliver Watkins impersonation. Not surprised Sandy left Danny at the drive-in, if he's as much a moron as Watkins. Why is he stranded when he's the driver?

Mr Walker's asking us how Spud's mum is. I'm filling him in on how Spud says the treatment is making her worse. Haystacks expresses our concerns about how angry Spud has been lately. Perhaps Mr Walker could talk to Spud. Like Cloughie sitting Justin Fashanu down and trying to calm him down.

Many of us could have predicted what happened next. Spud totally lost it! It was during the singing of *Grease Lightning* that he got all the words mixed up. They did restart the song twice for him, but

116

that just made it worse. The anger had built up so much that one more tiny mistake and Mount Spud would erupt. It wasn't a tiny mistake, though. The lyric should have been "With new pistons, plugs, and shocks". What Spud mistakenly sang would have had Mary Whitehouse penning a very strongly worded letter to Barry Took. A King Kong-like roar was then accompanied by a wild swing of Spud's left foot. Pity that this was the first time they were using the cardboard car prop that 2EK has finished painting today in their Art class. Paint was still wet in places.

Within seconds Spud had annihilated the blue cardboard car with the dramatic flame effect patterns on each side. Kicks were followed by punches. Mr Walker climbed quickly down the gantry ladder and was first to drag Pete away from the wreckage. Oliver Watkins misread the situation and tried to console Spud. Part of me wanted Spud to land one of his infamous headbutts on him. But I guess even perfect Oliver didn't deserve that.

It was an impromptu end to the rehearsal. Tucker thought also, the end of Spud's time as Kenickie. We wanted to help our mate. What could we do?

Saturday 28th November

7:45pm: Hope old Doris is okay. Odd that both her and Penny weren't there. Nice to have a bit of space on the front row. First time bushy eyebrow man has spoken to me. That's the best we've played all season. Take that, Mr Walker and Brain Clough. Looking forward to seeing Mr Walker at school Monday. Three-one! Peter Shilton stopped us scoring more. Pity Jimmy made that mistake for their goal. Fancy Des Bremner scoring two. Colin Gibson was definitely playing in midfield, but Eamonn still created the first goal. I love Eamonn Deacy. He doesn't look like a footballer. More like someone who has just asked if he can join in a kickabout in the park. He's on fire at the moment.

117

We all won today, even Walsall beat Bristol Rovers. Moving the Villa tab up to 13th. I think that's right. Ceefax haven't updated the league table yet. We have a zero goal difference. So, we are three places above Wolves. They have a rubbish goal difference. Confusing working out these three points for a win. The total games played for all the teams no longer is same as total points gained. Albion are a point below us and Wolves, but now three points above the relegation zone. The Bluenoses are now in the bottom three. Ron Atkinson's Man United just keeping winning at the top. That'll please Georgina Ramsey. Hastings did give her an option to go back out with him last week. If she goes back to supporting Albion and puts a Cyrille Regis poster in her locker by 1st December then he'll take her back.

December 1st is also the day Villa play at Wigan. Mr Hill didn't get lucky in the ballot. I'll be listening to it on my lucky radio.

Mum is back home today. In quite a good mood. Is resting though with her feet up. Catching up last week's *Dallas*. I can't remember a lot happening. JR was trying to frame Clayton Farlow, I think, the bloke who's played by Howard Keel. The singer in all those rubbish American musicals Grandad used to watch. Mark and I are going to help with the cooking. Well, getting things out of the freezer and putting them in the oven. Mum has labelled all the Tupperware containers in the freezer. Hope we can read her writing. Puddings are on a different shelf to dinners, so we shouldn't get too many surprises.

It's the curse of the *Aston Villa News and Record* that the player focus is Jimmy Rimmer, and today Jimmy made that howler. The other week it was Gary Williams and he ended up missing his first game of the season. Wow, you can get kids' Aston Villa pyjamas for Christmas for five pounds. Must show Mum and Dad that. Need to send a cheque or postal order.

118

Fascinating to read about Brian Little now. If it wasn't for his injury, he would have surely been going to the World Cup. He's still working for the club, despite retiring early. I didn't realise he was involved in the club shop and looking after the Villa lottery. He's been co-commentating on Radio Birmingham, sorry Radio WM, a few times this season. He seems to have taken over from the gloomy Larry Cannings. Brian really is a Mr Aston Villa. To think he nearly signed for the Blues.

1. Manchester United Pl: 17 Po: 32   +14
2. Swansea City   Pl: 16 Po: 30   + 4
3. Ipswich Town   Pl: 15 Po: 29   + 8
4. Tottenham Hotspur   Pl: 15 Po: 28   + 8

15. Aston Villa   Pl: 15 Po: 19   + 3

Villa November League Results

7th Arsenal (h) 0-2 Lost
21st Middlesbrough 3-3 Draw (Cowans, Withe, Shaw)
17th West Ham United (h) 3-2 Win (Mortimer, Geddis, Morley)
28th Nottingham Forest (h) 3-1 Won (Bremner, Withe)

Villa November European Cup Result

4th Dynamo Berlin (East Germany) (h) 0-1 Lost
[Villa won on away goals]

Villa November League Cup Results

11th Leicester City (a) 0-0 Draw
25th Leicester City (h) 2-0 Won (Cowans, Withe)

Chapter Six

December 1981

10:10am: In Chemistry, and Wendy McGregor slides something towards me. It's an envelope. With my name and two kisses on the front. I look at her in a state of confusion. She pats her blazer pocket. Possibly indicating I need to save it until later.

Spud's doodling something on the inside of his Chemistry exercise book. Seems to resemble a devil on a bicycle. Peter is quite artistic. He hasn't really spoken about the stage rage. It has been decided that he will not be playing Kenickie or any other part in the school musical. Also, he's in detention every night this week. Perhaps lucky he wasn't suspended.

12:46pm: How cold is it? Even with my jumper, blazer and coat on, I'm freezing. That sky looks full of snow. There was no heating in the Maths room either. Might bring my navy blue gloves to school in the morning. Playing football in so many layers is not easy and the icy patch to the left of Noddy's goal is causing problems. Haystacks went over twice there. His deadline for Georgina Ramsey returning her allegiances to his beloved Albion passed 45 minutes ago. So, Hastings is now on the lookout for a new lady. Says he wants an older woman this time.

That goal surely came off Tucker's hand. But Spud just doesn't respond. He's too busy watching Carrie Carrington. She is walking towards us. Totally ignoring the imaginary markings of our football pitch, she strides up to goalkeeper Spud.

'Do you want to go out with me?', Carrie asks in the direction of Pete, to everyone else's relief. 'Go on, then', he nonchalantly replied.

1:08pm: Seeking solitude in cubicle three of the boys' toilets. Resisting the urge to correct the grammar of the graffiti on the door referring to Mr Harpwell. Checking my homework diary to see what English homework I should have done. The toilet cubicles are only used for hiding in. The state of them, low centre of gravity and toilet paper that is so shiny nothing sticks to it, makes them impractical for bodily function purposes.

Remembering the envelope Wendy gave me, I take it out of my blazer pocket. Looks like she's used a fountain pen. Very dramatic "J" on the envelope. It's a Christmas card! Who sends Christmas cards on first day of December? Talk about being keen. I haven't even opened the first door on my stable-scene Advent calendar. With Mum's operation, Dad was slow getting the calendars down from the loft. Every year I know that behind window one is an angel. Yet it's still nice to get the first one open. Also, *Blue Peter* haven't lit the first candle on their Advent thingy yet. But here I have my first Christmas card of 1981. Not one of your bog-standard packs of twenty Woolworths ones either, or an Oxfam one. This one is Spiderman coming down the chimney like Father Christmas, with his sack of Spiderman goodies. "SEASON'S GREETINGS FROM MARVEL COMICS AND THE ELECTRIC COMPANY!" Wow, quite a card and not a little baby Jesus in sight. It looks like it's come from America. Wendy did say she had an uncle who lived in America. Inside the Christmas card she's written "To the very special Jonathan with love from Wendy xxxx". Four kisses, that's promising. What does "the very special" mean? I need to know if anybody else got a card. Has she given out

all her cards? I guess I'm going to have to get her an individual card now. Normally my mum gets all my cards.

That's the end of lunch bell. Followed by two crashing bangs on my cubicle door.

'Hugh! Hugh! You in there? shouts Tucker. 'Come on! Spud's been caught snogging Campton by Jock'.

7:34pm: Hopefully this'll be a routine win. No room for any giant-killing tonight. Let's not let Wigan Athletic be another Cambridge United. Lucky radio is tuned to Radio WM. Two League Cup games tonight on Radio WM. Our fourth-round tie and Baggies second third-round replay against West Ham. Haystacks was furious when it was announced they were playing it back at Upton Park instead of a neutral ground.

Can't believe they suspended Spud. Smashing up a car didn't get him suspended but putting his tongue down crazy Carrie Carrington did. Tucker says the film *Carrie* was based on Carrie Carrington. Although when I hear the name Carrie, I think of the Cliff Richard song. Can't believe 40-something Cliff is knocking off Sue Barker. No wonder British tennis is in such a mess.

Not sure how Spud's suspension will work. He won't be able to hide it from his parents. His mum stays in bed all day now. His eldest sister has moved back home to look after her. Spud and his sister, Valerie, have never got on.

No!! That can't be right. How can Wigan have scored? Less than ten minutes in. It's going to be another Cambridge.

8:25pm: It's even colder now. Can't believe it has snowed. Perhaps a snow blizzard might get this game abandoned. Mark has come to check on the score three times now. He's not normally so interested in the Villa score. If we lose to Fourth Division Wigan, then I'm not going to school tomorrow. Mark needs to focus on his Highway Code. It's his driving test in the morning. Could be useful if he passes. If Randy can eventually pass it, surely Mark should sail through it. To be fair, Mark has driven well the last two times I've been in the car with him. He only mounted the pavement twice last time. Harsh to include the one when he was swerving to avoid that hedgehog.

A penalty! At Springfield Park. But who to? Yes, Sid's scored from the spot. All-square. Come on, Villa. At least get them back to Villa Park.

9:08pm: A round behind everyone else, but looks like Albion are going through. They are winning 1-0 at Upton Park. Still goalless at Highbury. Arsenal against Liverpool. A late Arsenal goal would be good. A few minutes left in our game. Suppose a draw isn't a disaster. I can take the ribbing over that tomorrow. At least we are still in the cup.

The flipping goal horn. Mark comes charging into my bedroom. It's a third goal at Wigan. Surely a winner one way or the other. Mark's smirking. How can he know? This is unbearable. It must be a Villa goal. It is! Peter Withe has scored our second. Set up by Gary Shaw. There goes the final whistle. We are in the quarter-finals. Yes!!!

Thursday 3rd December

8:45am: With both Spud and Carrie Carrington now suspended for snogging in the Humanities block, it was time to act. Haystacks had called an emergency meeting of both form 4MC and 4WA in the locker area. We have formed a committee called "Justice4Snoggers". Noddy came up with the catchy name.

'Order! Order! shouts Hastings as he bangs on the nearest locker. It's chaotic with so many of us in such a small space. I decide to try to stand an equal distance between Wendy and Grace. Don't want to be nailing my colours to either of their masts yet. Haystacks asks for suggestions of peaceful protests. Tucker suggests a sit-in like they did in *Grange Hill* a few years back. Not a bad idea considering how cold it currently is outside. Grace makes the point that she can't afford to miss any *Grease* rehearsals. Louise Douglas is in favour of writing to our local MP. But nobody knows who our MP is and the MP probably won't care as we're not old enough to vote. In the end we agree that we'll start a petition to demand the end of the suspension for Peter Hogan and Carrie Carrington. Noddy had tried to push for it just being Spud, but that did seem unfair on scary Carrie Carrington. It takes two to French kiss. The challenge is to get 1,000 signatures by Friday lunchtime and then take it to the Headmistress. Making the petition Maths simple, there were 20 of us there. So, if we each get 50 signatures then we'd reach our 1,000. Allowing for our own names we only need 49 more each.

8:31pm: Would have thought my mum might have taken Spud's side. She is sympathetic to how difficult it is with his mum's cancer but says that kissing at school cannot be tolerated. Dad did sign the petition. I didn't tell him what he was signing. Just asked for his signature. He got a bit carried away. Think he thought he was giving an autograph. I now have 33 names. A good start. I'll get Asif to sign. Just need to find a way of sneaking out to see him. Noddy was bragging that he had collected over 60 names. Haystacks was really impressed until he started reading them. He questioned the authenticity of George and Mildred Roper's signatures. Wendy McGregor is doing well. Mr Walker might not have been brave enough to add his name, but Miss Tully signed it. Wendy also enticed all the boys in 2BE to put their names down. The hem of her skirt does seem to have risen again.

Still glad I didn't personally witness the passions of Carrie and Spud.

At least it's a home draw for us. Crystal Palace or Haystacks' Albion. Be interesting if we get to face West Brom. Either tie would be very winnable. Palace are struggling in the Second Division after finishing bottom of the First last season. Some decent teams left in. Spurs are at home to Mr Walker's lot. Ipswich are at home to Watford. Their manager Graham Taylor is doing well. Watford could end up in First Division next season for the first time. Ipswich should beat them though. Suppose the winner of the Liverpool-Arsenal replay will get through as well. They would only have to beat Barnsley at home. Looks like semi-finalists will be Arsenal or Liverpool, Ipswich, Spurs or Forest and hopefully the Villa.

Friday 4ᵗʰ December

11:39am: That was a waste of time. We have managed over 1,070 legitimate names on our petition, but the decision to allow the snogging couple to return had already been made. We were all set to march to the Headmistress's office at 2pm to hand over the many pages of our petition. Now Mr Walker is telling us that both Peter and Carrie are being allowed back to school on Monday. It appears that our Head has got some compassion after all. Mr Walker surprisingly says that Jock McGinn led the staff protests against the punishment.

My research on the Christmas card giving of Wendy McGregor has discovered that she has not yet sent anybody else a card. She has singled me out for her early season's greetings. It must be a sign. No more playing it cool. It's time to make my move. Grace Taylor was my summer girlfriend. It's time to get a winter girlfriend. I'm going

to ask Wendy out. It's a time for action, so next week I'm going to
do it.

Sunday 6th December

3:12pm: It's all Trevor Francis. He seems to have been Manchester
City's only forward. Amazed he didn't score. Dad's fallen asleep
during *Star Soccer*. Guess he deserves it after that great beef and
Yorkshire pud dinner he cooked. You can't beat a nearly cremated
parsnip. I wonder why Villa and Man City are wearing black
armbands. I don't know who died. It's a year this week since John
Lennon was shot but I don't think it's because of him.

We had our fair share of attacks. Allan Evans was unlucky not to
score then. Why hasn't the ref stopped it for Des Bremner's head
injury? There's blood, and Sid has stopped to help him. Manchester
City haven't stopped. That's their flipping goal. Dennis Tueart
header. That's not fair. It's just not sporting. The only goal of the
game and it shouldn't have counted. That was a clear foul. Come
on, show it again. How did Peter Withe miss that last-minute
chance? Can't believe we lost that game.

Sunday People shows we're 16th in the table. Champions and 16th.
Albion are above us now. We're only two points above the
relegation zone. This is crazy. We need Dennis Mortimer back. We
didn't seem to play that badly but still lost.

Paper is going on about a new disease called "AIDS". Odd name
for an illness. Seems to be a big thing that there are now cases in
England. Looks like it's a coming from America. Says people can
die from it. It talks about people who have unprotected sex being
vulnerable. I guess that means if they don't wear a rubber johnny or
the girl isn't on the pill. Maybe I should warn Mark to be careful
when bonking Sarah. We haven't seen Sarah lately. Mark keeps

127

going out to meet her, but she never comes back to the house. Mark passed his driving test on Wednesday. Don't we know it! Dad still hasn't been brave enough to let Mark go out in the Ital on his own.

Wednesday 9ᵗʰ December

9:35am: Madness! There's over a foot of snow and we're walking over three miles to school. The school bus couldn't run but us teenagers are expected to make this arctic trek. We need skis and husky dogs for this terrain. What do I get? My dad's old gardening wellies. Two sizes too big for me. Even with my two layers of socks. All the posh schools were read out on Radio WM as closed, but no mention of our school. Our purple-haired Headmistress is never going to close her precious school. Bet when we finally get there that half the teachers haven't managed to get in. Dad left for work early at just after 6am. No idea if he's arrived. It said on the radio that nothing was moving on the M6.

Nine of us started walking from the bus stop about half an hour a go. Only five of us left now. Not sure what happened to the third-year twins. I guess they aren't very tall and the snow has drifted. It's blowing in my face. It must be minus ten degrees. My foot feels cold and wet. Is that frostbite? No, I've just lost my dad's right Compo-style wellington boot. It's stuck in the snow six feet away. I'm going to have to go back for it. Hard to keep your balance on one foot. In twenty inches of snow. So much for camaraderie. They've left me to hop and recover my boot.

11:21am: At least it's warm in the sports hall, even if my sock is still wet. Only six teachers have got in. The first- and second-years have been sent home. The rest of us are in the sports hall studying. Noddy made it in, but no sign of the others. Spud is missing again. He still hasn't been in this week despite his suspension being over. Carrie Carrington came back on Monday and apparently was one of

the first ones here. Mind you, daddy has got a Land Rover. Nobody
has mentioned if there are any dinners. I can't smell that usual
unique odour of school dinners. Normally smells like a cross
between horse manure and strawberries. Nobody packed me any
sandwiches this morning. I might be forced to have it. If there is
any.

Hope Dad is okay on the motorway. He wasn't in a good
mood. Uncle Norman used to be great at shovelling snow off both
drives. He kept a giant red snow spade in his garage. Always cleared
our drive when he did his. Used to pile all the snow on our front
lawns. Mark, Carol and I used to then make fab snowmen with it.
Miss those days. Today, Asif's dad cleared the snow off their drive
and piled it all on our drive. It meant Dad couldn't get his car out of
the garage without first moving tons of snow. Which, of course, he
put back on the Mahmoods' drive.

Wendy McGregor and Grace Taylor are both here. They are
studying French vocab together. Pointless me going to try and help
them. I get so confused with the sexual orientation of the French
words. I am studying from afar which one has the prettiest mouth. I
have kissed Grace's. I think I need to kiss Wendy's to compare. Still
need to ask Wendy out.

'Do you think I should ask Georgina Ramsey out?' Noddy
asks totally out of the blue. I try to digest this random question.
Noddy was thinking of asking Hastings' Man United-supporting ex-
girlfriend out. Sounded crazy. It breaks the Local Gang team code
that Haystacks himself put in place in 1980. You cannot like the
same girl as another gang member. I think it's the Batson rule,
number three. We need to ask Hastings first if he still has an interest
in Georgina. Would she even say yes to Noddy? I can't ever recall
Noddy showing an interest in a girl before. Even though his pubes
are long enough to plait. A different shade of brown though to ones
on his head.

Grace has joined me. She's anxious about the school musical. Weatherman Michael Fish says that this snow will last until Friday. How will next week be? We have *Grease* shows on Tuesday, Wednesday and Thursday night. They have already called off tonight's rehearsal and Oliver Watkins didn't show up today. The Headmistress said that the parents of any absent pupil who isn't sick will receive a letter. Maybe Saturday's Villa-Albion match will be cancelled. It would be nice if they played it and used an orange ball. Mr Hill could offer to go and help clear the snow now he's retired.

Saturday 12th December

8:50am: It must be over two feet long. Now do tights go up or down? I suppose it depends if the girl is putting them on or taking them off. Knowing my luck, she'd be putting them on. I am sure it's stalactites that go down. So, these are massive stalactites coming down from my bedroom window. That would do somebody serious damage if that landed on them. Wonder if it would be sharp enough to go right through a person? It's going to be a long Saturday with no football. Really annoyed they called our game off against the Albion. The sun is shining now. There are only three First Division games left on today. Apparently, Coventry have got this clever under-soil heating. Another Jimmy Hill brainwave. Well, I hope Manchester City beat them.

Daily Express saying this week's snow was the heaviest since 1874. Wow, the year the Villa were formed. It's going to last until Boxing Day. We'll have a white Christmas. I guess I need to start thinking about Christmas now. I need to sort a Christmas card out for Wendy. Maybe I could ask her out in a posh Christmas card. The buses must be running today. So, I could go into Willenhall. Maybe see if Asif wants to come with me. Problem is, how do I let him know? We need to set a signal up. Maybe if I tap the wall three times then we both pick up the phone and talk on the party-line.

Problem with that is Asif's dad is continually banging on our wall. We need a code that we could use to write messages in the snow for each other. A code that Asif could easily decipher to mean "fancy going to Willenhall? Meet you at ten o'clock at the bus stop". I wonder how you send telegrams.

3:46pm: The Mander Centre is quite busy despite the compacted snow. Asif said he wanted to experience Wolverhampton shopping for the first time. His parents only ever take him to West Bromwich or Cannock. His parents don't know he's out with me. They think he is playing his violin at orchestra rehearsals in Walsall. Hence, he is now walking around C&A with a violin case.

Getting a message to Asif this morning had been a lot easier than I'd anticipated. I was in the garden trying to build a replica of Villa Park out of snow when Asif shouted over the wall. He did say he liked my snow fort. He'd been watching me from his bedroom window. I didn't say it was supposed to be Villa Park.

Asif's dad did drop him off in Walsall for his rehearsals, but then Asif got the bus and met me in Wolverhampton. He must be back at the concert hall before half-past five for his dad to pick him up.

Just checking the half-time scores on the TVs in *Radio Rentals* window. Coventry are losing and Swansea are beating Forest. Mr Walker won't like that. I need to find a soppy Christmas card for Wendy McGregor. Ideally around the 20p mark. Woolworths is probably a good shout for that or WH Smiths. Let's try "Woollies" first. We can check the singles chart out there as well.

Choice of Christmas cards is rubbish. All the romantic ones seem to have "Girlfriend" or "Wife" on. That's not appropriate. The "Special Friend" one with the lamb on the front is quite cute. Or do I go for funny?

'How about this one?' shouts Asif. He's holding one with a cartoon snowman on the front. It reads "What's the difference between Snowmen and Snowwomen?" I have no idea what the difference is. Inside it says, "snowballs". I love it. It's like the kind of Christmas cracker joke that my Grandad used to laugh at. It has really tickled Asif. There is a more religious serious "Mum and Dad" Christmas card that I decide to buy. Problem is cost. Need enough money left for some sweets from the Pick 'n' Mix and bus fare home.

'Give me them cards, Hugh', Asif whispered. This surprised me. Not only the lack of manners but because only members of Local Gang called me "Hugh". Asif's next action shocked me even more. He opened his empty violin case and placed the two cards inside it. Quickly he closed the case and we moved towards the Pick 'n' Mix. Chocolate limes are always my favourite. Followed by rhubarb and custard ones. Asif fills two paper bags full of sweets and then stows these away inside the loot containing violin case.

'Shall we check out the singles?' master criminal Asif says out of the side of his mouth. I'm not ready to go back inside a police van. Worrying that Asif is looking to add some 45s to his violin collection, I suggest it's time we paid and left. Knowing full well that this teenage Al Capone had no intention of paying.

8:12pm Feels wrong writing a stolen Christmas card to a potential girlfriend. Perhaps I should leave the price on the back, so she knows how much I intended to spend on it. Trying not to touch the card too much to avoid adding any fingerprints. What should I write? Seems a bit impersonal to ask a girl out in a card. 'To Wendy' is a good start. Forest came back to beat Swansea. That puts them ten points above us. Even though the Pools Panel put us down as a home win against the Albion for our postponed game. I am not putting 'love'. Going to go for "Have a lovely Christmas from Jonathan xx". Are two kisses too much? I think two kisses suggests

132

a level of romantic interest. I am going to be brave and add a PS. What have I got to lose? "PS Up the Villa".

Tuesday 15ᵗʰ December

7:13pm: Nearly time for the curtain to go up. I hope Oliver Watkins forgets his lines or falls off the stage. Decent crowd despite the wintery conditions. Really thought this morning they would postpone this. Nice of Mr Walker to let Spud join Tucker and me in the gantry tonight. I need to be alert. There are tons of lighting changes in the script.

Spud has the most crucial role tonight. He's responsible for my lucky radio. The Villa are playing at Swansea. The game starts at 7:30. I've handed Spud my radio and my Grandad's old earpiece. I cleaned it well before. As it still had some of his ear wax on it. It smelled like my Grandad too. Spud has agreed to be careful and give me a suitable thumbs up or thumbs down whenever there is a goal in the Villa game. We need a win. Too close to the bottom three. We should beat Swansea. Even Mr Walker's team beat Swansea.

Grace looks stunning as Sandy in that white summer dress. Chorus a bit flat on opening song. Needs more bounce. You can see the shine of Watkins' teeth from here. I bet he cleans his teeth with Crest toothpaste. Surprised you can't see his halo against the scenery. His hair looks so perfectly positioned as well. Maybe I need to flick some of my dandruff down on top of him. Time to change to the straw gel lights. I can really light up Grace here. I blow Grace a kiss which I know in the bright lights she'll never see. Tucker shakes his head.

I am multi-tasking now preparing to do the sound effects of the Rydell High School bell while changing the composition of the lighting. Spud is joining in with singing of the end of *Summer Nights*. A disapproving look from Mr Walker in his direction.

That sounded like a school horn from Spud's earpiece. I pause pressing the button for the school bell sound effect and watch Spud instead. His hand is coming out. Slowly, for dramatic affect he turns his thumb downwards. Must be a disastrous start at Vetch Field.

'Stadler! Bell!' yells Mr Walker to stares up to the gantry by the audience. I press the sound effect button. Then Spud spreads his arm out in horror. Now he's putting his thumb up. What is going on? Had he got it wrong? Was it a Villa goal? Tucker tells me to concentrate. How can I when I don't know if the Villa are losing, drawing or winning? Spud raises an index finger on both hands. I take this as a signal the score is in fact 1-1. Seems we were losing but we've equalised.

The cast are starting to warm up. Audience are being deliberately quiet, but clapping is getting more energetic. Grace is smashing it. She is so sweet in her white pyjamas with yellow flowers on. I think it's a bit obvious that I'm focusing on her on the stage. Only looking away to see if Spud is indicating any more goals over the Welsh border. Seems strange Villa playing a league game in another country. Spud is booing his Kenicki replacement, Richard Henry, whenever he comes on the stage. Poor Richard keeps looking up at the roof to see where the boos are coming from. Predictably, Tucker always calls Richard Henry Dick Emery, so is also hackling him with shouts of "Ooh…You are awful". To be fair, Richard Henry is doing a decent job. He's not a bad singer. Yes, he's a bit weedy and he's got even bigger ears than Noddy, but Dick's sound.

Curtain down and time for interval. Shame they don't have those little tubs of ice cream like they do in the theatre. Tucker and Spud are nipping to the bogs. I am catching up on the half-time report. Why didn't Spud tell me Swansea had scored again? We are 2-1 down. They took the lead just before half-time. Sounds like we are missing Peter Withe. David Geddis doesn't seem to be up to it this season. We so need the skipper back as well.

You can see right behind the scenery boards from up here. Grace is getting ready for second act. She sings the first song with the chorus line, "It's Raining on Prom Night". She looks extra nervous and is busy checking the words. I am looking forward to seeing her in those tight leather trousers at the end. To think she hadn't got time for me with her studying and yet here she is now being the star of the school musical production. Part of me is proud of her. The part that isn't totally furious for her dumping me. I do like Wendy McGregor, but is she my consolation prize? That's unfair. Surprised that either of them is interested in me. I'm not Oliver Watkins material. More on Dick Emery's level. If the Pools Panel were sitting and I was at home to Oliver Watkins, they would score it one and a half points for an away win. I think against Dick Emery we would get two points for a goalless draw. If it went to penalties, he would probably win because he's got quite a decent voice.

9:12pm: Guess that cut-throat gesture from Spud means it is all over. We have lost 2-1 to John Toshack's flaming Swansea. Who have Swansea got? Apart from the most Welsh named goalkeeper ever in Dai Davies. Sounds like he should be stoking the boiler of *Ivor the Engine*. Up front, how old is Bob Latchford? I thought he'd retired. Leighton James has played for loads of clubs. Swansea have gone top of the league. How crazy is that? They have gone above Ron Atkinson's Manchester United.

Need to focus on the finale. Lots of lighting changes. Need to forget about Villa's plight. Not to fixate too much on Grace's chest trying to escape from that tight top under her leather jacket. She really is stealing the show. Even Tucker gives me a "wow, she's hot" look. Watkins looks a right geek in his cardigan. Damn! He's

135

taken the cardigan off and looks cool again. Grace's heart better not be set on him. Wait, Grace has taken her jacket off. We can really see down her cleavage now from up here. To think my hands have fondled those breasts. The audience are on their feet and loving it. Spud is smiling for the first time in ages. He's singing all Kenicki's part. Possibly louder than Richard Henry is. Have a horrible feeling Spud's going to slide down the ladder and on to the stage. Mr Walker gives him a stern look.

The audience are all on their feet. It wasn't that good. I guess they are being polite as it's kids. Think if it was the West End, they'd be a little disappointed and some might want their money back. Big cheers for all the cast. Sandy *aka* Grace Taylor is now taking her bow. Big claps and cheers from up in our gantry. I would have given a wolf whistle but I have never been able to whistle. Why does Oliver flipping Watkins get the last bow? Would have thought Danny and Sandy would have gone together. At least it means Spud, Tucker and I can give him a loud "boo". Mr Walker is just shaking his head. I think he's given up on us.

What about us? The band, scenery makers and even the third-years who cleared the snow off the car park get recognition, but not the amazing lighting team. Without us, the whole performance would have been in darkness. Mr Walker promises he'll have a word so that we get a big mention tomorrow night.

The curtain falls and the audience are starting to leave after the encore of *Born to Hand Jive*. Luckily, Mr Walker has climbed down and is not watching Spud's X-rated hand jiving. I catch a glimpse of Grace at the side of the stage sharing a euphoric moment with her co-stars. For me, Grace was the star of the show. Watkins is a bit too close for my liking. No! No! They are kissing! On the lips!

'I think I might have had sex with Carrie Carrington', Spud blurts out.

Fridy 18th December

3:20pm: Still half an hour left of term. I'm ready for the Christmas holiday. I do like the snow. Be great if it's a white Christmas. But not too much snow as I can't wait for my first ever Boxing Day Villa game. Just imagine being at Villa Park on Boxing Day. It's only seven sleeps away. Can't believe my last lesson of 1981 is double French. What a rubbish lesson to end the best year of my life with. I've missed the opportunity to ask Wendy McGregor out. She's been off ill all this week. I guess that will have to go in my list of jobs to do in 1982. Along with seeing Ron Saunders' team playing in the European Cup Final in Rotterdam. Looks like I have missed any chance with Grace now perfect Oliver is on the scene. I did interrogate Grace about the first-night kiss, but she flatly denied it. Even accusing me of making it up and being horrible to her.

Still can't believe that Spud might have bonked Carrie Carrington. How can he not know? Said he wasn't sure if he was in when the spunk squirted. Spud said it was all Carrie's idea and he blamed his dad's homebrew. In fact, it was anybody's fault but Pete's. Perhaps scary Carrie but a spell on him. I can't believe he didn't use a rubber johnny. Hasn't he read the horror AIDS stories about unprotected sex? I tried to explain to Spud that he could be arrested. It's illegal to have sex at 15. He argued it was okay because Carrie Carrington is also 15 now. Hastings explained that coppers always take the girls' side in cases like this. Tucker pointed out that if one of Spud's tadpoles penetrated Carrington's egg that he could be a father by the first game of next season. We could tell Spud was bricking it, but he joked they could name the baby "Gary", after Gary Numan. Best if it was a boy then. Given Pete's obvious lack of the understanding of girls' bits, perhaps a boy would be best. At least Mrs Hogan was coming out of hospital for Christmas. Hopefully she can settle her wild son down. It's going to be weird seeing her with no boobs. I wonder what they do with the boobs they take off. Do they have a collection of spare nipples?

6:02pm: Snowing again. There are going to be a few games off tomorrow. I wonder what the weather is like in Liverpool. We could do with our game at Everton being on. We tend to do well at Goodison Park. Perhaps Tony Morley will score another goal of the season. This time with an orange ball. Guess more likely it'll be called off. Our lawn is still frozen under the snow. Dad tried to put a fork in it and bent his fork. The bird table is still so surrounded by icicles that it looks like a prison cell. Mark made a hole in the ice on the fishpond. By heating the bottom of one of Mum's saucepans on the gas hob. Took him ages to burn a hole to the water at the bottom. Poor fish only have about a foot of non-frozen water. Is it frozen water or ice? Suppose it's ice.

Mum is doing a lot better. We're now having to stop her doing things. Mark caught her putting the fairy on top of the Christmas tree on Monday. I think with a late fitness test she might be ready to do the Shake 'n' Vac on Christmas Eve. Dad has bought a "pine-fresh" flavoured one. So, people will think our plastic silver Christmas tree is real.

Express & Star is saying about the Chelsea hooligans. Following the incident at Derby, the Football Association have banned Chelsea fans from all the rest of their away games this season. How is that going to work? If they are playing another London club, like West Ham, how will you know if they are not West Ham fans? Keep telling my mum that football hooliganism isn't a problem at Villa Park. Think she worries when I'm there.

Dad arrives back feeling chuffed with himself. He has completed the set of six crystal tumbler glasses from the Texaco garage. Says we can use them on Christmas Day.

Saturday 19th December

6:41pm: This is getting serious. 17th in the league. Could we be the first champions to be relegated? Has that ever happened before? Beaten 2-0 at Everton. Admittedly, we almost fielded a reserve team. Noel Blake, Terry Bullivant, Terry Donovan, David Geddis and Ivor Linton on the bench. Four of those didn't play a single minute last season. Without Ken McNaught, Dennis Mortimer, Gary Shaw and Peter Withe, what chance had we got? Seems like Ron dropped Shaw, Williams and Deacy. Typical, only one of two games that survived this blooming weather and we lose. If that wasn't bad enough it's on *Match of the Day* tonight. So, we can be a laughing stock. At least no school again for nearly three weeks.

Snow has melted quite a bit today. Despite Mum's protests, Dad has let Mark borrow the Ital for the first time. He's taking Sarah to the ABC Cinema in Walsall. Old punk Sarah is going to get my 17-year-old brother into see the 18-rated film, *An American Werewolf in London*. Mum doesn't know it's an 18. I'm not letting on. Means I get an evening free from Mark's Villa taunts. It stars Jenny Agutter. Surprised it's an 18. She wasn't very racy in *The Railway Children*. Dad gave Mark lots of instructions about driving in wintery conditions. Dad even put a spade and a large rubber mat in the boot. Still think Mark in his suit and thin tie looked a bit overdressed for an encounter with the spikey-haired granny.

Can't believe *Roy of the Rovers* are copying *Dallas*. We know Roy Race can't be dead. There's no comic without the Melchester Rovers' player manager. Dramatic cover of him being shot though. Well, as dramatic as a cartoon drawing gets. In his suit, in his office. Copying how JR Ewing was shot. I don't think this whodunnit will quite grip the nation like the "Who shot JR?" campaign did. Let's work out who shot Roy Race then. Take my mind off Everton's player manager, Howard Kendall, getting one over the Villa. Roy has certainly lost his magic lately. Getting Melchester relegated. Then falling out with his wife, Penny. Even in a cartoon she looks

139

hot. The superstar boss has also angered several individuals with nasty tempers. Main suspect probably is teammate Vic "Superbrat" Guthrie who is suspended from the team for disciplinary issues. Is it motive to kill, though? Perhaps the shooter is from a rival comic like Judge Dredd from *2000AD*. Or maybe a character in another *Roy of the Rovers* cartoon strip. Perhaps Hot Shot Hamish, he's a bit of a loose cannon. I don't trust the actor who plays Roy in the television series they are filming about Melchester Rovers. Or maybe it's just copying *Dallas* and it will end up being Kristin Shepard. Perhaps I'm getting a little too old for *Roy of the Rovers*.

Sunday 20th December

4:45pm: It's not just outside it's so cold. The atmosphere in our lounge, as Dad is toasting a crumpet on the electric fire, is pretty frosty. Mark is in the bad books for not bringing Dad's car back until ten-past midnight. My parents refused to go to bed until he returned. Dad kept his corduroy trousers on so that he could put the Ital in the garage when Mark finally returned. Mum had been convinced that Mark had skidded off the road somewhere and ended up at the bottom of the canal. She'd made Dad lift the receiver on the phone twice to check that there was a dial tone. Needed to know the phone was working in case a hospital was trying to call us.

Mark makes things worse by announcing he isn't coming to the church "Carols by Candlelight" service. A family tradition I can never remember not happening. We always go together. It's the first one without Grandad. Mum plays the "It's the first one for me as an orphan" card. Mark isn't changing his mind though. Randy also tries appealing to Mark's better nature. Randy came for lunch. Dad went to pick him up, as Randy hasn't driven since the snow started. Although in that time, Randy has washed his car three times.

The highlight of Randy's visit was that he brought us a copy of the Christmas edition of the *TV Times*. First chance to see what's on ITV over Christmas. It runs from yesterday to New Year's Day. Fourteen days of telly. The sight of Harry Secombe in a Santa outfit on the cover, though, quickly dampened my festive excitement. The Christmas Day film is going to be *Dr No*, sounds like our doctor. Great picture of bikini-clad Ursula Andress with Sean Connery. She looks lovely. Apparently, she is known as "Bond's first bird". I didn't know she was from Switzerland.

Sharing our pot of tea, Randy and I dissect Villa's Everton defeat based on last night's viewing of *Match of the Day*. Both critical of the performance of young but massive Noel Blake. Who did look as if he was playing on roller-skates. The referee also got quite a slating. How many Villa players did he book? Randy agreed it was never a penalty but also thought it was funny the Everton player putting it wide. Randy is full of doom and gloom for the season. The football one, not the festive one. It's me who tries to bring out the positives. We are in the quarter-finals of both the European and League Cups. We are playing Albion now in the League Cup after they won 3-1 at Crystal Palace on Wednesday. Next year, 1982, could see us win a cup. Hopefully without getting relegated. Ron knows what he's doing. He'll get it right. We just need to be 110% behind him.

'Okay, I'll go. But only if I can drive'. Mark makes a complete U-turn and agrees to join us at the carol service.

Thursday 24th December

7:09pm: Never liked David "Kid" Jensen. What sort of middle name is "Kid"? I'm glad Human League are number one though. Glad Christmas *Top of the Pops* is including *Don't you want me*. My song of the year is probably Bucks Fizz with *Making your Mind up*. I think my favourite Christmas song is the Wizard one, *I wish it could* *be Christmas every day.* Don't know when you'd do your Christmas shopping though. I wonder what I'll get for Christmas. Guess a couple of Atari games. I've asked for the basketball one. Am so going to miss not having an ace present off Grandad. Used to be my favourite part of Christmas when we collected Grandad. We would bring him here and he would have brought us a great big pork pie for Christmas Eve tea. Tomorrow we'll have Grandma here and my Auntie Eve. Must make sure we put them in the right order. Auntie Eve is deaf in her left ear and Grandma in her right. Almost think we should leave two empty chairs: one for Grandad and one for Grandpa. We wouldn't have enough petrol garage glasses though if they were still with us.

Need to get my season ticket out ready for my first Boxing Day game. Southampton at Villa Park. Must be first time I have been wanting to get through Christmas Day and get to Boxing Day.

That's odd, my season ticket is there in my cashbox but where is my green Staffordshire Building Society book? I always keep it in there. I wanted to see how near I was to the £1,000 mark. Hoping that I might get some money that I can pay in. But where is it?

I'll watch *Only When I Laugh*. Recording *Are You Being Served?* so we can all watch it together after Dad has finished stuffing the turkey. It's young Mr Grace's 90th birthday.

I wonder what Grace Taylor is doing tonight. Bet she's on her own with her mum. Must be strange having parents in different houses.

Mark is overdoing the aftershave again. He's off to give Sarah her Christmas present. Without Dad's car this time. The elderly girlfriend is going to drive. She's picking Mark up on the corner of the street. Mum has wrapped a box of Black Magic up for Mark to give to Sarah from us.

Nicholas Lyndhurst – Rodney Trotter – is on *Give Us A Clue*. Quite a lineup with Terry Scott and Pat Coombs as well. Hope Una Stubbs' team beats Lionel Blair's.

It's snowing again. This is how Christmas Eve should be.

Friday 25th December

3:08pm: Didn't know it had been the "International Year of Handicapped People". Good of the Queen to tell us. Thought she'd mention Charlie's wedding. Can't say I understood much else of what Lizzie was going on about. Is "joblessness" even a real word? There must be a lot of people in Britain full of "joblessness" this Christmas afternoon.

Time for the rest of our presents from under the tree. We lost in the battle to record *Dr No*. Mum has decided we should record *Larry Grayson's Generation Game* instead. Grandma has fallen asleep, even though Auntie Eve is still chatting to her. Must be so hard for Grandma. First Christmas without Grandpa. They were married for over 50 years. She wrote on my Christmas card, "Love from Grandma and Grandpa x". She said she couldn't bring herself to write a card without Grandpa on.

Think both Mum and Dad are struggling without their dads this Christmas. Mum was tearful reading out a cracker joke. We all knew that Grandad could easily have written it. Dad never really shows emotion. I can tell he is struggling having just his mum. At least he's got siblings, unlike poor Mum.

Unwrapping a present that's obviously a selection box, I'm distracted by the two shoebox-sized presents that have suddenly appeared to the left of the Christmas tree. I had counted presents under the tree this morning. Mark had nine and I had nine. Now a tenth present for each of us had arrived. They were not in the same gold wrapping paper as the other presents.

Continuing to open my presents. Twice as fast as Mark. There was one pack of blank cassette tapes, a Villa book, Mastermind game, some Maths revision guides, the Villa pyjamas, a claret Villa V-neck jumper with the badge on, a PacMan Atari game and an Empire Strikes Back AT-AT Walker model.

Auntie Eve has got us all Terry's Chocolate Oranges but we must all pretend we don't know what it is when we're unwrapping them. Mum's busy swiping the wrapping paper off us, even before we have finished unwrapping each present. Determined to flatten it out so that she can use it again next year. She seems more interested in recycling the Christmas wrapping paper than her Eternal Beau oven gloves.

Mark's presents tended to match mine but with a Wolves theme instead of a Villa one. With the odd difference. Not sure he appreciated the sheepskin driving gloves. We are left with these two additional shoe-boxed sized presents and hopefully the traditional hidden combined present. Or, at 17, is Mark now too old to share a present with his little brother?

Looking suspiciously at Mum, both Mark and I start to unwrap the mysterious presents. It was too light for footwear. In fact, it was very light. Mine rattled slightly when I shook it. It was either broken or moving around. Hope it wasn't alive with the amount of shaking I had done. Pretty sure the two presents were the same. Our parents were smiling. Even Grandma was suddenly paying attention. Could I eat it? Mark opened his box first. Should have guessed, inside was a smaller box in the same wrapping paper. Mark suddenly looked up. He had been startled by something. I catch him up by releasing my smaller box. Then I see the reason for his startled look. The label on the second box. It read "To Jonathan from a Grandad who is very proud of you. Happy Christmas". It was Mum's writing. She had tried to disguise it and used a big lowercase "j" at the start of my name like Grandad always used to. I looked at Mum; she was giving nothing away. I was the one who opened my smaller box first. Mark watched intensely.

That's crazy! My Staffordshire Building Society book! Mum had taken it out of my locked blue cashbox and put it inside a Christmas gift. Makes no sense. Mark caught up. He also now had his Staffordshire Building Society book in his hand. Mark hadn't even realised his was missing. Still blank expression from our parents. They were giving nothing away. The boxes were empty, apart from the books. I flicked through the pages. How many times had "D Jukes" signed my deposits? Wait! That figure on the last entry. There was a new entry on 23rd December 1981. An entry that not only took my total over the long awaited £1,000 but took it to well over £3,000. There was a payment in of £2,500. Mark, of course, found the same in his book.

'A gift for you both from Grandad, to really help you get a good start in life', Dad finally broke the silence. Mum then explained that they had now got all the money in from Grandad's estate. I was confused that I had an estate when I thought it was just a semi. Mark explained that his estate is everything he had. Which it seems is all his cash, pensions and what they got from selling his house. 'Grandad would have wanted us to make sure his two favourite grandchildren were looked after.' We are his only grandchildren. 'So, we wanted to share £5,000 between you. It's to use for really important things in life. Not to be wasted. Perhaps a deposit for a house when you are older. Or buy a nice car.' Mum was now crying. She wasn't the only one. A special present from Grandad on Christmas Day. It's not about the money. It's about my Grandad. But I am now probably the richest kid in 4MC.

'There is a present between you both in the dining room, play fairly', Dad announced trying to refocus our "what can I spend £2,500 on" thoughts.

145

9:34pm: Mum appears with the turkey sandwiches just as I'm lining up to pot the all-important black on our new six-foot snooker table. Despite losing the first four games to Mark, I had pulled it back. The score was now seven frames all. It was a comeback that Ray Reardon would have been proud of. Now I had the chance to be crowned the Stadler Brothers 1981 Christmas Snooker Champion. I have chalked my mini cue. This was already the biggest break this table had ever seen. Twenty points, from the yellow to the pink. Trailing by five points now, this black for the championship. Turkey sandwiches can wait a few more minutes. Mark is tapping his cue loudly. Trying to psyche me out. This was my moment. I could hear my Grandad whispering "Go on, our Jonathan". The theme tune of *Pot Black* bouncing around my head. It's a straight pot. I don't want to follow it in. I'll hit the bottom of the white ball and screw back. Stop it going in the pocket as well.

Disaster! The black ball hits the side of the pocket and somehow stays on the table. Grinning, Mark gently rolls the cue ball against the black. The black ball rolls over twice before dropping into the pocket. Runner-up again. Beaten on Christmas Day by my older brother. I'd blown it!

Saturday 26ᵗʰ December

9:29am: Who rings this early on a Boxing Day morning? The ringing from the phone in the hall stops. I think Mum or Dad answered it. I did consider going down in my new Christmas Villa pyjamas. But what if it was bad news? Dad has just had a phone put in at Grandma's. What if she's in trouble? Or worse, Uncle Roger has gone in and found her dead in her bed. I can't possibly lose a third grandparent in 1981.

'I've got some bad news, Jonathan', Dad announces as he barges into my small bedroom. 'That was Mrs Hill'. Why is Mrs Hill ringing? Is it that Mr Hill isn't well? Is it that he's been rushed to hospital? Is he too ill to take me to the Villa? I suppose if that's the case, Dad will have to take me. 'Game's postponed'.

4:40pm: Rubbish Boxing Day. No Villa game because of a frozen pitch. Mark beating me again at snooker and now Albion have won at Coventry. Only two First Division games escaped the weather. Had to be Coventry again and Jimmy Hill's undersoil heating. Now even Albion are above us. Can't believe Dad set the chip pan on fire doing our traditional Boxing Day turkey and chips. Mum was furious that he used her Charles and Di souvenir tea towel to put it out with. Why don't Villa get undersoil heating? Or a giant balloon cover like Leicester City have got? I've lost two home games now in just over two weeks. It's not fair. Yes, I know they'll reschedule them, but what if I'm seriously ill that week? I could be lying in a coma missing a Villa game. Fixture congestion might interfere with our European Cup and League Cup campaigns. That's before we start playing in the FA Cup. The way it's going that third round tie with Notts County next Saturday will probably be off as well. It's like another flipping Ice Age. I'm sick of this cold weather. Can't remember the last time they opened the park.

5:21pm: Can't believe the only film on is a blooming *Lassie* one. Why not put on a *Carry On* film or a *Star Wars* one? Worse still, after Mike Yarwood is flaming *Gone with the Wind*. I think I am going to listen to the tape that Mark got me on my Walkman. Hedgehog Sandwich with all the best sketches from *Not the Nine O'Clock News*. Hope the song about believing everything apart from that Ronald Reagan is president is on it. Wonder what Wendy McGregor got for Christmas? So, need to ask her out in 1982.

Monday 28th December

4:35pm: Come on Villa, hold out. We desperately need these three points. Sounds a dirty game. That's the third Villa player in the book. How does the ref's book work? Does he have a new notebook each game? Or does he just keep one going for the whole season, a new page for each game? Hell, I'm nervous. Still 1-0. Tony Morley scored for us at Brighton. So important that Dennis is finally back. We've missed our number six. Still Geddis and Donovan up front, but the rest is more normal. Thought big Ken might have made it. Played in the reserves last week. Guess the pitch is still very hard, so Ron didn't want to risk it. No more goal horns please. Wolves are still losing at Man City.

6:02pm: Fourteenth place now. That was an important win. Three points above Wolves. Crazy that teams have all played such a different number of games due to the weather. We should have all played 21 by now. Half of the games. Instead, some have only played 16 and others as many as 20. We've played 19. Hastings' Albion have a game in hand on us and they're still two points ahead. We're only two points behind Liverpool. I'll ignore fact that they've only played 17 games. Can't believe Manchester City are top. I hate John Bond. What kind of manager buys his own son? Kevin Bond is rubbish. Trevor Francis scored again for them today, and Asa Hartford. Asa Harford's got a hole in his heart.

Thursday 31st December

10:10pm: I don't normally watch the news, but as I'm staying up to see the New Year in, I've decided to watch Richard Baker's last news bulletin of 1981. The lifeboatmen are not happy. An appeal fund after last week's disaster is not going to go to families who lost loved ones. That's dreadful. They are now refusing to operate the new lifeboat. Don't blame them. Maggie is telling us how good things are in industry despite so many people now being unemployed. She does seem to have a glow in her face every time she talks about the American President. Imagine what it would be like if Margeret Thatcher had an affair with Ronald Reagan. If they had a lovechild together. Sounds like the snow has thawed too quickly. We now have flooding everywhere. No guarantees football will be getting back to normal any time soon.

Watching *1981 Take 2* with Mark. Funny look back on the amazing last 12 months. Well maybe "funny" is a bit optimistic. It was billed as *Not the Nine O'Clock News* meets *Kick Up the Eighties*. I think it's lacking Rowan Atkinson. It's going through all the months of the year. How can they miss the Villa's title win? The July one about the Archbishop of Canterbury performing mimes to prompt Diana to get Charles's name right is funny. Dad is not impressed with the programme. He's not a fan of this new alternative comedy. He's even less impressed with the party going on next door at Asif's house. There has been music playing for over five hours now. Music that seems to have no lyrics just a very loud drum beat. Who would have thought New Year's Eve last year that twelve months later Uncle Norman and Auntie Mavis would have been replaced next door and that we would now be involved in a feud with our new neighbours. 1981 was certainly crazy. Full of personal highs and lows. I'll never forget 2nd May at Highbury, my first ever season ticket, getting an Atari, my maiden trip abroad, Ian Botham destroying the Aussies, fondling Grace's left breast and Bellington leaving for Coventry. The heartbreak of losing Grandpa in April and Grandad in June. Seeing Spud suffer with his mum's boob cancer. Villa starting this league season so rubbish, the disbanding of Ken's Mobile Trotters basketball club and being dumped.

Guess it's time to look forward to the World Cup year of 1982. Hopefully it will include my first Villa cup final. League Cup is probably the best hope. FA Cup would be amazing. Finally getting off seven FA Cup wins. We need to, as Spurs have got six now after winning last May. There is always the chance we could get to Rotterdam. I think we can beat Dynamo Kiev. Could do with avoiding Liverpool in the semis. What if everything goes perfect for me in '82? Villa wins all three cups, England win the World Cup, I get some pubic hair and Grace Taylor admits that Jonathan Stadler's are the only hands she wants playing with her boobs. No funerals and no blooming Saturday afternoon weddings would be great. The way my luck has gone the last six months, it's probably more likely we get relegated, Ronald Reagan accidently presses the red button starting World War III, Bellington comes back to school and Mark gets the old punk pregnant.

11:58pm: Ready to say goodbye to 1981. Bit of an anti-climax really. Just me, Mum and Dad. Mum even had to wake dad up. Mark is out with mad Sarah. Probably preparing for his midnight snog. We aren't even watching the Scottish chap in his kilt. Mum insisted on us putting on the special *This is Your Life*. So now we are stuck on ITV and *The Hogmanay Show*. It's pretty rubbish. As was Eamonn Andrews giving his flipping red book to Mickie Most. Never heard of him. Apparently, he's a record producer. Think Dad was disappointed. He thought it could be somebody really special like Pele, Prince Charles, John Noakes or Raquel Welch. Would have been more entertaining if it had been Mickey Mouse.

Out with the old and in with the new then. Grandad said you had to let the New Year in by opening all the doors, walking out the back door and then back in the front door. No idea why, but I guess an ideal time for burglars to nip in and steal your best stuff. Do we really have to link arms for *Auld Lang Syne*, Mum?

End of December Top of Division One

1.	Manchester City	Pl: 20 Po: 34	+ 7
2.	Southampton	Pl: 19 Po: 33	+ 7
3.	Swansea City	Pl: 20 Po: 33	+ 0
4.	Manchester United	Pl: 18 Po: 32	+13
14.	**Aston Villa**	**Pl: 19 Po: 22**	**+ 0**

Villa December League Results

5th Manchester City (a) 0-1 Lost
15th Swansea City (h) 1-2 Lost (own goal)
19th Everton (a) 0-2 Lost
28th Brighton (a) 1-0 Won (Morley)

Villa December League Cup Result

11th Wigan Athletic (a) 2-1 Won (Cowans, Withe)

Chapter Seven

January 1982

Friday 1st January

3:23pm: I'm bored. Why don't they play matches on New Year's Day? Expect because most of the players would still be hungover from New Year's Eve. Mark is feeling a bit delicate. He didn't get back until after 3am. Could hear him trying to get his key in the door for ages. He'll be 18 this year. Old enough the vote. One thing for sure, he won't be voting for Maggie. He'll be old enough to get married without needing Mum and Dad's permission either. At least if he gets mad Sarah "up the duff", he can make an honest woman of the old tart. Why have *Grandstand* on when there is no football? I don't even like horseracing. Why am I watching the Instasun Holiday Handicap Steeplechase? It's freezing outside, none of the horses look handicapped to me and where is the blooming steeple?

Telly tonight's no better. *The Superteams* should be good. No footballers competing though. Why do they always have rugby players? Usually Welsh. Ken Dodd is on after that. He never seems to have his Diddy Men with him anymore. Mum doesn't like him anyway, so we probably won't watch it. You can guarantee she'll be glued to *Wedding Day* at ten-to-ten though. It's 1982, do we really have to sit through the Charles and Di wedding again? The late film's *Up Pompeii*, one of my favourites. It's got Frankie Howerd in it and loads of boobs. I will have to set the video to record that. I can watch it when everybody is out and pause the naughty bitsSeems ages since I went to a Villa game. Last time was 28th November. Next possible home game is Sunderland, but that's

152

another week away. It'll have been over seven weeks since the last one. That's if the snow doesn't come again to postpone it. That's longer than the summer holidays.

Saturday 2nd January

12:38pm: Tin-pot Notts County! The weather isn't that bad. Surely, we could have played in this. Most of the other FA Cup games are on. Mark and Dad are going off to Molineux. If Wolves can get the game on, why are they calling ours off in Nottingham? Bet if we'd been playing Forest then the game would have been on. I don't believe it, Forest are playing at home and that hasn't been postponed. Brian Clough probably insisted. The groundsman is probably scared of him. Wouldn't dare tell Cloughie the ground's too hard to play on. Villa could have played in their trainers. Even non-league Enfield have got their pitch playable.

4:15pm: Goal horn again. Looks like Coventry are going through. Be good to draw them in the next round. We always beat Coventry. Another goal. Guess Wolves are going out. That's 3-1 to Leeds.

7:52pm: Hope Dad calls me in time for *The Two Ronnies*. This bath is going cold and the Matey bubbles have nearly gone. Can see my tiny willy. Really thought it would start growing this year. This is the last chocolate bar from my selection box as well, a Golden Cup. Haystacks ate four of these in one go last year. I wonder what all the gang are up to. Haystacks will be pleased that the Baggies got through against Blackburn. Mr Walker won't be happy though. Fancy Forest getting dumped out at home to Wrexham. Pity we aren't back at school on Monday. I could have really wound him up. Hope Spud's mum's doing better. With Wolves out of the cup, he

needs some good news. I suppose he would rather have his mum better than Wolves winning. Be interesting listening to the fourth round draw on Monday. Probably be listening on my own, as Mark won't be interested. Perhaps I could sneak out with my lucky radio and see Asif. Could give him his first ever experience of a Radio Two FA Cup draw. We need to avoid Liverpool. They stuffed high-flying Swansea today. Four-nil away. Glad the Bluenoses are out. Pity it was Ipswich who beat them. Spurs beat rivals Arsenal. Good that Arsenal are out, but we can't have Tottenham equalling our record seven wins. They only win cups in years ending with a one, so we should be safe. Elton John will be pleased with his Watford mob beating Ron Atkinson's Man United.

Nanny should be finished by now. What a waste of Wendy Craig. She was quite sexy in *Butterflies*. Didn't wear anything revealing, but you always felt she could be a bit wild. I wonder if I'll get to see Wendy McGregor's wild side. She certainly wouldn't be impressed with my lack of tackle. Maybe I should blame the cold water.

Monday 4th January

12:30pm: With a thin layer of snow covering the ground, Asif and I are sitting under the climbing frame listening to the draw for the fourth round of the Football Association Challenge Cup live from Lancaster Gate. I have explained to Asif that there are 32 balls in a bag. He understood the mathematics of a knockout tournament. Also said that he was pretty sure that Villa would be ball number two. But as we will be an "or" because we still must get past Notts County away, I think I might be wrong with this. Asif seems quite excited by what he's listening to. He doesn't really know who is in which division, but understands we need to avoid Ipswich, Liverpool or Manchester City. I wouldn't mind Albion as long as it's at Villa Park. We could play them in two cups in less than a week.

First out the hat is "Barnsley or Blackpool". That wouldn't be a bad tie. Asif is asking what kind of hat they use. I'm not sure. I think it's like a woolly hat. A top hat would be dramatic, but it would look too much like a magic trick. They are playing "Middlesbrough or Queens Park Rangers". They have got to replay.

Another "or" team. "Peterborough United or Bristol City". Their game was postponed. That's us! Will play "Notts County or Aston Villa". That's a good draw. Peterborough are in the Fourth Division. Bristol City are in the Third Division. It would be like playing Walsall. Asif oddly raises his arms in celebration. I think he is slowly morphing into a Villa fan.

Fairly easy draws for Liverpool and Ipswich against lower division teams. Not so easy for Spurs and Man City. Both are at home to lower placed First Division teams. Hastings will be pleased with being away to "Oldham or Gillingham". I explain to Asif that Gillingham starts with a "G" not a "J".

Asif is dreading going back to his grammar school on Wednesday. He really hates it there. Saying he might bunk off. Seems he skipped quite a few days off last term. Seems he has a supply of his dad's headed notepaper and has become an expert at forging notes from his dad. He's made up a range of illnesses, including bronchitis, scarlet fever and malaria. He missed four days with malaria. Says he just has no friends there. That even the teachers pick on him. He's dreading his report book that's due week after next. It will list the number of days he's had off. Asif's dad will be very keen to see it. He thinks Asif is the star pupil and each year takes great pride in showing everyone his son's report.

Wednesday 6th January

8:51am: I can walk into 4MC with my head held high. Six-nil. What a win at Notts County. There will be no Nottingham team in the fourth round of this season's FA Cup. We thrashed them. A David Geddis hat-trick. Just as I'm locking my locker, Spud appears. He

155

looks dreadful. I suspect asking if he had a good Christmas might not be appropriate. Neither would singing "six-nil, six-nil".

'She's not going to get better. The treatment ain't worked', Spud just announces about his mum. I can see Pete really wants to talk. We can't be late for Jock McGinn on the first day back. He's not exactly renowned for his pastoral skills. I promise Spud we can chat at lunchtime. With our gloves and scarves on we might just be able to brave outside for a kickaround.

10:59am: 'Do you fancy meeting in the library at lunchtime? Really missed you, Jonathan', a passing Wendy McGregor shouts out and blows me a kiss. Surely that's a sign.

It's been a long morning. McGinn was in foul mood. Paula Whittingham only asked him if he'd had a good Christmas. Perhaps she should have asked about his Hogmanay. Double English Lit was a struggle as well. I hate reading poems out loud. Especially lovey-dovey ones. Haystacks was making fun of me the whole time I was reading. At least in French I get to look through the glass at Grace. She keeps smiling at me. Not sure what to do at lunchtime now. Spud really needs me, but Wendy McGregor seems very eager to catch up. I need to do both. Perhaps Wendy first. I can explain that Spud is going through a hard time and I must go and see him. That might put me in the good light. She might see how caring and lovely I am.

12:31pm: 'How was your Christmas? Get any Villa stuff? Do you want to have lunch with me?', a gorgeous looking Grace, who's skirt seems even shorter than the 1981 version, whispers as I bend down to take my indoor shoes off. I'm certainly in demand today. Maybe it's my new navy school jumper. Or my New Year haircut. Only Noddy noticed the haircut. He said I'd been run over by a lawnmower. It cost nearly a quid at the barbers. I had been worried they had cut too much off and my fringe was too short.

Making my excuses to Grace. Telling her that Spud's mum is poorly and he needs a shoulder. Grace smiles and pats me on the arm whispering, 'Another time, sweetie'. I make my way to the library.

I find Wendy sitting on her own. At the table furthest from the famously nosey librarian, Ms Aspinall. Wendy has the big book of Shakespeare's sonnets propped up in front of her. She's seen me. Her eyes poked above the book and her eyebrows lift in a very suggestive way. Oddly not both at the same time. Wendy McGregor pats the seat to the right of her. Taking this as a sign that she wants the Stadler bottom on that seat, I sit myself down. Admittedly a little overdressed in my gloves and outdoor coat. It's then I notice that perched inside the open Shakespeare book is a copy of this week's *Look-In* magazine. She shows me the photo of Abba on the front cover and asking me a very leading question. 'Which of the women do you fancy the most?'. Now as Wendy is dark haired, it would make sense the say the dark-haired Anni-Frid. Although in reality it is Agnetha. It says on the cover that inside are "TOP STRIPS". This probably means cartoon strips. Not women stripping or even football strips. Can't believe *Look-In* is now 18p.

It's so easy and relaxed talking with Wendy, but I know I'll be in trouble if Grace shows up. Also, Spud is probably waiting for me outside. Feel guilty about revealing too much information about Mrs Hogan. Instead say I must go because I have promised to play football. Wendy looks disappointed, shrugging her shoulders and blowing a bubble-gum bubble. Ms Aspinall must have eyes like the Bionic Man to have seen that from her desk, but she's over in a flash to reprimand Wendy. I take this as my chance to make a quick exit.

1:18pm: Tucker's head has got a lump like an egg on now. Can't believe he tried that diving header on this frozen grass. Pity he got nowhere near the ball. Spud played well. Think he scored six. Tucker's gone to put some cold water on his head. Spud, Hastings,

Noddy and me are sitting on the concrete step outside the Science block. Talking about all the recent football postponements. Noddy brings up the conversation of Spud's mum.

Spud seems quite philosophical. Almost seems to be accepting that he won't have his mum for much longer. Difficult to know whether to give him hope or not. Doctors do such amazing things these days. If they can transplant a heart, then surely there is something they can do to stop Spud's mum's cancer spreading. They have already taken her boob off. I think it's only one. Not a question I feel I should be asking. To think Spud probably used to suck on one of those breasts. My mum couldn't breastfeed. I went straight on the bottle. Perhaps that accounts for my lack of expertise with the female mammary gland. Mrs Hogan is still receiving treatment. Some Mac nurses are going in three times a day. Not sure if they're Scottish.

'I got some big news too', Hastings butted in. I think Spud was relieved the conversation was moving away from him. 'Me mum and dad are getting a divorce. Dad moved out on Boxing Day'.

3:53pm: That's crazy! Waiting by the school gates in a gigantic duffle coat is Asif. What's he doing here? Guess he bunked off again. Time to introduce my newest secret friend to the members of the Local Gang. Well, all the members apart from Spud. He's walking home with Carrie Carrington. She said she had something she needed to talk to him about.

7:47pm: On the party-line talking with Asif while my parents are out at my grandma's. Asif is speaking quietly because his dad is asleep on the armchair in the lounge. The rest of his family have gone to Asda. For a first day of term, today had been mental. The shocking news about the Hastings, the seriousness of Spud's mum's condition and Asif turning up. He had played truant again and walked all the way from Walsall to our school. Asif hit it off with

Noddy, Tucker and Haystacks. He introduced himself as "a Villa fan who was the best under-16's chess player in Walsall". My work of indoctrinating him into the merits of supporting Aston Villa was nearly done.

The reason for our telephone call now was to produce a plan of action for an idea we'd all had to support Spud in his time of need. Asif was the brains behind the idea. He confirmed it was the MacMillan nurses that were looking after Mrs Hogan. Turns out Asif's mum is a MacMillan nurse. I didn't even know she spoke English. Asif filled us in on what they do. They look after people with very advanced cancer. Often ones that are going to die. It's a free service and they're a charity. So, they need a lot of fundraising. Haystacks was first to suggest we could raise money for them. We all agreed, but initial ideas were pretty rubbish. A jumble sale, car wash, disco and charity football match. Asif was then the bright spark and showed his grammar school education. Idea was a sponsored walk. Not any old sponsored walk but one between all our football grounds. Walk from The Hawthorns to Molineux then to Fellows Park and then finally to Villa Park. There was still some disagreement on the order. One idea had been to end at Spud's Wolves ground. Asif's sister has a typewriter, so he is going to type a letter to send to each of the clubs. Also put together a sponsorship form. There is a duplicator at our church that Dad uses. We can use that to print off copies of the sponsorship forms.

Studying Dad's AA Roadmap, it looks like the overall distance would be just under 20 miles. We could do that. Probably take us about five hours. More if they let us in to each of the grounds. Asif thinks we can write to the papers and the radio. He wants to tell his mum but knows then his dad would find out that we've been chatting. At least now I feel we're helping Spud. Just hope his mum holds out until we have done the walk. Will decide a date tomorrow.

Friday 8th January

12:55pm: Grace Taylor is well impressed when I tell her that the Local Gang, plus Asif, are going to walk over 20 miles to raise money for MacMillan Nurses. Although she has no idea who Asif is. She says she'll sponsor me 10p for every mile I do. I explain that we are doing sponsors per ground reached. So maximum is four. She agreed to make it 50p a ground. We are getting on well. No mention of Oliver Watkins. Grace says she is spending all her time studying now, but it would be nice to take a break occasionally. Not sure if this is a hint that she wants me to ask her out again. Probably reading too much into it.

We've agreed that the big sponsored "Local Team Walk" will take place on Sunday 7th February. Which gives us a month to organise it. Mr Walker is impressed by our plan and is not only up for helping but wants to join us on the walk. We have changed the order to make it an easier route and to finish at Villa Park. So now we are starting at The Hawthorns at either 10 or 11am. Then walking all the way to Molineux to Spud's Wolves. Then down to the Third Division and Fellows Park, before heading off to the home of the champions. Going through Perry Barr where Dad works. Avoiding the M6. Finally arriving at Villa Park, where I'm hoping Ron Saunders might meet us. Mr Walker says he's going to make a Maths equation to work out the total distance.

Spud is up for the walk. In fact, he wanted to run it. Hastings and unfit me soon put paid to that idea. Already I am worrying if I'm capable of walking 20 miles. My hugger jeans might cause some chafing. Spud is not himself. He seems even more withdrawn today. Perhaps his mum is worse. Wish there was some way to help him now.

2:39pm: 'Has Spud told you?' Wendy McGregor whispered across the blue flame Bunsen burner in Chemistry. I assume she's talking about his mum and I must have looked a bit perplexed. 'About him getting Carrie preggers'.

6:02pm: That's a shock! How is Spud going to take that news? Mark said he didn't expect it. John Barnwell resigning as Wolverhampton Wanderers manager. It's on *Central News*. Still can't get used to it not being ATV. Nothing seems to stay the same these days. It's only a year ago since Wolves were in Europe. I know they are near the bottom but still thought he would be there for longer. Albion, Walsall and now Wolves all changing managers in the last six months. Looks like Wolves chairman, Harry Marshall, is moving quick on Barnwell's replacement. He is trying to offer the job to the Aberdeen manager, some bloke called Alex Ferguson.

Been a crazy couple of days for Spud. Carrie Carrington told him she was late and was worried she was pregnant. Spud still doesn't know if they had sex or not. He hadn't seen Carrie since before Christmas. Not sure what happens if Carrie is pregnant. Guess she'll have to leave school. Surely, they won't arrest Spud. If they do, then on our sponsored walk we could wear t-shirts with 'FREE SPUD' on them. Must make it clear that we aren't giving away jacket potatoes. Carrie Carrington is evil. Fancy taking advantage of Pete in his current vulnerable state. What sort of offspring would Carrie Carrington produce? It could be like *The Omen*. When it's born, they'll be checking his head looking for 666.

Saturday 9th January

4:28pm: Apparently in Balmoral it was minus 27 degrees last night. You wouldn't want to be out in your kilt in that. At least with Villa's home game with Sunderland off I can stay under my Villa duvet keeping warm. Seems a long time since that last home game against Forest. Our Chairman, Mr Bendall, needs to seriously consider getting us some undersoil heating. At least when we start playing all these postponed home games, we will start marching up that table. I still think we can finish top six. Birmingham are losing at Forest. That should keep them below us. Be rubbish on *Match of the Day* tonight as only two First Division games survived. Wouldn't be surprised if they had no games at all.

I knew it was that actor who shot Roy Race. At least Roy is getting better now. Maybe it's time I cancelled my *Roy of the Rovers*. The stories all seem to be getting a bit silly now. *Express & Star* saying that Alex Ferguson has turned Wolves down. He says he has unfinished work to do at Aberdeen and thinks Wolves are not in a good position. They are looking at the Oxford manager now. If I was them, I would go for Graham Taylor at Watford instead.

9:15pm: I might not like her, but I don't want anything bad to happen to her son. Mark seems to think it's funny that his namesake, Margret Thatcher's son Mark, has gone missing. Him and his driver seem to be lost in the Sahara. Loads of conspiracy theories. Our Mark is back early from his date with crazy Sarah. He borrowed the Ital. Dad seems to be forensically examining his precious car now. He was rather perturbed by the reclined position the passenger seat was left in. Also, the cigarette lighter was not properly inserted. Surely Mark would not be dumb enough to let his ageing punk girlfriend smoke in Dad's car.

With Dad out inspecting his car interior for yellow cigarette stains, I take the chance to tell Mum about Spud's possible paternity situation. Not surprisingly, Mum is shocked. I didn't expect her question back, "do you know how that might have happened?" Was she about to finally tell me about the "birds and the bees"? I did try to defend Spud. Explaining how hard things are for him, with his mum so ill. I also made it clear that the main culprit was the evil Carrie Carrington. Predictably, Mum came back with, "it takes two to tango". I very much doubt Spud has an aptitude for ballroom dancing. Mum did reassure me that she felt it was unlikely that Peter would be sent to prison.

Wednesday 13ᵗʰ January

12:59pm: Mr Walker has confirmed my fears. He went to check on his car radio for me and Haystacks. The snow has struck again. Tonight's big West Midlands League Cup quarter-final tie has been cancelled. Yet again, I'm not going to Villa Park. They aim to try again next Monday. They'll be officially calling it Ice Age II soon. I'm sick of it. Forest tie at Spurs is off as well. The Ipswich-Watford one is also likely to be called off. Going to be a draw of "ors" for the semi-finals. Still can't believe Barnsley held Liverpool at Anfield last night.

With Spud and Wendy McGregor, trying to do our simultaneous equation Maths homework. Me and Wendy are flying through them, but Spud just doesn't get them. Even when we tell him the value of "y" he still can't work out "x". He seems more interested in talking about the state of Carrie Carrington's womb. Really fears there is a little Spud in oven. Talking about possible names for this yet unconfirmed baby. If it's a girl Spud wants to name her Annie after his mum. Thinks it's important the baby knows about her gran even though she might never meet her. It's not only Wendy who is close to tears as we are discussing a future without Mrs Hogan. Even when Wendy is looking her saddest, she still looks really attractive. Her lips are so well portioned with the rest of her face. It's time I made my move. Perhaps if Spud leaves us alone. If the baby is a boy, Spud is thinking of naming him after a Wolves player. He suggested Willie Carr, but we all thought Willie was a cruel name to give a little boy. Next, it was Kenny after Kenny Hibbitt. I stopped that idea by reminding him of Kenny Bellington. In the end, Spud decided he would name him after Peter Daniel. But call him Daniel so that he didn't have same name as him and confuse the postman.

'Pete, can we talk please?' Carrie Carrington ushers Spud away. Leaving me with the chance to be openly flirty with Wendy. Need to make it clear that I'm ready to commit. Not in a Spud-

Carrie way, but in a "going out" way. Wendy McGregor is so sweet about Spud's possible unintentional impregnation. She oddly suggests that they make a lovely couple. 'Perhaps they'll be the school's first wedding'. I remind Wendy that they are both only 15 and cannot legally wed, even with their parents' permission, until December at the earliest. Mr Hogan certainly doesn't need this with what's happening to his wife. Wendy's next question almost knocked me to the floor. 'Do you think you and Grace Taylor will ever have a baby?' Quickly, I re-emphasise that Grace and I are history. Wendy just smiles and ruffles my hair.

9:40pm: Still no sign of Mark Thatcher. Perhaps the whole car was abducted by aliens. Should be celebrating Villa reaching the semi-final now. Can't believe it's snowing again. Instead, I am watching the fat darts players on *Sportsnight*. What other sport do you get to drink beer whilst you are playing? "Crafty Cockney" Eric Bristow seems unbeatable. He has his little finger pointing out. Like a posh person drinking a cup of tea. You don't need to be fit to play darts. Unlike me, I need to be to walk this 20 miles around the football grounds. Haystacks says that The Hawthorns is the highest above sea-level football ground in England. Not sure what that means as Albion is miles from the sea. Really happy that Wendy is going to help me train. We are going to meet up Sunday afternoon and walk to Rough Wood and back. That's got to be about seven miles. More if we go via Wendy's house. I suggested it was a kind of date and Wendy laughed. We might have to walk in the snow. Will wear my trainers, though, not my wellies. Pity everywhere will be shut as it will be Sunday. Would have been nice to share a bag of chips.

Friday 15th January

8:55am: Can't believe I have got a hole in the bottom of my pump. That wasn't there when I put them in my locker yesterday. Haystacks is just showing us the League Cup semi-final draw in the

Daily Express. He stayed at his dad's new bedsit last night. So, his dad gave him a lift in and let him keep his paper. Mark Thatcher has been found by the Algerian army.

One of our teams could be playing Mr Walker's Forest. "Aston Villa or West Bromwich Albion" versus "Tottenham Hotspur or Nottingham Forest". As both Villa and Forest are at home in quarters, I think it will be Ron Saunders v Brian Clough. Two of the greatest managers of all time. The other tie will be "Ipswich or Watford" against "Barnsley or Liverpool". At least we avoid Liverpool until Wembley. Although hopefully Barnsley will finish them off next week. Still not sure the Villa v Albion game will take place on Monday. It's snowing again. At least the school heating seems to have been fixed. Yesterday you could see your breath when you answered questions in History.

Spud was telling us what Carrie Carrington had been talking to him about. I couldn't believe she hadn't told her parents that she might be pregnant. Spud was upset because she was talking about getting rid of the baby. She even said she'd heard that if you drink a bottle of whiskey, it can abort the baby. I think if she drank a bottle of whiskey she'd be in a coma. One of Carrie's mates has said she knows a house in Mossley where the old man there will carry out abortions for £15. He does a range of home medical treatments including teeth extraction and mole removals. Pete was trying to calm Carrie down. He's more interested in confirming if there is a baby or not first. Noddy told him that he'd heard you can do a pregnancy test with Colgate toothpaste. He said, "you squeeze some into a bowl and then put some drops of the woman's piss on it. If it froths up and goes a little blue, then she's up the duff". Haystacks seemed to have a better idea. He told us that you could test to see if a woman is pregnant using litmus paper. They have litmus paper in the Chemistry lab. None of us know what level of pH would indicate a life form was being created though.

A pleasant surprise for all us boys. French teacher Miss Tully enters 4MC. 'Bonjour, Monsieur McGinn'. Jock McGinn adjusts his tie as he greets Miss Tully. The pair then whisper and McGinn starts shaking his head. Miss Tully then addresses the class. 'Can I borrow Peter Hogan and Carrie Carrington, to help me with a small task please?' Spud and Carrie slowly get up from their seats and follow our sexy French teacher. This isn't a coincidence. Somebody has grassed. The staff know about the Hogan-Carrington immoral shenanigans.

Sunday 17th January

9:26am: Who knew Wendy McGregor had a blue Admiral England tracksuit. She looks fab in it. Reminds me of when Dee Hepburn is jogging in *Gregory's Girl*. I didn't expect Wendy to take it this seriously. Hopefully she knows we're walking, not running. I feel a little overdressed in my parka. It's so slippery underfoot. Compact ice. Maybe I should do some limbering up. Be good to get Wendy bending down and stretching. Might give her a kiss goodbye when we finish. If I have the stamina left. In that tracksuit and with her perm, she looks like a tall Kevin Keegan. Maybe best not to say that though. That new perm really suits her.

Rough Wood seems a lot closer on my Chopper. I don't remember it being so uphill either. At least being with Wendy makes it so much more enjoyable. I am not talking quite as much. Trying to conserve my energy. She's doing most of the talking anyway. Didn't expect that it had been Wendy who had spoken to Miss Tully about Carrie Carrington and Spud. Wendy said she was just trying to help. Thought Miss Tully would be able to help them. Spud did say that she had been really understanding. Miss Tully had arranged an appointment for Carrie at a family planning clinic next week. Odd being called family planning when that was the last thing they had been planning. Miss Tully is going to go with Carrie but is insisting that Carrie tells her parents over the weekend. Or she'll have to inform them. She promised not to mention Pete though if Carrie didn't want her to. Everyone felt that with Mrs Hogan's illness this wasn't news that Spud's dad needed to hear yet. No idea what kind of parents would have a child like Carrie Carrington. Hope they don't go ballistic.

Sitting on a log in Rough Wood, it's surprisingly romantic. So different to when I have been here with Mark and his mates. Wish I'd brought a Penguin or something. I'm starving. Wendy is not even sweating. She could probably walk 500 miles. Raise a lot of money if we did that. How many grounds could you cover in 500 miles? Could you do every ground in the First Division? I bet Sunderland to Ipswich would be the longest distance. Hope when we do the walk on 7th February that Spud's mum can see some of it. Ideally without the knowledge that a new generation of Hogans is growing inside a 15-year-old schoolgirl devil.

Wendy McGregor strokes my parka-covered arm and rests her head on my left shoulder. She says, 'This is nice. Thank you for inviting me'. Odd, as I'm sure it was Wendy's idea. I feel quite content. Forgetting for a moment about my worries about the Villa. Yesterday, only eleven days after winning 6-0 at Meadow Lane, we lost to Notts County in the League 1-0. Flaming Trevor Christie scoring with only five minutes left. Blinking rubbish Notts County have done the double over us. What kind of champions lose home and away to a team who last season were in the Second Division? It's crazy. Should never have played yesterday. Ron Saunders said the pitch was unplayable. What type of ref let's a game go ahead with a frozen pitch covered in snow? There wasn't even 10,000 people there. We so need to get Ken McNaught back. He hasn't played since Notts County crippled him in the opening game of the season. We're now only four points above the drop zone and we've played two games more than most teams. Despite having so many home games called off. We've played seven away games since our last home game.

11:48am: We arrive at Wendy McGregor's drive. It's been a lovely couple of hours. I'm knackered but it's been great. Time to ask Wendy out. See if she'll be my "official" girlfriend. Then I'll seal it with a kiss. I might even leave my mouth open like they do in the movies.

Not Mr McGregor's Ford Escort again? Yes, turning into the drive and ruining the moment again is Wendy's dad's car. Within seconds, Wendy's mum is calling Wendy to help carry the shopping into the house. Wendy turns, waving goodbye, and shouts, 'Had the perfect time, Jonathan. See you tomorrow at school.'

Wednesday 20th January

8:16pm: Doris is in a right tizz. She's convinced something has just happened with Tony Morley and the ref as they are leaving the pitch for half-time. I didn't see anything. She needs to calm down at her age. Her headscarf nearly came off. I'm sure she's still got a roller stuck in her hair under it. Ref Ron Chadwick has been pants. Albion shouldn't be winning this. Three times they have handled it in the area and I don't mean Tony Godden. That one just before half-time was a penalty all day long. We'll turn this around though. Hastings' lot didn't deserve that Derek Statham goal. I think it'll be 3-1 to us.

My feet have totally frozen. Hope my toes don't snap off with frostbite. I'm wearing two pairs of socks. Must be about minus ten. Decent crowd though. I think around 35,000. Not going to read my programme until I get home. No way I'm taking my gloves off in these freezing conditions. I'm sure Jimmy Rimmer is wearing long johns. Wish I was. Hope we manage to defrost Howard's car. Win this and only Tottenham can stop us getting to Wembley. The other semi-final is Ipswich against Liverpool. Liverpool won at Barnsley last night. Think I would rather play Ipswich in the final. Chance to avenge the three times they beat us last season. But we won the league. So, who cares. Let's just focus on beating the Baggies first. Too early to start planning my Wembley outfit.

That Bovril Doris is slurping smells disgusting.

Wonder how Spud's doing tonight. Probably relieved that it ended up Carrie Carrington not being pregnant. He had got quite fond of the idea of teaching a mini-Spud the art of head-butting. Miss Tully said there can be lots of reasons for girls missing periods. Apparently, stress is a major factor. I guess thinking you are pregnant is very stressful. Pete says he's not having any more sex until he's 16. Still seems to think Carrie is the girl for him. So complicated getting involved with girls. Perhaps I should wait until I'm 16 to ask Wendy out. It's only another 15 months away. Hopeful Ron will have won Villa some more silverware by then.

Here come the Albion players. They look determined to hold on to their lead. Looks like two of them have put gloves on. What a bunch of namby-pambies. Here come the Villa boys.

That's only ten players. Where's Tony? I guess he's having a late trip to the loo. Ron Saunders won't be happy with him. Surely the ref is going to wait for him. When you've got to go you've got to go. Come on, Tony Morley! We need you!

'Ref sent him off', Villa left-back Colin Gibson shouts back at Doris when she enquired about the absent Tony Morley. We are one down and a man down. How can he send Morley off at half-time? I hate this ref. Don't think a lot of the crowd have noticed yet. We can still take this to a replay. We don't need 11 players to score against Haystacks' mob.

Wednesday 20th January

8:53am: 'Baggies going to Wembley … You're not. You're not', Hastings is rubbing it in as soon as I arrive. Still don't know how we didn't equalise. Hope Spurs smash them in the semi. Tony Morley will be suspended for two games now, starting in two weeks' time. At least he can play in the FA Cup on Saturday. Then also against Liverpool the week after. If we beat Bristol City on Saturday, we're in the fifth round. I would much rather win the FA Cup than the Milk Cup. Mr Hill is going to take me all the way to Bristol for the cup game. If it's on, that is. Weather seems even colder today. I'll have to watch the weather on the news tonight and see what symbol they stick on Bristol. Not totally sure where Bristol is. I think it's west of us and down a bit. On the way to Ian Botham's Somerset.

2:47pm: Can't believe I'm beating Spud at badminton. He's moving so slowly around the court. He usually wallops me. Think he's really worried about his mum. Sounds like she's sleeping more each day. He said she was asleep before *Coronation Street* finished on Monday. There is no oomph in his serve. Normally you start feeling sorry for the shuttlecock when Spud is in full flight. If I can get two more points, I'll be in the final. Playing the winner of Noddy and Tucker. I don't know what's been wrong with those two this week. They've hardly spoken a word to each other. At lunch yesterday, when Tucker was captain, he had three chances to pick Noddy in his team. Just kept ignoring him.

3:00pm: Why did Carrie Carrington have to turn up? Spud was playing rubbish until then. I didn't think they were even still together, but just because she started watching, Spud became brilliant. It was like a badminton player that was a combination of Desmond Douglas and John McEnroe. I know, wrong sports, but I don't know any famous badminton players. The only sportsperson I can think of regarding badminton is Princess Anne. That's on a horse though.

Wendy McGregor is looking great in her pleated navy games skirt. Looks like she is giving Lucy Dobbin a good game. I had better concentrate on the Noddy-Tucker battle. Some anger in

Noddy's shots. Spud will now play the winner of these two. At least one of the Local Gang will be champion today. Sadly, not me! Spud says that Tucker has fallen out with Noddy because he kissed Emily Martins. Only a week after Tucker had told him he fancied her. Maybe Noddy has crossed the line. Didn't Tucker have first grabs? Does seem like the gang is imploding at the moment. Haystacks is not coping with his parents' separation. He's now blaming his mum and insisting on eating all his meals in his room. Spud is just not coping with his mum's illness. He keeps buying fags. Hardly mentions Wolves and I haven't seen his homework diary all term. Now we have Walsall fans Noddy and Tucker at war over flipping Emily Martins. Wendy says Emily Martins will kiss anyone for a finger of Kit Kat. Maybe our sponsored walk will bring the gang back together.

That's it! Tucker has won. Mr Marsh is insisting loser Noddy shakes Tucker's hand. Noddy is having none of it. The two mates are now scrapping. Tucker has smashed the metal edge of his racket against Noddy's shin. Bet that hurt. Got the feeling we aren't going to see the Spud-Tucker final. Marsh is doing his nut. Spud seems to be taking Noddy's side. He's squaring up now to Tucker. I'm not taking sides. This is stupid. No girl is worth falling out with your mates over.

Early end to Games. Marshy totally lost it. Tucker, Noddy and Spud have now been sent, still in their kit, to stand outside the Headmistress's office. Seems harsh on Spud and with his other recent antics, he could be in trouble. Perhaps I should have defended him more, but I was distracted by Wendy McGregor stretching to help take the badminton net down. I am sure her chest looked even perter than usual in her white polo-neck top. Notice Carrie Carrington didn't spring to Spud's defence either. Maybe us boys should give up girls for the rest of the football season. Life would certainly be easier.

7:39pm: Mark is watching *Doctor Who* again on the video. Whose idea was it to make Tristan Farnon the 5th Doctor? And why is he wearing cricket gear? My mum always gets Peter Davidson mixed up with the bloke who plays Rodney in *Only Fools and Horses*.

That looks serious. Parked outside our house is a Ford Cortina police car. Hope they aren't coming here. They are going next door. That doesn't look good. Perhaps Asif's dad is a master criminal. That's the real reason he keeps himself to himself. Wouldn't be surprised if they take him away in handcuffs. *Doctor Who* has been paused as the whole Stadler family peer through our living room curtains. More interested in the goings-on at number one than whether the Doctor will get Tegan home, or the frog-like monarch will take over the Earth. Looks like the police car is going. Think Dad is disappointed that Asif's dad is not going too. Perhaps he managed to make a quick getaway before they could get the cuffs on.

This is a turn-up! At our front door are Asif's parents, Mr and Mrs Mahmood. Surely Dad isn't going to let the enemy enter our castle. Are they raising the white flag? I can't see a flag. I'm being sent upstairs. Mark has got to turn *Doctor Who* off. This all sounds very serious. Is Mum about to offer Mrs Mahmood a cup of tea? I just don't get this.

Saturday 23rd January

1:20pm: Mr Hill seems much more relaxed since he took early retirement. I guess Maggie did him a favour. He's wearing a trendy Pringle jumper today and a cap. I wonder when I'll need a pair of leather driving gloves. At least the temperature is above freezing for first time in months. Mark is going with Dad to look at cars today. He's free because Wolves are out of the cup. Mark's going to spend some of the money Grandad left him. I think his idea of the type of car he's going to get is a bit different to Dad's. Dad is thinking that

Mark needs a trusty reliable car like a Morris Marina. Mark is thinking flashier. Like a Capri with some fluffy dice. Can see it now, Mark's name above the driver's side and old Sarah's above the passenger side.

I can see the floodlights. That must be Aston Gate. There's also Bristol Rovers, but I don't think their ground is as big as that. Would be great to go to all 92 grounds. Bet Mr Hill has been to over 50. He followed Villa in the Third Division. He's even seen them play at Walsall. Get through today and we'll be in the fifth round. Got a feeling this will be our season. Imagine if I see Villa win both the league and the FA Cup within 12 months.

Hope Asif is alright. Fancy being caught by the police playing truant. Surprised Mr Mahmood was so calm about it. Be odd if Asif does end up coming to our school. I think he's probably too much of a brainbox. His dad did want to know all about the school. Mum said he gave her a real interrogation on the pitfalls of comprehensive school education. Has he never watched *Grange Hill?* Mrs Mahmood seemed very anti the grammar school. She was blaming them for leading her good boy astray. From what they said, I think Asif is being expelled. At least Bellington isn't there anymore. He would have totally ripped Asif to pieces. It takes a special person like me to stand up to bullies like Bellington.

4:27pm: We're making hard work of this. Could easily be losing. Bristol City have had a few chances. Very strange them having a Gary Williams as well. He nearly scored. I like our Gary Williams, but he really isn't a centre-half. When will Ken McNaught ever be fit? Andy Blair's playing well, Des Bremner will struggle to get back in. I suppose a replay wouldn't be a disaster. Would mean I get three home games in a week. Wonder how the Baggies are doing at Gillingham.

"Gary Shaw, Gary Shaw, Gary, Gary Shaw. He gets the ball; he's bound to score. Gary, Gary Shaw". Even Mr Hill is joining in with the singing as we salute our golden boy giving us the lead. Sid played him in. That's Gary Shaw, not Mr Hill. That's Shaw's ninth of the season. Not bad when he's missed the first two months. Perhaps he can still get on the plane to Spain. Only about ten minutes to go. My grandad would say, 'best way to defend is to score another'. I'll take a scrappy 1-0. Get us into the fifth round. What I wouldn't give to see Dennis lifting the FA Cup up at Wembley in May.

Get the ball clear, Villa! I'm sure my digital watch has stopped. It seems to have been on 4:37 for hours. How can Howard Hill be so relaxed? Just pass it back to Jimmy Rimmer, Andy Blair. While it's in Jimmy's arms Bristol can't score. Now Kenny Swain passes it back to Jimmy.

5:40pm: Howard's not pleased. They kept us Villa fans in for over 20 minutes. Guess they were a bit peeved being knocked out of the cup. We missed all the reports on *Sports Report*. We're starting to work out the scores. Biggest shock seems to have been Oxford beating Brighton 3-0 away. Liverpool breezed past Sunderland. They're bang in form. We play them next week. They could win the lot this season. In the semi-final of the League Cup, the quarter-final of European Cup, marching up the league and now in fifth round of the FA Cup. Hope we don't draw them on Monday. Albion are through. So, Haystacks will bring his radio in. Watford knocked West Ham out. Maybe Elton John will need to start writing a cup final song for them. Our bogey team Ipswich thumped Luton Town.

'We need to hope Spurs lost. We can't have them equalling our record seven times'. Mr Hill was soon disappointed, as Mike Ingham announces, "Tottenham Hotspur 1, Leeds United 0".

9:11pm: Whose car is that parked on our drive? It's a bit late for visitors. A bright orange Ford Escort. With a black stripe on it. It's almost Wolves colours. I thank Howard for taking me to Ashton

Gate and wave him off. Mark comes out of house smiling. Oh no, he hasn't bought a car in the Wolves colours!

I am desperate for a wee, but Mark wanted to give me a ride in his new 'N' plate car. It's got black vinyl seats. Mum insisted on coming with us, even though Mark has already taken her for a spin. We did push her in the back. Think she wishes they had seat belts in the back. I'm fastening mine in the front. Mr Hill says it's going to become law next year that you must wear them.

Mark keeps putting the screeching windscreen wipers on when he wants to indicate he's turning. Really smells smoky. Bet the previous owner was a forty a day bloke. Grandad will be pleased Mark has used some of his money to buy his first car. Grandad didn't drive in later years because he never passed his test. You didn't need to when he was first driving. I wonder if I'll get to drive this car when I'm 17. Perhaps Mark will teach me. He'll probably be a better driver then. I'm sure he didn't mean to mount the pavement then. Wish all his heaters worked. The one by my arm is blowing out freezing air.

I shoot up the stairs. Thighs clenched together to stop me peeing myself. Thinking of Mark's number plate "WAS 433 N". Easy one to remember. "Withe and Shaw". Villa formation "4-3-3". "Never letting Mark drive me again". I wonder which cup games *Match of the Day* will have on tonight.

Sunday 24ᵗʰ January

2:29pm: I'm sure we're lost. Told Wendy we should have stuck to the main road. All these cul-de-sacs look the same. It's blooming cold as well. Now it's getting foggy. We need to be heading back. It'll be dark in two hours. Why is she staying so calm? Even with snot dripping from her nose, she's managing to smile. Hope the weather is a lot better than this when we do the sponsored walk.

Wendy McGregor has been doing most of the talking for the last two miles. I've been trying to conserve my energy. I do really like her though. Does this count as a proper date? Still haven't been brave enough to give her a kiss.

'Do you think you'll get any Valentine's Day cards this year?' Wendy surprisingly asked. What am I supposed to say to that? I go for the cool smile and "I hope so" response. Perhaps it was a gentle hint. I will buy her one, but I'm going to put my name on it in big letters. I'm not having her thinking it's from some other boy. Like Oliver Watkins. Bet he gets loads of cards. The postman probably has to go to Oliver's house twice. Hold on, 14th February is a Sunday. Week after the sponsored walk. There is no post on a Sunday. Do I need to give it to Wendy at school on the Friday? The day before Villa play the next round of the cup. Hope we get a home game.

How did we end up at Wendy's house? I've got miles to walk home now in the fog.

Called home and they are going to pick me up. Mr McGregor tried to explain to my dad how to get here, but Dad kept saying he'd look it up in his *A to Z*. No idea how he used to find anywhere before he had his *A to Z*. It must be older than me. I bet dozens of new roads have appeared since then. Our school isn't on it. At least the McGregors' house isn't a new one. Dad said he would be about half an hour, as he was just watching the end of *Carry On Nurse*. If he was able to set the video, he could record the rest of it. He seems to have a thing about Hattie Jacques. While I'm waiting for him, Wendy and I are going to work on our History homework. We're being allowed unaccompanied upstairs. Not only upstairs, but to Wendy's actual bedroom. The room where she sleeps and gets undressed. Wendy's gran is having a Sunday afternoon nap. So, it's thumbs up for crashing in Wendy McGregor's bedroom. Dad, please take your time. It's foggy out there. Please don't rush on my part.

I haven't been in many girls' bedrooms, but I did think they would be tidier than this. There are clothes on the floor. There are Wendy's pants! She took her tights and pants off together and just left them on the floor. Hopefully quite recently. I'll pretend I haven't noticed. I'll comment on the Shakin' Stevens poster instead. That's hardly cool. Very bad Blu Tack distribution as well. It's not straight and top left is four times fatter than the Blu Tack on the top right corner. Can't believe she's got a hammock full of Cabbage Patch Dolls. This is quite a mixed-up young lady. I like her even more. She's unconventional. I'm at her tiny desk. My bottom too big for the little stool. Wendy is lying on her bed. Boobs down. Her head only a few feet away from me. Neither of us has even mentioned History. This is the moment. Time to go in for the kiss. I need to be super-confident and masterful. As if I'm Gordon Cowans striding up to take a penalty. I know exactly where I'm going to place my lips. This is it! Move my head. Position my lips firmly against Wendy's lips and close my eyes. Bang!!

'What the hell are you doing?', yells Wendy as she pushes me away. What did I do? Had I bitten her lip? Before I could respond, an old lady, minus her teeth, barges in and starts bashing me with her slipper.

'Get away from my granddaughter, you beast'. Wendy McGregor's gran was now seriously walloping me. Wendy was just letting this assault take place. Now her dad has come up to see what the disturbance is. Hopefully some male solidarity. No, he's taking the old lady's side.

Quicker than a Bob Willis delivery, I am thrown out of the front door by Mr McGregor. Into the cold dark foggy night.

A bright orange car approaches. It's Mark. For once, I'm pleased to see him. Seems Dad had gone into a panic because page 14 of his *A to Z* had fallen out. So, Mark had offered to come and get me. Apparently one of his mates lives around here, so he knew where it was. Just a pity he doesn't know where the button for his fog lights is. It's getting foggier. Also, Mark says the petrol gauge doesn't work. Although it says empty, Mark is pretty confident it probably isn't.

Decided not to tell Mark about the bedroom incident. He hasn't asked why I was outside on my own. I just sit silent in the passenger seat, hoping that visibility is considerably better on the driver's side of the windscreen. Have I blown it with Wendy McGregor? At least it might save me buying a Valentine's Day card. The way my life is going now, I bet we draw Liverpool away in the cup. Although currently my biggest worry is ever getting home.

Monday 25th January

12:30pm: Need to forget about Wendy McGregor for now. Focus on what's important. The draw for the fifth round of the greatest cup tournament in the world. My post-snog debrief with Wendy can wait ten more minutes. Haystacks has managed to tune his tranny into Radio Two. This is it. Leicester out first. Wouldn't mind that one but really want to be at home. They're playing Elton's Watford. An all-Second Division tie. Be good to get the winners of that in the quarters. That hurt, Haystacks! He whacks me in the ribs as Albion come out next. Home to Norwich. The jammy gits. Norwich might get promotion back this season though. Ipswich away to Shrewsbury. At least we have avoided them.

Probably the tie of the round, but one we certainly didn't want. Hope Mr Hill can take me. Seven-time winners Aston Villa away to six-time winners Tottenham Hotspur. Glenn Hoddle against Gordon Cowans. The return of Archibald against Withe. Spud starts singing "Spurs are on their way to Wembley..." I hate Chas & Dave. Let's stop them making another rubbish cup final song this year. Lucky Liverpool have drawn middle of the Second Division Chelsea. I guess that's them through.

Wendy has got her arms folded. She doesn't look happy. Do I need to apologise? Not sure what for. Dad says, "if a woman is cross with you, best to apologise first and find out what you have done wrong later". One of us needs to talk. We can't just sit here in silence until the bell goes.

'What the hell were you thinking of? We're mates. We have a laugh'. I wait for Wendy McGregor to pause or at least take a breath before I can start my defence. Maybe I should bring up the four kisses Christmas card. 'I don't see you like that. I thought you weren't like all the other boys. Only thinking about one thing'. Decide not to mention that football isn't the only thing I think about. Although angry, I can't help noticing the heaving of her bosom. 'How could you ruin our lovely day by kissing me? What if Grace found out? Grace is my friend. I thought we were friends.'

I was about to begin my defence, but Wendy stormed off. As she was leaving, she trod firmly on a big toe. I will give her the benefit of the doubt. Even though there did seem a lot of malicious intent in it. She's probably bruised it. Had I totally misread the signs? Am I destined to be that boy that girls always want to be friends with but never want to be romantically linked to? First Tottenham away and then this. I hate Mondays.

4:15pm: Walking home from the bus stop. Still lots of snow on the ground. Horrible slush though. Some funny icy bits. Been a pretty rubbish day. At least Mr Mahmood has said Asif can come round after tea to help me with my Maths homework. That's crazy Sarah over there by Mr Moreno's shop. What's she doing there? Who is that bloke she's with? They look like they're more than just friends. He's got his hands all over her. Is she two-timing my brother? Maybe I should go over and confront the trollop. Protect the Stadler honour. He's got a motorbike. Two wheels less than Mark. My day can't get any worse. I'm going to go for it. I'm going to put an end to this punk taking my brother for a ride.

179

'Who are you? And who is Sarah?', the ageing punk seemed in total denial. Perhaps she had fallen off the bike and hit her head. She could be concussed. 'I'm sorry. I think you have got me mixed up with somebody else'. I most certainly hadn't. The voice didn't quite sound as annoying. She seemed posher. But it was Sarah. I explain that I'm Mark's brother. "One of your Art students". Still blank looks. Maybe it was her twin sister. I was starting to doubt myself. 'I'm an actress not a teacher. You really have got me mixed up with somebody named Sarah. My name is Rosanne. Rosanne Barkley, this is my agent Graham'. A real actress outside Mr Moreno's newsagents. I wasn't having this. I haven't seen her on TV. Documentaries or maybe she does dodgy films. Like the one that Noddy found in his parents' bedroom. No, this is Sarah. She's not fooling me. I would know those piercings anywhere.

9:12pm: I think with Mum gone for a bath, now is a good time to mention Sarah to Mark. *Three of a Kind* is on. The World's One Man Wrestling Championships was good but I do think Lenny Henry, Tracy Ullman and David Copperfield are running out of material. It seems quite dated compared to *Not the Nine O'Clock News*. How should I start the conversation? I'll say I bumped into Sarah today.

Wow! I didn't expect that response. Mark seems quite annoyed that I mentioned his girlfriend. Maybe all is not hunky-dory in the Sarah-Mark romance. He does say he is seeing her tomorrow night. He seemed totally uninterested in who she was with. He just told me to "shut it". I think I touched a nerve. Flinging a cushion at me, Mark stormed out of the living room. I seem to be making a habit of annoying people today. Asif got very frustrated trying to explain to me his unique way of solving quadratic equations. It was nothing like Mr Walker had taught us. I'm obviously going to be more influenced by a grown-up who supports a proper football team than an expelled grammar school teenager who didn't even know the rules of kerbie. Everyone knows you can only catch the ball in your half of the road.

Looks like Asif will be starting at our school in a couple of weeks. Mr and Mrs Mahmood went to see our purple-headed Headmistress, Miss Thatcher, today. Still scary that our Head shares the same surname with our Prime Minister. I'm sure they must be related. Both as frightening. Still think Asif will struggle to come down to our level. Not sure what went wrong at the grammar school either. I know he was bullied, but he's clever and I would have thought he could come up with a cunning plan to defeat the bullies. He's agreed to officially be an Aston Villa fan now. So, I can get him into the Local Gang. At the moment the gang is not really functioning. Tucker and Noddy are still not talking. Neither of them seems to have got any further with Emily Martins. Noddy even gave her a Curly Wurly, but still hasn't got her to go out with him. What kind of girl takes a boy's Curly Wurly and gives nothing in return? Can't believe they are 10p now.

Saturday 30th January

1:49pm: How much room do two elderly ladies need? I can hardly breathe here in the back of Mr Hill's car. It struggles to pull away as quick when they are going to the Bullring. Cold weather means they have got even more layers. Haven't they heard of Pac-a-Macs? Excited to be going to the first home league game since November, but why does it have to be Liverpool?

Main topic of conversation is about unemployment reaching three million. That's loads. I bet taking out the kids and the pensioners there is only about twenty-five million people in this country who could work. So Maggie has put more than ten percent of them on the scrapheap. Even poor Randy has been made redundant. He can only afford two pints a milk a day from the milkman. That scruffy Labour bloke, Michael Foot, says there are 32 people chasing every job. I guess by time we leave school there will be no chance of getting a decent job. Why am I even worried about my History homework? It's not as if I'll be the only one of the 2,000 of us going for a job who knows that Cleopatra wasn't actually an Egyptian.

Mark was in late last night after his alleged date with Sarah. I'm beginning to doubt he has a girlfriend anymore. Maybe I should have checked his passenger seat for clues when he dropped me off at the Hills. The car did still smell of fags. Mum got him a cherry flavoured dangly air freshener thing, but that smell combines with the cigarette smell to give an even more unpleasant odour. Wolves are at home to Sunderland today. Everyone beats Sunderland. They are three points behind us. Level on points if they win and Liverpool beat us. Would need to be a swing of 17 goals though. That ain't going to happen. Spud's not going to the game. He's looking after his mum today. His sister has gone away for the weekend. Apparently, he has to sit stroking his mum's hands. She sleeps most of the time. The MacMillan nurses come in four times a day now. Perhaps I can get Mr Hill's sister Peggy to sponsor me. She must shut up at some point so I can ask. Wonder if Noddy and Tucker will stand anywhere near each other at Walsall. They're at home to Oxford.

2:45pm: Today's game seems to be sponsored by a foreign fish company. Never heard of Sandvik. Sounds like one of the players who'll play against us in Kiev. Looking at Liverpool's 11 on the back of the programme. There are just no weak players. Probably the poorest one is Sammy Lee and he always looks decent. Ian Rush always scores against us. Why am I being so defeatist? We beat them last January. When we beat them 5-1 in 1976, they were European Champions. To think I'll be back here in three sleeps to see us play Sunderland. Be great if we took six points from these two games. That would certainly put us above the Albion and stop any crazy relegation talk. Good read about Tony Morley. He looks good in that England top. Interesting that he rates his Leeds League Cup goal above the Everton goal of the season or the Dynamo

Berlin one. He says that even though he's only scored six goals this season, he'll be disappointed if he doesn't get 15. I think a touch optimistic Tony. If you score one in the FA Cup Final that would do it for me.

That would be ace. Following England in Spain in the World Cup. Geoff Hurst, the '66 hat-trick hero is advertising his Sportsworld Travel in the programme. He is offering big discounts to groups of 20 people or more. You must send 19p in stamps direct to Geoff Hurst. Then he'll send you a full colour brochure. Be funny addressing an envelope to Geoff Hurst.

Not long now to the quarter-finals of the European Cup. Two whole pages on the four quarter-final ties. Dynamo Kiev don't seem that good. They haven't scored more than one goal in any of their games yet. I'm sure Liverpool will knock CSKA Sofia out. Red Star will beat Anderlecht. Red Star have already scored 14 times in the competition. No idea who UN Craiova are. Don't think they even appear on the Subbuteo teams catalogue. They are playing Bayern Munich. They won't be going any further. I think semi-finalists will be Liverpool, Red Star, Bayern Munich and us. Semi-finals would be impressive for our first season in the European Cup. Looks like Liverpool will retain the trophy. That would make it six straight England winners. That would be quite an achievement.

Ron is saying in his column that Liverpool are playing as well as ever at the moment. He's asking for the usual 110% but I do feel he is also fearing a defeat. At least Doris is more positive. She's got some mittens on that look like boxing gloves. Hope Asif is sticking to the plan. I have never trusted anybody before with my lucky radio. Really feel having it on will make all the difference. Come on Villa, we can do this!

3:03pm: I hate Ian Rush. I hate the Welsh. Just three minutes for him to score. Why was nobody marking him? I bet Asif was late turning the radio on. When will Ron realise Gary Williams is not a centre-half. Allan Evans is half the player without Big Ken by his side.

5:04pm: Good win for Walsall. Tucker and Noddy will be happy. But not together. I suppose it could have been worse for us. Losing 3-0 to Liverpool is not too embarrassing. At least Wolves lost at home to Sunderland. They really are in the relegation mix now.

End of January Top of Division One

5.	Southampton	Pl: 22 Po: 40	+10
6.	Manchester United	Pl: 22 Po: 39	+15
7.	Ipswich Town	Pl: 19 Po: 38	+10
8.	Manchester City	Pl: 22 Po: 38	+ 9
17.	**Aston Villa**	**Pl: 21 Po: 22**	**- 4**

Villa January League Results

16th Notts County (a) 0-1 Lost
30th Liverpool (h) 0-3 Lost

Villa January FA Cup Results

5th Notts County (a) 6-0 Won (Cowns, Geddis 3, Shaw)
23rd Bristol City (a) 1-0 Won (Shaw)

Villa January League Cup Results

20th West Bromwich Albion (h) 0-1 Lost

Chapter Eight

February 1982

Tuesday 2nd February

3:38pm: Must be home time now. This day has really dragged. Tucker and Noddy had another scrap in the playground. Jock McGinn says they are now on their last warnings. I'm not going to take sides. How dare Emily Martins break up our gang. She needs to decide one way or the other. Does she want to go out with Noddy or Tucker or neither? Neither would be the best result. Glad I am currently free from the complications of the opposite sex. Wendy McGregor is hardly talking to me. I got a nod in Physics. No eye contact. Villa home to Sunderland tonight so I need to focus. Can do my Chemistry homework on the bus in the morning.

Spud says his mum is worse than ever. All she talks about are depressing things. She was selecting funeral hymns the other day. Spud suggested hymns we sang in assembly, like "When a Knight won his Spurs" or "When Lamps are Lighted in the Town". We both agreed we didn't want any songs with Spurs winning in them. Spud's mum says she doesn't want people to cry but to be happy and remember the good times. If I die, I hope everybody will be wailing. I'd want the church flooded with tears so you'd need a canoe to be able to get out. Hope Mrs Hogan doesn't die. Certainly not before we do our sponsored walk next Sunday. That's going to be fun now, with Noddy and Tucker not able to be within ten feet of each other. Doubt if Wendy McGregor is going to come now. Haystacks is not his old jovial self either. He has taken his parents' separation very hard. Seems to blame his mum for kicking his dad out. Refuses to eat at the table with her. Has all his meals on his Albion tray in his room. With the amount of grub Haystacks eats, his mum must make about half a dozen trips to his room a day. Early on he really thought they would get back together. Now it's moved to divorce papers. Parents only communicate through solicitors. Haystacks did say his mum's solicitor was a stunning lady. He's caught a glimpse of her lacy bra a couple of times. Seems he only leaves his room when the solicitor is there. Georgina Ramsey wants to go back out with him despite his increasing waistline. She has even promised to take down her Man United posters. But Haystacks is too depressed to think about romance. He says he's never getting married. Mind you, with his lack of aerosol deodorant usage lately I doubt any prospective bride would be willing to get close enough for him to put a ring on her finger. If we win tonight, we go above Hastings' Albion. We will have played three games more. League table never lies though. Wolves are away at Arsenal. They'll probably get hammered. I hope for Spud's sake they pull off a shock result. He needs some happy news.

10:20pm: A win is a win. We weren't at our best. A scrappy 1-0 win. David Geddis getting the all-important goal. Early in the second half. After Peter Withe knocked it down. So many injuries. Brendan Ormsby, Gary Shelton and David Geddis all had to play. To think last season we used just 14 players. I wonder if Ron will drop Geddis for Shaw on Saturday. If Shaw is fit. How badly injured is Colin Gibson? Terry Bullivant did okay when he came on, but I wouldn't want him playing a whole game.

Pity Wolves lost 2-1 at Arsenal. Ceefax hasn't updated the table yet. But with 20 games to go Wolves are in the relegation zone. It's only because the Blues have also been so rubbish that they aren't further adrift.

Reading the programme and the youth team are doing well. Into the semi-final of the Southern Junior Floodlit Cup. Don't know how we're in a Southern tournament as we're from the West Midlands. At least our 2-1 win against Chelsea last week was played under floodlights. Pity Mr Hill doesn't go to the youth team games as well. A lad called Paul Kerr scored the first goal. We must play Birmingham now in the semi-final. Wow, this quiz of 50 Villa questions is hard. Most of them were before I was born. How am I supposed to know who our captain was in the '57 Cup Final? I'm sure Brian Little's England debut was against Wales. Why do I know that? Is it right? How can I possibly check it? Could be in my *Rothman's 1977 Yearbook*. Andy Gray joined from Dundee United. At least I know I've got one right. I know the last one too. I was there when Luton beat us 2-0 in 77/78 League Cup. I am not answering question one on principle. I have tried to put the 1980 FA Cup quarter-final defeat to West Ham out of my memory. Hopefully winning the cup this season will finally put that to rest. Only one question on our great 1980/81 season. Even that's a negative one. I'm sure the person who wrote this quiz was not a Villa fan. It was Leeds. That was the team we conceded our first penalty to last season. Less than two minutes into the season. Don't worry, Eamonn Deacy, I have forgiven you now.

Thursday 4th February

9:15am: Jock McGinn has just told us that a new boy called Asif Mahmood will be joining us after half-term. Disappointing that there were a few boos. I'm going to have to big Asif up a bit. Hope he doesn't come over as too much of a swot.

Spud's missing today. Hope he's not ill. We need him to be able to complete the walk on Sunday. Even if he needs a late fitness test. Haystacks has had a word with Noddy and Tucker. I think it involved physically banging their heads together. They have agreed that for Sunday they will call a 24-hour truce. Like the English and Germans did on Christmas Day in the war. There will be no mention of Emily Martins. They will march as fellow Saddlers around the West Midland football grounds. We have all decided to wear the scarves of each other's football clubs. I have got to wear my brother's flipping Wolves one. Tucker and Haystacks are wearing my Villa ones. I'll trust Tucker with my silk 1977 Wembley one. Haystacks can have the woolly one my mum knitted me last winter. Spud is going to have to wear a Baggies scarf. Hastings says he can have the one with Bryan Robson on as he refuses to wear it himself anymore. Noddy was struggling to find a scarf, so Mr Walker has donated his Nottingham Forest one. Seems a little unfair as both Forest and Walsall play in red.

Tucker seems more interested in talking about the wet dream he had about Gladys Pugh from *Hi-de-Hi!* last night than our upcoming fundraising event. Haystacks is more annoyed that West Brom didn't get a penalty against Spurs yesterday in the first leg of their Milk Cup semi-final. I watched it on *Sportsnight*, it was a dirty game. Two sendings-off and about eight bookings. I didn't see any penalty incident. Ossie Ardiles nearly scored a cracker with five minutes to go. I guess at 0-0 Spurs will be happier before the second leg at White Hart Lane. Don't think I could cope if the Albion won a cup. Would be much happier if Spurs won the League Cup and left the FA Cup to us. Maybe that's mean. Perhaps if we win the FA Cup then why not let Haystacks have some happiness. It might make up for his parents divorcing. I guess most likely is that Liverpool win the Milk Cup. They are 2-0 up against Ipswich. After the away leg. Liverpool could win all four trophies this season. A quadruple! At least we got half of the Charity Shield with Spurs.

Sunday 7th February

9:47am: Odd being at a football ground when there isn't a game on. Thought some Albion players might have turned up to see us off. Big Cyrille maybe. Asif had written to all the clubs. Seems only Walsall have written back. They are going to put on some sandwiches for us and manager Alan Buckley will be there. Hope they aren't tuna sandwiches. I get enough of those in my lunchbox each day at school. Twenty miles seems a long way. Can't believe we are about to walk from The Hawthorns to Molineux. Where's Spud? Asif is going to join us from the Wolves ground. He's given me strict instructions to start the stopwatch on my digital watch as soon as we take the first steps. Mr Walker had to pull out because he's helping with the third-years' Geography field trip, despite being a Maths teacher. Randy was going to follow us in his car. Then he found that he would have to do a very difficult right turn at Guns Village. I was hoping Wendy McGregor would have come and joined us. At least she is speaking to me now. Even made her laugh yesterday. I guess it's too early for a reconciliation.

Tucker is really looking the part in his red Umbro tracksuit. Haystacks has gone for the more casual jeans and ski jumper look. I'm sure he was a bit slimmer when he first had that jumper. The split with Georgina Ramsey has had an inverse effect on his waistline. It seems to be that for every week he's single he adds another inch to his waist. He's got a pump-bag full of goodies for the walk. I've already seen him munch down half a packet of Jaffa Cakes. He still holds the school record for the number of Jaffa Cakes in his mouth in one go.

That's unexpected! Grace Taylor has come to wave us off, with her mum. They've got buckets. No sure if they are expecting a leak or planning to raise extra money by washing cars. Oh, I see. They have "MacMillan Donations" written on the side. They are going to try to get us more money. They're wrapped up because it's freezing. Grace wears a bobble hat so well. Hope she likes my Villa

V-neck jumper. Wish I'd worn a coat. Where is Spud? We need to be starting soon. An old man and his dog now seem to be waiting to wave us off. I think he might be going to put some coins in Grace's bucket. Not surprised. Who can resist that smile?

Asif has calculated that if we all complete the 20 miles, we could raise nearly £200. Pete not here is going to knock us down. Perhaps he's ill. If I knew the Hogan phone number, I would have rung this morning. Haystacks' Albion scarf for Spud to wear is lying with my Pac-a-Mac and Tucker's Wembley Trophy on the pavement. Tucker thought we could dribble this along the route. The rest of us thought this was too ambitious.

'Four blooming one!' I had tried to avoid talking about our defeat yesterday at Old Trafford, but Noddy decides it needs mentioning. Really thought when David Geddis gave us the lead that we were going to win. Couldn't believe it when the goal horn went right on half-time and they had equalised. Totally rubbish letting United score three times in the second half. Bet Bryan Robson loved scoring against us. Poor Allan Evans did have his fifth centre-back partner of the season. Mind you, with Wolves losing 6-1 at Spurs, it's not surprising Spud couldn't face us. Haystacks must have been loving the Villa and Wolves scores yesterday. His mob beat Mr Walker's lot 2-1. Surprised Noddy brought yesterday's scores up after Walsall lost at Chesterfield.

No, don't cock your leg there! The old man's dog has just urinated all over Haystacks' Albion scarf and my Pac-a-Mac. I'm not wearing that mac now. Think I'll keep it quiet from Haystacks. Maybe it won't smell.

We can't hang around any longer. We need to start. Time to press the stopwatch button and start our 20-mile footballing hike. The four of us line up with the new Albion Halford Lane Stand behind us ready to be counted down by Grace, her mum and the old man. We are off. Quickly my nimble feet navigate firstly some white dog poo and then the remains of a hot dog sausage from yesterday's match. From the highest English ground above sea-level we march towards Wolverhampton. We certainly started with a marching pace. The panting noises and redness of Haystacks' face made us soon realise that we'd gone off too quickly. We waited until we were out of sight of the trio of cheerleaders before we reduced our pace.

Our mood in the first section of the walk was good. Haystacks asked us football trivia questions. Tucker and Noddy were friendly to each other. The sun even came out. One of Scott Hastings' questions was, "Who is the England player from the 1966 World Cup winners who everybody always forgets?" We started well; the two Charlton brothers, Geoff Hurst of course, Martin Peters, Nobby Styles without his teeth. I then said Gordon Banks, a great keeper even though he only has one eye. Noddy got the captain, Bobby Moore. Although he did originally say Roger Moore. Roger was a clue for me to add Roger Hunt. Tucker then said Alan Ball. He's playing for Southampton with Kevin Keegan now. Must be nearly 40 if he played in '66 World Cup. Out of nowhere, Noddy added George Cohen. That's ten of the eleven, but Haystacks said we still hadn't got the one everyone forgets. I tried Jimmy Greaves, even though I know he missed out and that's why he became an alcoholic. We were all quiet as we tried to think who the one was that nobody could ever remember.

'Do you give up?' Haystacks said, delighted that he felt he had beaten us. If I tell him that dog had taken a pee on his Albion scarf that might wipe that smile off his face. He had beaten us. We couldn't think who the player people always forget is. 'Ray Wilson is the one you lot certainly forgot'.

12:06pm: It's raining now. Morale is starting to drop. We need to remember we're doing this for Spud's mum. Wolves ground is not too far away now. We're approaching the Wulfrun Centre where C&A is. The place that changed my life. Where Grandad bought that purple tracksuit. The one he said was in the colours of the great Aston Villa. That was back in 1974. Ron Saunders had only just taken over as manager then. We were struggling in the Second Division. Now, eight years later, we are Champions of England and in the quarter-finals of the European Cup. What a journey me and Ron have been through. Bit of a blip in the league this season, but I still believe when everyone is fit, we are still a top team.

'Wait for me, you scumbags'. a heavy breathing Spud runs towards us waving a slightly damp West Brom scarf.

Spud had thought we were starting at eleven not ten. He's run most of the way from The Hawthorns. Apparently got lost twice trying to follow Asif's contoured map drawing. Didn't help that some of the ink had run in the rain. Spud's wearing his 1976 long-sleeved Wolves top. Sweat patches were now almost as long as the sleeve. But our gang was complete. The band were back together. Pete Hogan, the leader of our pack, was ready to lead us to Molineux. His second home. Apparently, he hadn't been off because he was sick. His mum had wanted all the family to have a short break together in Weston-Super-Mare. A place where the Hogans had enjoyed many family holidays. Normally in the summer though. Not in February when it is cold enough to make a penguin want to put a coat on. Maybe Mrs Hogan is getting better if she can manage a few days in Weston. Perhaps she won't need the MacMillan nurses much longer. Still think these nurses, like Asif's mum, need our support. I wonder why they must rely on donations. You'd have thought Maggie could have given them a bit of money. Suppose she's too busy finding all the extra dole money.

Tucker suggested that we do the last stretch to the Wolves ground in a line holding hands. Spud protested saying, "that's a bit gay". He's already wearing his rival team's scarf that smells of dog wee, so we'll save him the embarrassment of having to hold Noddy's hand. Waiting for us is a small group. Clapping, waving and shaking buckets. It's Grace, her mum and Randy. Randy opens his mack to reveal his white t-shirt. He's written in black marker on the front "GIVE US YOUR CASH". I think a "please" would have been nice. Grace is telling everyone around what we're doing and that we're raising money for MacMillan nurses. I can feel a big blister already on the heel of my foot.

Randy is going to walk with us to Fellows Park. He's come on the bus. I'm already knackered. Surly we have walked further than Asif had calculated. Was it really only 20 miles all the way?

2:54pm: Can't help thinking we've got our timings wrong. Our third ground reached and I'm on my knees. Poor Haystacks is even worse. He's eaten all his tuck and drunk a full bottle of Tizer, and not a small one. Now I wish I'd nipped behind the bushes in Willenhall Park for a slash like the others did. I'm bursting now. Maybe the Player Manager, Alan Buckley, can direct me to the bogs. The sandwiches are all curled over. The woman serving through the hatch moaned because we were over an hour late. Egg and cress isn't the best combo either. Especially with Tucker's guts.

Grace and her mum have caught us up again. Grace looks to be getting loads of money. Randy is a bit disappointed with Fellows Park. What did he expect from a Third Division ground? Tucker and Noddy are giving him a tour. One of the groundsmen is opening up for them to go on the pitch. I don't know if Walsall have got more than one groundsman. Kind of him to come along today. Alan Buckley seems a really nice bloke. Even if he has no idea where the Gents are.

We're going to be in the *Express & Star*. Their reporter is here. He's asking me lots of questions. Bet they spell Stadler wrong. Time for a picture for the paper. We need to get a move on. It'll be dark at 5pm. We still have to walk to the greatest ground in the world. Randy wants to be in the photograph. Think he wants to flash his slogan. I think Grace should be in. Pity Alan Buckley has gone. In the end it's just us five boys. Me, Noddy and Tucker kneeling on the front row. Haystacks and Spud standing behind us. I'm sure Spud would have pulled a funny face. Shouldn't the photographer have taken more shots just in case? I'm going to be in the paper looking like a drowned rat. Is this rain ever going to stop? Just need to remember that we are doing this for Spud's mum.

4:41pm: 'I can't go on. You'll have to leave me here in Perry Barr', Tucker dramatically announced as he collapsed to the ground. We'd all expected it would be Haystacks who wouldn't last the course. We still have probably a mile to go. We're all drenched. I suppose losing one of the five of us wasn't bad. Eighty percent making the finish line would be impressive. Haystacks has been running on empty for the last half an hour. Being Sunday, everywhere is closed. He looked longingly at the bags of pork scratchings in the window of the butchers we passed. What do we do about Tucker? His ankle really can't take any more. He twisted it jumping over a puddle.

'All for one. One for all', came Spud's rallying call. Haystacks and Spud went either side of Tucker. They lifted Tucker up between them.

5:05pm: It's getting dark. Pity the famous AV floodlights aren't on to light our way. Spud is now giving Tucker a piggy-back. Haystacks seems to have got his second wind. Must have been those egg sandwiches. We are in Witton Lane. We can see the home of the Champions of the Football League. What a glorious sight.

We've only gone and done it. The Local Gang have walked from The Hawthorns to Villa Park via Molineux and Fellows Park. I'm knackered, Noddy is hyperventilating and Tucker is unable to put his foot down. The five of us have faced the impossible and we conquered it. Divided by the football teams we support but united by our footballing bond.

In front of the iconic Trinity Road Stand, we are met by families and friends standing on the famous steps. Even Mr Hill is there. Probably telling everyone about the architectural splendours of the red-brick Trinity Road Stand, built to the designs of Archibald Leitch. My parents are looking very proud. Dad has even got his Kodak camera on a tripod. Pity it's so dark now. Grace is beaming. Delighted that we have accomplished this impressive feat. Grace sees a passing dark-haired gentleman and races towards him waving her bucket. Think he's someone to do with the club. He's got an Aston Villa tie on. He's wearing a light brown raincoat. Don't recognise him. Too old for one of the players. Not old enough for a director. He's putting his hand in his pocket though. Better than that he's going for his wallet. He's writing a cheque.

Grace runs over to me excitedly. 'Says he's a scout'. Looked far too old to be in the scouts to me. The cheque is for ten pounds and made out to "MacMillan Nurses". Dad will have to deal with getting that paid in. Name on the cheque is "A E Barton". No idea who he is, but what a kind bloke. At this rate we'll have raised over £200. They must be able to buy a month's load of nurses for that amount.

Where's Spud gone? He's always disappearing these days. Noddy gives me a nudge and points. Coming towards us is Spud and holding on to Spud is a very frail-looking Mrs Hogan. I recognise her but she looks nothing like the glamourous lady that I saw at Spud's 15th birthday party. I try not to look taken aback by her appearance. She seems to be smiling and crying at the same time. My mum now seems to be copying this mixture of emotions.

'You boys have done amazing. I can't believe you ever thought of doing this. Now you have done it. I hope you never have to find out just how wonderful these nurses are. Thank you so much'. Spud's mum then plants kisses on all of us. She gives us all individual hugs. I can feel her bones. I wonder what did happen to her old boobs.

Tuesday 9th February

9:23am: Hate being the centre of attention. Standing in front of the whole school during assembly in the Sports Hall. At least they're all clapping us. Suppose we are fundraising heroes. Never know what to do with my hands when standing in front of everyone. I guess the Prince Philip hands-behind-the-back way is best. Spud is really milking the cheers. Noddy and Tucker are back to being enemies. One is standing the opposite end of the line to the other. Can't remember ever having to shake the hand of the purple-haired Headmistress before. Her hands are a bit more lady-like than I expected. I didn't squeeze too tightly. Spud gave her a real good shake. Haystacks is the one who's going to make our speech. Thank everyone who sponsored us. And remind them they've got to pay up by Friday or Spud will head-butt them. Making it sound like a joke.

Mum was so proud of my photograph in the *Express & Star* last night. It's going in the family scrapbook. Next to the one of Mark performing a "Punch and Judy" show where kids brought silver foil bottle tops in aid of the *Blue Peter* Lifeboat appeal. At least this time they spelt Stadler right and even got my 14 age right. Unlike Noddy, who ended up being aged 71. Spud was called Peter Wogan. Never knew Terry was his father. He'll be doing the *Eurovision Song Contest* next.

On my way to Chemistry Wendy McGregor comes and congratulates me on both my Assembly appearance and for doing the walk. She gives me a five pound note from her mum and dad. Maybe there is still hope there. Perhaps I could send an anonymous Valentine's card. Perhaps send Grace one too. Perhaps you get discount if you buy two the same. Problem is, next week is half-term holiday. I'll be worried all week whether they liked them or not. At least they won't be able to compare notes. When we come back after the break, I'll have to be showing Asif the ropes. Need to brush-up on his Villa knowledge. See if I can get him to learn all the final venues of our 1977 League Cup success. It's the fifth round FA cup tie at Tottenham the Saturday before we're back. Be great if I could walk into school with Asif the first day back with our heads held high and gloating in being in the quarter-finals. Be great if Ron can add the FA Cup to our trophy cabinet. Would mean he would have won all the domestic cups with us.

2:10pm: This probability is so easy. Why aren't the others getting it? Mr Walker has explained it four times. If you toss a coin five times the probability of getting five heads is 1/32. Two to the power of five. How can Christine Price get 5/17? Hope she never ends up being a bookmaker.

What's old Jock doing here? He's coming over to me. What have I done?

'Jonathan, there is an important phone call for you in the secretary's office. The gentleman on the phone seems very upset. He says it's urgent he talks to you'. Unnerving that Jock McGinn is showing a sympathetic side. I don't like this. Mr Walker nods and pats me oddly on the shoulder. I follow Mr McGinn out of the classroom.

There is an urgency as McGinn, in silence, leads me down the stairs. Several pupils try to ask him questions, but he's on a mission to get me to the telephone. I feel a sense of doom.

We enter the secretary's office. Miss Parker's hand is over the receiver. She looks sad. I think she already knows the bad news I am about to receive. She passes me the phone.

'Be strong, Jonathan', Jock McGinn says and then bows his head.

'Is that you, Jonathan?" the familiar voice of Randy Nawas asks. He seems like he's been crying. What's going on? 'I'm so sorry. I can't believe it's happened. I just wanted you to know before you got home … He's gone'. Randy was making no sense at all. Who had gone? 'He's left us', sobbed Randy.

I walk slowly back to my Maths lesson. Trying to make sense of the tragic news I had just been given. Mr McGinn asked if I wanted to go home, but I needed to be strong. Maybe Randy had got it wrong. Maybe he was confused. Surely it couldn't be true. There is no way that Ron Saunders could have resigned.

6:20pm: I'm lying on my bed in the dark. I can't cope with people trying to console me. Even Mark seemed quite sympathetic after his initial jokes. Mum just doesn't get it. She said that classic "it's not like someone has died". It's massive and life changing. Our great manager has left us. The man who guided us to the League title. The only Villa manager I have ever known. Things will never be the same again. I might as well take my *Shoot!* League Ladder down now. We'll probably end up getting relegated with Wolves. Within three years we could be in the Fourth Division. Can't believe Haystacks celebrated when I told him the news. Why haven't they cancelled all the television programmes tonight? They should be playing sombre music instead.

A knock on my bedroom door. I told them I didn't want to be disturbed. I'm not going to eat anything. Perhaps I can do a hunger strike until the board convince Ron to come back. Hopefully that would only be a few hours. Not like the IRA hunger strikers. I can feel myself wasting away already.

'It's Asif. He's come to cheer you up', Mum shouts while continuing to knock, her painful words boring right through me. I don't want to cheer up. I want to wallow in this until somebody puts it right. This is the biggest disaster of my 14-year life. Villa without Ron Saunders would be like *Rainbow* without Bungle.

Asif does try to understand the severity of the news. I do appreciate his consoling words. Then he goes too far. He moves too quickly. Asif asks which manager could replace Ron. My tears finally come. I know that nobody can ever replace Ron Saunders. Even Brian Clough would struggle to fill his shoes. We need hope. A belief that Ron will have a change of heart. Perhaps the players could go around his house and plead with him.

9:19pm: That's just not fair. Mum says I can't stay off school tomorrow if I want to go to Villa Park in the evening. I must go to our game against Southampton. As a mark of respect to Ron. I need to be with other Villa supporters. I wonder who'll pick the team. Perhaps Dennis will be like *Roy of the Rovers* and be player-manager for the night. I can't concentrate on *Pot Black*. No idea if Eddie Charlton or Dennis Taylor are winning. Dad made me some tomato soup. Well, he poured the can into the saucepan. Comfort food is what I needed. I can't totally give up. It's not what Ron would have wanted. Hate the fact that we must talk about Ron in the past tense now. He's still our manager in my eyes.

Wednesday 10th February

5:52pm: How cruel is that? The board have painted over Ron's name on his parking place. Ron seems quite relaxed on the interview. Looks like he is taking it better than me. I haven't been able to focus on any of my lessons today. Nearly set fire to my blazer when I was reaching over the Bunsen burner in Chemistry. Why did the Chairman, Mr Bendall, have to change Ron's contract? Bet if we'd been top of the league again now, they wouldn't have done that. Even Bobby Robson, his nemesis, was totally shocked Ron had gone.

6:43pm: Mr Hill is more relaxed about Ron's departure than me. I suppose he's seen a few managers go over the years. Maybe he's just still in shock. Can't believe we're going to see Villa play without Ron as manager. It's going to be a very low crowd. We didn't even make 20,000 last time against Sunderland. Suppose at least today's a bit warmer. It's the players I feel sorry for. I'm sure they won't feel like playing. They probably got even less sleep than me last night.

I nearly raise a smile for the first time in 24 hours when Howard Hill announces he's got us two tickets for the cup game at Spurs on Saturday. I'd forgotten all about our upcoming FA Cup tie. The cockneys must be delighted that we are suddenly in such turmoil. To think the last time Mr Hill took me to London, we won the league. That seems a long time ago now. I think I need to get through today's game before I can think about a trip to White Hart Lane. This is going to be difficult. I just don't want to cry in front of Doris. Wonder if Steve Austin and Zippy will be there. They haven't been the last two games.

On the radio they're discussing possible successors. John Toshack, former Liverpool player who is doing so well at Swansea, is being mentioned. As is Elton's mate at Watford, Graham Taylor. No way can we consider ex-Wolves boss John Barnwell. Wolves sacked him so he's not good enough for us. The reporter says that one of Ron's assistants, Tony Barton, is going to be caretaker manager, while the club looks for a new permanent boss. Never heard of him.

7:17pm: More here than I thought, but it's like a morgue. Not that I've ever been in a morgue. Doris and Penny were blubbering when they walked to their seats. Seems to be quite a hostility against the board. Feeling if we go behind it could turn nasty here. Bushy eyebrow man says a protest group has been formed. They're starting a petition.

That's quick. The inside cover where Ron's manager notes always are. I thought it would have been too late to remove them. But they have. It's the ticket details for the Dynamo Kiev game instead. Just above a profile on Ivor Linton. Must get my dad to go and get my ticket. Three pounds, doesn't seem to be a juvenile reduction. Voucher number 26. They haven't taken that picture of the great man out of the next page. I suppose that's difficult, as he's behind Peter Withe's handshake with a police inspector who retired. I wonder how many hooligans he nicked during his time at Villa Park. That basketball player is huge. Must try to get Dad to take me to see Team Fiat play again at the leisure centre. Got a bad feeling that Kevin Keegan will score against us today.

Here come the players. Quite a good reception for them. My heart just doesn't feel in this. I think we should have a minute's silence before we start to allow us to remember our legendary boss in silence. Finally, Ken McNaught is back. No Morley or Shaw. Guess that's four in midfield.

It's that bloke who gave Grace Taylor a cheque. He's walking to the dugout. That must be Tony Barton. That's a turn-up. Hope he gets a win in his brief moment of glory. All the Villa fans are singing "There's only one Ron Saunders". Pity, if there were two, we'd have the ideal replacement. I have never known old Doris to sing so loudly.

The Holte Enders are making it clear whose side they're on. Shouting Ron's name and booing the board. One of the chants sounds like "We won the league, we won the cup, now Ronnie Bendall has mucked it up!" I don't think it's "mucked" though. Sounds like it's to the tune from *Citizen Smith*.

8:15pm: Nearly half-time. That was classic Steve Austin saying that was a Villa throw-in right on the opposite side of pitch to us. There were at least four players in his way. Does he really think the linesman can hear him from here? It's been a dull game. Perhaps appropriate in the circumstances.

No! No! Don't you dare! Flaming Kevin Keegan. I knew he would score. This week just keeps getting worse. Why couldn't he have stayed at flipping Hamburg?

Half-time and we are losing to Lawrie McMenemy's lot.
You'd have thought our former captain Chris Nicholl would have
helped us out. We could have done with one of his infamous own
goals. The fans are certainly letting rip at Bendall and Kartz now.
Feel sorry for that nice Tony Barton bloke being dropped into this.
Although I would give absolutely anything to be Villa manager for
just one game.

So, we play Spurs at home next Wednesday whatever
happens. If we draw in the cup on Saturday, next Wednesday will be
the replay. If it's not a draw, then a week today we'll play them here
in the league. Our next two games are against Spurs and I'll see
them both. Be great if Ron was back in charge for Saturday. I have a
feeling he might be. The board must do whatever they can to take
him back. Perhaps I could help with the petition. If I can get 50
people to sign about a snogging suspension, then bet I can get 100
to reinstate Ron Saunders. Asif will be up for helping. Mr Hill must
know lots of people. Pity he doesn't work anymore. My dad works
in Birmingham. He'll be able to get me a few signatures.

9:14pm: Glad that's over. The booing is deafening. Goes right
through you. It's for Ron Bendall, though, not the players. We at
least showed some fight second half. Nearly won it at the end. That
was a good chance. I'll take a 1-1 draw, thanks to Peter Withe's goal.
We missed Tony Morley. I wonder if the Albion managed to
equalise in the League Cup. Bushy eyebrow man said it was 1-0 to
Spurs at half-time. If that's the case it will be a Liverpool v Spurs
final. I suppose a Spurs win today is the best result for us. They'll be
so busy celebrating getting to Wembley that they'll take their eyes
off Saturday's game against us. Also, probability-wise it's unlikely
you would be successful in two cup tournaments in four days. But
Albion might have equalised.

Thursday 11th February

12:48pm: That was a nasty challenge by Haystacks on Noddy. I think he's still annoyed about Albion losing last night. He really was expecting to finally be seeing them at Wembley. Noddy and Tucker have both agreed to ask Emily Martins out. No more animosity. It was my idea. They have agreed that whichever one Emily decides to go out with, the other one would accept it. No idea which one she will choose. But the gang is back together. Spud is in a better mood too. He's decided that he's going to start playing for the school team again. He went into retirement last March after a difference of opinion with Mr Aitken over tactics. Mr Aitken did not want Spud to stamp on the Pool Hayes star striker in the first minute.

Miss Cresswell is standing by our goal. Think she's trying to attract our attention. Standing there with those fabulous legs certainly has my attention. Noddy is trying to look brave and not limp too much following his encounter with Haystacks. Spud seems in his own world. We have all stopped to acknowledge Miss Cresswell, but Spud is curling a shot into Tucker's unguarded goal. It seems it's Peter Hogan that Miss Cresswell wants to speak to. Lucky Spud.

Spud leaves with Miss Cresswell. As they walk away Spud turns and gives us a fist pump gesture. I wonder what Miss wants with him. Guess without Spud it's pointless carrying on the game. I've lost count of the score anyway.

1:32pm: That's odd, Miss Cresswell in our Form Class. Where's old Jock? That would be a stupendous change. Cracking Cresswell instead of moaning McGinn. Why isn't Spud with her?

'4MC, I'm sorry to say I have some very sad news. Peter Hogan has been taken home. You all know Peter's mother has been very poorly. We had a phone call about an hour ago to say that Mrs Hogan has sadly passed away', Miss Cresswell was trying to tell us

204

the bad news in the gentlest of voices. This was a lot to take in. I had only hugged her four days ago. My mate had lost his mum. How is he going to cope? What are we supposed to say to this news?

Friday 12th February

3:45pm: Only just caught the school bus. I'm sure the driver deliberately leaves earlier on a Friday. Probably wants to get home for his tea. End of another half-term. Halfway through my fourth year. What a horrible week it's been. Ron resigning and then the news about Spud's mum. I know it's mean but I'm glad I've got a week off before I must face Pete. He'll probably not be back until after the funeral. I might ask Mum if we can go to the funeral. Try to support Spud. Mum was going to get a sympathy card from Mr Moreno's today. Apparently, that's what you do when somebody dies. Seems like the last thing somebody who is sad because someone close has died would want is a depressing card. I'm glad Mrs Hogan came to Villa Park. Don't know how I'd cope if my mum wasn't here. Who would empty my lunchbox? Might give her a hug when I get in.

The state of the ripped plastic seats on this bus is disgusting. Think most of the seats are only being held together with chewing gum. I hate this bus. Even the graffiti is badly spelt. How is Asif going to cope with this? That small girl with the broken hospital glasses on is target practice for the lads towards the back. They are blowing chewed-up bus tickets through the cases from their biros. What if Asif gets bullied? He can probably stand up for himself. I can imagine him opening his violin case and getting out a mini machine-gun. He could then flip and take out the whole bus.

I hope Wendy and Grace are looking in their school bags tonight. Just my luck if they throw them in the cupboard until a week on Monday. Knowing the state of Wendy's bedroom that bag could disappear under any amount of discarded clothes. It took a lot of skill to plant those two Valentine's Day cards. Easier with Wendy McGregor as her bag was wide open in Physics. Challenge was not letting Noddy see what I was putting in. I deliberately chose small cards. Not only because they were 5p cheaper. Decided in the end to go for two slightly different ones. I think on the romantic scale they were both on a similar level. Wasn't going to be completely anonymous. So put "From 'J' xx" inside both. I did write "Love From 'J' xx" in Grace Taylor's originally. Then decided against it and tippexed the "love" out. Hope Grace finds the card in her Home Economics basket. I was assuming that as she would have to take home the Victoria Sponge cake she'd made, then she would empty the basket when she got home. Did look tasty, that cake. I'm starving. Be great if it was a fish shop tea tonight, but that would mean we won't eat until after six when Dad's back. Last episode of *Shine on Harvey Moon* tonight. Hope they make a second series. Still don't know if I really like or not. Wonder what time we'll have to leave for White Hart Lane tomorrow.

Saturday 13th February

11:12am: I'm sure this is the M1 service station we stopped off at last May. Loads of Villa fans again. Must be a lot of fun on one of those coaches. Some of the fans look to have had a tank full of booze already. They must have started with some with their Frosties. So, if this is the same service station that we stopped at before the Highbury match, is it lucky or unlucky? We did win the league, but also lost the match. Impossible in the cup. Without Ron, I'm not confident. No offence, Mr Barton, but what do you know about winning cup ties? You haven't got Ron Saunders' pedigree for cup success. I would take another draw like in the Charity Shield. Get them back to our place.

2:10pm: It's a bit of a rough area this. Mr Hill tells me to leave my scarf in the car. What good is that when you're supporting your team? I put it on the backseat. It's covering up my sponsor form and the sponsorship money Mr Hill and his family have given me. At least we found a space to park. Hope Howard knows where the ground is from here. Or do we just follow that group of Tottenham fans? They must be going to the game. The one lad has a cardboard cup covered in silver paper. Pretty rubbish effort. Looks nothing like the FA Cup and he's only covered half the back of it. Wish I'd put my old shoes on with all this mud. Will have to make sure I wipe them off before getting back in Mr Hill's Ford Cortina. I'm the only one of the Local Gang going to a cup game today.

Haystacks isn't going to the Albion-Norwich tie. Says his mum won't pay for him and he can't afford it. His dad has now got a new woman and she's got a toddler. Haystacks is worried that his dad might start to prefer the little kid to him. Don't think Spud will be going to see Wolves. They are at home to Man United in the league. I bet there's quite a lot to do when your mum dies. Suppose they need to decide if they are going to bury her or burn her. Mark's going to the Wolves game. Noticed he had a card in the post this morning. It looked like a Valentine's. The lipstick mark on the back was a dead give-away. Quite a nice colour lipstick though. Not like the fluorescent pink ones that crazy forgetful Sarah wears. It was a Walsall postmark. Disappointingly there were no cards for me. Only post was from Julien, my French pen pal. Can't believe he's still writing. I haven't replied since second year. He still insists on writing half of it in English and half in French. I've stopped even trying to translate the French bits. There is a reason why I'm in the CSE French group. Mind you, his English makes no sense either. No idea what he was on about with the marrow and the croissant. He never even mentions Saint-Étienne anymore.

2:55pm: Here goes, then. Spurs fans make a lot of noise singing the rubbish "Glory, glory, Tottenham Hotspur". Be good to cut them down to size. Surprised Archibald is on the bench for them. Glad the only Argentinian playing is Ardiles. Don't want someone named Villa playing against us. BBC cameras are here. So, *Match of the Day* have chosen this game. I guess it is the tie of the round. League Champions against the FA Cup winners. Glad Tony Morley's back. Can't believe Ron transfer-listed him after their fallout. We're nearly at full strength. Only Gary Shaw missing through injury. Tony Barton has had an easy first team selection. Just hope Ken McNaught remains fit. Tony Morley looks like he's dyed his hair blond. Difficult to tell him and David Geddis apart. Except for Geddis's enormous moustache.

We've started well. Good chances for Evans and Morley. Tony Morley looks like he has a point to prove. The pitch is dreadful. So much mud. I think we played on better pitches than this when I played for the Boys' Brigade team. Poor Des Bremner is caked in mud already. That was never a foul by Gordon Cowans. I hate Keith Hackett. Spurs have done worse fouls than that. This is more like the old Villa. Guess they are doing it for Ron. Well, apart from Tony Morley. He probably was least upset with Ron resigning. Think they had a love-hate relationship. The Villa fans are starting to make all the noise now. "We are the Villa. We are the Champions".

They don't deserve that. One-nil Spurs. It's blooming Falco again. The one who scored two against us at Wembley. Typical of this horrible week. A long way to go though. Mr Hill just shakes his head.

4:59pm: Will I ever see us win the FA Cup? Maybe it's jinxed. Knocked out again, beaten 1-0 away for the third year running. West Ham, Ipswich and now Tottenham. Spurs might have edged the first half, but we were the better team in the second half. Allan Evans was fantastic. The dream is over. We'll have to wait until next January before we can try again. Just hope Tottenham draw

Liverpool or Ipswich in the next round. Anything that will stop them equalling our seven wins.

So much mud on my trainers. Will try to scrape some off before I get into Mr Hill's car. Lots of glass on the ground here. Certainly a rough area. Looks like someone has been smashing bottles. That glass by my door wasn't there before. Where's Mr Hill Cortina window gone? Some scummy Tottenham fan has smashed the back window on the passenger side. This day just gets worse. At least Howard Hill has noticed before I have to tell him. He's staying quite calm about it. I hope he's in the *AA* or *RAC*. I don't remember passing a phonebox. If we do find one it will probably have a vandalised phone in anyway. I hate London. Why do we never score here? People are much friendlier in the Midlands.

I suppose it was quite kind of that Spurs fan to find us a sheet of polyethylene. He only charged Mr Hill a quid for it. Still blinking cold on the motorway. Especially my side. It was very difficult to hear the scores on the radio as well with the loud flapping noise. Bet if we'd have won today and got through to the quarter-finals that there wouldn't have been so many shocks. How can Ipswich have lost at Shrewsbury? Crazy. And how the hell did Second Division Chelsea knock out Liverpool? It all makes no sense. Haystacks will be getting excited. Albion beating Norwich and now one of only three First Division teams left in. Apart from Spurs and Albion there's only Coventry City. They never win anything. This was our chance. Perhaps if Ron had still been here, we'd have done better. The board need to get it sorted. Either get Ron back or start looking for a top replacement. Still hope Saunders comes back. The petition is going well. Both me and Mr Hill signed today. I wrote my name in big capital letters to make it fill two lines.

Wolves lost again. Really does look as if they are going down.

Tuesday 16th February

12:51pm: Asif has just finished counting the money. We have raised an incredible £273.38½. Not sure who gave the halfpenny. That's more than I expected. Mr Hill did replace the money that was stolen from his backseat. I do feel guilty about that, though. If I hadn't left it on view, they might not have broken his window. I now have a painful neck from sitting in a draft for three hours. Hope the window is fixed for the next Villa-Spurs game tomorrow night. Spurs fans will be full of themselves. In the final of the Milk Cup and now only have to overcome Chelsea to be in FA Cup semi-finals. And they're in the quarter-finals of the Cup Winners' Cup.

Quite a shock in *Daily Express* today to read that the Blues have sacked Jim Smith. Thought he was doing okay with them. Considering they haven't got any decent players. A draw on Saturday at West Ham wasn't that bad.

Asif is going to type a letter to the MacMillan people telling them about our fundraising and then Dad's going to put a cheque in. Mum thinks she can talk Dad into rounding it up to £300. She's going to cook him his favourite hotpot for tea.

Who's that ringing our bell? I don't recognise that ring.

Very surprised to see Spud in our porch. Looking in need of a shave and his hair less manicured than normal. Being mean I had hoped I wouldn't see him for a bit. Just no idea how I should react. Is the appropriate welcome to a grieving pal a pat on the back, a hug or just a gentle nod? I go with gentle nod followed up with the dumbest of questions, "How are you doing?" Why isn't Mum here to take over? She'd know what to do or say. Should I mention his mum? Is it okay to talk about the current Wolves demise or the Jim Smith sacking?

'I'm just bored. Nothing to do. Everyone keeps fussing. Bringing us shepherd pies. I can't stand shepherd pies', Spud says, showing no real emotion. 'Carrie sent me a Valentine's card. She put a smaller sympathy card inside to save postage'.

I decide the best approach is to get my football out and take Spud and Asif round to the park for a kickabout. Much easier than talking about feelings and stuff. Spud smiles at the suggestion.

With Asif in goal, we played three-and-in. Not surprisingly, this meant that within minutes Spud was in goal. He claimed an Andy Gray hat-trick. More than Andy Gray has scored this season for Wolves. Spud did seem his old self. You wouldn't know he'd just lost his mum. Although with his scruffy facial hair he could probably have passed for somebody in their 30s. Not a 15-year-old. I don't think Carrie Carrington would be that keen to have intercourse with him in his current state. Suppose he might get the pity vote.

'Funeral is Friday. Will you come please, Hugh?' goalkeeper Spud said as he collected Asif's tame shot.

Defeat to Spud was expected, but to find myself trailing 2-1 to Asif was disappointing. He had got lucky with the second. My shot was just going wide when somehow it struck Asif's large nose and deflected past Spud's outstretched hand. Asif hasn't quite mastered all things Aston Villa because he claimed he was Jimmy Rimmer. Oddest part was that he didn't seem to be in pain after being struck quite hard on the nose.

This was my chance to equalise. One-on-one with Wolves' Paul Bradshaw. Despite the tarmac, Spud bravely dives at my feet. With the poise of Johan Cruyff, I sidestep the keeper and roll the ball towards the empty climbing frame. What the … Goal-hanging Asif arrives and toe-pokes the ball over the line. I've lost again.

Thursday 18ᵗʰ February

6:40pm: I must be on an episode of *Game for a Laugh*. This can't be right. The *Midland's Today* reporter is saying that our Ron Saunders is the new manager of Birmingham City. This must be a Jasper Carrot windup. No way would Ron go over to the dark side. This is the worst month of my life. Their chairman, a Mr Coombs, is saying "It's the greatest day is the club's history".

The way this month is going, I'm surprised we grabbed a draw against Spurs last night. Really though when Garth Crookes scored with about 20 minutes to go that we were doomed. I suppose at least we showed character to come back and equalise. Guess it's the end of the "We want Ron back" campaign. Time the board started putting together a shortlist of winners. We can't keep on not winning. We're still only 15ᵗʰ.

With typical Ron Saunders' flamboyancy, Saturday is the Villa v Birmingham derby. That will be an interesting atmosphere.

Friday 19ᵗʰ February

11:23am: Glad Mum came. I don't know anybody here apart from Spud and his dad. A lot of people. I guess the younger you are the bigger crowd you get. At least most of your friends are still around. I wonder if I'll get to go to Spud's funeral. I hope it's that way around. First time I've been to a Catholic service. Lot more formal than our Methodist ones. They like to shake the incense around. Perhaps the priests go to "incense-swinging" classes. Must be a bonus the priest doing a service that they actually know they'll have one of their own one day. They won't have a wedding and almost certainly not a christening. Although with not being allowed to use contraception they'll need to be extra careful to avoid becoming a different sort of "father". I didn't even know the Hogans were Catholic.

Lots of people crying. They obviously didn't get the memo from Mrs Hogan saying no tears. Pete was going to see his mum last night. His dad was insisting the whole family went. Spud didn't really want to go. He was worried that seeing his mum's body lying there might make it all real. At the moment he just felt she'd gone away somewhere. I wonder how they fasten the lid of the coffin down. You want it to be quite firm. Maybe it's a lock and key. But then where do they put the key. Life isn't fair. Spud's mum in that box, only in her 30s and still in her sexual prime. Then you have that ancient priest still alive. He must be in his 80s. If Heaven is so wonderful, how come this deeply religious bloke has resisted going there for so long?

My mum's crying now. That makes no sense. She never met Spud's mother. Maybe I should try and manage a couple of tears. Focus on something really bad maybe. Like the rabbits in *Watership Down* that didn't make it. Spud looks smart. He's had a shave. He's singing quite loudly to "O Jesus I have promised".

That is confusing. The hymn says, "To serve thee to the end". When is the end? Is it when you die? In which case Mrs Hogan has to serve no more. Bet she won't miss having to wash Spud's smelly undies. Or is it the end of your time in Heaven? But then that's eternity. So that surely never ends.

I guess this funeral puts things into perspective. Maybe there are some worse things than the greatest ever manager leaving. Perhaps my time of mourning my loss needs to come to an end. It's time to move on. Ron is moving on. I must too.

Saturday 20th February

3:11pm: Kenny Swain off already. That's not good. Terry Bullivant at right-back. Good that Gary Shaw is back playing. At least Ron hasn't officially taken over manager of Blues yet. Expect he's still having some influence on team selection and tactics though. He knows the Villa players better than anybody. We can't afford to lose today. I've changed the batteries in my radio in case the old batteries were losing their luckiness. Maybe our poor season is due to Radio Birmingham's name change. Perhaps I should swap to BRMB today. No, let's stick with WM.

4:13pm: Goal horns everywhere but St Andrews and the Hawthorns. Maybe a draw isn't too bad. Wolves are getting thumped by Notts County. Didn't expect 3-0 there. Liverpool are taking their FA Cup defeat revenge out on Coventry. Ian Rush has just scored their fourth.

I think I get more nervous waiting for the goal horns than I do when I go to the game. There goes the goal horn. Off to St Andrews.

Well done, Peter Withe. That's one in the eye for Ron. Goal created by Tony Morley. Still over 20 minutes left, but at least we are winning. Another goal horn, already! That's good, it's back at Meadow Lane. Crickey! Wolves are four down. What's going on with them?

6:23pm: Mark says that's Tammy Wynette in *The Dukes of Hazzard*. No idea who she is. Marks says she's a singer. I am more interested in watching Daisy Duke in those very tight jeans. We're not allowed to mention football. I'm just inwardly glowing with the fact that we beat the Blues 1-0. An important win. We are still 15th but now ten points clear of the 20th placed team. Which are Mark's Wolves. We are two points clear of the Baggies. There is a small matter of the fact we've played six games more than the Albion. At this rate Haystacks' lot will still be playing while the rest of us are watching the World Cup. Wolves have played 26 games like us. Leeds, the team just above the relegation zone, are four points better off than Wanderers and have played two games less. Good to see Mark's team struggling but I hope they don't go down. I really enjoy playing them at Molineux and beating them.

8:05pm: Need to focus on my Maths homework. Try to get it done before *Dallas* starts. Wish I'd written more detail about what it was in my homework diary. I was in too much of a rush for the half-term break. I'm sure Mr Walker set us something to do. Wasn't there a slip of paper? Let me search around my school bag. How long has that white sock been in there? Now a smelly white sock with blue patches on as one of my ink cartridges has leaked. What's this envelope? It's got a question mark on the front. Looks like a Valentine's card. Aren't you supposed to put the question mark inside? Bit of a thin cheapo card. Must be for me, though, as it's in my bag. Maybe it's from Wendy or Grace.

Aged 14 and my first ever real Valentine's Day card. Might be six days late opening it, but I'm still going to display it on my bedroom windowsill. It's a groovy kind of card with a big red lick-stick print on the front and the words "Valentine's Kiss ????" I wonder if it's too late to claim it. They haven't even written inside. This is a girl (hopefully) who is playing hard to get. Absolutely no clues. Just a big question mark on the front. How can I concentrate on my Maths homework, if I even knew who it was, with this hanging over me? Was it Wendy McGregor regretting spurning my kiss? Grace Taylor wanting me back? Or a new admirer? The third option seems unlikely. Probability-wise, it's extremely likely that one of the girls I sent a card to has sent me one back. Monday at school will be interesting even without putting Asif's 4MC debut into the equation.

Monday 22nd February

8:25am: Asif certainly looks the part in his new school uniform. Shoes so shiny we'll be able to see the bus coming in them. He seems to be taking it all in his stride. I do fear it won't end well. People as brainy as Asif don't go to our school. Asif needs to keep a low profile early on. I need to make sure he blends in.

The school bus is late again. Should have been here ten minutes ago. I'm used to it, but poor Asif is starting to panic. Suggesting he'd rather not go at all than be late on his first day. I can't let him escape now. It's my responsibility to get him there on his first day.

8:59am: Made it with a minute to spare. Can't remember the last time I had to run so fast. Didn't expect Asif to turn into Daley Thompson on that run from the bus stop. The way he hurdled over that first-year boy's satchel was phenomenal. I don't know how I kept up. Asif isn't even out of breath while I sound like an obscene phone-caller. Here comes Jock. What's he going to make of Asif?

'Ah, Master Mahmood. Welcome to our humble class. Ready to outshine this rabble?' Jock McGinn addressed the terrified Asif. There were murmurs from Asif's new form mates. Could hear words like "swot" and "grammar school dropout" being used. As well as pupils making reference to Asif's skin tone. Spud's back and he's put a chair by our desk for Asif.

'As if I wouldn't make room for Asif', Spud becomes the first, today, to joke about Asif's name. Spud means well, but I think our new form grew tired of this joke a few years ago. I'm disappointed that Asif rejects Spud's offer and instead goes and sits in the vacant chair by Wendy McGregor. He's unaware of who Wendy McGregor is and the significance of his seating position. Perhaps I should have briefed him more on my romantic involvements. Maybe I was wrong to prioritise him knowing the names of the Villa back four in the 1975 League Cup Final win over which girls in 4MC were off limits. Wendy is certainly making him very welcome. Can't believe she's letting him use her protractor to underline his name with.

10:40am: Who'll be the first one to throw something at Asif? I
know he's clever and that to him this is stuff he probably covered in
his second year, but he's ruining our Maths lesson. There hasn't
been a single question Mr Walker has asked that Asif hasn't
answered. Please give the rest of us a chance. When Mr Walker set
us on that algebraic fraction exercise, I think he was hoping it would
give him a peaceful 20 minutes to read his paper. The look of
horror on his face when after less than five minutes Asif put his
hand up to say he had finished. Made worse with Asif explaining
that Mr Walker had written question three incorrectly.

Disappointed that neither Grace nor Wendy have commented
about receiving Valentine's cards off me. Should I bring the topic
up with one of them?

12:35pm: Haystacks is happy with that draw. Avoiding Spurs and
getting a home tie against Coventry in the quarter-final. I still can't
believe how many rubbish teams are left in the FA Cup. At least
half the semi-finalists are going to be from outside the First
Division.

'I got a Valentine's', Noddy surprises us all by announcing. 'It
didn't say who it was off. Think it was Emily Martins. She hid it in
my sports bag. Mum found it when she was putting my games kit in
the wash. She made me put it up in the lounge'.

'I thought mine was off Emily', Tucker interrupted. 'It had a
question mark on front of the envelope. Nothing written inside'.

The more Tucker and Noddy described their cards, the more
they sounded identical to one I had received. Further investigation
found they were the same cards. More bizarrely, Haystacks had also
received one. His was inside his homework diary. We did a straw
poll of a few of the other boys in 4MC. All of them had received
similar cards. Although Derek Fieldmount had no idea what we
were talking about until he looked in his bag. Who was the
"Phantom Valentine's Sender" of 4MC? Was it some huge prank or

just a desperate girl? A girl from our Maths class working on the rules of probability. If you give out 15 cards, then very probable that you would gain at least one admirer. Problem is none of us know who it is. More likely it's some lad having a laugh. The only lad who doesn't seem to have got one is Spud, but then he wouldn't as he was off after his mum had died. This is a mystery I need to crack.

Not sure what's going on in Spud's head. Everyone is being so nice to him today. He's just so nonchalant about it all. In some ways he seems the old Spud, but then he's just being so soft. His edge has gone. Still think he could erupt at any time.

'Why did you send me a card?' I felt like I under interrogation by Wendy. It was as if I had done something really mean. 'I've told you I don't see you like that. I just want us to get back to being mates'. At least I know she found the card. It does seem to have moved us back to me being in Wendy McGregor's bad books. Not sure I want to just be her friend. Boys have needs. It's not just football we need. If I want a friend, I've got the boys in the Local Gang. What is it that girls find so repulsive about me? Is it my rubbish kissing technique? Or that my teeth aren't as bright white as Oliver Watkins? I really like Wendy. I wrongly thought she really liked me. Well, if she doesn't want my stinking card, she can give it back and I'll find a girl who really appreciates it.

4:22pm: Walking back down our street with Asif. He seems to have really enjoyed his first day. Seems to think he was quite a hit with the ladies. Very taken with Wendy McGregor. He's welcome to her. Also, Asif is excited that he had his first kiss. First day at a mixed sex school and he got a kiss. Didn't take me long to work out who the lucky girl was. It was Emily Martins. Apparently, it only cost him a finger of Fudge. Everyone kept asking him where he came from. He varied his answer from Darlington to the planet Zog. To be fair to the people asking, they were just curious. I don't think they had met many people like Asif. Carrie Carrington has asked

Asif to join the "Debating Society". I never even knew we had one of those. Asif has been put in the top set for all his subjects. He's joined Grace and Wendy in the top O level French class. He's been quite a hit with Miss Tully. They shared a joke in French in front of me. I laughed, but had no idea what they were going on about.

My dad and Mr Mahmood are suddenly best mates. The wall at the front that divides our pathway is being knocked down. I thought there was more chance of the Berlin wall coming down. Mrs Mahmood keeps bringing around these sweets she's made. I think they are made of condensed milk. They are so sickly sweet. We fed some to the cat. But the cat has started refusing them now.

7:09pm: Looks like the players are all behind Tony Barton. The board saying they are in no rush to make a permanent appointment. Looks like Mr Barton might still be caretaker manager when we play our European Cup quarter-final in Russia.

Why are all the newspapers now doing these bingo cards? Must check Mum's for both *Daily Express* and *Sunday People* numbers in the *Express & Star*. Takes longer to do this than it does to read the articles about the Villa. Says Tony Barton is going to take a squad of 16 to Russia next week. In the Central League tie tonight against Blackburn, Colin Gibson, Terry Bullivant and David Geddis will get a chance to prove their fitness. Ken Swain is already a doubt having come off against the Blues. Seems the game won't be played in Kiev, though. That's strange. Reason seems because it's too cold. Currently averaging about minus 8 centigrade. Like here before Christmas. Looks like it will be switched today to somewhere called Sebastopol. Never heard of it. They wanted us to go near the Chinese border to Tashkent. But have agreed that is too far. I know my Geography is rubbish, but since when has China been in Europe?

Good to see Ron Greenwood is giving Tony a go tomorrow night. The England team for tomorrow night is on the back of the

paper. Says big chance for Brighton's Steve Foster and Villa's Tony
Morley in the game against Northern Ireland. Trevor Francis and
Keegan up front. Surprised Cyrille Regis didn't get the nod. The
midfield is Robson, Wilkins and Hoddle. Guess Trevor Brooking is
still injured. Everyone seemed to want Greenwood to give Hoddle
another chance. Pity it's Ray Clemence's turn in goal. I think Peter
Shilton is a better keeper. It's unusual there are no Liverpool
players. Viv Anderson is right-back. That'll please Mr Walker.
Kenny Sansom on left of defence. How old is Dave Watson? He's
getting his 64th cap.

An auto cruiser around Italy and France for £72 with Riveria
Holidays, that seems quite reasonable. Bet Wendy McGregor would
be happy to go out with me if I took her on a holiday like that. I
could afford that with Grandad's money. Must book it around the
Villa games though. A bit more exciting than going to Scotland. It
says in the advert you get "reclining seats" and "a full-length video
film". Maybe "Auto Cruiser" is a coach not a boat. That's a bit of
luck. The bingo numbers are right by a picture of topless Tricia
Welsh. She's an actress. This isn't *The Sun* so the picture is from the
side. No nipples on display. Wow, Mum's got number 77 and
number 42 on the *Daily Express* one. I wonder how much you win.
How can all these newspapers give all this money away? Strange
that you don't even need to buy the paper to find the numbers out.
The Spot the Ball is on the same page. Perhaps there should be an
advert for Gamblers Anonymous on the next page. It's the Wolves
v Manchester United game at Molineux. I think the ball is just
above Wayne Clarke's hand. £26,000 to be won and a new Metro.
Dad would want to win the 100 gallons of petrol.

Wolves manager Ian Greaves admits he was wrong to waste
Andy Gray's talents in midfield in the hammering by Notts County
on Saturday. What planet is he from? Andy Gray is an old-fashioned
centre forward. It would be like the Villa wanting to play Des
Bremner as a striker. I suspect his reign as Wolves manager might

be one of the shortest on record. Up there with Brian Clough at Leeds. Walsall aren't happy. No wonder Noddy was moaning. It says their joint manager Neil Martin is being reported to the FA over his protests at ref Daniel Vickers giving Lincoln that controversial last-minute penalty. I bet they get dread refs in the Third Division.

Flipping Jimmy Hill is at it again. Who does he think he is? He's chairman of little Coventry City, not one of the big clubs. He wants to save football. Return it to the days of Denis Law and Bobby Charlton. He led a meeting of the club chairmen in Solihull yesterday. That's near the Villa training ground. He wants football like it used to be. Well, perhaps he shouldn't have brought in this crazy three points for a win rule. He's worried about falling crowds. How TV and the football pools are subsidising the game. He's putting together a "think tank". Why can't he just keep his big chin out of it? They're going to try to stop cynical fouls, time wasting, offside traps, dissent and overcrowded midfields. This isn't America. It's not all about entertainment. We love the game as it is. Apparently, they decided to keep the silly three points for a win system next season. Also, all payments must have 50% paid in the first six months and the rest over the next nine months. How can teams afford to do that? I'm sure Wolves are still paying us for Andy Gray.

That's just showing off. On the front page a lad from Queen Mary's sixth form has just broken the world record for doing the Rubik's cube one-handed. Richard Hodson did it in just one minute 22.51 seconds. Have to see if Asif can beat that.

Thursday 25th February

7:42pm: How does Asif manage to do his History homework so fast? I've been working on this for three nights now. Need to get it done before 9pm. Three things I like to watch at the same time: *Call*

My Bluff, Shoestring and *Shelley*. Mark is out so he's set the video to record *Shoestring*. So do I watch *Call My Bluff* with my parents or watch *Shelley* on my portable? Shelley's baby is six weeks old now. According to the description of today's episode in the paper. Six weeks is a very important milestone for new fathers. It's officially the day that "conjugal rights" return. It says that the newborn's non-stop crying means Shelley must call the doctor out. Unfortunately, a locum that he doesn't know comes instead. Confusion seems to happen as a double-glazing salesman arrives at the same time. I guess he thinks the double-glazing salesman is the doctor. Hardly seems worth watching now I've read all that. I'll watch Frank Muir doing *Call My Bluff* instead. I'm sure they make some of those words up. That is if I get this History homework done. Why did I let my desires for Miss Farrington talk my third-year self into doing History? I am sick of analysing the Industrial Revolution. This jenny must be dizzy with all this spinning.

Guess Maggie is reversing the Industrial Revolution now. The front page of tonight's *Express & Star* includes several foundries making redundancies. Looks like she's investing in transport, though. A staggering £30million has been put aside to build a new superhighway through parts of the Black Country. That's 20 Bryan Robsons! It's going to be a fast road that goes through Bilston. Past the derelict steelworks where Grandad used to work.

Not sure Tony Morley did enough on Tuesday night to convince Ron Greenwood. He had his moments but got taken off for Woodcock midway through second half. Easy 4-0 win for England. We looked good. Can't believe that Northern Ireland have qualified for the World Cup Finals. Apart from Pat Jennings and maybe Martin O'Neill, they've got nobody. How can Chris Nicholl still be playing for them at 36? It would be like England bringing back Alan Ball. Mind you, Noel Brotherton looks even older even though he's only mid-20s. He's got a receding hairline to compete with my dad. Hope I don't inherit that.

Should have accepted Asif's offer of finishing this History essay. Miss working with Wendy McGregor on our History homework. Not that we actually got much homework done. It's easy without the complication of trying to understand the female brain. I can concentrate on the important things. Like my O levels, getting Villa to Rotterdam and helping my mate Spud work through his grief. I think Miss Farrington was unfair with the comment in my report, "Jonathan is easily distracted". Should I tell Dad that I really don't like the new pickled onion flavoured crisps he keeps putting in my lunchbox?

Friday 26th February

1:10pm: 'They can't cane us anymore without our parents agreeing'. Noddy was filling us in on the news that corporal punishment in schools was changing. Some European Court has decided that beating schoolchildren against their parents' wishes is a violation of the Human Rights Convention. They have been battling for four years. Seems now it's up to the parents. Knowing Noddy's dad, he would probably insist on extra strikes of Noddy's buttocks if the school requested permission from him. I'm pretty sure that nobody at our school, since it opened in 1978, had been caned. Don't recall even seeing a cane in the Headmistress's office. I guess the company that makes school canes will be disappointed by this new ruling.

Finally finished my History essay with five minutes to spare before the lesson. It's still four pages shorter than Asif's. Hope Miss Farrington marks mine before she sees Asif's. If not, I'll be up against a high bar. What does Wendy McGregor want?

'Jonathan, can I ask you something in private?' Wendy is being mysterious. I agree and go into the corridor with my former love interest.

'I don't want to upset you, but…..' Wendy's opening prepared me for bad news. 'Do you mind if I go out with Oliver Watkins? He asked me yesterday'. She was seeking my permission!

7:42pm: This is the future then. 3D TV. Two sets of glasses between the four of us. Well, cardboard shaped glasses with coloured plastic over the areas where our eyes go. We are about to witness the first ever 3D broadcast in Britain. These red/green 3D glasses, given away in the *TV Times,* are going to let us see the picture coming out of the telly. TV makers Philips are going to show us footage shot in Holland that will be in 3D. Obviously only black and white but soon this might even work in colour. Mum is struggling to balance her 3D glasses on top of her glasses. I am a little disappointed it only lasted a few minutes. It wasn't all that clear either. Think it will be a long time before *Coronation Street* is in 3D. Imagine Stan Ogden coming out of the telly.

Saturday 27th February

2:58pm: Need Kenny Swain fit for Wednesday. Hope Mark Jones does okay on his debut today. At least we always beat Coventry City. Doris is feeling confident. She thinks it will be 4-0. Bushy eyebrow man is saying that it's odds-on now that John Toshack is taking over next week. Seems he knows somebody whose uncle is one of the match-day stewards.

That wasn't supposed to happen! Garry Thompson putting them ahead. He's a player I wouldn't mind seeing at Villa. Be a good understudy to Peter Withe. Bet Jimmy Hill is celebrating that goal. There's only two minutes gone. So much for Doris's prediction.

Must be a penalty! That was a blatant push on Shaw. Come on, ref. Steve Austin has no doubts. Yes, ref's given it.

Sid Cowans never misses from the spot. Five minutes gone and two goals. Well, Jimmy Hill wanted entertainment.

Mark Jones is playing well. Another good cross in. Nodded down by Peter. Has to be! Gary Gary Shaw!! What a game!

Sunday 28th February

2:20pm: 'He had to go for that', Randy agrees with the referee for sending Garry Thompson off as we watch the highlights on *Star Soccer*. 'An important win. We can concentrate on Europe now'.

Watching the game back I'm surprised how on top we were. Should have won by more than 2-1. Even against ten men, I was nervous towards the end yesterday. Nice that Randy came for Sunday lunch. Even though he dipped his tie in the full Eternal Beau gravy boat. Randy is quite excited because he's starting a new job tomorrow. He's joining a growing industry. He's going to work at the Job Centre. Only three days a week at the moment, but it's a start.

'I am working Wednesday but I should be home to listen to the second half', Randy reminded me of the fact the game in Russia was kicking off at 5pm our time. Randy will be driving home from work during the first half. He's still not brave enough to turn the radio on while his driving. He did try it on Radio Four the other week but quickly had to pull over when the play got too exciting.

I'll be home from school in plenty of time to listen to the game. I think if we don't lose by more than one, we'll be in a good position. An away goal would be good. A Tony Morley special maybe.

Wolves did well to beat Ipswich yesterday. They're still in the bottom three, but it gives them a chance. Ron Saunders' first real game for Birmingham didn't go well. Beaten 3-1 at Southampton. Lawrie McMenamy's side are now four points clear at the top. Swansea are second. Would be a shock if one of them won the title.

225

I wonder if Swansea are allowed to represent England in the European Cup. Good to see we are the top West Midlands club.

Was I right to say that I was happy for Wendy to go out with cheesy-grin Oliver Watkins? Don't think I really had a chance. Just hope she doesn't want the three of us to hang out together. I'm officially off the market until Villa get knocked out of the European Cup.

End of February Top of Division One

1.	Southampton	Pl: 28 Po: 53	+13
2.	Swansea City	Pl: 27 Po: 49	+ 6
3.	Manchester United	Pl: 26 Po: 47	+19
4.	Liverpool	Pl: 25 Po: 45	+24
13.	**Aston Villa**	**Pl: 27 Po: 33**	**-3**

Villa February League Results

1st Sunderland (h) 1-0 Won (Geddis)
6th Manchester United (a) 1-4 Lost (Geddis)
10th Southampton (h) 1-1 Draw (Withe)
17th Tottenham Hotspur (h) 1-1 Draw (Withe)
20th Birmingham City (a) 1-0 Won (Withe)
27th Coventry City (h) 2-1 Won (Cowans, Shaw)

Villa February FA Cup Results

13th Tottenham Hotspur (a) 0-1 Lost

Chapter Nine

March 1982

1:26pm: Mr Walker is never wrong. That's madness! How can they change kick-off time the day before a game? Mr Walker says that Dynamo Kiev have brought the game forward two hours tomorrow. Now it is 5pm their time, not 7pm. Due to poor floodlighting. Seems that they are two hours ahead of us. This means the game will kick-off at 3pm. When I'm supposed to be in Metalwork. I need to think how I'm going to listen to the game.

Tucker is going on about how brill the new TV football drama was yesterday. It was good. Theme tune was ace. Didn't see much football though. Might be a made-up Fourth Division club but still looking forward to the next episode of *Murphy's Mob*. Haystacks says it is all filmed at Watford's Vicarage Road ground. Think it's trying to teach kids that they shouldn't be football hooligans. Seems a bit like a footballing *Grange Hill*.

6:45pm: Mr Walker was right. Villa are really cross about the kick-off change. It's on the back page of the paper. They're saying the floodlights are not good enough. How can that suddenly be the case? Tony Barton says if they had known about the earlier kick-off, they would have arranged to fly back to Birmingham straight after the game instead of leaving the next day. Seems the hotel they are staying in is of very poor standard. He describes it as YMCA-style and third-rate. They have taken their own supply of food: 150 fillet steaks, breakfast cereal and bacon with them. Looks like both Allan Evans and Kenny Swain are major doubts.

Robert Maxwell, chairman of Oxford United, has decided not to sue Wolves over poaching their manager, Ian Greaves. Maxwell has now appointed former Blues manager, Jim Smith, so I think Oxford got the better of the deal. Says that Blues have swapped Frank Worthington with Leeds. Blues have taken someone named Byron Stevenson in exchange. I thought Worthington was their best player. Perhaps Ron Saunders has only joined the Blues to deliberately relegate them.

Tomorrow I'll have to borrow Mark's small radio. It will fit in my blazer pocket. If I take Grandad's earpiece I can listen to the commentary during Metalwork. I can feed the cable up my blazer sleeve and into my left ear. I'll use the 206 medium wave frequency for Radio WM instead of the FM. If I do FM, I need to put the aerial up and that would be a dead giveaway. Hopefully I can run to the bus stop during half-time.

Wednesday 3rd March

12:44pm: Haystacks has decided he's not seeing his dad anymore. He'll have to go to Albion games on his own. Big news is that Hastings found out last night that his dad is the dad of the toddler. The small boy belonging to his dad's new girlfriend is his half-brother. The affair was going on a lot longer than Haystacks or his mum had known.

Tucker is trying to cheer Haystacks up. He's just announced that he's got a video recording of Erika Roe's streak at Twickenham in the England v Australia rugby match in January. His dad had recorded the whole game on a 180 tape. It's not even recorded on long player.. So, it can be paused in colour. Generous Tucker is offering to bring it in for Haystacks tomorrow. We all want to see it though. We agree a rota. Asif will be last as he's only just joined the Local Gang.

Spud is struggling with his sister Valerie. She's stayed on to look after him and his dad after the funeral. It's only supposed to be temporary, but Spud feels she's taking over. She forced him to turn his Gary Numan tape down yesterday. Carrie Carrington rang the house and Spud's sister said he was unable to take the call because he was still eating his pudding. Valerie is even forcing Pete to have three baths a week.

Difficult seeing both Haystacks and Spuds struggling so much. What can I do to help? Haystacks doesn't like going to the football on his own. He doesn't make friends like I've done with Doris, Penny and bushy eyebrow man. My suggestion is that Spud and I should go with Scott Hastings to the West Brom v Coventry FA Cup quarter-final on Saturday. Villa are away at West Ham so I can go. We can also pay on the day on the terracing. Haystacks doesn't think it will be a sellout, but we can go early just in case. Last time I went to a match at The Hawthorns was our 0-0 draw last season. When I went with Tucker and his annoying little brother Sammy.

2:53pm: Rubbish reception. I guess it's a long way to Russia. The Americans are probably stopping any satellite links leaving the USSR. Spud is on lookout for Mr Harper. I'm balancing the radio just under my armpit. Quite an annoying squeak on the transmission. Pretty sure that's Brian Little co-commentating.

Sounds like Kenny Swain is playing. Think Andy Blair is playing centre-half. Here comes Mr Harper. Need to get back to working on my clamp. Oh no, I've pulled the headphone lead out. The whole table can hear the crackling commentary. Spud starts to whistle to cover the noise as I quickly turn the volume dial, initially making it louder before turning it down. Mr Harper is loitering. He knows something is happening. Come on, I need to get back to the match.

No idea if any goals. Come on, Brian, tell us the score. Sounds like the Kiev crowd is making lots of noise. Keep losing the tuning. All I keep hearing is that Blokhin's name. I'm sure he plays for the national team. No mention of any Villa forwards. Good to finally find out it's still goalless. Must be nearly 15 minutes gone now. Where's Colin Gibson?

Asif is at the door to the Metalwork room. He's mouthing something towards me. Think he's asking me for the score. What's all that cheering? Is it a goal? It's gone quiet. The reception has gone again. This is impossible. It's back. Blokhin has hit the post. Great save by Jimmy Rimmer now. We need to get the ball off them.

Chance for Tony Morley. Go on Tony …

'Stadler! Turn that radio off now! This is a place for craftsmen, not listening to rubbish pop music', Mr Harper shouts in my ear without the headphone piece inserted.

4:06pm: I can't get any reception at all now on Mark's crappy radio. This bus needs to get me home quickly. No idea what the score is in Sebastopol. Asif is trying FM now and holding the radio out of the upstairs bus window. They'll be into the second half now.

4:50pm: That's it. We come away unscathed. Sounds like we rode our luck. Didn't get the away goal, but I'm happy with no goals. Sounds like Gary Shaw had a great chance late on. Everyone saying how amazing Blokhin was. Guess I'll get to see him first-hand in two weeks' time. I think getting my lucky radio on for last 20 minutes helped. Asif was sitting on my bed listening too. He still had his school bag round his neck. Think he was even more nervous than me.

9:45pm: Must put my portable on quietly as Mum doesn't think I should stay up to watch *Midweek Sports Special* on a school night. Pity the European games aren't on *Sportsnight* as that's already started. I'll watch the end of *Minder* first then go upstairs.

11:45pm: Can't believe they didn't show any highlights from the Villa game. They said it was a good result though. Liverpool seemed to make hard work to beating CSKA Sofia. Only 1-0 at Anfield. They beat them 5-0 last season. At least they didn't concede an away goal. Looks like Bayern Munich are as good as in the semi-finals. They won 2-0 away. Two West German international stars, Breitner and Rummenigge, scored the goals.

Tottenham did well in the Cup Winners' Cup. They beat West German team Frankfurt 2-0. And Dundee United won 2-0 in the UEFA Cup. Good night all round for the British teams. None of us conceded any goals. Need to turn my brain off now and stop thinking about the football. Got a Maths test tomorrow. I'll make sure I'm sitting near Asif.

Friday 5th March

9:13am: Fellow Villa fan Julie Duggan is very chatty this morning about our performance on Wednesday. She saw an item on *Central News* yesterday about the broken toilets and the cockroaches in the rolls in the hotel we had to stay in. For a girl she seems quite knowledgeable about football. She even seems to get the offside rule. It's like talking to a boy. I guess in 1982 girls can like football too. Doris's daughter Penny in the Trinity Road talks a lot of sense. Odd that I haven't spent more time with Julie Duggan. We even went to the same primary school. To be fair she's always seemed a bit scary. She plays quite a lot of sport and used to be top scorer in the netball team. Mainly because she was goal shooter and in netball there is this unfair rule that only certain players are allowed to score.

Julie Duggan has always been quite muscley. She once beat Noddy in an arm-wrestle. Wouldn't call Julie pretty but she can look nice from certain angles, in the right light. I've just never really got to know her. No idea why she supports the Villa.

1:05pm: A new school rule is in. It seems rather harsh. Jock McGinn announces that all radios are now banned from all classrooms. They can be brought to school but must be kept in lockers and can only be listened to in the playground or the Common Room. Spud gives me a knowing look, but none of the others realise that I am the culprit here. Instead, they are complaining about this infringing on their home rights. Walkmans are being banned as well. There will be a distinct lack of pop music now in our school.

Friday 5th March

3:19pm: Feels odd being at The Hawthorns when the Villa aren't playing here. Feels like I am being unfaithful. I guess worse for Spud. Albion are Wolves' rivals. Think Spud is just glad to have escaped his sister Valerie. He's hoping she's going back home tomorrow. His dad is as desperate for her to leave as Spud is. Think Spud's dad wants to be left alone to grieve for his wife. Spud said his dad was cross yesterday; Valerie started to sort through his mum's clothes. Guess she was only trying to help.

Surprised the place isn't packed for an FA Cup quarter-final. Getting wet here on the terrace. Spud is oddly joining in with some of the Albion songs. Including the anti-Villa one. Need to try to find out how Villa are doing at West Ham. There's always some bloke with a transistor. I know on the half-time scoreboard they'll be the "H" score. Don't want to wait that long.

Wow! That was a cracking goal. A Cyrille Regis special. He hits the ball so hard. I've never seen Haystacks jump so high. Even when we had our basketball team. Rain really coming down now.

Typical, our view is now blocked by two umbrellas. At least one is a clear one.

I'm sure I heard that old bloke say, "sodding Villa are winning". Probably best to not look too interested. Nearly half-time now. Hold on, the old bloke who said Villa were winning is now doing a high five with the bloke next to him.

Can't believe Spud has just lit a fag. His mum has recently died of cancer and here he is smoking. Doesn't he know smoking causes cancer? I don't think Mrs Hogan smoked, but I know Spud's dad smoked in the house.

We are drawing 1-1. Haystacks said that a chap in the bogs told him West Ham equalised with a Ray Stewart penalty. I don't believe it. It's the 1980 quarter-final all over again. Bet this one wasn't a penalty either. Why does nobody save blooming Ray Stewart penalties? No goals in Wolves' game at Ayresome Park. I joke with Spud that Bosco Jankovic might score in the second half.

'He doesn't play for 'Boro anymore', font of football knowledge Scott Hastings announces. 'After winning your lot the league, he was going to give up football to become a lawyer. Instead, he went to play for some French team'. I had no idea. Anyway the 14 Villa players and Ron Saunders won us the league, not Bosco Jankovic.

I'm getting soaked. Missing my Trinity Road. Even though I still get drenched there when it rains. The old bloke with the radio is cheering again. Corner here for Albion. Right in front of us. How did that go in? Nice skill by Gary Owen but Jim Blythe shouldn't be letting that in. Even on this muddy pitch. Suppose I had better look like I'm celebrating. Coventry haven't been very good. Albion are heading for the FA Cup semi-final. Perhaps they'll hold it at Villa Park. They always have one semi at our great ground.

Sunday 7ᵗʰ March 1982

6:18pm: What is the point of *Stars on 45*? If I wanted to hear a medley of Stevie Wonder hits, then I'd buy his album. The charts shouldn't have songs that aren't original. Now *A Town Called Malice* by The Jam, that's more like it. Odd name for a town, but good tune. Suppose there are a lot of towns with funny names. Aston, Willenhall and Ipswich are probably as odd as Malice.

Albion must have a good chance of winning the cup now. It's them or Tottenham. Pity Spurs won at Chelsea yesterday. Two Second Division teams left. QPR and Leicester City. Shrewsbury put on a spirited display against Leicester before eventually losing 5-2. I bet the semi-final draw is fixed to keep the First Division teams apart. The FA would prefer a Spurs v West Brom final. Wembley would be empty if it was QPR against Leicester. Although Albion was nowhere near sold out yesterday.

Glad Peter Withe got us that 2-2 draw yesterday. We're still unbeaten under Barton. Pity only one of the games has been a win. A draw is not as good with this daft points system. I'm glad Coventry are out of the cup. It would have been unbearable had "Chinny" Hill's lot got to Wembley.

"Who broke my heart, you did, you did". Naff lyrics but I do like *Poison Arrow*. ABC didn't spend very long choosing their band name. Just chose the start of the alphabet. Unless it's named after the Wolverhampton cinema. Don't think they are local.

I wonder if any of the girls in our year will end up being a *Centrefold*. Probably my favourite song out now. Never heard of any other J Geils Band songs. It's up to number five this week. I think Tight Fit will still be number one this week. Appropriate "the lion sleeps.." with Aston Villa beings the lions. Guess this season we're sleeping a bit too much. Always sounds like "win away" in the song. Perhaps I could make the words fit the mighty Villa. I could start singing it in the Trinity. Get Doris, Steve Austin and Tim to join in. I hope Haircut 100 aren't number one. I can't stand them.

Thursday 11ᵗʰ March

12:39pm: More kids in the library than usual this lunchtime. Must be because there were no school meals. Seems silly no dinners when it's the teachers who want more money not the dinner ladies. Seems they are working to rule. Which is why Spud's school match tonight has been cancelled. Grace is helping me with my English Lit homework. Trying to tell me why Simon is the visionary of the group in *Lord of the Flies*. She says he's like me. Is that a compliment? I suppose I watch *Tomorrow's World* more than the rest of the Local Gang. Still think the *Jetsons* cartoon shows the future. It was produced in the 60s but several things have already come true. Not sure we'ill see aerocars with a transparent bubble top before the year 2000 though. I am trying to take in what Grace is explaining, but hard to concentrate when I'm remembering the joys of caressing that boob. I'm still determined to stay off girls whilst Villa mount their European Cup challenge. Would that get derailed if the chance to again touch Grace Taylor's nipples popped up?

Oliver Watkins and Wendy are huddled closely together at the next table. Bet she's sharing her latest copy of *Look-In* with loverboy. Will he be allowed to kiss her? I'll snuggle up close to Grace. Maybe make Wendy McGregor a bit jealous. Grace isn't retreating. Our arms are touching now.

An excited Asif hurries in and plonks himself in the seat next door.

'You'll never believe it. We have finally managed to make a test-tube baby in the West Midlands', Asif seems more excited about this news than the rest of us. 'They are keeping the baby's identity a secret. It's a boy'. I do get how a test-tube baby works though. We had to explain it to Noddy a few months back. He thought they stayed in the test tube. Haystacks did try to kid him that every month they got moved to a bigger test tube. The reason for Asif's unexpected excitement was, apparently, because at his old school the test-tube baby pioneer from Cambridge had come and given them a talk. I don't think he'll be coming to our school. He seems to have made quite an impression on Asif and is the main reason Asif wants to be a doctor. He even remembers his name was Patrick Steptoe. I wonder if he was Harold's uncle. Be funny if when he met infertile fathers, he said, "you dirty old man".

7:48pm: Thanks, Simon Bates. That's all I need. Haircut 100 on *Top of the Pops*. It was bad enough having to sit through that World Figure Skating Championships after they shortened *Nationwide*. That was dancing, not ice skating. Torvill and Dean are no Robin Cousins. Don't know why my Mum was wowing about them. She won't be so happy when Kenny Everett comes on next. You can guarantee within two minutes she'll be saying "turn that rubbish off". She'll be wanting to turn over to watch that boring Russell Harty instead. Hope this new Channel Four station that's coming soon has more programmes like *The Kenny Everett Television Show*.

Saturday 13th March

2:19pm: Appropriate that Gordon Cowans is on the cover against Wolves. After he scored two goals against them last time. I'm not normally here before bushy eyebrow man. Must be because I came with Mark. He certainly drives quicker than Mr Hill. Quite nice to come the Aston Expressway for a change. See the ground in all its glory. Hope Mark doesn't regret turning that "mind your car gov" lad down. He didn't look happy. Might have been better if Mark had agreed to pay him afterwards, then said no when he got back to the car. It's definitely a Wolves coloured car. I felt quite conspicuous in it. Was nice to walk through grounds of Aston Hall for a change. Mark insisted I walk four paces behind him. It'll be hell travelling back with him if we lose. Defeat is unthinkable. Told Asif that if we lose, we'll have to keep a very low profile at school on Monday. We shouldn't lose. Players warming up look up for it. They've had a week without any games for once. Where is Peter Withe? I've seen eleven players but no Withey. We could do with no injuries today. Need to have everyone fit for Kiev on Wednesday.

'No Peter Withe then', Doris greets me with team news. 'Donovan number nine. At least Evo is back'.

The normal crew of fans all seem very relaxed. They haven't got the family and friends pressure that I have resting on this league game. Spud was quite cocky about it yesterday. He's here with his dad. They're in one of the posh executive boxes in the North Stand. A mate of Spud's dad is a Villa fan with some big company. They've hired a 16-seater box. They get a 4-course meal. Can't wear their colours. Spud is going to have to wear a shirt and tie. He says he's going to pretend to be 18 so that he gets one of the cigars and a glass of brandy provided. The only time we see brandy in our house is when we light the Christmas pud. Pete says he'll still celebrate every Wolves goal. At least Andy Gray isn't playing. Think their forward line will be Richards, Eves and Clarke.

Wolves seem to have players who been around for ages. Willie Carr, Kenny Hibbitt, Derek Parkin, Geoff Palmer and John Richards have played for them as long as I've known. I thought they were selling Willie Carr.

Can't believe there isn't more people here. It's a big local derby. It's not even half-full. Grandad used to talk about days when there used to be over 50,000 here.

3:42pm: Great goal! Tony Morley's back to his best since Tony Barton became caretaker manager. Hope Ron Greenwood got one of his scouts here. Great knock-back by Gary Shaw. Two-nil. We are cruising. Mark is not going to be happy. They've had chances, but Jimmy is too good.

Bet Spud celebrated that one. How can we let Wayne Clarke score against us? It's not like playing against his brother Allan. Wayne Clarke was born near our school. Wake up, Villa. We can't give them another chance. Doris is livid. She almost choked on her aniseed ball. We shouldn't have given the ball away. Didn't they hear Tim shouting "Time. Time"?

Looks like the reserves are scoring goals for fun in the Central League. Programme says they have scored 24 in 5 games. That's virtually 5 a game. Terry Donovan has scored 18 in 18 reserve games this season. That means with his 6 first-team goals, including today's, he's scored 24. Maybe he's better than I thought. Tony Barton is praising the reserves as well in his piece. He seems quite pleased that crowds have been around the 25,000 mark since he took over. He thinks that's good in the current financial situation.

That's pants! The Swansea game that was the day before my birthday has been cancelled. The last day of me being just 14. It's because we are hosting the Spurs v Leicester FA Cup semi-final. Why do they always put us at home when semi-finals are on? They know that as we have the best ground, it's going to be used. They haven't even found a new date yet for the Swansea game. I'm sure that's me on the top picture of Dennis shooting against Coventry. Just above the "D" in MIDLAND BANK. Can see Doris's big hat as well. Emlyn Hughes is doing better than I expected as manager. He won 8 out of 8 games for Rotherham in February. Took them from 20th to 4th. Surely they can't end up in the First Division next season. Who's ever heard of Rotherham United in the First Division? Maybe Emlyn will end up managing Liverpool one day. Or Wolves. Alan Brazil scored a hat-trick in just five minutes against Southampton. He ended up scoring five.

That's loads of money. Manchester City season tickets have gone up to £90. Chairman Peter Swales is trying to defend the price rise. He's saying Maine Road is one of the best grounds in the country. Well, Maine Road isn't hosting a semi-final. I thought he was old. Derek Parkin signed for Wolves in 1968. When I was one!

The "Letters" section in the programme is always one of the funniest sections. Some moaning old codgers write in. The kind who write to Barry Took about the BBC programmes. Tom Hassall, 38 Pingil Close, Pelsall, Staffs, WS4 7AJ is having a moan about the pre-match pop-music. Tom wants the five minutes before kick-off to be music-free. Let real fans soak up the atmosphere and "enjoy the repartee between rival fans".

Jimmy Rimmer and Gordon Cowans are now our only ever-present players this season. Couldn't imagine playing without Jimmy Rimmer.

Wow, that would be amazing. The Villa Cubs are going to start letting cubs be mascots at games, from Wednesday. Every game a cub will be chosen at random to lead the Villa players out. They get to walk on the Villa Park pitch. I must join the Villa Cubs. Perhaps that could be one of my birthday presents.

Nigel Spink is in focus on the back two pages. Don't know much about the Villa reserve goalkeeper. I know he has only played one game. Against Forest on Boxing Day in 1979. Seems happy being the number two number one. An easy way to make a living. Says that even in the reserves he rarely has to do anything because the Villa reserves are so good. He gets to sit on the bench in the European games. In the last ten months he has clocked up 11,000 miles. Guess he hopes Jimmy will retire in about four years' time.

Players starting to come out for the second half. I'd forgotten Liverpool were playing Spurs today in the Milk Cup Final. If it's a draw, then the replay is here on Monday 29th March. I'll ask Doris if she's heard the score.

Spurs winning 1-0. Archibald the scorer. I bet Ray Clemence is enjoying that one. At least Kenny Bellington won't be happy.

4:36pm: This is too nerve-wracking. We must hold out. Been 2-1 for ages. John Richards just went close. We deserve to win. Need to fast-forward time to twenty to five. Come on, Villa. Bushy eyebrow man saying Ronnie Whelan has equalised at Wembley. As long as no one equalises here.

Wolves want a push on Wayne Clarke. He went down very easy. Go on! Gary Shaw has done it! Three-one to the Villa. Now I can relax.

5:03pm: At least the car is still there. Mark is in a foul mood. Thinks it was a blatant push on Clarke and that Wolves should have had a penalty when Des Bremner pushed old Derek Parkin. I'm staying quiet until we're safely back at home. We've beaten Wolves four times this season. A clean sweep. I can go to school Monday morning with a spring in my step. Spud might well have had his fancy dinner and liqueurs, but we've taken six points off them this season. We're now 13 points ahead of them with 13 games to play.

We sit silently in the traffic waiting to join the M6. Mark turns on the radio. There's commentary of extra-time in the Milk Cup Final. Looks like Villa Park will not be needed this time. Ian Rush has just made it 3-1. Looks like they are retaining their cup. Puts them one behind our record three League Cup wins.

Tuesday 16th March

2:55pm: This just isn't working. Asif is far too clever for us. He's bored. Feels the teachers just aren't pushing him. Some of the lads in Chemistry are getting quite brassed off with Asif answering all the questions. He didn't help himself by saying Ian Matson's answer was stupid. If he goes on like this, he'll get his head pushed down one of the bogs. There are only so many times I can play the "he's new" card. Even the other lads in the Local Gang are struggling with him. Noddy thinks we should give him his final warning. Tell him one more put-down of any of us and he's off. I seem to have to be the mediator. I've been elected as the person to have a quiet word with Asif.

'Are you going tomorrow, Jonathan? Wish I was going.' Surprisingly Julie Duggan is being nice to me. 'I think we can do it. Get to the semi-finals'.

Wednesday 17ᵗʰ March

8:44am: European Cup quarter-final day. Asif seems more excited than me about our game tonight. I'm more nervous. I didn't get much sleep. Kept imagining Blokhin scoring past Jimmy Rimmer.

Trying to tell Asif he needs to cool it a bit, to not appear so keen. Not sure he's really getting it. Perhaps I ended up being too blunt. Telling Asif he needs to reign it in or he's out the gang and to lay off Emily Martins. Think I've annoyed him now. Asif looks upset. He can't get off the bus now! We are not at school yet. Come back, Asif. Should I go after him?

9:05am: Jock McGinn doesn't look up. So, when he calls Asif Mahmood's name in the register, I foolishly shout "here". Spud gives me a look, but nobody else seems to realise. I didn't even disguise my voice. No idea where Asif has disappeared to. I do feel responsible. Where could he have gone?

12:55pm: Still no sign of Asif. Not sure what I should do. I can't risk answering his name again on the afternoon register. But if he's suddenly absent, how do we explain him being here this morning? Noddy, Tucker, Haystacks and Spud all seem to think this is my problem. They think square Asif deserves all that's coming to him. So much for "All for one. One for all". I don't need this mess now.

Enough to think about with a finely balanced European Cup quarter-final tonight. Perhaps I should own up. I'm not the one who's done a bunk.

Jock won't fall for it twice. I'll just stay quiet.

'Mahmood?' McGinn calls Asif's name.

'Here', Spud surprisingly answers. Trying to throw his voice and making Asif sound a little girly.

'Your balls will drop one day Mahmood', Mr McGinn jokes about the Asif high-pitched response. Others start to become aware that Asif is missing. Dave Ports goes to put his hand up to inform Jock of the absentee, but his arm is quickly wrestled to the ground by Haystacks.

6:21pm: This is new territory even for Mr Hill. For the first time this season I can feel his nerves. I guess at his time of life he didn't expect to see Villa so close to the semi-final of Europe's elite trophy. All level from the first leg. This really was our big chance. The radio might have settled us down a bit, but instead Howard Hill for once drives us with the radio firmly turned off. He asks unimportant questions about my O level studies. Asks about my parents. Everything apart from what really matters. He seems to be deliberately avoiding the most important question. Can we beat Dynamo Kiev?

7:21pm: Too nervous to even read my special souvenir programme with the odd pink and yellow cover. I hold it tightly trying to take in the enormity of the next 90 minutes. Maybe 120 minutes. Perhaps it will go to penalties.

Doris hasn't spoken. Even Steve Austin looks deep in thought.

7:35pm: What a start! A superb solo goal by golden boy Gary Shaw. Maybe it went through the keeper's hands, but Gary still beat him well at his near post. This is going to happen. We can do this.

What sort of thicko does bushy eyebrow man think I am? I know that if they equalise, then they are winning on the away goal rule.

8:15pm: Our first corner at last. Be a perfect time to get a second. Right on stroke of half-time. Come on, Gordon. See if you can find Allan Evans' head. That'll do. Ken McNaught rises high and heads the ball down passed the Kiev keeper. Two-nil. Two blooming nil. I'm being bear hugged by Doris. This is it. We're on our way to the European Cup semi-final. I can't believe it. Please don't mess it up now.

Hope Dad is going to record *Sportsnight*. This occasion needs marking. We're in control. Nothing silly in the second half.

9:43pm: That's a major shock. I never saw that coming. It's all down to us now. We're England's sole remaining team in the 1982 European Cup. CSKA Sofia have beaten Liverpool. Two-nil. They have knocked them out 2-1 on aggregate. If England are to keep the European Cup on our green and pleasant land for a sixth year, then it's up to Aston Villa FC.

Mr Hill says our 2-0 win was never in doubt. I think even he is starting to believe that we could yet go all the way to Rotterdam. Is it too early to ask if he'll take me? Bayern Munich, Anderlecht or Liverpool's victors CSKA Sofia will await us in the semi-final. Be good if we were at home for the second leg. The atmosphere tonight was incredible but would be even better if it was the game that took us to the final. Still can't believe Liverpool lost. The European Champions and League Cup winners out. While Villa go marching on. What a performance. Oleg Blokhin didn't have a sniff. Mr Hill lets me hang my scarf out of his car window. This is a very special night.

11:00pm: I can't believe nobody bothered to record *Sportsnight*. How hard is it to press the OTR button? Dad was even watching it. Must wait until *Midlands Today* tomorrow night to see Gary and Ken's goals. They didn't even show the goals at the end after the boxing. Instead, they show Spurs going through in the Cup Winners' Cup. We are the only British teams left in Europe now. Dundee United blew their two-goal first-leg lead.

Now Mum wants a serious talk with me. At after 11pm. She's never awake this late. It must be serious. Not serious enough to interrupt *Sportsnight* or to have a tannoy announcement at the game. That would have been crazy. No way I'd be leaving the game in the European Cup quarter-final. Still, must be a bit serious. Nobody is crying, so nobody has died. Maybe I should check on the rabbit. Dad is joining in now. They've obviously planned what they're going to say. Frantically trying to think what I might have done wrong. I did drink some milk straight out of the bottle in the fridge, but I'm sure I didn't leave any evidence.

11:45pm: That's so unreasonable. How do my parents expect me to stay away from Asif? We catch the school bus together. We're in the same class. We play footie in the same park. It's not very Christian. Can't believe he was caught by the police again. Feel a bit to blame, after our talk this morning ended with him not going to school. I'd forgotten that Spud and I covered for him in front of old Jock. Do I need to confess that to my parents? The school are bound to get involved. Why was Asif stealing from WH Smiths? If you're going to steal, there are shops with better stuff. Surprised he got caught. I wonder what they caught him stealing. Hope it wasn't a "How to be cool at school" book. I can't just desert him. Guess we'll have to go back to meeting in secret. How can my parents think he's a bad influence? I'm old enough to make my own decisions. Just because Asif is a thief doesn't mean I am going to become one. How can I sleep with this and Villa's victory whizzing around my head. I'm going to be knackered in the morning.

Friday 19th March

3:49pm: Three years and six months I've been at this school. Now for the first time I'm in detention. Can't believe it. Still don't think there was enough evidence. I suppose I deserved it. I had to own up. Jock McGinn was going to put the whole of 4MC in detention otherwise. Wendy McGregor looked at me with pleading eyes. She'd got a date with Oliver Watkins this evening, so was desperate not to be in detention. Truth was that I did pretend Asif was here on Wednesday. Mr and Mrs Mahmood came in yesterday. They had a long talk with Miss Thatcher and Jock. Asif is back today, but has been warned about his behaviour. The police say they aren't pressing charges, this time. We walked home from the bus stop separately. We did chat on the bus though. He says it wasn't my fault he went on the rob. Says he always does when he gets cross. That boy has got issues. Could have a whole episode about him on *Grange Hill*. He needs Mac from *Murphy's Mob* to take control of him.

Just me and the annoying third-year Patterson in detention. At least it's Miss Tully doing it. She's letting us do our homework. So not all bad. Downside is that I still don't know how the European Cup semi-final draw went. Hope we have avoided Bayern Munich. They've got half the West Germany team playing for them. Spud offered to wait for me. Told him it was okay. Think he felt bad for not owning up to the afternoon call. Silly both of us being in detention. Will have to walk home as the school bus has gone. Be time for tea by the time I get home.

5:29pm: Straight through the door and head for the *Express & Star*. Look at back page. There it is. Far right. I'll take that. "Villa face

Belgium Champs". Silly they put "Champs", everyone in this tournament are champions of their leagues. Anderlecht! At home first. That's a pity. Draw was in Zurich. I suppose Switzerland are neutral. So never any chance of foul play there. You can trust the Swiss. Bayern Munich are away first against CSKA Sofia. Be great if they got knocked out and we got to the final. Suppose CSKA must be good if they can beat Liverpool. Spurs have got Barcelona in Cup Winners' Cup.

They are still reporting on England cricketers who have gone on the rebel tour of South Africa. Glad that Ian Botham didn't go. Graham Gooch is 50 not out.

We might get a few days off school. Teachers are going to strike. Maggie won't give them the 12% pay rise they want. I bet if all teachers were on strike our Headmistress would still insist we came in. Just below the teacher strikes article it says MPs are going to vote on bringing back the death penalty. That's one way of stopping the strikes. I guess as I'm still aiming to be a teacher, as the job of Villa manager is unlikely, then I should be backing the strikers to get the 12%. Mum is in a union that doesn't strike. Not sure what the point of a non-striking union is. I suppose they can just act very disappointed.

Why do I never get to watch the programmes that Mary Whitehouse sees? She's always going on about the amount of sex on TV. Looks like she lost her legal battle today. Mary Whitehouse was charging a National Theatre director for gross indecency. His play *Romans in Britain* was apparently quite explicit. I guess it was on the stage, not TV. If it had been on TV, then Tucker would have definitely videoed it. Wonder when it's my turn to get the Erica Roe tape? Probably get more people turning up to *Romans in Britain* now it's been condemned by the moral campaigner. I always get Mary Whitehouse mixed up with Barbara Woodhouse.

Saturday 20th March

1:52pm: This just isn't fair. Having to go and visit my mum's old college friend in Chesterfield, on a match-day. It we'd been at home they wouldn't have got me here. Mark avoided it because Wolves are at home to Swansea. Just because of my detention they have forced me into an afternoon of rock-hard homemade biscuits and weak Ribena. Wouldn't be so bad if their fit daughter Marie was here. Seems she got a better offer. She's out with her mates. The husband of my mum's friend has absolutely no understanding of football. He says he has no interest in watching 22 scruffy men chasing a leather ball around. Leather ball! What age is he living in? If I was at home now, I would be finding out the team. Surely this is the day we finally beat those tractor boys. Put Wark, Butcher and longhaired Mariner in their place. Guess my parents didn't trust me to be left home alone. They thought I would sneak off and see master-criminal Asif. Why has nobody told Mrs Robinson she can't cook? Even her custard has to be bitten into. Wish Dad didn't always have to sing that old song by Simon and Funky-something every time he greets her. She has such an inane giggle when he does it. They've also got this gigantic dog with a flatulence problem who slobbers all over me. I'm just not in the mood for this. I know they mean to be friendly.

3:45pm: Everyone is looking at the crocked spire on the cathedral. Mr Robinson has got his old camera out. Me, I'm looking at the clock on the spire. Quarter to four! It's half-time. I have no idea how the Villa are doing at Portman Road. Why aren't we at least by some shops where there could be a telly? I try suggesting a nice cake perhaps. Hoping to entice the group into the town to find a tea shop. One that was near Radio Rentals.

4:12pm: That plan backfired. We are now back at the Robinson's. I am sucking on one of Mrs Robinson's supposed sponge cakes and trying to taste even a smidgen of blackcurrant in this weak Ribena. I know from experience to decline any offers of a cup of tea. Still haven't recovered from the one Mrs Robinson served me three years ago. I'm sure I could have had her under the Trades Description Act. She hadn't even bothered to put the tea in a bag. It was loose floating around in the milky hot water. Perhaps I can hide this inedible cake in my jeans pocket? Or feed it to the smelly dog?

With cake in pocket, I have nipped to the bathroom. My plan is to take a wrong turn. Mistakenly end up in Marie's bedroom. I'm sure it's second on the left. If I'm lucky I'll find what I'm looking for. If I'm quiet, I might even get it working. Bingo, she's got one. It's just at the bottom of her bed. It's bigger than I expected. Now how do I turn it on?

'Jonathan, are you alright in there?' my concerned mum starts shouting at the bathroom door. I'm forced to retreat from Marie's room. Claiming I'd taken a wrong turn. Mum looks at me suspiciously. No idea what bizarre conclusion she's coming to for me being in Marie's bedroom. 'What's that bulge in your trousers?' I've been caught. Forced to reveal my hidden rock-like sponge cake. Mum smiles. Takes the uneaten cake. Opens her handbag and puts it with her own uneaten cake.

My mission to Marie's bedroom had been a failure. I hadn't managed to turn her TV on. I hadn't managed to find out if she had Ceefax. I hadn't been able to go to page 300 to find the latest Villa score.

4:41pm: 'I guess you'll be wanting to see how your football team did, young Jonathan', Mr Robinson states the bleeding obvious. My over animated response surprises even my dad who spills the cup of tea he's been nursing for the last half an hour.

Grandstand is on, the Teleprinter going already. This is torture. The results are slowly being typed on the screen. No order. The odd goal, but mostly results. "Leeds United 1, Nottingham Forest 1". It seems stuck on "4:43". Here comes another one. It's only a Scottish one. "Wolverhampton Wanderers 0", oh dear, "Swansea City 1". Still waiting on the Villa score. Six score draws so far. Here's the Albion score. One-one against the Blues. Haystacks will be disappointed by that. That's all Division One games out apart from us now. It's "4:47". What's going on? This is it ...."Ipswich 3", damn, "Aston Villa 1".

Totally gutted. Nobody else is even taking an interest. Dad is too busy dabbing tea off his shirt. Our first defeat since Ron left. We have lost to flipping Ipswich Town again. Five times in a row they've beaten us.

Sunday 21ˢᵗ March

8:24pm: This is the moment, Spud says, when they escape outside the dome. Then Jenny Agutter – Jessica 6 – takes her flimsy dress off. She certainly got that short green dress very wet and torn. You can see right through it. No undies at all. She's certainly grown up since the *Railway Children*. Wish more young ladies dressed like that. It's set in the future but looks like the kind of things they wore in the swinging 60s. Perhaps she burnt her bra. Wish I was that lizard. He's climbing right up. Well, I guess it's a male lizard. Shouldn't she have stripped off by now? Interesting concept having to be killed when you hit 30. I suppose by the time you turn 30 you'll have had all your fun anyway. It would mean I wouldn't make the year 2000 though. That would be a pity as we buried that time capsule at church.

'You won't see her boobs, perv. Not before the 9pm watershed'. Mark was obviously reading my mind. 'They'll cut all the nude bits out'. Mark seemed to know all about it. Bit unfair calling me "perv". 'In cinema this film was two hours long. They have knocked over five minutes off for the telly.' I bet the bloke who had to spend time cutting out the naughty bits had a fun time. I didn't know that the one-off *Charlie's Angel* was in this. She's hot as well.

Not surprised Logan is asking if he should take his clothes off when Farrah Fawcett invites him to lie on the table. She's Farrah Fawcett-Majors now, although Haystacks says he read in *The Sun* that all is not well between the Angel and the Bionic Man, Lee Majors. Spud said if she's back in the market that he wouldn't mind giving her a go. As if a Hollywood star like Farrah Fawcett would be seen dead in Willenhall market.

Wednesday 24th March

10:19am: A boring week with no football. Need to get my head round this Chemistry exam. Getting a good mark in this will help my chances of being in the top set next year, when it gets serious. I keep thinking about Jenny Agutter and that green piece of cloth.

"$Zn + 2HCl \rightarrow ZnCl2 + H2$", that's zinc and hydrochloric acid. Nasty stuff if you spill it. I remember what it did to Tucker's lucky ruler. H2 is hydrogen. How am I supposed to know what "The rate of the above reaction will be greatly increased by…" is? Guess process of elimination. Bit unfair having five multiple choice options. Asif is flying thorough his paper. I've told him not to put his hand up as soon as he's finished. He's going to wait until somebody else has finished first. Wendy McGregor is using her rubber a lot. I wonder how her date with Oliver "goody goody yum yum" Watkins went. I think it's A: "The Zinc is in powder form". Makes sense it would react quicker if it was in powder form instead of metal. Who's heard of powdered zinc? I'm going A. I haven't got time to read all the other options. It must be A. Grace Taylor would look great wearing just a green sheet with a belt.

12:48pm: With the rest of the Local Gang, including Asif, comparing our Chemistry answers. Checking them off against what Asif put. Spud didn't seem to have had his mind on it. He said he'd gone with "ABBA ACE DA DA CAB". Spud was delighted when Asif said he'd actually got five of them right. Not so pleased when

Asif told him if he'd put C for all of them, he would have got seven. You'd have thought the people writing the questions would try to spread out the letters better. Shocked Spud put "ABBA ACE"; he hates Abba.

Playing Knockout with Tucker in goal. Surprisingly Asif scores first. He does seem to be improving. Haystacks is next through having sent the ball through Tucker's legs.

'Can I join in?' We are all surprised to witness Julie Duggan asking for a game. At first, Spud dismisses her request. The feisty girl is having none of it. She runs towards him. Before he knows it, Julie Duggan has dispossessed Spud. He's not happy. Tackled by a girl. Noddy is the next one she beats. I'm not tackling a girl. Julie has a chance to shoot at goal. She strikes the ball. Her high-heeled shoe comes off and follows the trajectory of the Wembley Trophy. Tucker doesn't know which one to save. He takes evasive action and just ducks. Both the ball and the impractical shoe end up in the goal, between the jumpers. I guess Julie Duggan is through to the next round. That leaves Spud, Noddy and me. I'm determined not to be knocked out. The pride of the Villa behind me. Sadly, Spud then takes everything out on the ball. He kicks it so hard it sails through Tucker, through the goal and through the window in the Music Room. You'd have thought classrooms would have tougher glass than that.

The six of us are facing the music. Not the tuneful music of xylophones of the Music Room, but the wrath of Jock McGinn. Ball games at lunchtime are now going to be banned. All thanks to Spud. Interesting that Julie Duggan was nowhere to be seen. She quickly disappeared at the sound of the breaking glass. I am fearing detention number two. Jock is showing that unnerving kind nature again. If we help the caretaker to board up the window, then he'll forget all about it. This is very unJock-like. Maybe there's a new woman in his life. We've never been stupid enough to enquire about mad Jock's home life. Was there a Mrs McGinn? We all assumed he lived a life of celibacy. Like a mad monk.

'I'm going out with my new girlfriend tonight', Haystacks says out of the blue. This news prompts looks of surprise. What girlfriend? Was he back with Georgina Ramsey?

7:56pm: What's Brian up to in *Coronation Street*? He told Gail Tilsley he was working. Now he's on the loose in Cairo.

I didn't know there was football on tonight in *Sportsnight*. They are showing highlights of England playing Athletic Bilbao last night. At the ground where they will play their group games in the World Cup. I don't even know what the score was.

Still trying to work out how Haystacks met a sixth-former from Frank F Harrison. Thought he was spending all his time in his room. She doesn't even like football. He says she's nearly 18. Nearly old enough to vote. Why is she going out with a chubby 15-year-old? It makes no sense. He says she's learning to drive. Doing A levels in Physics, English Lit and French. Quite an odd combination. What's she got in common with Haystacks? She must be desperate.

9:48pm: They didn't show much of that. Bit of a non-event. I'm sure England let them equalise. One-one was probably the agreed score before they started. No Villa players. Decent free-kick worked between Keegan and Brooking. Strangest part was number of cigarettes that bloke on the Bilbao bench got through. You wouldn't catch Tony Barton having a crafty fag in the Villa dugout.

Saturday 27th March

11:23am: The end of an era. Feels like a part of my childhood is ending. The 146th and last episode of *Multi Coloured Swap Shop*. I never did get through on the phone to talk to Noel. Quite bizarre having Barry Took on, with Christmas tree tinsel wrapped round his neck. That was quite a funny joke from Ben. "What do you get if you cross the Atlantic with the Titanic?" Answer: "half-way".

The "Swap Trek" sketch was a bit cringe-worthy. Suppose they wanted to do something different to mark the last episode. John Craven as Mr Spock didn't really work. Feel sorry for John Craven. Has to do his *Newsround* every night and then they bring him back for a whole Saturday morning. Suppose Keith Chegwin is busy too. With this and *Cheggers Plays Pop*. Wonder which teams the presenters support? Maybe QPR, as it's filmed in Shepherd's Bush. That way they would have no problems getting to the game after they'd finished filming.

Interesting swap. Warren Parson is offering "Scalextric 300, with 2 Minis & BMW"; he wants "anything to do with snooker". Samantha Leonard wants "Sindy clothes + furniture" and is offering "Tomahawk bike". Assume the furniture is dolls' furniture.

Margo from the *Good Life* answering children's questions on the posh telephone. She looks oddly sexy in those knee-length black boots.

2:50pm: Five more minutes trying to learn these crazy Physics formulae before the game starts. They are all so similar. Why did Newton do so many laws? He could have just done one and then retired. Pressure is "F" over "A". Where "F" is force. What the hell is "A"?

Not sure we'll get much at Highbury. Both Mark Jones and Terry Bullivant playing. As well as Pat Heard in for Dennis Mortimer. No Pat Jennings for Arsenal. George Wood is a Scottish goalie. Hopefully he'll be rubbish.

Why do we need a third temperature scale? What sort of name is "Kelvin"? Bad enough old people still talking in Fahrenheit. At least on the weather they now do it in centigrade. Which is also called Celsius. Now we need "absolute Celsius" called after some bloke. I guess all I need to know is to add, or is it take away, 273.

Goal horn already! At Highbury! I'm worried. Right to be worried. Former Wolves player Alan Sunderland has given the Gunners the lead. It could be a long afternoon. Maybe I should continue with my Physics revision. Thinking my 15 predictions on Guess the Goals was a bit low. Walsall are losing at Newport County now.

4:16pm: The paperboy is early tonight. Might as well go down and get my *Roy of the Rovers* comic. Don't want to hear a fifth Arsenal goal. I thought when Morley equalised at 2-2 that we might win. Now suddenly we are 4-2 down. Could be a pounding. Not another goal horn!

At least we are showing some fight at 4-3. Nice to see Pat Heard score. Still no goals in the Coventry v Wolves game. Or at The Hawthorns. Thought Spurs would smash Haystacks' lot. With the goal Birmingham have scored and the three at Newport County, that makes eleven. Villa just need to score two more and both Wolves and Baggies let a goal in. Another goal! Come on Villa, let's be all square.

'And it's all square now' the presenter starts to say, and I start to jump. 'At Newport, Walsall have equalised and made it 2-2'. We're still 4-3 down. I go to the porch to pick up *Express & Star* and *Roy of the Rovers*. Wow, David Geddis is on the cover against Spurs at Wembley. Must be the Charity Shield. Says colour picture of Dennis Mortimer inside. Pity neither of them are playing today. I still think we're going to equalise. This team are fighters. They have the spirit of Ron Saunders.

Back page of the paper says that the two Ronnies are fighting. Ron Atkinson and Ronnie Allen it means. I wouldn't fancy Ronnie Corbett's chances in a fight with Ronnie Barker. They both want to sign Lawrie Cunningham from Real Madrid. Ronnie Allen wants to bring him back to the Albion. His former boss wants to take him to Old Trafford. I wouldn't mind him at the Villa. He'd be a good understudy for Tony Morley. Good old *Express & Star*, reminding us on the front page to put our clocks forward tonight. A big photograph of a pretty blonde girl holding a cuckoo clock. It got my attention. Means the park will be back open until 8pm next week. The goal horn!

At least Haystacks will be happy. Didn't expect them to beat Tottenham. Not to be for us, but we weren't embarrassed. Albion at home next.

Looks like Wolves really are hard-up. It says, next to the stunning blonde, that they are going to sell part of their new two-million-pound stand. How is that going to work? Chairman Mr Marshall says, "Ours is a very serious financial problem. We are under a lot of pressure from our bank". It's the offices under the stand they're selling. Not parts of the seating. The Poly currently rent them, but the club is going to sell them instead. The club is losing £20,000 a week. That's careless. Their gates are only around 12,000.

Sunday 28th March

3:40pm: Randy's right. It says so in the *Sporting Star*. In Tuesday's fixtures, "Aston Villa v West Brom (7:30pm)". It was definitely Wednesday last time I looked. Guess they have moved it forward to give Albion more time to prepare for Saturday's FA Cup semi-final. Gives us an extra day before the much more important European Cup semi-final. Can't wait to see us play Anderlecht. My 15th birthday before then.

Randy was late coming for dinner. He obviously didn't see the blonde on the front page holding up her clock. He forgot to wind his watch forward.

'Will you go to Rotterdam, if we get to the final?' Randy asks the million-dollar question. In earshot of Mum. Quickly I respond with a "you bet". Mum raises her eyebrows. I'm sure Mr Hill wouldn't miss out on this once-in-a-lifetime opportunity. Education-wise I think a couple of days taking in the culture of Holland would be beneficial to me. I have tried not to think about the possibility of us being in the European Cup Final. Maybe I do need to bring the subject up with Howard Hill on Tuesday night.

Studying the league table in the *Sunday People*. It's so close between us and Albion. We are one place above. Two points ahead, but they've only played 28 games. We need to beat them. When Randy's gone, I'll update my *Shoot!* League Ladder. I haven't done it for over a month. Crazy when everyone has played a different number of games. Despite Wolves getting a point yesterday, it's looking very bleak. They've only got 10 games left. In the relegation zone on goal difference. But Leeds have still got 13 games left. The next team up, Coventry, are four points ahead. Very tight at the top. Five points separating the top six. Tottenham seventh. If they win all their games in hand, they'll be top. I think Liverpool and Ipswich are the two most likely to win the title though. Hope Ron Atkinson's Man United don't.

Tuesday 30th March

3:35pm: Be glad when this test is over. I thought History would be easier than this. Final one of our tests at least. We should start getting the results tomorrow. Grace Taylor said the Biology test covered lots of stuff they hadn't done. She said she thought the teacher had given them the wrong paper. I do miss Grace. Maybe when the season is over, I'll look to rekindle our romance. I'm sure not being a star at Biology won't affect Grace's journalistic ambitions.

Haystacks wants a wager on tonight's match. He's going with his dad. Haystacks has decided football is more important than his dad's infidelity. He's not planning to talk to his dad though. Bet will be the loser buying the other a Mars bar and a packet of Golden Wonder Smokey Bacon crisps. Despite Haystacks' romance with the Frank F Harrison sixth-former, he doesn't seem to be watching his weight. Maybe she likes her men chubby with plenty to hang on to. Not sure if I want to make this bet. I'm not overly confident.

7:21pm: Well, Mr Hill didn't say no to Rotterdam. He just wants to wait and see if we get there. Surprised that next week's Anderlecht game isn't all-ticket. Hope we get over 40,000. I know there is a lot of unemployment, but the players need a big crowd. Looks just over half-full tonight.

Why would I want to come to Tottenham against Leicester? I will allow somebody else to sit in my seat for the FA Cup semi-final on Saturday. Day before my birthday. Last birthday we played Leicester. Won 4-2 to go top and stayed top for the rest of the season. Can't believe Easter holiday is a week after my birthday this year. Wish they would settle on a set weekend for Easter.

Here comes skipper Dennis. Glad he's back. Kenny Swain too. Only Des Bremner missing.

8:18pm: Doris must have been bursting for the loo, the speed she pelted out at on the ref's half-time whistle. We haven't really been at it today. Looks like I'll be providing Haystacks' snacks this week. Silly goal to concede, so early on. Albion will go ahead of us if the scoreline stays the same. Bushy eyebrow man lost his voice midway through the half. Don't know why he was giving Tony Morley so much stick. Can't see Haystacks. You'd have thought you couldn't miss someone his size amongst the Albion fans. Hope Tony Barton isn't being too nice with the Villa players in the dressing room. They need a good shouting at. Looks like their minds are on next week's game.

8:51pm: That'll do! Peter Withe! 2-1 Villa! Tim is bouncing up and down. Steve Austin is making quite unsavoury gestures towards the Albion fans. Still 20 minutes to go, but we are the team in the ascendency.

Wednesday 31st March

8:52am: Asif joins in the gloating in front of Haystacks. The Mars bar and Golden Wonder Smokey Bacon crisps belong to me. Villa are the victors by two goals to one. Julie Duggan gets in on the act. Easy to forget she's a girl at times. She's taunting Scott Hastings even more than we are. I'll share some of the crisps with her when Haystacks pays up.

Wendy McGregor is being extra friendly. Do I really want to hear about her boyfriend, Oliver Watkins? Seems he does like football after all. He had to be a glory-hunter. Wendy is telling me she's happy his team Liverpool won last night. Bet he's never been to see them. I can probably name more Liverpool players than he can. With Swansea losing last night, it means Liverpool are now second. Ipswich won so they are third. I still think it's between those two. Now I know Watkins is a red, I'm all behind Bobby Robson's lot.

'Oliver says he's struggling to really fit in with the boys'. I'm already fearing where Wendy is going with this. 'Likes football, so couldn't he join your bunch?' "Bunch"? We are a "gang". Also "Local Gang" because we support local teams. Teams within a 20-mile radius. Mark unfairly says Villa are not local. We're always in the *Express & Star* and covered by Radio WM. Liverpool certainly is not local. I'm not falling for white-teeth shining Oliver Watkins being "Billy-no-mates". Isn't he happy enough with all the female attention he's getting?

2:44pm: I can't believe Asif. I said don't draw attention to yourself. How can anybody get 100% in a Physics test? Second highest was 62%. Couldn't he have deliberately got one question wrong? Tucker only got 29%. Looks like he'll be doing the CSE exam next year. I'm quite chuffed with my 57%. Asif might as well do the O level exam now. I guess he's exposing the current flaws in the Comprehensive educational system.

3:51pm: Be rude to say no. I accept the lift home with Mr Mahmood. He's come to collect Asif. Mr Mahmood is very proud of his son's 100% mark. Seems that Asif is back in his dad's good books. I'll be home a good 20 minutes earlier now. Be back before Mum and Mark.

Wish Mr Mahmood would put Radio One on. This station plays really strange music and I don't know what the DJ is saying.

'How did you do in the Physics test then, Jonathan?' Asif's dad seems genuinely interested. I told him "57%". 'Not bad, only 43% less than Asif. He went to the grammar school you know'. Yes, and he was expelled. At least I'm not wanted by the law.

Getting the spare key out of the rusty tin in the garage. That's odd, it's not there. Somebody didn't put it back. I can hear noises coming from inside the house. Somebody must be in. I ring the bell. Nobody answers. It's all quiet now. Maybe it's burglars. More likely I was just imagining the noises. I decide to walk up the road and see if I can catch my mum walking down.

I know that girl over the road. The one who's walking extra quickly. What's she doing around here? I'm going to catch her up. Been ages since I last saw her. Just need to cross over.

Where's she gone? How can I have lost her? Maybe I was wrong. Perhaps it wasn't Carol who used to live next door. It did look like her. Here's Mum.

That's odd, Mark was in all along. Why wasn't he at College? Why didn't he let me in?

End of March Top of Division One

	Team	Pl	Po	
1.	Southampton	33	58	+11
2.	Liverpool	30	57	+32
3.	Ipswich Town	30	57	+15
4.	Swansea City	32	56	+ 8

14. Aston Villa **Pl: 32 Po: 40 -4**

Villa March League Results

6th West Ham United (a) 2-2 Draw (Cowans, Withe)
13th Wolverhampton Wanderers (h) 3-1 Won (Donovan, Shaw, Morley)
20th Ipswich Town (a) 1-3 Lost (McNaught)
27th Arsenal (a) 3-4 Lost (Shaw, Heard, Morley)
30th West Bromwich Albion (h) 2-1 Won (Withe, Shaw)

Villa March European Cup Results

3rd Dynamo Kiev (USSR) (a) 0-0 Draw
17th Dynamo Kiev (USSR) (h) 2-0 Won (McNaught, Shaw)
[Villa win 2-0 on aggregate]

Chapter Ten

April 1982

Saturday 3rd April

10:28am: This is madness. The last day of my 15th year and I think we are at war. Trying to get my head around this. Argentina, where the last World Cup was held, have invaded a British island. Not an island like the Isle of Wight, but an island 8,000 miles away. Technically more than one island. Called the Falkland Islands. Up until 24 hours ago, none of us had heard of. Now it's been invaded by the Argentinians. They caught us off guard. Not surprising, as the Falklands is only 800 miles from Argentina. It does seem as if the inhabitants of The Falklands consider themselves British. They watch the Queen on Christmas Day and supported Daley Thompson in the 1980 Olympics. This just doesn't seem real. Are we in Willenhall in any danger? Maggie is not taking it lying down. She's sending our Navy to sort them out. Oddly, she's sending Prince Andrew, second in line to the throne to be sub-lieutenant on the HMS Invincible. He will set sail on Monday. Two days before Villa play Anderlecht. Surely the Argentinians would never attack a British royal.

What about the Argentinian footballers? Ricky Villa and Ossie Ardiles are supposed to be playing in the FA Cup semi-final today at Villa Park. Is Villa Park safe?

4:09pm: Pity Bob Champion and Aldaniti fell at the first in the National. They said last night the race was in danger because animal protesters had set fire to the fence they call the Canal Turn. I've never seen a canal on the course. Be funny if a canal barge suddenly came along, just as the horses were jumping over the fence. Not many horses left now. Royal Mail and Monty Python were the two I was shouting for. Grittar is going to win. The jockey is nearly 50. He's older than my dad. Back to the football now. See how the Albion are doing in the semi. Odd having no Villa game. Sounds like Ossie Ardiles is having a tough time at Villa Park. Everyone is suddenly very anti-Argentina. I'm sure he's never even been to the Falklands.

West Brom playing Second Division QPR at Highbury. Haystacks and his dad have gone. Haystacks is still only grunting at his dad. Former Wolves player Bob Hazell is playing for Rangers. QPR's leading goal scorer this season, Simon Stainrod, has scored 20 goals. His manager, Terry Venables, thinks he's going to be a top player. Still no goals. Listening to the commentary on Radio WM.

Goal at Villa Park. Garth Crookes has given Spurs the lead. Set up by the unpopular Ardiles. I think it'll be an Albion-Spurs final. The two First Division teams will win.

Wolves are doing well to hold Arsenal at Molineux. Another goal at Villa Park. Second for Spurs. An own goal this time. Looks like only Albion can stop Spurs equalling our historic seven FA Cup wins now. Oh, there's a chance. Surely Bob Hazell can't score. It's in. Clive Allen, the former million-pound teenager, has scored. It's Queens Park Rangers 1, West Bromwich Albion 0. Not long to go and the Second Division team are on the brink of breaking Haystacks' heart. Albion are about to be beaten semi-finalists in both domestic cups.

That's it. Albion have lost. Tottenham Hotspur, with their Argentinians, will play fellow cockneys QPR at Wembley in the FA

Cup Final. There's going to be another blooming Spurs cup final record. Probably not focusing on Ossie this time.

Sunday 4ᵗʰ April

7:33am: Probably not cool to be awake this early on your 15ᵗʰ birthday. Perhaps I shouldn't be this excited. Maybe give my parents another half an hour before I find a way to indicate that the birthday boy has surfaced. Going to be odd not having that special birthday present from Grandad. Would have been his birthday next Saturday. Bet they don't celebrate birthdays in Heaven. Maybe the day you get let into Heaven becomes your new special day. If I get over £20 birthday money, I'm going to buy myself a metal detector. Like this one in the Argos Catalogue, page 85. Asif said there are lots of Roman coins if you look hard enough. It would be an investment. Be odd not having Auntie Mavis and Uncle Norman popping round to give me something smelly. I'm still sure that was Carol I saw the other day. The dartboard in a cupboard, on page 87, looks good. This bedroom is probably too small. It's got chalk boards on the inside of the doors. Only £17.99.

To think that this time next year I'll be old enough to have sex. Provided my genitalia have caught up. Old enough to nip off to Gretna Green to get married. Think I had better get my O levels first. Will we still be at war? Still think it's odd that nobody had ever mentioned The Falklands before. Never heard Judith Chalmers mention them as a a possible holiday destination. I can hear my dad in the bathroom.

'Happy birthday to you. Happy birthday to you. Happy birthday dear Jonathan, Happy birthday to you', Mum and Dad sing joyfully together to mark the 15ᵗʰ birthday of their youngest offspring.

12:41pm: Nice to have Randy here. His naff jokes remind me of Grandad. Today's Sunday lunch is a bit different. Grandma is here, as well as Randy. Mum has also invited Asif and his parents. Seems that the "Asian Artful Dodger" has been forgiven. Now after his 100% Physics score, he's seen as a good influence. I got to choose the menu. Perhaps went a little left-field with toad-in-the-hole. With chips cooked in Mum's new Teflon deep fat fryer. A deep fat fryer that's electric. It's enclosed, so it doesn't catch fire as often. Does take about 20 minutes to melt the fat and come up to the right temperature. Another of my mum's gadgets. Hopefully it will get more usage than the Soda Stream, yogurt maker or waffle maker. Mum did worry about Hindus and toad-in-the-hole, but I checked with Asif and it's okay. Randy wasn't so sure. He was happier when we reassured him that no toads were involved. Although, to be fair, I had been up for giving it a go.

Happy with my presents. Loving the Atari Winter Olympics game. Great to finally have a copy of *Rothmans Football Yearbook 1981/82*. It's got Gordon Cowans on the front. In a game we lost to Ipswich. Sid is wearing blue shorts. Must have been away. A dimmer switch for my bedroom light. How ace is that? That's going to impress the ladies. A new Aston Villa duvet set. With "Champions" on it. Birthday cash campaign is doing well. Managed to find £12 in my cards so far. Pound note from Grandma. She treats all her many grandchildren the same. She's up to seven now. Mark even put a fiver in his card. Cheeky git did have a player in a Wolves-like kit on the front. Still signed it "From Mark and Sarah". Something isn't right about that. A card from Wendy McGregor. She must have come round and pushed that through the letterbox. At least it's just from Wendy not from "Wendy and Oliver". Only two kisses.

Randy hands me a present. 'It's not much. But didn't want to come empty handed'. He's right, it isn't much. It's a *Look In* magazine. Not even the current one. It's dated 13th March. Centre colour poster of flipping Torvill and Dean. There is a League Cup Final preview. Spoiler alert – Liverpool win in extra-time! Glad to see that Randy thinks I'm worth 18p. At least more than a penny a year.

On the back page of *Look In* is a quick question-style thingy with Bjorn from Abba. The third in a series of four Abba ones. Trust me to get one of the bearded blokes. Looks like Bjorn has moved on. A new wife already, called Lena. Claims he has blue eyes. They look brown in that picture. At least he's got some taste. His favourite TV Show is *Fawlty Towers*. Not sure if they translate it into Swedish. Would Manuel be as funny saying "I'm from Barcelona" in Swedish? The *Cannon and Ball* comic strip isn't particularly funny. More Randy's humour than mine. I could try and win a bike in the special Bird's Instant Whip quiz. You only seem to have to know your Green Cross Code. Three Denim bikes for girls with shopping bags on and three sporty Grifter bikes for the boys to be won. Problem is the closing date is 29th March! Everyone knows that Darth Vadar and the Green Cross Code man are played by the same man. Jayne Torvill looks very flat-chested. Suppose big knockers would get in the way when ice skating. They might distract Christopher Dean or flip up and strike him in the eye.

4:08pm: 'Someone to see you, birthday boy', Mum over-eggs the introduction of the visitors gathered in the porch. She's shouldn't have had that second Babycham.

Shocked but really pleased to see our old neighbours. Auntie Mavis and Uncle Norman had made the effort on my birthday to come and see me. Carol is here too. Looking extra hot. Tight black leather trousers really suit her. Even Asif has noticed. To think she used to get undressed in his room. I hate opening birthday cards in front of the giver. You must shake it quite discreetly to see if any money drops out, without looking too disappointed if it doesn't. No money this time. A second envelope though. It's a two-pound book token. Guess I'll have to be buying a suitable reading book. The *Roy of the Rovers* annual, or are there any new Villa books?

Uncle Norman quizzes me on Villa's chances on Wednesday night. I try to come over as confident. In truth I have absolutely no idea. I don't know if Anderlecht are any good. They must be of a decent standard to have reached the European Cup semi-final. Asif and Randy are even more positive than me. Suggesting we could take a three- or four-goal lead back to Belgium. Mark has disappeared. Obviously didn't like the Villa chat. Perhaps he's gone to help Mum light the 15 candles on my cake. Hope it's a chocolate one. Carol says she's going to help in the kitchen. A pot of tea is being made. Although I think Mum's going for another Babycham.

Going to get my *Rothmans Yearbook* to show Uncle Norman. It's on my bed.

'Let Mark know we're ready to light the cake', Mum shouts to me, as I'm climb the stairs. I guess he's not in the kitchen.

I knock on Mark's bedroom door. Shout to tell him cake's ready. Bit of a muffled response. Not sure what he said. So, I open his door. I make a quick U-turn.

Blowing out my candles I try to think how best to play things. Perhaps I can use this new information to my advantage. Obviously, this is a big secret. That was not a one-off. That was not the first time that Mark and Carol had snogged. How far away was Bridgenorth? Why is there always one candle that just won't blow out?

Wednesday 7th April

10:45am: Last day of term. Disappointed with my Maths test result. Really thought I would be near the top. Guess I made a few silly mistakes. I need to focus more. Couldn't believe I beat Asif. Even allowing for him completely missing out section D's questions he still underperformed. He claimed they taught Maths in a different way at the grammar school.

Tucker and Noddy have fallen out again. They've decided to give in with Emily Martins. Problem is that Tucker is now making a move on Georgina Ramsey, Haystacks' old third-year girlfriend who Noddy now fancies. Noddy thought he was getting somewhere until Tucker moved in. I think Georgina really wants Haystacks back, but he is too besotted with the six-former from Frank F Harrison.

Spud has dumped Carrie Carrington. Claims he doesn't like her friends and apart from Gary Numan they have nothing in common. Resisted telling him that we all could have told him that back in first year. Spud's coping well, though. Seems to be less volatile now. Can't remember the last time he intentionally nutted anyone. He even wished me luck tonight. Said he hopes the Villa do it. Mr Walker also said he'd be rooting for us. He wants the European Cup to stay in England. Odd to think that when we come back after the Easter holidays, I could be a supporter of a European Cup finalist.

3:50pm: That's it! Time for the Easter holidays. A well-deserved break after an exceptionally long half-term.

'Jonathan. Can we talk?' Wendy stops me as I'm walking towards the school bus stop. Sounds like a private conversation. I let Asif go on ahead.

6:45pm: Walking with Mr Hill to the ground it feels different. This doesn't feel like a normal under the AV floodlights game. There's an extra buzz in the air. A confidence and belief we are about to witness something special. Lost count of the number of times I checked my zipped coat pocket for my prized ticket. A ticket stub that hopefully I'll want to keep forever. In my blue cashbook with the one from Highbury last season.

Think it was a mistake not making it all-ticket. The queues at the Holte End are all the way around the ground. Even at our Trinity Road entrance there are longer queues than normal. Everyone ready for the first match of the Tony Barton era. Think it was the right decision by the board to make his appointment permanent. Still wish Ron was in charge.

7:18pm: Don't think I've ever felt this nervous. My stomach feels like it's twisted more than Dawn Smith's plaited hair. How can Doris look so calm?

Still don't know why Wendy McGregor felt she needed to tell me that she'd finished with Oliver Watkins. Why would I be interested? I've got more important things on my mind today. Hope these Swedish officials haven't been bribed by the Belgians. I don't know any of the Anderlecht players. Maybe recognise Morten Olsen, but I thought he was a speedway rider. There are very few famous Belgians. I can only think of Tintin. Was Jacques Cousteau from Belgium? Or was he French? I'm sure the bloke in the Agatha Christie films with the moustache came from Belgium.

Says in the souvenir programme that their striker Willy Geurts is top scorer in the competition. Allan and Ken will stop him. Good to see we are finally at full-strength. This is our Championship-winning team. Back to Bremner, Mortimer and Gordon in midfield. Gary Williams back at left-back. The Withe and Shaw super combo up front. I'm feeling good about this. Do I need a quick wee? Nerves might get to me otherwise. No, I can't risk missing them coming out. Leon Hickman says in the programme that Anderlecht's "defensive methods are highly controversial". What does that mean? He describes an "offside steel-trap" and "mass defending". It sounds like at least they won't be attacking much. Hickman finishes up by saying "we must hope good football is the winner". Here come the players. They're all in white. That's odd. They've made us change our shorts. Quite like our blue shorts. We're at home though. They should change.

Good early chance for Gary Shaw. Just over. We've started well. Peter Withe winning everything against that blond defender. Pitch looks quite hard. No grass in the centre. Suppose we have played a lot of games on it lately. Kenny Swain seeing plenty of the ball. Peter Withe wins a knock-down for Shaw again. Corner to Villa. I think we could score here. Come on, Gordon.

Yet another foul. He was all over Withey. Allan Evans has it by the penalty spot. Real chance. Not to be.

This is it. Tony's clean through. They gave it to him. Morley's put it wide! That's a bad miss.

Good save from Dennis. We are doing okay. Just need to be more clinical. Anderlecht aren't really interested in attacking. One long-range shot is all they've really offered.

Suddenly they've got a three-on-one. What's happened? Great save by Jimmy. Where did that attack come from.

7:57pm: Lovely skill Gordon Cowans. He plays it to Gary Shaw. Great layback to Cowans. Fab ball into Tony Morley. This time, Tony. Go on. YES!!!!! Tony sweeps the ball on the ground across the keeper. Off the post and into the goal. What a noise! A kiss from Penny and bushy eyebrow man has slapped poor Doris, right on the back. You can feel the relief.

Thursday 8th April

10:03am: Watching last night's recording of *Sportsnight* for the sixth time. Watched before *The Banana Splits* and now after it. Any excuse not to watch *Why Don't You…?* This time, I'm reliving the highlights of last night's 1-0 win with Asif. I've played Tony Morley's goal so many times that the tape is already starting to wear out. I'm going to take the tab out of the video cassette, so nobody can ever record over it. This is a piece of history. The commentator is right when he says, "I've never heard Villa Park so loud". It was incredible. I thought my eardrums were going to burst. What a save that was by Jimmy Rimmer. World-class! Their striker thought he'd equalised. Jimmy and Tony have been the real stars of this European Cup run.

Jimmy Rimmer's only let one goal in all tournament and he stopped a penalty. Well, with the help of a post.

Asif is in awe of the highlights. So jealous that he wasn't there. I feel my whole life had been building up to Wednesday 7th April. Just as I think Asif has finally got the intricacies of European football, he asks a question like that: "So, who do Villa play in the final?" It's only half-time. We still have to go to Belgium. Good news is we didn't concede an away goal. I thought I'd taught Asif the "away goal rule". If we lose 2-1, 3-2, 4-3 or even 5-4, we win because our goals count double. Which doesn't mean 5-4 becomes 5-8. In all the excitement, I hadn't checked the score in the other semi-final. I assume Bayern Munich will have won. Although Tony Barton did say he was glad we had avoided CSKA Sofia.

Asif is frantically skimming through the sports pages in the *Daily Express*. Spending too long reading the Gambol cartoon. Still think it's funny the wife is named "Gaye". Gaye Gambol. Sounds like something Noddy does in PE. I'm searching Ceefax for the Bayern score. Asif finds it first. That's unexpected. "CSKA Sofia 4, Bayern Munich 3". Plenty of goals. I guess CSKA are favourites now. Although, the Germans scored three away goals. Who would I rather play in the final? CSKA Sofia, obviously.

Spurs held Barcelona, 1-1. In the Cup Winners' Cup semi. Think that might just give Barcelona the edge. I want all British teams to win the European trophies. For once I'll be supporting Tottenham in two weeks' time. Wish I could just go straight to Wednesday 21st April now. I can't wait 14 days for the second leg. Asif is blown away by the European Cup trophy pictured on the front of last night's programme. I can't answer his question, "What is the exact scale?". It always looks a very big and heavy cup when I've seen Liverpool and Forest winning it.

Sunday 10ᵗʰ April

6:15am: I should watch the sunrise more often. It's a great sight. Glad Mum talked me into getting up and coming with them up this beacon. To celebrate this Easter morning. Quite a religious experience. Bet loads of Christians are up beacons all over the world doing this. Holy Communion to start our Easter Sunday off. Might go back to bed later. Mum says we get a hot cross bun and a bacon sandwich back at the church. When I get home, I'm going to crack open the first of my Easter eggs. Probably the Crunchie one. Great how Christians mark every occasion with some tasty food. Turning the Crucifixion into a toasted tea cake was a masterstroke.

Easter started well with us walloping high-flying Southampton yesterday. That 3-0 win at the Dell puts an end to any dreams Keegan and Co. had of winning the title. Villa are back! We are going to march up the league with Tony's army. Guess Liverpool are title favourites now. They scored five at Man City yesterday. Ipswich lost to Spurs. Maybe Tottenham still have a chance. Think I'd rather hand our trophy back to Liverpool than let a London team win it. Mark was in a good mood with Wolves winning at Mr Walker's Forest. Or is he pleased because he had a snog with Carol? I think there is something going on there.

Very small measures of wine you get at sunrise on a Sunday morning.

The way Villa are playing now, I think I'll see a few goals against Brighton in tomorrow's Bank Holiday Villa Park game. Perhaps 4-1 again like we did against them last season to go top. Hope Steve Foster isn't playing. I hate him and his headband. Haystacks says the other Brighton centre-half is England cricketer Mike Gatting's brother. Think he's joking though.

Monday 12th April

7:18pm: Changing the team on back of the programme. Crossing out Gary Shaw and putting in David Geddis. He deserves to be acknowledged when I reread this programme in years to come. Two goals today for Geddis. A big reason for our 3-0 win. Two 3-0s in 48 hours. Brighton & Hove Albion couldn't live with us. Three second-half goals past the unfortunately named Perry Digweed. Evo getting the third.

Wolves are certainly putting up a fight, despite their financial problems. The League has banned them from buying players, but a 4-1 win at home to Manchester City today will have cheered their fans up. Rubbish Easter for Man City fans, nine goals conceded since Jesus rose from the tomb. We are only four points behind them now. Tottenham are still in with a chance of catching Liverpool. Bet their fans are celebrating winning 3-1 today at rivals Arsenal.

Getting more worried about the Argentinians. Says in the paper that if Britain's task force enters the "special operations" zone around the Falklands, they'll be entering a minefield. Seems 9,000 soldiers from Argentina will be on the main island from next week. I wonder how big the island is.

This is a waste of *The Two Ronnies*. Why can't they stick to their sketches? Like "Four Candles". This seaside one-off is rubbish. More like Benny Hill sort of slapstick humour. I can tell Mum wants us to turn it over.

Thursday 15th April

4:25pm: That's sad. He wasn't even that old. The voice of the *Mr Men* and Captain Mainwaring in *Dad's Army*. He died in Birmingham this morning. He'd been performing at the Alexandra Theatre.

Seems he had a massive stroke. Not sure if he had finished his part. Paper says he was a 66-year-old star. But papers do have a habit of getting people's ages wrong. Guess that's the end for the *Mr Men*. Oh, his understudy went on instead after they found he'd had a stroke. Bet the audience were disappointed that Arthur Lowe was missing. Probably be more understanding now that they know he died. It says he was in *Coronation Street*. I don't remember that.

The Falklands conflict has now reached the global stage. Ronald Reagan is now getting involved. I think he's on our side. Well, I think he's got a thing for Maggie. President Reagan is telling the Russians to "butt out". He claims Moscow is "evidently" providing intelligence to Argentina. Why does everything have to be about Russia and America?

8:41pm: My final descent then. Mark managed 57.3 seconds. I can beat that. Need to just not go too wide on the bends. On my own I've gone faster than that. Need to be straight off on the bell. My Atari skier is ready for the slalom. Don't know why I'm pretending to be David Geddis. Suppose he looks a bit like a skier. Perhaps I should be Konrad Bartelski instead. I'm sure that's a made-up name. It doesn't sound very British. It even ends with "ski". I wonder if he's a Russian spy.

Ignore the time at the top. Just be natural. Love the sheesh sound effects when you go round the poles. This is fast. I'm going to smash Mark. That's the last pole. I've surely done it. No!! How can I fall now? Yards from the line. There was nothing near me. David Geddis, what have you done?

Mark is being too nice to me. For once not gloating. Guess it's a good time to mention the Carol kiss. With nobody else around I bring up what he knows I saw. He's not denying it. More surprisingly he says they've been seeing each other for nearly a year. It started before Uncle Norman and Auntie Mavis moved. This is crazy. Mark's rubbish at keeping secrets. He couldn't fool me for that long. What about mad Sarah? That was only about six months ago.

So, Sarah was all pretend. A girlfriend of one of his mates. The one on the motorbike outside Mr Moreno's. He got her round to put Mum off the scent. Stop her asking for him to bring girls home. Not sure my mum wanted Mark to bring girls plural home. Just one nice one would have done. The girl who played the part of punk Sarah was a drama student. Still don't get why he didn't mention him and Carol being together though. Mark says that the thought of Auntie Mavis and Mum matchmaking would have driven him mad. They would have had them married by now. I don't know how I feel about Mark and Carol. We all used to play together. Yes, Carol is much nearer Mark's age but still I couldn't get my head round him seeing Carol in that way. I guess the fact that I was always "piggy in the middle" makes sense now.

I'm glad that my older brother is confiding in me. Maybe only because I caught them in the embrace. Guess I was right about seeing Carol walking away last week. What had they been up to? I don't want to think about my brother having sex. Surely, he wouldn't do in our house. I don't think there's been any sexual activity in this house since I was conceived during the 1966 World Cup Finals. Okay, an exaggeration. I know my parents did it, but I don't want to think about it.

'Why don't you come roller skating with me and Carol next week', Mark took me by surprise. I went for the casual "maybe" reply. Truth was, I didn't know. It's nice to be included and it would be good Stadler bonding, but would I be a gooseberry. Would I again be "piggy in the middle"? Worse still was the horror of being on roller skates. Not something I have ever mastered. I didn't even know my brother could roller skate. I guess he's good at most things, so he's probably mastered the art of roller skating. Perhaps Mark and Carol are Willenhall's answer to Torvill and Dean on wheels. More I think about it, the more I think this would be my worst nightmare. What if I ended up in a coma in hospital on the day of the Anderlecht v Villa second leg?

Saturday 17ᵗʰ April

12:03pm: Hope that clock is right. Can't believe the battery on my Casio digital watch chose today to pack up. Batteries don't last like they used to. When the bloke said come back in 40 minutes, I was worried. Need to be at Mr Hill's for ten to two. I like the Golden Egg restaurant, but had we really got time to be served and gulp down our egg and chips? Dad has got to get out of the Mander Centre Car Park and then it's a good 15 minutes to the Hills. I can do without my watch. Don't know why it will take him so long to fit it.

At least the food arrived quickly. Now how fast can I eat this? No time for chatting, Mum. We're in a rush.

1:14pm: Since when has 40 minutes been one hour 20 minutes. If I'd known he was going to be that long, I could have had a pudding. Those banana splits looked incredible. Bet I've got to reset the date now as well. We need to be getting a move on. Villa v Middlesbrough waits for no man.

Who has Mum stopped to talk to now? Hold on, that's Grace Taylor's mother. I didn't even know they knew each other.

'Hi stranger. Fancy seeing you here. How've you been?' Grace seems quite excited to see me. Good to see Grace as well. That's quite a tight t-shirt. I like her hair tied up. Shows off her neck. I need to focus. I have a game to get to. Come on Mum, stop nattering.

'I miss us spending time together'. Grace seems in no hurry to terminate our conversation.

2:39pm: Make sure I use the same turnstile as I have the last two games. We won them both, so must be a lucky one. Buy my programme from the same programme seller. Took me ages to find that loose 5p. Forgot these jeans had a hole in the left pocket. Luckily it had rolled down my trouser leg and ended up in my sock. Can't believe this is the 24th home game of the season. Still don't know if I should be cutting these vouchers out. Maybe I'll need to take them all in. When I go to collect my European Cup Final ticket. Mr Hill still isn't committing on the final. I think he's going to go. If we get there. Maybe he doesn't want to be responsible for a teenage boy in a foreign country.

Impressed at how brave I was. Asking Grace Taylor out on a date. That wasn't in the plan. Hope Mark is okay with it. I remembered the *Blue Peter* Bring 'n' Buy sale last year. When Grace donated her roller skates because she had outgrown them. What quick thinking to have the brilliant idea to ask Grace Taylor to accompany me to the roller drome. I won't be a gooseberry and it'll be a great excuse to hold on to Grace. I did nearly say the wrong name. Don't think Mum noticed. She was too busy admiring Mrs Taylor's fake fur coat. Very quickly changed "Mark and Ca…." into "Mark and Crazy Sarah". Grace looked confused. I'll fill her in on Wednesday. She'll like to be in on the secret. Don't think she's ever met Carol.

Guess they've run out of first-team players. Seems mean only giving them half a page each on Focus. Not heard of either the two Central League players before. Paul Birch doesn't seem very tall. Tony Barton says he should be playing more games in the Central League, but lately Gary Shelton, Andy Blair, Terry Bullivant and Pat Heard have been keeping him out. I guess even Villa reserves need to play matches. Ray Walker apparently first went to the Villa training ground when he was nine. He signed schoolboy forms when he was just 14. Walker seems quite a prospect. He's played six times for the England Youth team.

4:35pm: I can't see Middlesbrough equalising. We just need to be careful. Can't afford any injuries for Wednesday night. I thought that when Allan Evans scored in first half it would be another 3-0. It's been quite comfortable. Be our fifth straight win, if we get it. Would mean Tony Barton still has a 100% record since he got the job. What a turnaround since the start of February. Who would have thought super Ron Saunders would be managing a team in the relegation zone and his scout would be marching the Villa up the league. Hopefully Tony is just resting Des and Dennis. Need them on the pitch in Belgium. I guess Gary Shaw is still a big doubt. Geddis has done well again today.

That's it. Three more points. I'm getting used to saying that. Only one away from 50 points. With only seven games left though, we can only get 70 points. So, if Liverpool won today we can no longer retain the title. "Attendance 21,098" – that's not bad. It looked a bit less than that. Surprised bushy eyebrow man wasn't here.

5:08pm: A win for Liverpool at home to Hastings' lot. So, we are giving our Championship trophy back. Perhaps we can swap it with Liverpool's European Cup. A point for Ron Saunders' Blues at Wolves. Spurs finally losing. Guess that means nobody is going to stop Liverpool. It said on the radio that Rush and Dalglish have scored 40 goals between them this season.

Mention Rotterdam to Mr Hill again. To my delight he says he's decided that if we get there then he's going. Even better, if my parents agree he will happily take me. Says I'm his lucky charm. What a nice man.

8:19pm: That's madness. No way Noddy and Tucker are going to traipse all the way to Wolverhampton to watch their Saddlers play. Seems Walsall fans have started a "Save Walsall" action group. Perhaps Noddy and Tucker should join it. I didn't know Walsall were in so much financial trouble. Them and Wolves. Suppose the idea of a ground share makes sense. Be funny if Walsall ended up getting better gates for their games at Molineux than Wolves did. Walsall fans are going to vote on the idea of going to play at Wolves. At least the 529 bus goes from Walsall to Wolverhampton. Oh, the "Save Walsall" group say they'll take legal action against sharing with Wolves. Harry Marshall seems to be pushing the idea of them becoming Walsall's landlords. Walsall Chairman, Ken Weldon, also seems to be in favour. How can two teams play at the same ground? What about the corner flags?

So, the Argentinians are claiming we have put a 200-mile "no-go" area around the Falklands. Prince Andrew must be doing well. Not only does he get all the best girls because he's the best-looking prince, but now he's becoming a war hero. No wonder he manged to pull model Koo Stark. Still don't remember hearing about the Falklands before all this started. Perhaps Maggie made them up, trying to win a few more voters. I'm going to see if they get a mention in the encyclopaedias. This one covers F. Wow, it's there! Everything is in the *Encyclopaedia Britannica*. "Falkland Islands [fawlk'land] Archipelago in the southern Atlantic". Population of 2,100. Plenty of potential Tory voters. Pity sheep can't vote, as there are 600,000 of them. That's nearly 30 sheep per person. They'll need a lot of mint sauce. Not surprisingly their biggest export is wool. There's an island off it with the brilliant name of South Sandwich. How much fun must that discoverer have had naming it that? You could have North Chocolate Mini Roll nextdoor to it.

Wednesday 21st April

10:53am: There is Grace Taylor waiting for us. She's keen. I thought we were early. Mark did seem to drive quicker than normal. Probably trying to impress Carol. I did feel like a gooseberry in the back seat. They seem very relaxed together. I did want to puke when Mark put on their special cassette. On the inset card he had written, "Romantic Songs for the One I Love". Currently it's playing *Romeo and Juliet* by Dire Straits. Hope Mark knows where to park. It looks a bit rough around here.

I hadn't given this morning and my "date" with Miss Taylor much thought. Guess I've been too nervous worrying about the most important game of my life tonight. Couldn't sleep last night. I was going through all the games we had ever played. None of them compared to a game that was just 90 minutes from Aston Villa being in the European Cup Final. It was almost impossible to comprehend. We just must not lose. Then I'll be going to Rotterdam on 26th May. Pity today isn't tomorrow. If we did fail tonight then I would still have Grace Taylor to help dull the pain. I can't think about defeat. Don't know how I'd cope. Would I start crying and never be able to stop? Is today the one chance I'll have in my life for my team to reach a European Cup Final?

11:42am: I haven't quite mastered to art of skating to the music. I'm managing to walk around on the skates. Even went nearly a metre away from the edge at one brave point. Why do they make the entrance gaps so wide? I had to just lunge then to get back on to holding the edge as I was losing my balance. Think I'm quite pleased that Grace Taylor isn't that good either. She is at least jigging to *Kids in America*. Mark and Carol keep disappearing. Not sure I've even seen Mark on the rink yet. Carol did do a few quick laps early on. She even managed to go backwards at one point. Mark very generously paid for all of us. Was surprised he asked for size 10 skates. He is always an 11½. He's got massive feet. No way he's getting those plates into size 10 skates. Maybe he didn't want Carol to know he's got big feet. They do say "big feet, large willy". I fear that isn't true for Stadler men.

You would think people would move out of the way when they see a novice hurtling towards them.

2:14pm: I'm knackered. Didn't know skating was so physically demanding. Think I'll stick to my Chopper. It's been strange, but nice, spending time with Grace again. Not sure if she would be interested in rekindling our romance. No room now for thoughts like this in my head. I need to focus. In just over five hours my team are going for glory. The Champions of England could be on the verge of being Champions of Europe by 9:30 tonight. Maybe a goodbye kiss would be appropriate. Grace Taylor has stopped me being a gooseberry. She possibly deserves the lips of Jonathan Stadler. I did buy her a milkshake. Is that sufficient reward? Waiting for Grace's dad to come and pick her up. Carol and Mark have disappeared again. Think there is some snogging activity going on somewhere. Need some polite conversation now while we wait. I'll ask how Grace's exams went. That man's waving at us. Must be Grace's dad. Yes, recognise him from *Grease*. Does he know that his daughter and me have history? Hopefully he doesn't know that my hand has explored his daughter's bra. Bet he didn't get to explore Mrs Taylor's bra until they were married. Unless they were part of the "Swinging Sixties". The gentleman walking towards us doesn't look like he was part of anything that was particularly wild. He was probably more into his Airflix models, like that chap in *Carry On Loving*.

'Hope they do it tonight, Jonathan', Grace shouts as she leaves. I'm delighted that she understands the importance of the day. Disappointed that I didn't go for the kiss before her dad appeared. Guess I just need to wait for Carol and my brother to resurface.

'Fancy seeing you here, Mr Stadler', I turn round to see the other girl of my 81/82 season affections, Wendy McGregor. What are the odds of that happening? It's like the *Hitchhiker's Guide to the Galaxy* infinite improbability drive had been at work.

Wendy was here to skate. She's brought her own skates. She looks hot in those Daisy Duke-style denim shorts and long pink socks. With her blouse tied at the front. You can see her belly button. Can't see any fluff. Wendy McGregor is followed by her even hotter looking auntie. Linda McGregor looks so hot she could catch fire. A short turquoise skirt, a stripey multi-coloured top and a colour-coordinated headband. She's going to get a lot of attention in the roller drome.

As they queue, Wendy and I chat about our Easter holidays. I had three more Easter eggs than Wendy. She seems disappointed that I'm going. I explain that I have an important game to get to. I think she thought I was going to be flying over to Belgium. How fab would that be? Then I receive an unexpected invite. Wendy McGregor and her auntie Linda have booked a badminton court in our school sports hall on Friday morning. Wendy asked if I wanted to join. If I could bring somebody else along, we could play doubles.

Finally, Mark and Carol appear. Looking as if they have been quite busy. Should I tell Carol that she's lacking one of her shoulder pads?

A very excited, hot-looking, Linda races straight towards her former classmate, Mark. She jumps on him. Wrapping her legs around his waist and gives him a smacker right on the lips. She's delighted to see my brother for the first time since he left school. This is not going down well with Mark's secret girlfriend. Carol looks furious. She has no idea who this sexy lady kissing her boyfriend is.

'Jonny, you must bring your brother to play on Friday. Be a great double', Linda beamed.

7:07pm: I need a sign on my bedroom door saying, "do not disturb". The next two hours could define our season. I can hardly move. Still 20 minutes to kick-off. Maybe I need to just take some deep breaths. To think by the time I play the McGregors at badminton my team could be in the European Cup Final. Or I could be heartbroken and not want to even leave my bedroom. Still need to find a partner for Friday. Maybe ask Spud or Haystacks. There was no way Carol was letting Mark play anything with stunning Linda McGregor. Can't wait to see Linda stretching on the badminton court. Would have been nice for once to have played with my brother instead of against him.

Talk of some fighting before the game. Hope it isn't our fans. Sounds like they're not very well segregated.

10:34pm: Still nervous now watching the highlights. Mark says it's pointless as the game isn't going to count. He says they'll have to replay it. Can't believe some idiots could have ruined it for all us Villa fans. Need to see for myself. Certainly heroics by our defenders. Being at full strength certainly helped. Looked as if all the players knew their roles and gave their all.

We had a few chances. Tony Morley looked lively. Allan Evans was not being beaten. At least the players were doing England proud. Anderlecht weren't going to score past Jimmy. Wish Mark didn't keep making such negative comments. His Wolves team will never be in a European Cup semi-final. Allan Evans did well to get there in front of their two strikers. This was the Withe chance. Keeper dropped it at his feet. He just couldn't pull it across to Gary Shaw. Got a corner though. On the radio it sounded like we were defending more than this. This is when the problems started. They are fighting behind Rimmer's goal. Lots of Union Jacks. That was a close shot by them. Fighting seems to be getting worse. This must be about the time that thug invades the pitch. Bet he wasn't a Villa fan. The police are in the crowd now. It looks nasty. People being pushed against the barriers. Why do the English always fight abroad? Police are using riot weapons. I'm glad I'm not there. Hope this doesn't stop us getting through. They should have stopped the game now.

Crazy that nutter is on the pitch right by Jimmy Rimmer. This is the chance Anderlecht are complaining about. Ref should have stopped it by now. That was a great chance for Anderlecht, but they put it over. I don't think the forward was put off by the idiot in the six-yard box. Mark disagrees. He would. He says they would have scored. Dad is staying impartial. About six police with batons dragging the disgraceful fan away. He can't be a real supporter. Hope he is never allowed in a ground anywhere in the world again. Glad they don't seem to be hitting him with their batons though. What are the Anderlecht fans chanting? It doesn't sound very nice. The bloke is lying on the floor now. He's lucky there aren't police dogs. The police have got him again. Carrying him like a star. His legs wide apart. Commentator saying Jimmy Rimmer has now gone into the crowd to try and calm things down. Still can't believe these are Villa fans. There is never any trouble at Villa Park. It's not like at St Andrews or Elland Road. Game was stopped for seven minutes as more police came and stopped the fighting.

Villa starting to get on top. Off the line from Withe. The flag went up for offside. I think Villa were the better team that half, but all they are mentioning is the trouble. Yes, Mark, I know you think the game will be replayed. Just stop going on about it.

What a great run by Dessie Bremner. He's quicker than he looks. Would have been a great goal if Shaw could have kept that shot down. What a challenge by Ken McNaught. We played so well. Just over by Peter Withe. It's a pity we couldn't score. So important Tony Morley scored in the first leg. That's it! Tony Barton raises his arm in triumph. I don't care what Mark says. Villa are going to Rotterdam. That goalless draw was a brilliant performance. A masterclass that Ron Saunders would have been proud of. I'm still celebrating. Nobody is taking this away from me. One month into the job and Tony Barton has achieved the impossible. He's taken Villa to the European Cup Final.

They can't get the match replayed because of one idiot. I don't think it stopped a goal being scored. I guess if the worst happens and it is replayed, then Villa will be even more fired up. This Anderlecht team are never going to score past us. I'll be going to Rotterdam. Watching Aston Villa in the European Cup Final. Against the great West German side Bayern Munich. Bayern overturned the first-leg deficit to thrash CSKA Sofia on aggregate 7-4. They won 4-0 today.

Thursday 22nd April

5:28pm: No, Mark, I'm not ashamed to be a Villa fan. Reports and pictures in the paper from last night's game are shocking. Front page of *Express & Star*, "VILLA GLORY AND SHAME IN CUP CLASH". David Harrison is pulling no punches in his article, "RIOTING FANS who brought shame to Aston Villa's night of glory were today limping back from Belgium". Fifty fans were arrested. Hope they are never let into Villa Park again. Does say the troublemakers travelled separately from the official supporters. Says they didn't even have tickets. Why did Anderlecht let them in? Why did they mix all fans together? Says most of the injured were wearing claret and blue. So that must mean the Anderlecht fans were mainly to blame. UEFA investigating the incident. That doesn't sound good. It says they have the powers to expel a team from the competition. That surely can't happen. Anderlecht are out. They can't put them in the final instead of us. It was their fault anyway. That's more hopeful. It says, "Villa are likely to escape the ultimate penalty since much of the blame was being levelled at Anderlecht for not segregating the fans and selling tickets immediately before the match". See, Mark, it wasn't our fault.

The pictures look horrible. I'm not sure if I really do want to go to Rotterdam now. Holland is next door to Belgium. What if the Anderlecht fans turn up again wanting revenge?

"Pressure grows for World Cup ban". Surely our hooligans aren't getting England knocked out of the Spain World Cup as well? No, it's the English FA wanting the Argentina team banned because they invaded the Falklands. Would certainly help Ron Greenwood's team's chances if the World Cup holders were not allowed to compete. We would just need Brazil to invade an island and get them thrown out too. Imagine if Villa win the European Cup in May and then England win the World Cup in July. 1982 would then go down as the best football year ever.

Friday 23rd April

11:05am: Asif reminds us that today is St George's Day. Seems that the Saint of England defeated a mythical dragon. Trust us to have a made-up saint. Asif is full of useless information today. He claims Willam Shakespeare was born on this day. Asif also says he died on this day. Dying on your birthday, that's a bit unlucky. Hope he got to blow out his candles first. Asif might be a brainbox but is he any good at badminton? I know Wendy is decent. Not sure how fair a match is between the McGregor family and the Stadler/Mahmood partnership.

Nice to see Mr Walker here. He's been playing squash with Miss Morgan. I think something might be going on between those two. Did chat with Mr Walker about the Villa getting to the final. He said he had heard UEFA were going to decide Villa's fate next Thursday. I can't wait that long. Mr Walker says an MP named Denis Howell, a Villa fan, is fighting Villa's corner. Mr Howell had been Minister for Drought in the hot summer of 1976.

Wish Spud had been in when I called. He would have made a much better badminton partner than Asif. Obviously, grammar school education does not produce star badminton players. We're getting hammered. Not doing our gender proud. Linda is lethal with that shuttlecock. I think we are also too nice. That last shot Wendy

McGregor played looked out to me. We gave her the benefit of the doubt. The two ladies certainly look the part in their white pleated skirts. Unlike Asif, in his tatty red t-shirt with the hole under his left armpit.

So difficult to give badminton my all when I don't know if Villa are in the European Cup Final or not. How can I wait another six days to find out? This is torture!

Wednesday 28th April

12:38pm: It's been a funny first week back at school. Everything seems to be quite bitty. Results all in from pre-Easter tests, reports due out to parents next week and several of our year currently on the French trip. Nobody has been gloating about the football. Saturday we could only draw 1-1 with Mr Walker's Forest. Wolves and Albion both lost. The Villa game didn't seem important with the UEFA decision following Anderlecht's appeal still hanging over us. Suppose at least we got a point.

Crazily Asif has challenged Wendy McGregor and her auntie to a rematch. Not sure I'm up for that. Yes, it was nice to have the two ladies jigging up and down against us, but embarrassing losing to girls. I have decided that it's Grace Taylor that I really want to relight the fire with. I came to this decision on Monday night, while watching *Hill Street Blues*. I did a deal with myself. If UEFA make us replay the game, or worse, knock us out the competition, then I'll ask Grace Taylor out. If they say we are definitely in the final, then I'll stay single until next season.

10:33pm: What a rubbish night. The worry about the UEFA decision must have got to the players. That was the worst we've played all season. Bushy eyebrow man was booing before we'd even got to the hour mark. Leeds were no great shakes. Geddis even gave us the lead. Fancy losing 4-1 to that lot. The only bright spot was young Mark Walters coming on for his debut. He looks quite a talent. Tony Morley will have a fight for his place if Walters keeps improving. To be fair, Tony did play the whole 90 minutes for England last night. In the Home Internationals win against Wales in Cardiff. No wonder he had to come off today. Peter Withe played all of the two games. Pity he didn't score for England. Not sure he did enough to get in the World Cup squad. Think Francis and Mariner are ahead of him.

Mr Hill was so negative about our chances of being allowed to play in the European Cup Final. Almost seemed to think we should forfeit the tie due to some of the hooligans being Villa fans. Worst of all, whatever UEFA decide, Mr Hill is not going to go to Rotterdam. He says it isn't safe and certainly wouldn't be prepared to take me.

Both Spud's Wolves and Haystacks' Albion are now in the relegation zone. Shame we didn't have our bet this season. It's so tight at the bottom though. Only two points between 21st placed Albion and 16th placed Birmingham. Bottom placed Middlesbrough look doomed.

Says on the back page of tonight's paper that Albion's Derek Statham is in trouble. He's reached 40 disciplinary points for the season. Already been suspended at 20 and 30. He'll be in for a big ban.

Wales manager Mike England doesn't think England have got a hope in the World Cup. That shows how rubbish his Wales team must be. England, the team, could have won by more than one yesterday away to his mob. Hope Kevin Keegan's injury isn't too bad.

That's crazy. He's only eleven years older than me. How can Bjorn Borg be retiring now? Just because he lost to John "tantrum" McEnroe in last year's Wimbledon Final.

Thursday 29th April

2:38pm: Julie Duggan seems even more nervous than me about Villa's fate. She's asked me four times already today if I've heard any news. She's wearing her lucky Aston Villa badge, under the lapel of her blazer. She'll have to wait like me until she gets home.

Just double Maths left and then I can get home and ring Randy. He said he'd have all news on the radio all day. Hope Mr Walker goes easy on us today. We are ahead in the curriculum.

'Before we get on with the Maths, we have some news. News that I know Mr Sadler has been waiting for', Mr Walker had something to tell us. Something to tell me. Did he know? 'I've just heard the decision that UEFA have come to regarding Aston Villa'. Julie Duggan is on her feet. 'Have you heard the news, Jonathan?' He did know. Come on sir tell us the decision. 'I'm sorry. It's not good news. You are out'. The juggernaut hit me. 'Only kidding. You're in the final. Just a fine and your next home European game must be played behind closed doors'. Fantastic news. The relief is unmeasurable. Uncontrollably, I run to embrace Mr Walker. Julie joins in the hug and celebratory jig. Asif then dives in as well. Most of the class look on bemused. Unaware of the significance of the news that has just been exchanged. Aston Villa Football Club are in the European Cup Final. An event in Rotterdam that I want to be part of.

End of April Top of Division One

1.	Liverpool	Pl: 36 Po: 75	+14
2.	Ipswich Town	Pl: 37 Po: 71	+15
3.	Swansea City	Pl: 37 Po: 66	+16
4.	Manchester United	Pl: 37 Po: 65	+11
15.	**Aston Villa**	**Pl: 37 Po: 50**	**0**

Villa April League Results

10th Southampton (a) 3-0 Won (McNaught, Morley, own goal)

12th Brighton (h) 3-0 Won (Evans, Geddis (2))

17th Middlesbrough (h) 1-0 Won (Evans)

24th Nottingham Forest(a) 1-1 Draw (Cowans)

28th Leeds United (h) 1-4 Lost (Geddis)

Villa April European Cup Results

7th Anderlecht (Belgium) (h) 1-0 Won (Morley)

21st Anderlecht (Belgium) (a) 0-0 Draw

[Villa win 1-0 on aggregate]

Chapter Eleven

May 1982

Saturday 1ˢᵗ May

1:35pm: Randy drops me off at the Hills. It's a shopping day for Mrs Hill and Peggy. Randy is off to be a Morris dancer in Bilston town. He's been practicing in his front room all week. It will also involve some dancing round the maypole. He's a little worried because he gets dizzy quite easily. The Hills' dog gives me a big licky welcome.

Mrs Hill is excited that the first test tube twins have been born. Peggy Doubleday thinks it's unnatural and the start of the end. Seems to think that within 20 years the country will be overrun with test tube babies. Apparently, there's a reason that God makes some women barren.

Peggy is now warning me to stay away from any of the Villa hooligans. She says you can spot them because they have tattoos. Mr Hill just turns his classical music up three numbers higher.

2:40pm: Doris seems really excited to see me. We discuss Rotterdam. For some reason I tell her I'm going. She thinks that's wonderful news. She's planning a whole new outfit to wear to watch the final on the telly. Bushy eyebrow man starts reeling off the international players that Bayern Munich have. He's expecting us to get hammered.

Manchester City today. We should win this. Great pictures in the programme of the players preparing for the Anderlecht game. Good to see a picture of kit man Jim Williams. He always seems a jolly chap. They all seem very relaxed. Even the subs in their suits. Easy job for reserve goalkeeper Nigel Spink in these European games. Probably gets paid a bonus just for sitting on the bench. The players are going to be busy this week. Tony Barton says they have got the Supporters' Player of the Year Bowen Terrace Trophy tonight. Wonder who will be player of the year. Think I would give it to Gordon Cowans. He hasn't missed a game and has put in some good performances. Then tomorrow they fly out to Morocco. I'm sure that's a good distance away. We're playing matches to mark the opening of the Moroccan National Sports Week. We are going to earn around £10,000 playing these games. Need to be back in time to play at Stoke City on Wednesday.

Good that Steve Stride, the secretary, has said next season the season ticket prices are not going up. Mine is still £40. Not sure if Dad will pay that. I can use some of Grandad's money if needed. The poshest bit of the Trinity Road is £101. I don't think I would swap my front row seat for that.

Our average attendance this season is 5,000 down on last season's. I guess we were winning a lot more games then. The Albion and Ipswich sellouts helped. All teams are down this season. Arsenal 8,000 down. Their average is only 24,610. Wolves have dropped down to just over 15,000. Biggest rise is Spurs. Up 6,000. Suppose they've had a good season. Most teams are down. I guess with high unemployment it's not surprising. Maggie needs to help subsidise football. Today's mascot is Alistair Dykes. It says "Alistair (188) lives in Chase Terrace". I guess 188 isn't his age but his Junior Supporters Club Membership number. I so need to become a Junior Member.

Pat Heard is number six with Andy Blair as sub. Need to cross out David Geddis and write in Gary Shaw. Former Villa player Bobby McDonald is playing for them. Half their team has changed. I can't hear some of the names. I'll write them in at home. See the manager has picked his son again. No Trevor Francis. That's good news.

5:26pm: I'm sure Peggy has put on weight while she's been at the shops. I can hardly breathe. Sounds like they had some nice cream horn cakes. The ladies enquire about the score. They say from our expressions there are no clues. Mr Hill tells them it was goalless. In truth neither side looked like scoring. 'Who won then?' Peggy asks.

7:15pm: Watching *321*. For some reason two ladies are dancing in schoolgirl outfits on a railway station platform under a sign saying "Wet Paint". They can certainly kick their legs high. Trying to discretely see if I can see their knickers. It could be a vital clue. The dark-haired one is gorgeous. Libby from dance group Lipstick has brought the clue. She's leaving a metal bucket. As always, Dad shouts "Dusty Bin". "Lipstick got quite steamed up. So might you with this. Some might say you'll clean up. Dry your eyes if you miss". Still, Dad is adamant it's the bin. I'm saying more a carpet or curtain steamer. Mum says she would love a carpet steamer. Mark isn't impressed. Contestants are oddly thinking dishwasher or a Turkish bath. Not sure how they would take a Turkish bath home. Mark is in a dreadful mood. Seeing Wolves lose at home to rivals Albion was painful. Especially as it puts the Baggies above Wolves. Made worse with news that Ron Saunders' Birmingham had won 4-1 at Notts County. Table looking very bleak for Wolverhampton Wanderers.

It wasn't Dusty Bin. It was a steam iron, but also with a dishwasher, washing machine and fridge freezer. That's some prize they have just rejected. Dad is not impressed. He's going up for his bath. That's the telephone ringing. Mum goes to the hall to answer it, putting on her telephone voice as she recites our telephone number.

'I've decided to tell them about Carol', Mark surprisingly informs me. 'They're going to find out at some point anyway'. I am somewhat shocked by this revelation. I ask him "what about Sarah?"

Having chatted with Auntie Mavis on the phone for the last 40 minutes – so long that the Richard Burton film has started – Mum is now consoling her eldest son. Who has just revealed that Sarah has dumped him. Surprised Mum used terms like, "cradle snatching" and "Jezebel". I'm starting to feel sorry for the fraudulent crazy punk.

This battle with Argentina is getting out of hand. The Argentinians are claiming they have shot two of our Harriers down. A place called Port Stanley on the Falkland Islands is where all the fighting seems to be taking place. This is the first real war I've known in my lifetime. It says in the paper that Mrs Thatcher and her cabinet have sent orders to bomb Port Stanley.

Looks like former Black Sabbath front man Ozzy Osbourne is going to divorce his wife and marry his manageress, millionaire's daughter Sharon Arden. Hope she knows what she's letting herself in for. His current wife is citing "unreasonable behaviour" in the divorce. I'm pretty sure he once bit a bat, so she might have a point. Says he's from Birmingham. Wonder if he follows the Villa.

Tuesday 4th May

10:17am: I'm sure this Chemistry experiment shouldn't be doing this. Smells rancid. Even worse than when I forgetfully left that half-eaten egg sandwich in my bag for three weeks. What's that odd crackling noise?

Good to see Noddy and Tucker working together again. Seems they have been united by the "Save Walsall" group. They are both vehemently against the idea of playing their home games at Wolves. Ken Weldon still wants to sell Fellows Park and move in with Wolves. Noddy says that private investment is being considered. Tucker says his dad has been part of a committee looking at this. They want to buy the club from the greedy Weldon. Tucker says former Wolves player Derek Dougan is involved. The "Save Walsall" group is now known as "SWAG". It stands for "Save Walsall Action Group". Noddy and Tucker have both got t-shirts with "SWAG" on the front. Admittedly written in thick black marker pen. It's just great that they are mates again.

Wednesday 5th May

7:43pm: Didn't expect Asif to score from there. Jimmy Rimmer was half asleep. Guess that's Wales 1, Aston Villa 8 then. Perhaps I should have had my hand on Jimmy's rod. Asif is busy celebrating his first ever Subbuteo goal against me. I'm not used to playing someone left-handed. Trying to listen to the report from the Villa game at the Victoria Ground. Sounds like we're playing well but still no goals. The goals do seem to have dried up lately. Hopefully we are saving them for the European Cup Final.

Asif is around because our parents are at Parents' Evening. We had our reports last Friday. Mine was okay. Still said "Jonathan is easily distracted". What do teachers expect when I have teenage hormones and the excitement of Villa's European adventure to cope with? Asif's first report at a comprehensive school was a mixed bag. Several teachers seemed amazed by his knowledge. I do think Mr McGinn was harsh using the word "cocky" though.

Asif is getting very worried about the fight in the Falklands. He said that 87 of our Navy were dead or missing. Mrs Thatcher says there will be no ceasefire until the Argentine forces withdraw. I guess there will be lots more dead. This could go on all year. As a pacifist, I cannot condone any of this.

Blooming heck! Thought we were on top. Now 1-0 to Stoke. Plenty of time to come back. Perhaps I should call time on this game with Asif. Maybe 13-1 is a bit humiliating. Perhaps let Gary Shaw score his seventh first.

10:00pm: My parents seemed pleased with the chats with my teachers. They are going to pay for me to do the English Literature O level. Still don't know why I was put in the CSE group for English Lit in the first place.

Looks like the Villa have forgotten how to score. Only three goals now in the last six games. Really thought we would win today. A 1-0 defeat to Stoke City is poor. Our failed title defence now consists of 13 wins, 12 draws and 14 defeats after 39 games. I suppose if we win one more and draw two then it will be total symmetry, 14 of each.

Haystacks will still be worried about going down. Albion beaten at home by Ipswich. We've got to play West Brom on Saturday. We could do Spud's lot a favour by beating them. Even though we lost tonight I'm still going to update the league ladders. Need to check that Ceefax includes tonight's games.

Friday 7ᵗʰ May

12:59pm: Haystacks is full of doom and gloom today. He's convinced Villa will stuff Albion tomorrow. Hope he's right. His dad isn't going. So, Hastings isn't going. He doesn't think he will get to another home game. He's convinced Albion are going to get relegated. He fears he might never see another First Division game at The Hawthorns again. Haystacks put the blame solely on Ron Atkinson deserting them. To make things worse for Scott Hastings, he is now single again. His Frank F Harrison sixth-form girlfriend has dumped him. She said he was too moody and never smiled. What does she expect from a Baggies fan in their current perilous position? Haystacks says he's done with women and football. Mostly women.

Spud is prepared for Wanderers being relegated. He says he's looking forward to games against new teams next season. I try to give him hope. Although, with only two games to go it's unlikely. Normally 32 points is enough to stay up, but now with Jimmy Hill's three points for a win it's probably at least 40 points.

All the Local Gang are girlfriendless. It feels good. We are united by our lack of romantic involvement. How do I feel about the real possibility that next season I'll be the only member of the Local Gang who supports a top division side? At the start of the season there seemed no way that Wolves and Albion might be fighting relegation. Like there was no chance that we wouldn't all still have two parents. Now Spud is half-way to being an orphan and Haystacks' dad has done a runner.

'Are you going to Rotterdam then, Hugh?', Tucker asks the all-important question. I really wanted to even if the thought of going scared the hell out of me. Was it realistic? Probably not, with Mr Hill not going. My parents would never allow me to go on my own especially after the events of the semi-final. How would I even get to Holland? It's a school day as well. Can't exactly just leave when the bell goes. Bullishly, I tell my mates that I'm determined to go. Explaining the obstacles I must overcome.

'This might be your only ever chance to see your crappy team in a European Cup Final. You have to go', Haystacks says. What I suspect the rest of them are thinking. He's got a point.

Saturday 8ᵗʰ May

4:39pm: A point isn't a bad result. Gives Albion a good chance of staying up. Will be our third game in the row that we haven't scored. Sounds like it's been an even game. By the time I've finished "You are the Ref" in my *Shoot!* magazine, it should be full-time. Mark, I think, will be happy with Wolves getting a draw at Goodison. Gives them a chance next Saturday. "The goalkeeper has the ball kicked out of his hands by an opponent. Do you…." That must be a foul if the keeper has it in two hands. But is it a direct or indirect free-kick?

That's late for a goal horn. The Hawthorns! Must be the last kick. Come on, who has scored? There's a lot of noise. Must be Albion. No, it's Villa. Pat Heard of all people. Dennis Mortimer passed a free-kick to him and Heard found the net. I didn't hear Cyrille Regis getting sent off. When did that happen? That's the final whistle. Sorry, Haystacks.

Thursday 13ᵗʰ May

7:48pm: So, Mark chooses the Yazoo song on *Top of the Pops* to tell my parents the news that he has started seeing the former girl next door, Carol. Interesting that he is suggesting this is a new romance. I pretend to be shocked by this revelation. Mum is surprised. She drops one of her knitting needles. Dad seems more perturbed that the Scotland World Cup song is three places higher than the England one. I must admit I prefer the dramatic Scotland *We Have a Dream* one. The actor from *Gregory's Girl* sings it well. Talking more than singing. Allan Evans looks to be really enjoying singing the chorus. England's *This time (we'll get it right)* is probably catchier but it's less dramatic. Think Peter Withe sings on it. Does seem to be the Kevin Keegan show.

Expected more interrogation about the Mark-Carol relationship. I have a feeling that my mum already knew. She's not letting on. If she did. At least all the excitement is over and done with before *It Ain't Half Hot Mum* starts. I certainly wouldn't cope in all that heat.

Am I destined not to be able to focus on any television tonight? Dad's now reading aloud articles from the *Express & Star*. Shifting quickly to how John Ireland is trying to wrestle control of Wolves back from Harry Marshall to the latest casualties in the Falklands war. Now he's going on about Pope John Paul being indestructible, like Captain Scarlet. Seems a mad priest tried stab him today. Less than a year after the Pope survived a previous assassination attempt. I wonder what rank you must reach before a murder attempt becomes an assassination attempt.

Unable to concentrate on Captain Ashwood falling in love with June Whitfield, I decide to test the Rotterdam water. My dad is only half listening. He might agree without even knowing. Mum is going to be harder to convince. I need to find if there is any chance they would let me go to the European Cup Final on Wednesday 26th May. Perhaps best to make them think that Mr Hill is going to take me. This might help my case later when I reveal Mr Hill can no longer go. Perhaps Dad would then agree to step in and play the hero.

8:20pm: Not even a "we'll think about it". Instead, just a "No! No! No!" Followed by a dramatic "Over my dead body". I managed a few fake tears before storming upstairs. Now watching Ronnie Corbett's *Sorry!* I know how Timothy feels having a controlling mother. I need to rethink my approach to getting permission to go to Rotterdam. Need a plan.

Friday 14ᵗʰ May

12:51pm: The next time we have a lunchtime kickabout both Haystacks and Spud could be supporting Second Division teams. Albion's 3-0 pasting by Ron Atkinson's United has moved them dangerously close to the trapdoor. For Spud's Wolves, all they can do is win at West Ham tomorrow and then pray that other results go their way. I hope for my friend's sake they do. Let's get Birmingham City relegated instead.

'STREC?' Tucker continues to suggest acronyms for our new committee. The latest one stood for "Stadler to Rotterdam European Cup". None of us were convinced. It's more important to me for us just to come up with a plan. We need a means to get me there and a cover story. Many crazy ideas were floated. Asif wanted me to hitch-hike. Haystacks suggested a stowaway approach. All totally mad ideas.

We decided that a further meeting of the provisionally called "STREC" committee will be held at 12:45pm on Monday 17ᵗʰ May, when I would hopefully have further travel information from tomorrow's matchday programme. The current meeting closed with Spud chipping the ball over goalkeeper Noddy, as Noddy was bending down to make some meeting notes. It was then proposed that all notes be destroyed as they could later be used in evidence against us.

6:38pm: Good to see that both Allan Evans and Des Bremner have made Jock Stein's provisional 40-man Scotland squad for the World Cup. Be surprised if Des makes the final cut, though. He only has one cap and that was when he still played for Hibernian. Surprisingly, Andy Gray is also included. He's been rubbish for Wolves this season. Always seems to be injured lately. He should never have left the Villa. With Gary Shaw joining Morley and Withe in the England 40 possibles for Spain, that means five Villa players with a chance of making it to Spain this summer.

Ina Botham got 63 for Somerset but they still lost in the Championship to Derbyshire. The Embassy Snooker World Championships is looking exciting. Must watch that tonight with Dad. The semi-final between Jimmy White and Alex Higgins is now level at 11-11. Not sure who I want to win. They both seem a little crazy. Especially compared to the trusty other semi-finalists, Ray Reardon and Eddie Charlton. Is Eddie any relation to Bobby and Jackie Charlton?

Forgotten it's Mark's 18th birthday next week. Going to look in the Argos catalogue if there any car-related things for him. Where is that Argos catalogue? I'm sure it was in the dining room last week. It must be in Mark's room. Am I brave enough to go in there?

Mark's room is very tidy. No clothes lying around. You can tell he's been entertaining a girl in here. Maybe the Argos catalogue is underneath his pile of Wolves programmes? Wow, that's interesting. Mark's collection of *Amateur Photographer* magazines. There is a totally nude woman on the front of that one. Pity she's facing the sea. What a lovely bottom. She's stunning. Superb composition of the photograph. I didn't know these magazines had so many naked ladies in. They are borderline pornographic. No wonder Mark keeps his collection next to his bed. That Lord Lichfield chap really is a dirty old man. There are pages of topless women and naked ladies' front bottoms in the article about Lord Lichfield's calendar shoot. He doesn't need much from the wardrobe department when composing his shots. I need more time to read these magazines. Perhaps I should take more of an interest in photography. Maybe Grace Taylor might agree to pose for me one day. I could say the pictures would be artistic. If I used my polaroid, I could see the pictures in 30 seconds. Think I'll borrow a couple of Mark's older magazines. He won't notice if they are old ones. I can hide them under my mattress. Then flick through them at night using the light from my wind-up torch, under my Villa duvet. I'll take this one from January 1981 with the Lord Lichfield special in.

Saturday 15th May

2:36pm: Bingo! Just what STREC needed. In the middle of the programme is a four-page form. Right in the centre of an Everton away team article. A form listing all the official travel options for Rotterdam. The club are only selling tickets to people travelling with the official travel club. This is brilliant. It tells me all the prices, times and what I need to do. Chairman Mr Ronald Bendall is saying "…the club has taken every precaution possible to prevent the small minority of people, who claim to be football supporters, from damaging the good name of Aston Villa Football Club".

Looks so real seeing it written down, "European Champions Cup Final ASTON VILLA v BAYERN MUNICH WEDNESDAY 26th MAY 1982 at THE FEYENOORD STADIUM ROTTERDAM, HOLLAND Kick-off 20.00 hrs". That's 8pm normal time. Aren't they an hour ahead though on the continent?

So, I can go by plane. Flying out on Monday 24th from either Castle Donnington or Birmingham Airport. I didn't know Castle Donnington had an airport. I thought it was just a castle. I think having to have four days off school makes that option impossible. It is £225, plus if I have a single room it's another £10. That's more than I was thinking. Better bet, I think, will be to go by boat. There is an option for coach or train with the ferry crossing. I'll take my programme to school on Monday and see what the lads think. I do need to be in possession of a valid passport. That could be difficult. I don't think I've got a passport.

Penultimate home game of the 1981/82 season. Last one on a Saturday. Seven points behind Everton. Even if we win our last two games we will still be a point behind them. At least I can relax today, unlike Spud and Mark who are both at Molineux. Even if they beat West Ham and results go their way today, they will still have to wait for other games later this week. Even Noddy and Tucker are sweating on their result at home to Doncaster Rovers. Walsall should be safe though. Even if they lose. One of either Swindon or Wimbledon would need to win for them to be relegated to the Fourth Division. I guess even playing in Fourth Division next season is dependent on them not being wound up in the summer. With Albion in danger too, it's a depressing time for West Midlands football. Well, apart from the flagship team being in the final of the European Cup.

Here comes Tony Barton in his pin-striped suit. He's being given an enormous bottle of Bells Whisky. Penny says it's for winning the April Manager of the Month.

Speaking Clock Tim is on transistor radio watch today. Keeping us up to date with latest scores. Most people in the Trinity seem more interested in the relegation fights of local rivals Birmingham, Albion and Wolves today than what's going to go on in front of them. The greatest desire seems to be that Ron Saunders gets fierce rival Blues relegated. I have checked the league table several times in the programmes and to me this still seems unlikely. There is a much higher probability that Wolves or Albion will be in the Second Division next season.

3:07pm: Tim is jumping up and down. He's joined in celebration by Steve Austin. Penny is quick to find what's going on. Seems Wolves have scored. In fact, they have scored twice already. Bad news for Albion and Birmingham. Maybe the great escape is on. Tim is off again. More misery for Ron's team. Albion are now winning as well.

3:50pm: Liverpool aren't losing that lead. Normal service has been resumed. Liverpool will be champions again. It was good while it lasted having claret and blue ribbons on that famous trophy.

304

We have played some great football today. Pity we let that Graham Sharp score. Bushy eyebrow man said Villa nearly signed him two years ago, before Everton gazumped us. Gordon Cowans has been brilliant. Can't believe he isn't in the England 40. They don't deserve to be level. Wolves 2-1 up. With Leeds not winning, they've got a chance.

5:05pm: It's on *Sports Report* so it's official. Wolverhampton Wanderers have been relegated. They beat West Ham, but with Leeds ending up winning, they are down. Even before Birmingham scored that late winner at Coventry. Ron Saunders has managed to keep our rivals in the First Division. Still doesn't seem right him working across the city. Albion won, but so did Middlesbrough and Sunderland. Incredibly the bottom six all won! Liverpool are champions. Bobby Robson's Ipswich are bridesmaids again. Bizarrely, they are saying Stoke are now in the bottom three. Mr Hill is getting confused. He thinks Albion are down. The presenter now explaining that only Wolves are down. The other two places will be filled by Albion, Stoke, Leeds or Middlesbrough. No idea how Boro are still fighting. Guess it will be a long time before they tell us the fate of Noddy and Tucker's Saddlers.

Graham Taylor's Watford have been promoted. So, Luton Town, Watford and Norwich City will be gracing Villa Park next season. That should be a guaranteed nine points.

With all the end of season relegation and promotion proceedings, Villa's defeat to Everton seems insignificant. We should have won, though. Silly goals to concede.

Monday 17th May

9:14am: Spud is wearing a black armband. Jock tried to get him to take it off. Spud said he was in mourning. Think McGinn thought it might have been Pete's mum's birthday or something. Instead of the true reason, which is to mark the relegation of his beloved football club. From League Cup Winners just over two years ago to a Second Division club in danger of falling into administration. It's been a dramatic slump. A slump that might be matched this week by Haystacks' Baggies. West Brom were fourth last season. Only eight points behind champions Aston Villa. Now they are fighting for their First Division life. Two games in the next four days will decide Albion's fate. Leeds and then Stoke both at home. Three points will guarantee their safety.

Noddy is trying to explain to Asif the Walsall situation. Seems that after their goalless draw on Saturday, they've played all their games. They must just wait now. If Swindon win tomorrow night, Walsall are down. Or if Swindon don't win and Wimbledon win by 14 goals, Walsall are also down. Oddly, Asif asks, 'what are the chances of Wimbledon scoring 14 goals?'

12:48pm: Not sure who elected Asif STREC secretary, but he is busy taking notes. Asif is using his invisible ink pen from his *Yes & No Quiz Book*. Preventing us from leaving any secret information as clues. Haystacks has studied the Official Travel pullout pamphlet from my Villa programme.

'I think the best option, Hugh, is tour number AVCBI', Haystacks informs the meeting. 'Go by coach and boat'.

Reading the details I see it costs £31 plus £8 seat ticket. No hotel involved. I'm going to be knackered. Noddy says I can sleep on the coach. Haystacks has gone for a seat ticket. He thinks it will keep me away from any trouble. He says the fighting will be on the terraces. I guess £39 isn't bad. Probably need a bit of spending money as well. I would want to buy a programme. Tucker starts to plan how they can get me to the Villa on Tuesday evening, 25th May. He seems to think I can go straight from school. Yes, I'm sure my parents will agree to that.

'You get back 10am Thursday morning. We can get you back to school for lunchtime. You'll only be missing a day and a half of school', Spud is next to chip in.

I do feel the lads are overlooking some important details in this plan. I don't have a passport, my parents will never let me go and I need to call in person to the Travellers Club office.

3:15pm: 'Are they really going to smuggle you to Rotterdam, Stadler?' Julie Duggan asks me during Biology. So much for it being a big secret plan. I tell Julie to be quiet. A big ask. 'I can help', she loudly whispers.

Why am I only finding this information out now? Julie Duggan's brother is taking a coachload of Villa fans to the final. He runs the Cannock Aston Villa supporters club and has permission by the club to take fans. To get a match ticket, though, fans must be Villa Travellers Club Members. This changes everything. Maybe this could be the answer. Her brother is 22, so he will be a responsible adult. I need to quickly fill the gang in on this development. Julie Duggan is going to ask her dad tonight and then if he's happy she'll give me a call tonight. I give her our phone number. We concoct a cover story for the phone call. Julie is going to say she needs to know what the Biology homework is.

7:11pm: Mum is engrossed in BBC1's *Triangle,* so answering the phone is much easier than I had anticipated. I knew Julie was going to ring just after seven.

Trying to appear to stay calm as Julie Duggan gives me the fabulous news. Her brother Steve is happy to take me. He'll only charge me £30. Happy to get me there without a passport as well. Makes me sound like a master criminal. I just need to get a ticket and also must have a Villa Travellers Club membership card. I can manage this. Then the killer blow. Julie Duggan told me her brother will only agree to it if he can talk to my parents. So near yet so far. I say goodbye and put the phone down.

'Who was that, love?', Mum asks but doesn't take her eyes off sailor Matt Taylor. Still think it's funny that the bloke who plays him is named Larry Lamb. Interesting that the ferry in *Triangle* is heading for Amsterdam.

Mum wasn't really interested in my story of Julie Duggan wanting to know what our Biology homework was. She was more focused on the telly. Mark, however, was. He followed me upstairs. He suggested that I was being secretive. That I hadn't mentioned Biology homework once on the call. He didn't even believe it was a girl. So much for your powers of deduction, Mark Stadler.

8:44pm: It's a gamble, but I reckon he owes me one. I decide to confide in my older brother. After all, I hadn't mentioned Wolves' relegation once. As well as keeping his Carol and crazy Sarah secrets. Mark might be able to help.

Mark is quite understanding. He does think I should go to Rotterdam. If only to see my "bunch of losers get smashed by Bayern Munich". He also knows that Mum is never going to agree to it. We must keep it secret. But Mark is going to help. He says he will pretend to be Dad and phone Julie Duggan's brother. He will also drop me off and pick me up. Make sure I am safely on the coach. That must be as far as his involvement goes. Mum and Dad are never to find out he was part of it.

Tuesday 18th May

7:07pm: Randy can't believe he is here. His first ever game at Villa Park. When I had told him Mr Hill had suggested he came with us, Randy did a little dance. It might not be a real game, but for Randy this was as good as being at the cup final. We were among around 10,000 other people. All of whom have come to play tribute to one of Randy's all-time heroes, Brian Little. This is Aston Villa v

England for Brian Little's Testimonial. I've given Randy the full tour of the Trinity Road Enclosure.

Time to take a chance again. I need Randy's help with my Rotterdam plan. I know it will put him in a difficult situation, but hope he'll do it for Grandad. I want him to bring me to Villa Park tomorrow after school. Well, via Woolworths. I need to register for my Villa Travellers Club Membership and buy my European Champions Cup Final ticket. I feel bad asking Randy to do this, but who else can bring me. He doesn't even have to lie to my parents. We can say he's bringing me to the club shop so we can both buy new scarves to wear when we watch the European Cup Final.

To my delight, Randy agrees to be my accomplice. He'll collect me from school tomorrow and take me to Villa Park. If he doesn't have to drive on the motorway. We must go to the club shop though and then he doesn't have to have to tell any lies.

Here come Dennis Mortimer and Kevin Keegan leading the two teams out. Randy is up out of his seat. Not only does he get to see the Villa but also wave England off on their World Cup adventure. Villa are at full strength. Only change is at number eight. Instead of Gary Shaw there is the man himself. The one who walks on water. Brian Little. He looks fit. Difficult to believe he was forced to retire injured two years ago. Villa have a sponsor on their shirts. I wonder if that's the new one for next season. It's got a tree and says "BARRETT" on the front.

7:32pm: He's scored! Against England! Two minutes in and Aston Villa are beating England. The goalscorer is Brian Little.

8:01pm: The crowd rise as the legendary Brian Little leaves the pitch. Randy is in tears. What a half an hour of Little magic. He scored two goals. Villa leading 2-1. On comes David Geddis.

8:28pm: To think a week tomorrow I'll (hopefully) be at the European Cup Final. I managed to get Steve Duggan's phone number and this afternoon Mark was as good as his word. He rang Julie's brother and impersonated our dad. As Dad, Mark gave full approval for his son, Jonathan Stadler, to go on the coach and ferry to Rotterdam. With my birthday money and this month's pocket-money I've got enough cash to give Julie Duggan. But then what am I going to buy the ticket with?

Here come the players for the second half. Looks like Villa are going to make a couple of changes. I suppose at 3-1 up we can take it a little easy. Jimmy Rimmer is coming off and so are Gary Williams and Ken McNaught. Keep them fresh for Swansea on Friday. Nigel Spink, Colin Gibson and Pat Heard are coming on.

10:20pm: Pity there wasn't a bigger crowd tonight for Brian. Guess having a home game last Saturday and then another on Friday makes it quite an expensive week. Good game though. Randy certainly enjoyed it. Villa took it easy second half. England players were all trying to make sure they gave Ron Greenwood reasons to put them in his final 22. Still, Villa 3, England 2 sounds good.

Pleased Albion and Walsall both stayed up tonight. Sounds like Newport left it late to beat Swindon and keep Walsall up. Haystacks will be happy with Albion beating Leeds. Cyrille Regis getting his 25th goal of the season. Means Stoke City will go down unless they beat Albion on Thursday night.

Just can't sleep. Too much going around my head. I don't think I'm good at deception. Dad was puzzled when I said Randy was taking me to the Villa shop tomorrow after school. Not surprisingly, he asked why we couldn't go before the game last night. I said Mr Hill was running late. Mr Hill never runs late. Going to read my *Shoot!* magazine for a bit. A lot about the World Cup in it. Only three weeks until England's first group game against France. Hope France aren't as good as the Villa. Ten First Division players are picking their starting England eleven. Interestingly, four of them have picked Tony Morley. Including former Villa full-back

John Gidman. Nobody has gone for Peter Withe. The last selection is by David Geddis. Can't believe he's chosen no Villa players. Seven of the players have put Peter Shilton in goal. Only two for Ray Clemence. Think I agree with that choice. The other one, Billy Bonds, stays loyal to his West Ham goalkeeper, Phil Parkes. You see, David Geddis, that's how you pick your team. Ooh there's a free World Cup wallchart next week. I must get that.

Shoot! "World Cup stars to watch" is all about Karl-Heinz Rummenigge of West Germany, who plays for our Final opponents Bayern Munich. European Footballer of the Year in both 1980 and 1981. Sounds like he's really been banging in the goals of late.

Good to see Villa in full colour on a centre-page spread. Great headline "Villa Glory". It says, above Villa's celebrating semi-final players, that "Liverpool and Forest have kept the European Cup in England for the last five years … now Aston Villa can make it six in a row". I'm feeling sick with nerves already.

What's that picture of Peter Withe doing on the letters page? The Star Letter of the Week is from Tony Goldingay of Streetly, West Midlands. He wins £10 for being Letter of the Week. He's saying a big thank you to Peter Withe, who he met at his dentist's when he was having four teeth taken out. Peter put his mind at ease. Tony told Peter he was an Ipswich Town fan. Why was he living in Streetly then? Peter Withe promised to send him a signed picture and an Aston Villa team poster. A few days later, Tony, minus his teeth, had a call from the dentist saying Peter had left some items for him. Super Peter had got all the Ipswich Town players to sign a ball, an Ipswich poster and an Ipswich shirt.

Wednesday 19th May

5:23pm: That's it. I'm a member of the Villa Travellers club. Now queuing for my European Cup Final ticket. Well, queuing to pay for it. You don't get it until you get to Holland. Randy has been brilliant. He picked me up from school right on the bell. He drove me to Woolworths. Nearly reached 25mph at one point. Randy even paid for the passport photographs. He did insist on being in the third one. We got to Villa Park quite quickly as well. Guess we beat the rush-hour traffic. Forgot I needed an extra £1 for the membership fee but Randy managed to produce a pound note from his purse.

Quite a few Villa fans in this queue. Mostly older than me. Guess I'll see some of them again at the Feyenoord Stadium. Was quite a struggle at school to raise the money for the ticket. The gang all helped have a whip-round. They manged to get £5. So, I am going to be standing on the terrace instead of sitting in the safer seat. Asif wouldn't say how the lads raised all the money. But I know Grace Taylor put some in and that Haystacks took some empties back to the off-licence. I'm not even going to have to touch my Grandad's money. That's a bonus.

6:17pm: That's it! I now have proof in my hand that I've paid for a ticket for the Aston Villa v Bayern Munich European Cup Final. Something that I must keep secret from my parents. Finally going to a cup final that will feature my club. Randy is finding it all too much to take in. He wants to feel the piece of paper Villa have given me but is also dreading ever facing my parents again.

Spud will never believe this. If only I'd got my polaroid. Am I dreaming? Standing about ten yards in front of me. On the steps of the Trinity Road Stand. It can't be!

Thursday 20ᵗʰ May

8:57am: 'Don't believe you!' Tucker, like the others, was not buying my claim of what I saw last night. I did. I saw Erika Roe in a new Villa shirt with the word "DAVENPORTS" emblazoned across her ample bosom. The bloke there told Randy they were doing some marketing shots to promote Villa's new £100,000 sponsorship deal. Next season we will have a name on the front of our shirts. Jimmy Hill has made it so teams can now have sponsors' names on the front. Not sure if I'm in favour, but Twickenham streaker Erika Roe certainly made it very appealing.

I hand over £30 to Julie Duggan. Hope I can trust her. She seems to just put the cash loose in her blazer pocket. I ask her why she isn't going to Rotterdam. She says she's never been to a football match. Her dad is very strict and doesn't allow it. Her brother, though, gets away with everything. There's something quite sweet about Julie. I've never noticed before. She's not as hard as I thought.

1:01pm: Haystacks has devised a plan to minimise suspicion when I go missing the day of the European Cup Final. Haystacks' mum is so worried about him never coming out of his room, except when the hot solicitor turns up, that she'll give him almost anything he wants. Usually Mars bars, but next Tuesday night he's going to say he wants his friends to stay over. A "sleepover" like American girls have. Glad I won't be there because the idea of sharing a bedroom with Noddy, Tucker and a sweaty Spud is not my idea of Heaven. It's a good plan, but what if my parents check to see if I'm there? Scott Hastings has thought of this. It's perfect in its simplicity. His mum has never met me. She's also never met Noddy. The idea is that Haystacks introduces Noddy to his mum as "Jonathan Stadler". This means if anybody asks who stayed, then Haystacks' mum will say Jonathan stayed. It's brilliant. That covers night one but what about the night of the final?

'We might have to extend it to a second night', Tucker suggested. I'm not convinced. I think my parents would get suspicious. 'We could claim we had caught some tropical disease and had to go into quarantine'. Haystacks asked Tucker what kind of tropical disease you could contract in Willenhall.

'Does it matter?' Asif stuns the group. He explains that if my parents found out teatime on the day of the match, so what. He suggested that apart from getting Interpol searching for me there wasn't a lot they could do. By that time, I'd be safely in Rotterdam. He had a point, but had he ever seen my mum crazy cross? Guess they're always going to find out that I went at some point. Going to see my club in a European Cup Final would be worth any punishment they dished out to me.

Friday 21st May

7:03pm: Glad I'm queuing up at the Trinity Road Stand now, having said goodbye to Mr Hill. Really felt bad not telling Howard the truth. Having to talk about next week's final as an event I will only be witnessing on the television. Not letting on that under my mattress, with several X-rated copies of *Amateur Photographer,* was a piece of paper that entitled me to a Rotterdam ticket. I hadn't even been able to share with Mr Hill my brief encounter with the large-breasted Erika Roe.

Last time I'll be ripping tickets out of this season ticket book. Will make sure I keep this book, my first ever season ticket, as a souvenir in my cashbox. If I have a season ticket every season until I'm 84, I'll end up with 70 books. Might need a bigger cashbox. I guess the first season and we reach the European Cup Final is an impressive start. Odd how quickly Doris, Penny and bushy eyebrow man have become my Villa friends. Doris always seems so pleased to see me. Hope they are all still here next season. I don't want any of them going the way of old Mr Warrington. Not much grass left on the pitch. It has certainly seen a lot of games this season. Think the best one was the quarter-final against Dynamo Kiev. The League Cup comeback against Wolves was pretty good too.

Just one last game left, against Swansea. Be good to go off to Rotterdam with a top performance. I'm telling everyone in the Trinity that I'm off to the final. Haven't let on to Doris, though, that I'm going on my own. I don't want the old lady worrying. Bushy eyebrow man says, "bring back the cup".

I expected more from the souvenir programme. Seems fewer pages in than normal. At least it says, "Good luck Villa!" on the front. Guess they've been busy this week with the Everton game and then the Brian Little Testimonial. Disappointed no pictures of Erika Roe.

Worrying that Gary Shaw is still missing. Everybody else is playing. Apart from Bob Lachford and Robbie James I don't recognise any of the Swansea players.

8:13pm: Nice goal, Des Bremner. Wonder if Bayern have sent a scout. Hope if they have that Villa have given them a rubbish seat behind a pillar. We're playing well, 2-0 and passing the ball around nicely. Not sure how a team as good as us are only going to finish 11th. At least in the top half. Swansea are 6th and they just don't look in our league. Like dirty Leeds won't be next season after Stoke beat Albion last night.

8:46pm: That's number three. Peter Withe's 10th league goal of the season. That's half the number he got last season. Doris thinks we'll score five.

9:13pm: I wonder how many of these fans will be there next Wednesday night? We're all giving the players and Tony Barton a terrific send-off. Nice to end with a 3-0 thumping. Hope we're at home first game next season. Hopefully with Dennis parading the giant European Cup around the pitch. I know it's going to be a very hard game. Bayern Munich are full of West German internationals.

Feel quite tearful walking away from the ground. Mr Hill waiting for me as always. Can't believe it's going to be three months before I next go to a game here. Perhaps I should have given old Doris a hug.

Saturday 22nd May

11:04am: Just time to watch a recording of last night's *Soap* before Cup Final Grandstand starts. See what happened to Jessica's kidnapped baby.

Looks like no Villa today. Ricky Villa has decided not to play for Spurs at Wembley. Due to all the hostility over his country invading the Falklands. So, no Argentinian players. Ossie Ardiles never came back from international duty due to the conflict. Spurs are letting him play for French club Paris Saint-Germain. Maybe with their two star men missing, Spurs might not equal our record. They should beat Second Division QPR. Saying that, Southampton won it in '76 and West Ham in '80 both as Second Division teams.

Leicester's Gary Lineker is on back page of this week's *Shoot!* He says his favourite ground is Villa Park. Good taste in TV as well. His favourite show is *Not the Nine O'Clock News*. Will struggle to reach his personal ambition. He wants to play for England. After playing he aims to become a bookmaker. Good choice in the "which person in the world would you most like to meet?" category. He's gone for Victoria Principal. Can't believe Asif has never watched the FA Cup Final build-up. Can't believe he's never heard of Victoria Principal either.

That's annoying. No mention of Villa's European Final in the *Shoot!* Magazine. At least I've got my World Cup wallchart. Not putting it up until I get back from Rotterdam.

2:36pm: Must be great to sing *Abide with Me* at Wembley. Seems to be more poignant this year with us being at war.

Mum has finally agreed to me staying over at the Hastings' house on Tuesday night. Even though it's a school night. She said she knows Mr Hastings and used to go to his butchers. Not sure Haystacks' dad was ever a butcher. Thought best not to mention that Haystacks' dad walked out on them at Christmas. She is insisting Mark drops me off. Mark is not happy about this at all. He thinks it's getting him more and more involved.

Not sure who Princess Anne supports. She seems to be smiling more at the Spurs players. No, Asif, I don't know why both teams are wearing their away kits. Who's that at the door?

Uncle Norman is keeping the tradition alive. He has come to watch the Cup Final. Pity he's brought Auntie Mavis. She will talk all the way through it. A dilemma for Mark. Carol is here as well. He's gone for the public kiss. That's brave. Obviously, everyone knows now. Mark wants Carol to sit on his lap while he watches the final. Dad's not happy with that. At least Auntie Mavis and Mum have gone into the kitchen.

4:42pm: One of dullest Cup Finals I can remember. Hucker has made some good saves for Rangers but not many real chances. Simon Stainrod had a late shot but Ray Clemence isn't being beaten from there. Another 30 minutes then to try and get a goal. An endurance test. Mark and Carol gave in just after half-time and disappeared upstairs. Asif lasted about an hour before he went home to work on his French vocabulary homework. Just need QPR to pinch a goal. Maybe John Gregory can sneak one in.

8:25pm: I guess our final will not be the last game this season now. With Queens Park Rangers' Terry Fenwick late equaliser, there'll be an FA Cup replay at Wembley on Thursday. Pretty sure by then my parents will know I skipped the country. I'm sure I'll be grounded for the rest of the year.

Carol is still here. Auntie Mavis seems quite excited about this new connection our families have gained. I do hope it works out between Mark and Carol. She was like an older sister to me growing up. Be great if she became my sister-in-law.

Monday 24ᵗʰ May

6:50pm: If anybody is going to give our secret away, it's Randy. He's just all over the place. Every time Mum directs a question at him, he reacts like a rabbit caught in the headlights. Mum only asked him if he wanted a fig roll with his cup of tea. You would have thought by his nervous response that he was watching his egg fall off the wacky contraption he had built on *The Great Egg Race*. I'll be happy once I'm on that ferry. Feel bad including Randy and Mark in my deception. Maybe I should back out.

Randy came especially tonight to bring me a copy of *Sports Argus* European Cup 1982 Special. Peter Withe, Allan Evans and a very small child on the front. The small child looks as petrified as Mr Nawas did when Dad asked him how he was finding the new neighbours. I need to get one of those Villa hats. Still haven't decided what I'm wearing for the big day. I'm going to need to travel light. It must fit it into my school bag. Looks like Bayern's star men are Paul Breitner and the beans bloke Karl-Heinz Rummenigge. We've got good players too. Oh, the kid on the front cover is Allan Evans' 18-month old son. That makes more sense. Says the Bayern Munich manager, Uli Hoeness, was a member of the Bayern team that won the European Cup three years running in the '70s. It says he's only 30 years old. That's very young for a manager. Bet if they beat us he'll be youngest manager ever to win the European Cup. Good to see Ron Saunders saying, "I expect Villa to win". Kenny Swain is certainly up for it, "Apart from perhaps appearing in the World Cup Final, I can think of nothing better than playing in the European Cup Final". That's it, Kenny! There's no going back. I'm going to Rotterdam and we're going to keep that big cup in England. Where it belongs. That's a good coloured-poster. I'm going to Blu Tack that to the inside of my bedroom window. Would be great to put a sign up saying "Gone to Rotterdam". Time to pack my bag. Need to try and sneak some orange Club bars out from the kitchen. Randy gave me a tenner.

That should pay for any food and snacks I get. Worried about my lack of a passport. Julie Duggan says that won't be a problem. I've got my Villa Travellers Club Membership card. I look like the Mona Lisa with that odd smile in the photo. I'm going to secretively hide my lucky radio in Randy's car. He has promised to have it on during the Final. He's going to turn the volume off on the ITV commentary. Even though Brian Moore is his favourite commentator.

That's heartbreaking. It says on front page a soldier from Sutton Coldfield has been killed on his 18th birthday. His mum said he hadn't wanted to go to fight in the Falklands. This war must end soon. Why can't they negotiate peace?

Tuesday 25th May

12:01pm: Is there anybody in this school who doesn't know I'm off to Holland? Even Mr Walker seemed to give me a knowing look. Julie Duggan seems to be almost stuck to me. A little odd her giving me that rabbit's foot. Relieved to see she had cut it off her toy bunny. Why should a rabbit losing a leg be lucky? I've promised to keep it in my pocket during the game. I must have checked 20 times that I have the slip of paper to claim the ticket. Tucker seems quite excited to be going for tea at Haystacks'. Noddy is extra excited because he's going to be pretending to be me. Oddly, he says he's been practicing the voice. Spud seems quite calm about it all. I'm the one who is a gibbering wreck. I really am scared. I don't know if I'm going to be able to cope with this. I won't know anybody. Feel I can't let the lads down now. Feel like I could puke at any time. What if there was fighting? I'm a pacifist. I wasn't born to fight. What will my parents do if they find I'm missing? What if I'm seasick on the ferry?

'I think you are so brave, Jonathan. I've got you two Tip Top drinks for the journey'. Grace even gave me a big hug. Perhaps when this is all over, we can make a go of it. Hope nobody else will have got their hands inside her bra.

Gifts keep coming. Wendy McGregor has got me a FOUR-finger Kit Kat. She oddly said, "think of me when you break a finger off". Maybe she's regretting giving this brave adventurer the elbow.

3:50pm: Time to say goodbye to my mates. I can see Mark's bright orange Escort car parked by the school gate. I almost feel jealous that the rest of the Local Gang, even Asif, are going to be together tonight. I'll be alone amongst a coachload of people I don't know.

The gang are ready. Each of them knows exactly what they must do. Noddy has to pretend to be me. Haystacks needs to make his mum believe that Jonathan Stadler is there. Spud must get me marked as present on the register tomorrow. Tucker is going to record the final for me. Asif is going to make everyone believe that we are playing together after school tomorrow.

6:47pm: We arrive at a deserted road in Cannock. Mark is checking Dad's *A to Z*. Making make sure this is the road that Steve Duggan said. Thought there would be a few Villa fans here. It's certainly the right day. We're ten minutes early.

A group of four middle-aged men is approaching. I can see claret and blue silk scarves around the wrist of one. Did think there would be a lot more than this. No coach in sight. Perhaps the Duggans have conned us out of our £30s. I can hear what sounds like Villa songs. They're coming from that dodgy-looking pub down the road.

Mark looks very worried. I think he wants to take me home. I sit in the passenger seat with the window down. I'm so scared. Hoping that it's all a con. That I'll be able to go back to my mates at the Hastings'.

Is that it? Coming towards us is an old coach. A coach that looks like it belongs in the Steptoes' scrapyard. It's an "F" plate. That's about as old as me. How is that going to get us to Rotterdam? Looks like it's only the rust that's holding it together.

It's our coach. A young, long-haired chap with a clipboard descends the steps. Seems to be the driver and the organiser. Mark gets my bag from the boot. Can't believe I'm still in my school trousers. Can't I just stay here in the car? Mark drags me towards the bloke with the clipboard. Confirms that the man is Steve Duggan. Gets a reassurance that I'll be looked after. Do I want to be "looked after"? The Villa singing is getting louder. I look to see a large crowd of Villa fans leaving the pub and walking towards the old banger. Clear that several of these travellers have had several pints. Look of horror spreads across Mark's face. But he retreats, leaving me to climb aboard. I plonk myself halfway down the coach. No idea how, or if, I should interact with the embarking drunken rabble. I can see the orange Escort reversing away. This is not a time for tears. I need to be strong. I pretend to be busy searching for something in my bag. Anything to avoid eye contact with my fellow passengers. I put the bag by the side of me. Making it less appealing for anybody wanting to sit next to me.

'Is this seat taken, mate?' It's a familiar voice. A voice I would know anywhere. Standing there is Peter Hogan. My best mate, Spud.

10:52pm: Spud's snoring was getting louder, but I didn't care. The couple opposite can stare all they want. This is a true friend. He could see earlier in the week that I was brickin' it. So, Spud had paid Julie Duggan £30 to come with me. As he said, "someone's got to protect you against those Germans". He hasn't got a ticket. He's just come for me. Has no desire to see the Villa in a final. His dad thinks he is at Haystacks'. Anyway, his dad is away working this week. Spud has been left to fend for himself. Left plenty of money for takeaways, but Spud gave money to Wendy Duggan instead.

Seems all the lads had been in on this. They knew I'd never agree to the idea. Now I was just delighted that I had a companion. Starting to chat to the fellow Villa passengers and join in with some of the songs. Even singing a few of the naughty words. The older spectacled bloke behind us is quite chatty. Asked me, "You Jonathan, then?" How did he know me? His reply surprised me even more, "we all know Jonathan Stadler". The mysterious man didn't give much away. Apart from that he went to the 1957 Cup Final. Steve Duggan did refer to him as Mr Boating.

Despite its advancing years, our old rundown coach was passing several more modern Villa coaches. We saluted each Aston Villa fan we saw. Even normal people in cars and lorries sounded their horns as we overtook. Aware that we were going off to represent our great nation. Hopefully continuing the tradition of English European Cup winners. Could we possibly do it?

11:50pm: How has Spud got his passport? That picture looks nothing like him. Pre-Gary Numan dyed hair. Spud had said he would make me a fake passport in Technical Drawing. An offer I didn't take up. Nervous here, as we wait to drive onboard the ferry at Dover. Steve Duggan collected all the passports. The security guard seems to be going through all of them. He's going to see there's one short. Hope I don't get arrested and end up in some darkened Dover jail.

The security guard is happy. He hasn't even looked inside the coach. He's walking away and Steve is getting back up. Julie Duggan's brother gives me a thumbs up. I'm in the clear.

The coach parks up inside the ferry. We're soon crossing the Channel. The boat is packed with Villa fans. Different ages. Some nice-looking girls in straw boaters with claret and blue ribbons on. Mr Boating is sitting on his own at a table behind us. Seems to have a flask full of soup. He's tucked a napkin into his collar to protect his Villa tie.

The captain announces over the crackly tannoy that the bar has had to close. The Villa fans, apart from Mr Boating, collectively groan. The captain then makes a second announcement, 'It's your fault. You've drunk the bar empty'.

It's choppier than I expected. Don't remember it being this rough when on the school trip to St Malo last year. Lovely smell of vomit this end of the ferry.

Wednesday 26ᵗʰ May

6:14am: Must have been asleep. Not sure if we're still in France. Spud is asleep again. He'd been flirting with the two women on the back row with the Villa rosettes last time I looked. That arm is a bit too close to me. Wednesday 26ᵗʰ May 1982. Will it be a date that Villa fans will celebrate for years to come? Could this be the day that sees us become Champions of Europe? Still find it odd being on the wrong side of the road. This old banger is travelling at a fair pace. I've got a feeling this is Belgium. Mr Boating offers me a Murray Mint and informs me that the water to our left is the Lys river.

7:50am: Spud has eaten my last bit of chocolate. He's also knocked back three cans of Carlsberg Special Brew he had hidden in his duffle bag. Hope there's a toilet stop soon. I'm bursting. Bloke in front says we're in Holland now. It even says something that looks like Rotterdam on the road sign.

'I asked Emily Martins out. She said yes', Spud just drops into conversation. I guess the Kit Kat triggered his memory. I suppose she's an upgrade on Carrie Carrington.

I'm aware that Spud and I are conspicuous by our lack of Villa clothing. Relieved that Spud hasn't made it public that he supports Second Division Wolverhampton Wanderers. Perhaps he did arise some suspicion when the old chap in the Villa bowler asked him for his prediction. He seemed quite taken back when Spud said 4-0 to Bayern.

1:27pm: I guess the rest of the gang are at afternoon registration now. Hopefully my parents are none the wiser. No, it's only just lunchtime there. Forgot we are one hour ahead of England. It's only half-twelve back at home. I changed my digital watch on the ferry.

I can see the floodlights. We must be here. Excitement spreads around the coach. It even wakes up Spud. The driver follows the view of the floodlights. Travelling through some quite minor roads. Finally getting near the ground. Not very impressed with the stadium. It doesn't look grand enough to host a major European Final. Reminds me more of Bilston's non-league ground. Guess grounds in Holland aren't as good as in Britain. Surprised by the lack of activity around the ground. Where are the television vans and how was our old banger the first coach to arrive?

'This isn't the Feyenoord Stadium', Mr Boating protests. Driver and organiser Steve Duggan has found somebody to ask. Unfortunately, the international language of expressive hand gestures only results in shakes of the head by the confused passerby. Mr Boating is now getting off the coach. What's he up to? He's found a Dutch policeman. The copper is now rudely laughing at poor Mr Boating.

Mr Boating returns to tell the coach driver that this is the ground where school children play. We are still five miles away from the international stadium.

3:45pm: Precious green ticket collected. No idea what it all means as it's in a foreign language but trust the Villa chap has given me a legit ticket. Pity Spud won't be with me in the ground. He seems quite happy drinking beer. They wouldn't serve pre-pubescent me, and anyway I need to focus on the game. Still over four hours to kick-off. Plenty of red-and-white Bayern Munich fans around. Mr

Boating seems to be on his own, so we're letting him tag along. He insisted on buying me a Villa sunhat. I agreed only if he got himself one as well. Mr Boating now wants us to call him George.

Walking around the stadium. It looks like it was made from large Meccano pieces. The large letters on the front saying "stadion feyenoord". My mum wouldn't be impressed with the lack of capital letters.

Mr Boating is chatting with a local Feyenoord supporter. Oddly in French. Well, it sounds like French. As he moves away the Feyenoord supporter shouts "Villa! Villa!". We quiz George about this. Seems the Dutch are supporting us tonight. They don't like the West Germans. Still haven't forgiven them for beating them in the 1974 World Cup Final.

We come across what looks like the official Feyenoord training pitches. There's quite a large game of footy going on. Spud is keen to join in and show off his footballing skills. As we get closer, we see more people are starting to join the game. It's Mr Boating who first notices the differing attire of the two large masses. One side in familiar claret and blue and the opposing team featuring a lot of red. There was no structure, but this was very much Villa fans against Bayern Munich fans. It was a friendly yet competitive affair. Reminiscent, I suspect, of the Christmas Day First World War game between the rival forces. Tackles were flying in and not all Football Association rules were being adhered to.

Spud is oddly joining in with the West German supporters. He can't be associated with us Villans. Mr Boating and I are chasing the ball for the Villa boys. Mr Boating is now taking a breather. I can't get anywhere near the ball. Rumour is that the score is currently level. Suggestion of next goal wins. I'm sure that's a rule all nationalities follow. I've just been kicked by Spud. The ball was nowhere near.

Pressure here from the Bayern fans. Think we're outnumbered. Some of the local police are joining our team, though. Spud has suddenly got the ball. How did that happen. Despite the excessive amount of Special Brew he's consumed, he's showing some fancy moves. Nobody seems to want to challenge him. Admittedly there is some confusion over which side Spud is actually on.

What was the Villa keeper doing? Nipping back to finish his pint. Spud's being mobbed. He's won the game for Bayern Munich. Unbelievable! That shot should never have gone in. Peter mishit it. Hope that's not an omen for the real game.

Catching up with Mr Boating, who is puzzled at Spud's defection. 'I've got a surprise for your mate. Not sure he's going to want it after seeing him scoring for our opponents', Mr Boating offers more mystery.

7:21pm: Walking into the arena. This is special. The three-tier open oval ground of the Feyenoord Stadium. So many fans decked in claret and blue. Union Jacks everywhere. Many Villa fans already stripped to the waist apart from their Villa hats. I'll certainly not be joining them. My chubby little boy-boobs are not for public view. Bad enough when they make me be on a team that is "skins" in games. I feel so nervous. No idea what the next three hours of my life will bring. Not sure what time the telly for the match starts in England. Hope my dad doesn't see me in the crowd. Feel quite homesick. Good that I'm with Spud. Fancy Mr Boating doing that. He's a strange chap. Very kind, though. Swapping his seat in the stand for two tickets here on the Villa terrace. Think Spud is happier to be in the ground with us. He doesn't give much away. Spud's chin is getting quite stubbly. Sun is quite strong. Strange smell. Smells of rotten fish.

Every game of the last two years has been building up to this moment. Do wish Ron Saunders was still in charge. Trust in Tony

326

Barton. A banner nearby reads "BARTONS TASK FORCE
SINKS BAYERN".

8:11pm: We are belting out the National Anthem. Hope the Queen
is tuned in. I feel so proud to be British and a Villa fan. Our players
look up for it. In our classy white Le Coq Sportif shirts. Wish I had
one of those. Full strength. This is the team that won us the league.
Now go on lads, pull off the dream. Mr Boating might have listed
Bayern Munich's ten internationals. Yes, they might never have lost
a major final. But they haven't been up against Mortimer, Cowans,
Morley and Co. This is what I dreamt about. Dreams can come
true.

Spud shakes his head. Showing that he fears I'll leave this
place heartbroken. I won't. Whatever happens, I'll be proud of my
team. Proud of the part I played, shouting from the Lower Trinity
to get them here. This is a time to be positive. Villa will do it.
They'll do it for Doris, for Mr Hill, for bushy eyebrow man and for
the many other Villa fans around the globe. George Boating just
says, 'be patient'. He's already told us the five Villa players who are
lined up to take penalties. It's Gordon Cowans, Allan Evans, Kenny
Swain, Peter Withe and Gary Shaw. I don't think my adolescent
heart could take a penalty shootout. If it gets that far then I'll put
my faith in Jimmy Rimmer.

Bayern Munich to kick off in their red. Come on, Villa. More
empty seats than I was expecting. Can't see many neutral people.
I'm sure that's Central TV's Gary Newbon on the Villa bench.
What's he doing there?

Close by Allan Evans. Pity that header couldn't have dipped a
foot lower. I think we've started well.

That's a nasty foul on Des Bremner. This is a chance to get it
in the box. Gordon needs to put a good ball in. Go on, Peter! That
was a good chance once Peter Withe had won the header.

What's going on? Why is Jimmy walking towards the sideline? He's taking off his gloves. Shaking his head. Villa fans have gone silent. Jimmy Rimmer is coming off! We are changing our goalkeeper after just nine minutes. Didn't see him get injured. Why is he coming off? This is dreadful. Nigel Spink has only ever played one real game for us. We lost that one. It was over two years ago. This can't be happening. Jimmy never misses a game. Why now?

8:36pm: Spink is doing okay. Bet he's nervous. All Bayern at the moment. We're just not creating. Looks like we're shell-shocked after losing Jimmy. Good save by Nigel Spink. Then the shot is blocked by Allan Evans. The noise in the ground is so loud. That's never a foul. Rummenigge dived. Don't get fooled by that, ref. Even Spud is calling him a cheat. Mr Boating seems the calmest person in the ground. Nigel Spink is certainly the busiest.

9:00pm: That's half-time. Thought the ref might have added some time on. Glad he didn't. Tony can settle them down now. We've played alright. It hasn't been one-way traffic. Wonder what they're saying at half time on the TV. Someone said that Brian Clough was going to be in the studio. Cloughie will tell it like it is. At least if we do lose now, it shouldn't be by too many. Spud still thinks Bayern will score a couple in the second half. The Villa fans made lots of noise that half. I just have no idea what the next 24 hours are going to bring. Will we do it? I would take penalties now. What reception will await me back at home? Hope Mum and Dad aren't panicking too much. Hope they haven't called the police. Surely Mark will have told them the truth before it got to that. What could my punishment be? I don't care. I'll take whatever comes my way. I just want my Villa to be taking the European Cup back to Birmingham.

9:24pm: I can't take much more of this. The Germans are on top. They're making a change now. Bringing on their number 16. He's not a goalkeeper like our number 16. Feel the nerves growing around the crowd now. Thought they would score there. Glad that went past the post.

Brilliant save by our young keeper. He probably isn't that young. Seems to have been playing in the Central League for years. He grabbed hold of it as well. We need the ball up this end. Spud, shut up! Support the club representing England.

No! Yes! Off the line! Who was that who headed it off the line? Think it was Gary Williams. Or was it Allan Evans? Heroic defending. Jump on it, Nigel. He's doing brilliant. Bet he didn't think last night that he'd be on the pitch today.

9:35pm: Well, we've survived three-quarters of the game without conceding. Unless it goes to extra-time. How has Spud gone for a slash now? I guess a lot of beer swirling around his bladder. That was a wild shot, Tony Morley. At least we saw the ball down this end.

Nice play between Williams, Cowans and Shaw. This is interesting. Take him on, Tony. You can beat him. Chance! He's missed it. No, it's gone in! We've scored! Peter Withe has scored right in front of me. I don't believe it. I thought it had hit the post. I don't know what to do. Villa fans are going totally crazy. Shaw, Cowans and Peter Withe are just hugging each other. Mr Boating is in a full embrace with a bare-chested sweaty fan. Getting pushed towards the fencing. I don't care. We are winning. We've scored in a European Cup Final. Need to stay calm. Long way to go. We need to focus. I need to make sure Spud can find us. We're winning!

Spud arrives and asks what all the racket was about. I think he's joking. He's smiling. Think deep down he's happy we scored. I suppose I did celebrate Andy Gray's League Cup winning goal when I was in with the Wolves fans at Wembley.

'If you can keep them down to one goal, you can take this to extra time', Spud says. My Grandad said once you have scored one, you have to go and get a second. Easier said than done.

9:47pm: Why aren't the minutes in the middle of that electronic scoreboard changing? It's said "29" for at least five minutes. I check with Mr Boating. He confirms that the number of minutes is correct. I feel so hot. I'm burning up inside. Well done Nigel Spink, again. He looks nearly as calm as Mr Boating.

They are bringing on a number 13. Hope that isn't unlucky for us. Last ten minutes now. We're going to do this. Evans, McNaught, Williams and Swain are defending so well. Throwing their bodies in front of everything. Suppose it is the last game of the season. Doesn't matter if they're injured.

No! No! Save it, Spink! No! Guess it's been coming. Maybe we'll need penalties after all. I cover my face with my hands in disappointment. All I can hear is the roar of the celebrating Bayern fans. Cheers are dying out. Being replaced by Villa fans cheering.

'Linesman's flag is up, Hugh. It's offside. You jammy lot', Spud relays the good news.

I make it two minutes left. Need to get it away from our penalty area. Gary Williams has been immense. They all have. We just need to keep going. Use every strain of energy. I'm doing my bit with singing my head off. "It's Aston Villa. Aston Villa FC. They're by far the greatest team the world's ever seen". Mr Boating is joining in. He's got his tie tied around his head now. The seconds on my digital watch are in slow motion. Still Bayern Munich attack. Allan Evans gets it away again.

Peter Withe has it near us. Hold it up, Peter. He's won a throw-in. Thought that vicious police dog was going to burst the ball then. Kenny Swain not rushing to take the throw. Hope the ref doesn't add on too much. McNaught wins the header. Now

Bremner wins the next header. Now Sid Cowans wins a third header. It's like head tennis. Gary Shaw has it by the corner flag. Only a few yards from us. Spud is screaming for him to keep it there. Oh, Withe has lost it. Their keeper Muller has got it now. Guess one more attack. Only 30 seconds left on my stopwatch. We all start to whistle. Sadly, I can't, so I make more of a mooing noise.

Karl Heinz-Rummenigge has got it in our half. Tackle him, Gordon! He's still going. He's got passed Dennis and Des. He's in the penalty box. Surely not! Don't foul him. A chance! What a challenge by Bremner. Injury-time now. Tony Morley on his way. He's really motoring towards us. He passes it to Peter Withe. I can hear Trinity Road Tim in my head shouting at his telly "Time! Time!" Why has Peter played that long pass? Didn't need to. What's Kenny Swain doing up here? He wants to be a hero. Swain has gone for the shot. They've blocked it. It's back with Des Bremner. Blow, ref. Please just blow. Keep it, Sid. Has the ref blown? Gordon Cowans has scored! No, referee had already given a foul against him. Uses time up at least. Guess the West Germans will kick it long. We are so close. I'm not going to breathe again until the final whistle. Ref checks his watch. He's played 45 seconds of injury time. How much more is he going to play? He's blown! Aston Villa. My Aston Villa are European Champions! I support the best team in Europe. This is incredible. The celebrations in our end are even wilder than at Highbury 12 months ago.

Mr Boating is being lifted aloft by two quite muscular young ladies. Firecrackers are going off. Spud is snogging quite a fit-looking Villa lady in a straw Villa boater. His hands are enjoying themselves. Bet he hasn't told her he's a Wolves fan. A bloke nearby has inexplicably thrown one of his trainers into the Bayern Munich fans. Not surprisingly, the despondent defeated fans did not return it.

I'm just standing motionless. Tears in my eyes. I just can't take this in. I don't know what I'm supposed to do. This is something that happens to Liverpool, Real Madrid and Bayern Munich fans. Not teams who until last season had not won the league for 71 years. To think when Grandad gave me the greatest gift of all, a Villa coloured C&A tracksuit in 1974, we were a lowly Second Division team. I owe so much to you, Grandad, for making this possible. For making me a Villa fan. Dreams do come true for teams like Nottingham Forest and Villa when they have very special managers. Thank you, Ron Saunders.

The players in their all-white kit are embracing the unused subs in their blue tracksuit tops. In our white away kit, we look like Real Madrid. Today we played like them. Could this be the start of a Villa European Cup dynasty? We're now back in Europe next season. There's Jimmy Rimmer embracing goalscorer Peter Withe. Looks like Jimmy has got a support around his neck. Peter Withe and Gary Williams are running towards us, arms aloft. Acknowledging the part we have just played in this historic win. Some of our players have swapped shirts with the Bayern team. It's weird seeing them in red tops.

9:58pm: I bet Randy is dancing around his garden. Pity Grandad isn't in the next garden to witness it. Struggling to see Dennis walking up the steps. Can see the beautiful cup though. There it is, being held above his head by our skipper Dennis Mortimer. Bet that feels heavy after playing 90 minutes of football. Kenny Swain is next to raise it up in his Bayern top. Dennis is having none of it. He has taken it back before any of our other players can have a moment of glory. Our skipper wants to bring the massive trophy to us, the supporters. Here comes the cup.

11:46pm: Twelve real heroes today: Rimmer, Spink, Swain, Williams, Evans, McNaught, Mortimer, Bremner, Shaw, Withe, Cowans, Morley. Names that will go down in Villa folklore as the first Aston Villa team to conquer Europe. It wasn't just the twelve though. The nine games it's taken to win the famous trophy has seen others play major roles. Terry Donovan's goals against Valur. Brendan Ormsby, two defensive clean sheets. Andy Blair, his great performance in Kiev. Ivor Linton, whose afro froze in Reykjavik. Colin Gibson, a hero of Berlin. Then there are the two subs who never got on the pitch, but still played their part: Pat Heard and David Geddis. Perhaps the biggest unsung hero of all was our manager, Tony Barton. The man who had been so kind to give us a donation for MacMillan nurses only just over three months ago. He has now joined the immortal names of British European Cup winning managers. Jock Stein, Sir Matt Busby, Bob Paisley and now Tony Barton. A manager for just over a month and now part of an exclusive European Cup winning club. Pity the match programme listed the Villa manager as Ron Saunders.

The coach is buzzing. I think Steve Duggan is just running on adrenaline now. Hopefully in a fit enough state to drive us cup winning supporters back home. Still waiting on a few revellers to return. Spud seems to have found another crate of beer. He said it was a gift from the Germans. Not sure what that means. George Boating looks completely frazzled. It's a lot for somebody in their 50s. He is claiming it's the best day of his life. He also seems to have acquired one of Kenny Swain's sweat-drenched socks.

Looks like we will have to leave, four passengers short. We've waited an extra 40 minutes for them. They'll be out celebrating. Aston Villa Champions of Europe. I really am in a daze. Knackered, delirious with joy and dreading facing my parents. Whatever punishment awaits will be worth it. Just hope I haven't caused too much upset.

Thursday 27th May

6:55am: On the ferry I set my digital watch back one hour. Everybody wants to share memories of the great night. Even spotted the bloke who threw his trainer into the Bayern fans hopping around the boat. Everyone here seems to be a Villa fan. A few didn't even get into the game, but still had a great time. I just don't know what awaits me at home. Or at school tomorrow. I'm not going to pretend I didn't go to Rotterdam. I want to talk about this all summer.

'It would have been Mum's birthday today', a subdued Spud informs me. 'She would have turned 40. Bet we would have been having a big party'. What words could I say to console Pete Hogan? He had been there for me in Rotterdam, but all this time he has been grieving. For him, 1982 will always be remembered as the year he lost his mum.

5:02pm: Final stop before home. Just haven't been able to sleep. My head so full of Peter Withe's mishit goal and the fear of what lies at home. I've always liked service stations. Something magical about walking in the air across the motorway traffic. Carpark was full of Villa coaches when we arrived. Not sure what's keeping Julie Duggan's brother's eyes open. He seems to be drinking a gallon of coffee. Looking at the back pages of the national newspapers in WH Smiths. They're all celebrating my team's achievement.

7:36pm: This is it, time to face the music. Find out from Mark what I'm going home to. Lots of cars are here to meet us. Horns being hooted in celebration. Flags being waved and loads of claret and blue on display. Imagine the welcome the players will get at Birmingham Airport when they return with the cup.

Why can't I see a bright orange Escort? Don't say Mark has deserted me. Perhaps he's just running late. That looks like my dad's Ital. That's not good. There are Mum and Dad. Dad has got his arms folded. At least Spud is with me. Perhaps I should make a run for it. Mustn't forget my programme. Mr Boating shakes Steve Duggan's hand and passes him a five pound note. A chorus of "we won the cup" breaks out as we start to leave the coach. What a 48 hours that has been. Seems like I've been away for weeks.

We walk, heads down, towards my parents. Trying to think of an appropriate phrase to greet them with. All I could muster was "sorry!" To my astonishment, Dad just greets me with a big hug. Mum grabs hold of a startled Spud.

'Champions of Europe, hey, and you were there to see it', Dad says with a broad grin. This was better than I expected. But I was waiting for the follow-up. I nervously said "Hope I didn't cause you too much worry. I didn't mean to".

'Oh, we weren't worried at all. Glad of the peace and quiet', Mum replied. Something wasn't right about this. My parents aren't this hard. They would have been going out of their minds.

'Hi George. Great result. Thanks for everything. See you at work tomorrow', Dad shouted at the passing Mr Boating.

9:36pm: Well, that's it. Our record seven FA Cup wins must now be shared with Tottenham Hotspur. We need to win our eighth one next year. It's the only trophy now we haven't won in my lifetime. An early goal by Glenn Hoddle in the replay was enough to beat QPR.

Dad recorded the European Cup Final for me last night. Says I can watch the last 30 minutes now before I go to bed. School tomorrow. Can't believe Mark snitched on me. That my parents knew my plans all along. Why didn't they say? Would have meant a lot less worry for me. They didn't know that Spud was going to turn up, though. Bet that surprised Mr Boating. How sneaky of them to get him to be my chaperone. No wonder me and Spud couldn't shake him. Seems Randy was in on it too. Good to talk to him on the phone just now. He was so excited you'd have thought he was the one who went to Rotterdam. I'm so glad Mark had my back. He really is a great brother. Even though he never lets me win at anything. Mum said you could hear the screams from Asif next door when Villa scored.

Until now, there had been no mention of punishment. I had been expecting it to come. So now was the time for Dad to hand out my punishment. No pocket money until the new season starts! That's three months away! Also, I must clean both Dad's and Mark's cars once a week until the summer holidays. Hopefully they'll forget about that one in a few weeks' time. Especially if I do a rubbish job the first time.

I'm going to save tonight's copy of the *Express & Star*. It says our win will be worth a million pounds. We are going to play Barcelona in the Super Cup. I might get to see Maradona at Villa Park. Also, we have a chance to rule the world. We get to compete for the World Cup Championship against the South American Champions. Imagine that, being the Champions of the World. We can really sing the Queen song then. Need to remember that the Madness song *House of Fun* was number one when Villa were crowned Champions of Europe. That seems appropriate. It says Villa's win created history. For the first time ever, the trophy will stay in the same country for six years. Beating Spain's record. Let's make it seven next season. England will have two chances in us and Liverpool. We could be Champions of England, Champions of Europe and Champions of the world next season. Is that a bit greedy for the 1982/83 season? Going to be difficult to focus on my O levels, girlfriends and getting through puberty with so much football going on.

Time to watch the ITV coverage then. Thanks, Dad. You're the best!

10:23pm: Nigel Spink showed no nerves. Brian Clough knows what he's talking about. All his comments are so relevant. I do like Brian Moore as commentator. This must be the goal! It is. Get in! That's me in behind the goal. I'm rewinding that. Going to play that goal over and over again.

"Shaw, Williams, prepared to venture down the left. There's a good ball played in for Tony Morley. Oh, it must be! It is! Peter Withe!!"

End of Season Top of Division One

1.	Liverpool	Pl: 42 Po: 87	+48
2.	Ipswich Town	Pl: 42 Po: 83	+22
3.	Manchester United	Pl: 42 Po: 78	+30
4.	Tottenham Hotspur	Pl: 42 Po: 71	+19
11.	**Aston Villa**	**Pl: 42 Po: 57**	**+2**

Villa May League Results

1st Manchester City (h) 0-0 Draw

5th Stoke City (a) 0-1 Lost

8th West Bromwich Albion (a) 1-0 Won (Heard)

15th Everton (h) 1-2 Lost (Cowans)

21st Swansea City (h) 3-0 Won (Bremner, Withe, Morley)

Villa May European Cup

26th Bayern Munich (Rotterdam) 1-0 Won (Withe)

[Aston Villa European Champions]

Acknowledgements

This book could have been written by many Villans of a certain age. Hopefully it is more than just an Aston Villa book. It is a nostalgic look at what football was like in the early 80s and the banter that existed between school friends supporting different local teams.

It has been a sheer pleasure to write and to pay homage to some real Villa legends. Many of them I have been lucky enough to meet. They have been so supportive of my Villa projects. These legends have a bond similar to the lads in the "Local Gang".

Since I wrote 'Just 14' in 2015 I have always wanted to continue remembering the very special Aston Villa journey. But the journey that I have personally been on, since releasing 'Just 14', has been mind-blowing. From sharing the stage with Gary Shaw, Tony Morley and Colin Gibson at the book launch to attending the Cannes Film Festival. It's all been crazy.

With the help of West Midland film company Mockingbird Films Co and the brilliant local director Steve Broster we produced a promotional trailer for 'Just 14 the Movie' in the Autumn of 2022. If you haven't already you can watch this trailer at just14themovie.com. The trailer amazingly includes cameos from three of Villa's European Cup winners. The trailer was premiered on 23rd October 2022 to a packed venue, which included many of the West Midland 1980s football legends. It was the night when

Brian Little took the mic to announce that Aston Villa football club had appointed their new manager – Unai Emery.

Since that remarkable day, many wonderful people have contributed to bringing the 'Just 14' Movie closer to fruition. Although we're not there yet, with Bart Films now managing production, I am confident we are nearer than ever before.

In March 2023, we selected 14 outstanding individuals as Just 14 The Movie Ambassadors. They have been incredible supporters and are all legends in their own lunchtimes.

So, here are the 14 'Just 14 The Movie' Ambassadors, whose inspiration made this sequel possible.

- **Carter Carrington** (*'Carts' always stealing the limelight*)
- **Marie Bushell** (*and her son Connor Sherry who have been brilliant*)
- **Mike McKiernan** (*'SOB ON THE TYNE' banner writer*)
- **Jason Quek** (*travelled thousands of miles to meet Villa legends*)
- **Peter White** (*former writer for the Sports Argus*)
- **Claire Donnelly** (*and her inspirational son Alfie*)
- **Village Podiatrists** (*Just look at their reviews on Google*)
- **Darren Wootton** (*had to include a Wolves fan*)
- **Kevin Boucal** (*part of a whole village of Villa fans in Gambia*)
- **Kenny Swain** (*a true gentlemen, who likes to sing*)
- **Harper Mills** ('Harps', *surely a future Villa ladies star*)
- **Aston Villa's Cornwall Lions Supporters Club** (*thanks Dave*)
- **Prone to Mischief** (*Chris and Gemma certainly are*)
- **Alan Crampton** (*The best Villa Park model maker*)

Other Andy Dale Books

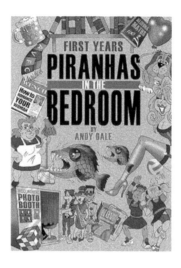

First Years Piranhas in the Bedroom

It's 1986, and 19-year-old Jonathan gets quite a culture shock when he leaves home to start his First year teacher training at Derbyshire College of Higher Education. Living in a large white (unmissable) student house full of lads, ranging from a posh boy from Kent to a northerner with anger issues, he must negotiate the perils of student life, which include seven-legged pub crawls in the dead of winter, fishnapping raids and cereals in the bedsheets, all at the same time as trying to woo a pretty blonde from Rochdale. Set in a time when cassette players were cool, contact with home was a red phonebox, but alcohol, lingerie and high jinx were still the order of the day, First Years: Piranhas in the Bedroom is written with a great British dry wit. Its nostalgia for all things 80s as well as its "will-they-won't-they" romantic comedy gives it a really broad appeal: The Young Ones meets High Fidelity.

Just 14

Fiction and fact merge in this story of a teenage boy (Jonathan Stadler) following his beloved Aston Villa's glorious 1980/81 season. As he turns 14 (one year for each of the Villa players) his life begins to change in many different, funny and unexpected ways. Step back to a time of; Big Ron Atkinson's flamboyant Albion, Andy Gray's Wolves League Cup winner, Cloughie conquering's Europe and Star Soccer on TV. This is a must for anyone who followed Midland football in the early 80's. It will bring memories flooding back of a time when a staggering eight Midland teams were in the top division. A time when going to school on Monday was a nightmare if your team had lost on Saturday. But this isn't just a football book.... 'Just 14' really has it all; from the shooting of John Lennon, the ripping skirts of Bucks Fizz to a guest appearance from Pele this book will make you laugh, smile and probably even cry.

All Andy Dale's books are available from Amazon, Waterstones, Imgram Sparks and direct from Andy Dale's Bookshop

9 781666 410884